Praise for

EYES GLOWING AT THE EDGE OF THE WOODS

———

"Beautiful and important."

—Silas House, author of *Clay's Quilt*, *The Coal Tattoo*, and *Eli the Good*

"This book is a literary treasure for West Virginia and the rest of the Appalachian region. It is a rumination on what it means to be of a mountain place in this day and time. In vivid, fresh language West Virginians explore place, identity, family, and so much more. A rich and important addition to mountain letters, I think this book will be regarded for a long time."

—Crystal Wilkinson, author of *The Birds of Opulence*, *Water Street*, and *Blackberries, Blackberries*

"Never sentimental or clichéd, this essential collection captures the complexity and richness of West Virginia today. Revealing a deep, sometimes uneasy connection to home, these stories and poems carry us into the coalfields and hollers, cities, and small towns across West Virginia and take surprising turns along the way to illuminate its beauty, darkness, violence, and grace."

—Carter Sickels, author of *The Evening Hour*

"Representing the rich diversity of West Virginians, these writers offer historical, contemporary, and timeless reflections of life and death in the great mountain state through poignant, at times haunting, poetry and prose."

—Theresa L. Burriss, Radford University

EYES GLOWING AT THE EDGE OF THE WOODS

Fiction and Poetry from West Virginia

Edited by

Laura Long and
Doug Van Gundy

VANDALIA PRESS

MORGANTOWN 2017

ISBN:

paper   978-1-943665-54-9
epub   978-1-943665-55-6
pdf   978-1-943665-56-3

Library of Congress Cataloging-in-Publication Data is available
from the Library of Congress

Book and cover design by Than Saffel / West Virginia University Press

Irene McKinney

TO MY READER

———————

There's a passage through the night
where someone awards me, hangs
the tassle of distress off to the side
and replaces it with a badge
indicating that I did one thing
right by continuing what
I'd started when I didn't know
it had begun, and I was sure
of no reward. Blessings were not
forthcoming, daily distress.
The path is aerial seen from
above. I startle myself
and feel I have no choice but
to proceed by inches. I pull down
the magic curtain, uncurb the car,
get in and drive, coaxing
the pattern to relief.

And you have been with me
through the long and hateful night
although you are only a shadow.
You have stayed behind
my shoulder and I've sheltered
you there, made a place for

you in my mind. In loneliness,
in rain, in the loss of breath,
you have been with me
and I have not failed you
because I continued to speak
when you begged me not
to inquire further and I spoke
to your fears in a voice of grief,
saying, yes they are gone and
will not return, but you
are still breathing. And I sang
you a song that came through
a trail of nerves down the generations
through all we have read together
and all we have remembered.
Remember the words, and I'll remember you.

EYES GLOWING AT THE EDGE OF THE WOODS

———————

CONTENTS

INTRODUCTION

This anthology presents fiction and poetry by sixty-three contemporary writers who have called West Virginia home. Some of these writers were born and raised in the state, while others came to live here as children or adults.

Twenty-seven fiction writers and thirty-six poets are represented here. Their writing speaks eloquently to the spectrum of experience possible for West Virginians, both at home and away. In the process of editing, we considered the many ways in which people understand and interpret this place. In the end, we made our selections based on the bold and authentic artistic vision of each author. It is our intention that this collection defy easy categorization: a mosaic crafted from many voices, united by this place, and the quality of the work.

When we first set out to gather recent writing by West Virginians, we did not realize what richness and diversity we would discover. We contacted established and emerging writers, most of whom had published at least one book, and asked them to send us fiction and poetry connected to a West Virginia sense of place, however they might define that. We requested work first published since 2002.

The writers responded generously. We then selected either one work of fiction or one or two poems from each author. Though some of the writers had published in both genres, we limited our final selection to one genre per author. We would have liked to have included work from more authors but were limited by space.

We have many people to thank. The influence of former West Virginia Poet Laureate Irene McKinney, who was a friend and inspiration to both of us (and to many of the other authors in this volume), can be found throughout this book. The title, *Eyes Glowing at the Edge of the Woods,* comes from a line in a poem of hers not collected here: "Handholds." Her poem "To My Reader" introduces our anthology. And her wonderful "Homage to Hazel Dickens" can be found amid the other poems and stories.

We are grateful to all the hardworking editors who first published these pieces in magazines and books. We thank everyone at West Virginia University Press/Vandalia Press, especially Abby Freeland, for their unwavering support of this project.

Most of all, we are grateful to the writers, and we hope readers will seek out more of their work.

Laura Long, Fiction Editor
Doug Van Gundy, Poetry Editor

OLIVES

———

In the supermarket where I shop there is a new feature: at the end of the deli counter, where ham haunches wait to be sliced and cheeses and breads are heaped as in a European market, is a counter made to look like a surrey cart. Under its fringe are galvanized buckets filled with false grapes and plastic bins the size of troughs; most of these bins are filled with olives. The ones on the end present mixes of peppers and onions and mushrooms, but the inner containers hold olives only. How beautiful they are! So glossy they hardly look real.

I bought two tubs of them; so many they'll probably never be eaten, but I put them on a plate and admired their differences: the plump, slick, khaki ones, the eggplant-dark that look like small prune plums or deepest bruises, and the strange, shriveled ones, the cadavers of the olive world. They look like mummies' eyes and their taste is oily and musky at once.

I bought so many because olives are what must be bought when I want to remember my mother; when I want to ask myself what I am doing with my life; when I want to be thankful that I was born in America.

My mother was born into a poor family in the village of Aelintakos on the edge of Greece that borders Turkey, a paring of land so poor that the earth is bleached as white as the sky; yet even now, battles rage over who will own it.

"It seems," my mother once said, "that when the sun fled to rest, the earth became its rightful color—the red of blood." So I buy olives to remember all those lives lost to strife and hardship and the wearing away that a hard life brings. Aelintakos was a poor village and it was not redeemed by kindness. Poverty rarely ennobles or enriches the spirit of man.

"Only those who have a soul can feel it move for the pity of life." That too was something my mother said.

Sometimes as I lick the olive's thick matte skin or sip the brine that puddles in the bottom of a dish, I imagine I hear my mother's voice in a slow murmur behind the door. She prayed every night and there was not only a click of beads, but a strange thump and then a soft thud that I later learned was the beat of her fist at her breastbone, the lowering of her head against the floor.

From my mother I learned that olives were life, to be eaten every day; to eat the fruit and the oil and with them the staff, which was bread, baked each morning, a flat round the size of a wheel, a rude cross cut into its face. And, also necessary, coarse salt, and water carried from the town's well, which sat squat in the center of the square, its circle of chipped blue and white tiles glistening; its cool slosh a promise of some deep, unquenchable freshet beneath the parched earth that would provide as the heavens did not.

The olives arrayed on the majolica plate seem to me like the girls of that village. My mother told me their names: hers Melaina, her best friend Irina, her sister Zoe. Daphne, Cleota, Olympia; these are the names of maidens in myths, nymphs or mortals stolen away from their homes by the gods. Ariadne and Danae, Elektra and Chloe. In this fruit's progress I see the girls of Aelintakos as they emerge into first womanhood: thick fuzzy braids tied with twine, a perfect line of brow above dark eyes filled with life. I see them wear down until in their forties they are kerchiefed crones, like a Greek chorus. They are the tragedy's keening; they are the harpies shrieking; they are the dark and shriveled flesh I lift to my lips.

"Dark bitterness—it's delicious," my mother said of these wrinkled olives that she most loved. And it's true. This taste is the essence of years: salt and lime, earth and must, and at its core the hardness that will break into flower.

Beyond the hills of that village, olive groves appear in the dusk as one great tangle; and when I dream of Aelintakos in the nights when my mother is still alive to me, there is a stand of women arrayed against the rise. What an odd gate it makes, those pickets in black. But against that parched white earth, those dark green vines, these dreamed black sentries are my link to memory, and my link to all those other lives when mortal women spurned Elysian lovers and were thus transformed: *spider, laurel, willow, olive, echo echo echo.*

Maggie Anderson

AND THEN I ARRIVE AT THE POWERFUL GREEN HILL

———

Up, up, I follow
    the creek bed through downed branches
        on spongy leaves, rimed and slippery.
The way is clear because
it is late winter,
    wet snow patches
      the runoff cold, cold to the touch
      a tang of ice still in it.

And then I arrive at the powerful green hill,
my place, my exact location,
    where I began and started from
      where I will end beneath this ground.
I have brought everything I've left undone—
letters and resolutions, almost loves,
    hard grudges—to give to the wind that takes them up,
    tosses them down, down until
my hands are empty and I am as thin and light as a girl.

A BLESSING

———

Inside the mind there is a balm
I know it and I say hello.

—Irene McKinney

Translucent braid gelled to silver at first light,
the valley's work, the white, the shining.
An entrenched meander cuts sharp
shoals into the narrow sluice
of the gorge. Clouds like ether rise
from the sandstone up the sheer, simple
mountains, dark-graded with pine.
I come to this water
for the rustle and hiss at the falls,
for the fast train sound when
the traps of the dam open up downriver.
I come for the limestone outcroppings—
the blue stone—and the shift
of the midwinter sandbars after
a summer of drought. I come for
the silence of amber, the flicker
of brook trout over the rapids,
to the soft banks of sand
where the stiff-necked sumac release
and fall over into what's left of the river
at the end of the dry branch.

Pinckney Benedict

MERCY

The livestock hauler's ramp banged onto the ground, and out of the darkness they came, the miniature horses, fine-boned and fragile as china. They trit-trotted down the incline like the vanguard of a circus parade, tails up, manes fluttering. They were mostly a bunch of tiny pintos, the biggest not even three feet tall at the withers. I was ten years old, and their little bodies made me feel like a giant. The horses kept coming out of the trailer, more and more of them every moment. The teamsters that were unloading them just stood back and smiled.

My old man and I were leaning on the top wire of the southern fenceline of our place, watching the neighbor farm become home to these exotics. Ponies, he kept saying, ponies ponies ponies, like if he said it enough times, he might be able to make them go away. Or make himself believe they were real, one or the other.

I think they're miniature horses, I told him. Not ponies. I kept my voice low, not sure I wanted him to hear me.

One faultless dog-sized sorrel mare looked right at me, tossed its head, and sauntered out into the thick clover of the field, nostrils flaring. I decided I liked that one the best. To myself, I named it Cinnamon. If I were to try and ride it, I thought, my heels would drag the ground.

Horses, ponies, my old man said. He had heard. He swept out a dismissive hand. Can't work them, can't ride them, can't eat them. Useless.

Useless was the worst insult in his vocabulary.

We were angus farmers. Magnificent deep-fleshed black angus. In the field behind us, a dozen of our market steers roamed past my old man and me in a lopsided wedge, cropping the sweet grass. They ate constantly, putting on a pound, two pounds a day. All together like that, they made a sound like a steam locomotive at rest in the station, a deep resonant sighing. Their rough hides gleamed obsidian in the afternoon sun, and their hooves might have been fashioned out of pig iron.

The biggest of them, the point of the wedge, raised his head, working to suss out this new smell, the source of this nickering and whinnying, that had invaded his neighborhood. His name was Rug, because his hide was perfect, and my old man planned to have it tanned after we sent him off to the lockers in the fall. None of the other steers had names, just the numbers in the yellow tags that dangled from their ears. Rug peered near-sightedly through the woven-wire fence that marked the border between his field and the miniature horses', and his face was impassive, as it always was.

The teamsters slammed the trailer's ramp back into place and climbed into the rig's cab, cranked up the big diesel engine, oily smoke pluming from the dual stacks. The offloaded horses began to play together, nipping at one another with their long yellow teeth, dashing around the periphery of the field, finding the limits of the place. Cinnamon trailed after the others, less playful than the rest. Rug lowered his head and moved on, and the wedge of heavy-shouldered angus moved with him.

Another livestock van pulled into the field, the drivers of the two trucks exchanging casual nods as they passed each other. I was happy enough to see more of them come, funny little beggars, but I had a moment of wondering to myself how many horses, even miniature ones, the pasture could sustain.

More of the midgets, my old man said. What in hell's next? he asked. He wasn't speaking to me exactly. He very seldom addressed a question directly to me. It seemed like he might be asking God Himself. What? Giraffes? Crocodiles?

This valley was a beef valley from long before I was born. A broad river valley with good grass, set like a diamond in the center of a wide plateau at twenty-four hundred feet of altitude. For generations it was Herefords all around our place, mostly, and Charolais, but our angus were the sovereigns over them all. My grandfather was president of the cattlemen's association, and he raised some trouble when the Beefmasters and Swiss Simmentals came in, because the breeds were unfamiliar to him; and my old man did the same when the place to our east went with the weird-looking hump-backed lop-eared Brahmas. But they got used to the new breeds. They were, after all, beefers, and beef fed the nation; and we were still royalty.

Then the bottom fell out of beef prices. We hung on. Around us, the Charolais and Simmentals went first, the herds dispersed and the land sold over the course of a few years, and then the rest of them all in a rush, and we were alone. Worse than alone. Now it was swine to the east, and the smell of them when the wind was wrong was enough to gag a strong-stomached man. The smell of angus manure is thick and honest and bland, like the angus himself; but pig manure is acid and briny and bitter and brings a tear to the eye. And the shrieking of the pigs clustered in their long barns at night, as it drifted across the fields into our windows, was like the cries of the damned.

Pigs to the east, with a big poultry operation beyond that, and sheep to the north (with llamas to protect them from packs of feral dogs), and even rumors of a man up in Pocahontas County who wanted to start an ostrich ranch, because ostrich meat was said to be low in fat and cholesterol, and ostrich plumes made wonderful feather dusters that never wore out.

The place to our west wasn't even a farm anymore. A rich surgeon named Slaughter from the county seat had bought the acreage when Warren Kennebaker, the Charolais breeder, went bust. Slaughter had designed it like a fortress, and it looked down on our frame house from a hill where the dignified long-bodied Charolais had grazed: a great gabled many-chimneyed mansion that went up in a matter of months; acres of slate roof and a decorative entrance flanked by stone pillars and spear-pointed pickets that ran for three or four rods out to each side of the driveway and ended there; and gates with rampant lions picked out in gold. That entrance with its partial fence made my old man angrier than anything else. What good's a fence that doesn't go all the way around? he asked me. Keeps nothing out, keeps nothing in.

Useless, I said.

As tits on a bull, he said. Then: Doctor Slaughter, Doctor Slaughter! he shouted up at the blank windows of the house. He thought her name was the funniest thing he had ever heard. Why don't you just get together and form a practice with Doctor Payne and Doctor Butcher?

There was no Doctor Payne or Doctor Butcher; that was just his joke.

Payne, Slaughter, and Butcher! he shouted. That would be rich.

———

The horses started testing the fence almost from the first. They were smart, I could tell that from watching them, from the way they played tag together, darting off to the far parts of the pasture to hide, flirting, concealing their compact bodies in folds of the earth and leaping up to race off again when they were discovered, their hooves drumming against the hard-packed ground. They galloped until they reached one end of the long field, then swung around in a broad curve and came hell-for-leather back the way they had gone, their coats shaggy with the approach of winter and slick with sweat. I watched them whenever I had a few moments free from ferrying feed for the steers.

I would walk down to the south fence and climb up on the sagging wire and sit and take them in as they leaped and nipped and pawed at one another with their sharp, narrow hooves. I felt like they wanted to put on a show for me when I was there, wanted to entertain me. During the first snow, which was early that year, at the end of October, they stood stock still, the whole crew of them, and gaped around at the gently falling flakes. They twitched their hides and shook their manes and shoulders as though flies were lighting all over them. They snorted and bared their teeth and sneezed. After a while, they grew bored with the snow and went back to their games.

After a few weeks, though, when the weather got colder and the grass was thin and trampled down, the horses became less like kids and more like the convicts in some prison picture: heads down, shoulders hunched, they sidled along the fence line, casting furtive glances at me and at the comparatively lush pasturage on our side of the barrier.

The fence was a shame and an eyesore. It had been a dry summer when it went in five years before, when the last of the dwindling Herefords had occupied the field, and the dirt that season was dry as desert sand, and the posts weren't sunk as deep as they should have been.

They were loose like bad teeth, and a few of them were nearly rotted through. I was the only one who knew what bad shape it was getting to be in. My old man seldom came down to this boundary after the day the horses arrived, and nobody from the miniature horse farm walked their border the way we walked ours. We didn't know any of them, people from outside the county, hardly ever glimpsed them at all.

It wasn't our problem to solve. By long tradition, that stretch was the responsibility of the landowner to the south, and I figured my old man would die before he would take up labor and expense that properly belonged with the owners of the miniature horses.

————

Cinnamon, the sorrel, came over to me one afternoon when I was taking a break, pushed her soft nose through the fence toward me, and I promised myself that the next time I came I would bring the stump of a carrot or a lump of sugar with me. I petted her velvet nose and she nibbled gently at my fingers and the open palm of my hand. Her whiskers tickled and her breath was warm and damp against my skin.

Then she took her nose from me and clamped her front teeth on the thin steel wire of the fence and pulled it toward her, pushed it back. I laughed. Get away from there, I told her, and smacked her gently on the muzzle. She looked at me reproachfully and tugged at the wire again. Her mouth made grating sounds against the metal that set my own teeth on edge. She had braced her front legs and was really pulling, and the fence flexed and twanged like a bow string. A staple popped loose from the nearest post.

You've got to stop it, I said. You don't want to come over here, even if the grass looks good. My old man will shoot you if you do.

————

He surprised me watching the horses. I was in my usual place on the fence, the top wire biting into my rear end, and he must have caught sight of me as he was setting out one of the great round hay bales for the angus to feed from. Generally I was better at keeping track of him, at knowing where he was, but that day I had brought treats with me and was engrossed, and I didn't hear the approaching rumble of his tractor as it brought the fodder over the hill. When he shut down the engine, I knew that I was caught.

What are you doing? he called. The angus that were following the tractor and the hay, eager to be fed, ranged themselves in a stolid rank behind him. I kicked at Cinnamon to get her away from me, struggled to get the slightly crushed cubes of sugar back into my pocket. Crystals of it clung to my fingers. He strode down to me, and I swung my legs back over to our side of the fence and hopped down. It was a cold day and his breath rolled white from his mouth.

You've got plenty of leisure, I guess, he said. His gaze flicked over my shoulder. A number of the miniature horses, Cinnamon at their head, had peeled off from the main herd and were dashing across the open space. What makes them run

11

like that? he asked. I hesitated a moment, not sure whether he wanted to know or if it was one of those questions that didn't require an answer.

They're just playing, I told him. They spend a lot of time playing.

Playing. Is that right, he said. You'd like to have one, I bet. Wouldn't you, boy? he asked me.

I pictured myself with my legs draped around the barrel of Cinnamon's ribs, my fingers wrapped in the coarse hair of her mane. Even as I pictured it, I knew a person couldn't ride a miniature horse. I recalled what it felt like when she had thrust her muzzle against my hand, her breath as she went after the sugar I had begun bringing her. Her teeth against the wire. I pictured myself holding out a fresh carrot for her to lip into her mouth. I pictured her on our side of the fence, her small form threading its way among the stern gigantic bodies of the angus steers. I knew I would be a fool to tell him I wanted a miniature horse.

Yes sir, I said.

He swept his eyes along the fence. Wire's in pretty bad shape, he said. Bastards aren't doing their job. Looks like we'll have to do it for them.

He shucked off the pair of heavy leather White Mule work gloves he was wearing and tossed them to me. I caught one in the air, and the other fell to the cold ground. You keep the fence in shape then, he said. The staples and wire and stretcher and all were in the machine shed, I knew.

Remember, my old man said as he went back to his tractor. First one that comes on my property, I kill.

———

On the next Saturday, before dawn, I sat in the cab of our beef hauler while he loaded steers. There were not many of them; it would only take us one trip. I couldn't get in among them because I didn't yet own a pair of steel-toed boots, and the angus got skittish when they were headed to the stockyard. I would have helped, I wanted to help, but he was afraid I would get stepped on by the anxious beeves and lose a toe. He was missing toes on both feet. So he was back there by himself at the tailgate of the truck, running the angus up into it, shouting at them.

Rug was the first, and my old man called the name into his twitching ear— Ho, Rug! Ho!—and took his cap off, slapped him on the rump with it. Get up there! he shouted. I watched him in the rearview mirror, and it was hard to make out what was happening, exactly, because the mirror was cracked down its length, the left half crazed into a patchwork of glass slivers. The other angus were growing restive, I could tell that much, while Rug balked.

My old man never would use an electric prod. He twisted Rug's tail up into a tight, painful coil, shoving with his shoulder, and the big steer gave in and waddled reluctantly into the van. The truck shifted with his weight, which was better than a ton. The rest followed, the hauler sinking lower and lower over the rear axle as they clambered inside. My old man silently mouthed their numbers, every one, as they trundled on board, and he never looked at their ear tags once. He knew them.

When they were all embarked, when for the moment his work was done, his face fell slack and dull, and his shoulders slumped. And for a brief instant he stood still, motionless as I had never seen him. It was as though a breaker somewhere inside him had popped, and he had been shut off.

———

I made my daily round of the southern fence, patching up the holes the horses had made, shoveling loose dirt into the cavities they carved into the earth, as though they would tunnel under the fence if I wouldn't let them break through it. They were relentless and I had become relentless too, braiding the ends of the bitten wire back together, hammering bent staples back into the rotting posts. The sharp end of a loose wire snaked its way through the cowhide palm of the glove on my right hand and bit deep into me. I cursed and balled the hand briefly into a fist to stanch the blood, and then I went back to work again.

The field the horses occupied was completely skinned now, dotted with mounds of horse dung. Because the trees were bare of leaves, I could see through the windbreak to the principal barn of the place, surrounded by dead machinery. I couldn't tell if anyone was caring for them at all. I don't believe a single animal had been sold. Their coats were long and matted, their hooves long untrimmed, curling and ugly. A man—I suppose it was a man, because at this distance I couldn't tell, just saw a dark figure in a long coat—emerged from the open double doors of the barn, apparently intent on some errand.

Hey! I shouted to him. My voice was loud in the cold and silence. The figure paused and glanced around. I stood up and waved my arms over my head to get his attention. This is your fence!

He lifted a hand, pale so that I could only imagine that it was ungloved, and waved uncertainly back at me.

This is your fence to fix! I called. I pounded my hand against the loose top wire. These here are your horses!

The hand dropped, and the figure without making any further acknowledgment of me or what I had said turned its back and strolled at a casual pace back into the dark maw of the barn.

————

Most days I hated them. I cursed them as they leaned their slight weight against the fence, their ribs showing. I poked them with a sharp stick to get them to move so that I could fix the fence. They would shift their bodies momentarily, then press them even harder into the wire. The posts groaned and popped. I twisted wire and sucked at the cuts on my fingers to take the sting away. I filched old bald tires from the machine shed and rolled them through the field and laid them against the holes in the fence. The tires smelled of dust and spider webs. This was not the way we mended fence on our place—our posts were always true, our wire stretched taut and uncorroded, our staples solidly planted—but it was all I could think of to keep them out. The horses rolled their eyes at me.

And I tossed them old dry corn cobs that I retrieved from the crib, the one that we hadn't used in years. The horses fell on the dry husks, shoving each other away with their heads, lashing out with their hooves, biting each other now not in play but hard enough to draw blood. I pitched over shriveled windfallen apples from the stunted trees in the old orchard behind the house. I tried to get the apples near the sorrel, near Cinnamon; but as often as not the pintos shunted her aside before she could snatch a mouthful.

————

You know why we can't feed them, don't you? my old man asked me. We were breaking up more of the great round bales, which were warm and moist at their center, like fresh-baked rolls. The angus, led not by Rug now but by another, shifted their muscular shoulders and waited patiently to be fed. I could sense the miniature horses lining the fence, but I didn't look at them.

They'd eat us out of house and home, he said. Like locusts.

Behind me, the hooves of the horses clacked against the frozen ground.

———

One morning, the fence didn't need mending. It had begun to snow in earnest the night before, and it was still snowing when I went out to repair the wire. The television was promising snow for days to come. Most of the horses were at the fence, pressing hard against it but not otherwise moving. Some were lying down in the field beyond. I looked for the sorrel, to see if she was among the standing ones. All of them were covered in thick blankets of snow, and it was impossible to tell one diminutive shape from the next. Each fence post was topped with a sparkling white dome.

I walked the fence, making sure there was no new damage. I took up the stick I had used to poke them and ran its end along the fence wire, hoping its clattering sound would stir them. It didn't. Most of them had clustered at a single point, to exchange body heat, I suppose. I rapped my stick against the post where they were gathered, and its cap of snow fell to the ground with a soft thump. Nothing. The wire was stretched tight with the weight of them.

I knelt down, and the snow soaked immediately through the knees of my coveralls. I put my hand in my pocket, even though I knew there was nothing there for them. The dry cobs were all gone, the apples had been eaten. The eyes of the horse nearest me were closed, and there was snow caught in its long delicate lashes. The eyes of all the horses were closed. This one, I thought, was the sorrel, was Cinnamon. Must be. I put my hand to its muzzle but could feel nothing. I stripped off the White Mule glove, and the cold bit immediately into my fingers, into the half-healed cuts there from the weeks of mending fence. I reached out again.

And the horse groaned. I believed it was the horse. I brushed snow from its forehead, and its eyes blinked open, and the groaning continued, a weird guttural creaking and crying, and I thought that such a sound couldn't be coming from just the one horse, all of the horses must be making it together somehow, they were crying out with a single voice. Then I thought as the sound grew louder that it must be the hogs to the east, they were slaughtering the hogs and that was the source of it, but it was not time for slaughtering, so that couldn't be right either. I thought these things in a moment, as the sound rang out over the frozen fields and echoed off the surrounding hills.

At last I understood that it was the fencepost, the wood of the fencepost and the raveling wire and the straining staples, right at the point where the horses were gathered. And I leaped backward just as the post gave way. It heeled over hard and snapped off at ground level, and the horses tumbled with it, coming alive as they fell, the snow flying from their coats in a wild spray as they scrambled to get out from under one another.

The woven-wire fence, so many times mended, parted like tissue paper under their combined weight. With a report like a gunshot, the next post went over as well, and the post beyond that. Two or three rods of fence just lay down flat on the ground, and the horses rolled right over it, they came pouring onto our place. The horses out in the field roused themselves at the sound, shivered off their mantles of snow, and came bounding like great dogs through the gap in the fence as well. And I huddled against the ground, my hands up to ward off their flying hooves as they went past me, over me. I knew that there was nothing I could do to stop them. Their hooves would brain me, they would lay my scalp open to the bone.

I was not touched.

The last of the horses bolted by me, and they set to on the remains of the broken round bale, giving little cries of pleasure as they buried their muzzles in the hay's roughness. The few angus that stood nearby looked on bemused at the arrivals. I knew that I had to go tell my father, I had to go get him right away. The fence—the fence that I had maintained day after day, the fence I had hated and that had blistered and slashed my hands—was down. But because it was snowing and all around was quiet, the scene had the feel of a holiday, and I let them eat.

———

When they had satisfied themselves, for the moment at least, the horses began to play. I searched among them until finally I found the sorrel. She was racing across our field, her hooves kicking up light clouds of ice crystals. She was moving more quickly than I had ever seen her go, but she wasn't chasing another horse, and she wasn't being chased. She was teasing the impassive angus steers, roaring up to them, stopping just short of their great bulk; turning on a dime and dashing away again. They stood in a semicircle, hind ends together, lowered heads outermost, and they towered over her like the walls of a medieval city. She yearned to charm them. She was almost dancing in the snow.

As I watched her, she passed my old man without paying him the least attention. He wore his long cold-weather coat. The hood was up, and it eclipsed his face. He must have been standing there quite a while. Snow had collected on the ridge of his shoulders, and a rime of frost clung to the edges of his hood. In his hand he held a hunting rifle, his Remington .30-06. The lines of his face seemed odd and unfamiliar beneath the coat's cowl, and his shoulders were trembling in a peculiar way as he observed the interlopers on his land. I blinked. I knew what was coming. The thin sunlight, refracted as it was by the snow, dazzled my eyes, and the shadows that hid him from me were deep.

At last, the sorrel took notice of him, and she turned away from the imperturbable angus and trotted over to him. He watched her come. She lowered her delicate head and nipped at him, caught the hem of his coat between her teeth and began to tug. His feet slipped in the snow. Encouraged by her success, she dragged him forward. I waited for him to kill her. She continued to drag him, a foot, a yard, and at last he fell down. He fell right on his ass in the snow, my old man, the Remington held high above his head. The sorrel stood over him, the other horses clustered around her, and she seemed to gloat.

The Remington dropped to the ground, the bolt open, the breech empty. Half a dozen bright brass cartridges left my old man's hand to skip and scatter across the snow. The hood of his coat fell away from his face, and I saw that my old man was laughing.

Laura Treacy Bentley

VOW OF SILENCE

To a mind that is still,
The whole universe surrenders.

—Chuang Tzu

Distant brush fires seam
the mountainside—

smoke erases the moon.

Deep in the forest,
mute songbirds

settle in windless trees.

Under the earth,
tap roots

ration autumn rain.

Beneath the waves,
silent fish wait

for the lake to freeze.

Michael Blumenthal

STONE-HEARTED

———

"Hide your God, *for as He is your strength, in that He is your greatest secret, He is your weakness as s oon as others know him.*"

—*Paul Valery,* The Art of Poetry

I like working at a university where
there's a building called *Mineral Industries*
and another called *Pharmaceutical Studies.*

It assures me there won't be too much poetry
around, that I can wake and say to my beloved,
"Hey, let's go check out some coal" instead of

How do I love thee? Let me count the ways.
It assures me I won't have my heart battered
by too much sentiment, that I'll be able

To live in peace with my private gods,
with only a few miners and pharmacists
to disturb me. Don't get me wrong:

I like poetry well enough, I just want to
keep it a private matter. Yesterday I went
to the drugstore, then visited a mine.

There was something poetic about it all.

Today, no one harassing me with a sonnet
of their own, I may write one myself,

Fourteen lines rhyming *abab*, and let the
last two lines go wherever life takes them.
Who knows? Maybe my poem will end

With the words *bauxite*, or *gneiss*. But
if not, what the hell?—*aspirin* will do.

Ace Boggess

"WHAT IF THERE WEREN'T ANY STARS?"

————

—William Stafford, *"What If We Were Alone?"*

The astrologers find other jobs:
mining the veins of umber leaves
for information, predicting futures
by digging graves—the easiest answer.
Captains of ships, stranded
in an age before technology,
refuse to sail at night, directionless,
each a compass in a room full of magnets.
No philosopher muses on the Infinite.
No scientist measures the speed of light.
No father, lying back on a beat blue Dodge,
says, "Look, there's Orion's belt,
the big & little bears, & there,
that's the face I drew for your mother
so long ago when we still loved each other."

Mark Brazaitis

THE RINK GIRL

Her family moved to town from Omaha on Christmas Eve. Her father and mother are the new managers of the Sherman Ice Arena, which, thanks to the coal-baron millionaire who owns it, is open all year. It is mid-January now, skating season. Half the town goes to the public skate on Saturday afternoon, the experience like walking down aisles of a sold-out show. Excuse me. Sorry. Hey—watch it!

Walt waits in the long line to rent skates. Behind the counter is the Rink Girl. She isn't pretty. This is what every boy in the tenth grade says. Acne coats the sides of her face like raindrops on a window. Her brown hair looks oily, and its curls are petals of a wilted flower. Her eyes, however, are a dazzling hazel.

"Size?" she says. She looks him over. "Wait. Aren't you in the geography class before mine?" Geography, a tenth-grade elective. His parents insisted he enroll so he wouldn't be ignorant of the world. "Walt, right?"

"Yeah."

"What size, Walt?"

He tells her and she retrieves a pair of night-blue skates from the shelf behind her. The skates are the newest the rink owns, she says. "The gray ones have been here since 1947. The brown ones? Since the Civil War."

She looks to her left, out the windows of the double doors and onto the rink. Ten minutes after the start of the session, it's packed. Shaking her head, she turns back to him. He hears someone grumble in the line behind him: "What is this, the post office?"

"How much do you like skating?" the Rink Girl whispers, her voice as intimate as a lullaby.

"I like it fine," he says.

"Come back at midnight."

"Is there another public skate?"

"Come back at midnight," she repeats.

He wakes up as if to an alarm. The red numbers of his digital clock radiate the time: 11:42. He fell asleep convinced the Rink Girl wasn't serious about midnight. There's only one way to know for sure, however. He exchanges his pajamas for the clothes on his floor. His house is asleep. Silver, his dog, acknowledges him with three thumps of his tail before closing his eyes again. He steps outside.

The rink isn't more than a mile from his house. Because the night is clear and full of stars and the roads are free of snow and ice, he rides his bike. He makes it to the rink in minutes. But of course the door is locked, and when he taps like a hopeful fool, no one answers. If Brian and Ben could see him now, they would laugh all week. They were supposed to join him at the rink this afternoon, but they watched football instead.

"Hey." He turns to the voice behind him. "You're early." The Rink Girl smiles. In the bright-dark night, in her gray overcoat and bowler hat, she looks like a bohemian detective. She inserts a key into the rink's front-door lock, turns it, and pushes the door in. "After you."

It is darker than night inside. Then it's as light as a party. The Rink Girl calls him over from her spot behind the counter. "Do you want the same boots?" she asks.

"Sorry?"

"The same skates. Do you want the same skates you had on today?"

"Sure," he says.

She places the night-blue skates on the counter. Her own skates are white, with red hearts on the toes. As she laces them up in the lobby, he stares at them. "It was either hearts or skulls," she says. "Next time, I'm going with skulls."

She kills the lights in the lobby and clicks them on in the rink. She pushes open the double doors and leads him to the gate. She snaps it open and draws it in. "Gentlemen first," she says. He isn't prepared for how smooth the ice is—he is used to it being gnawed by a hundred blades—and he finds his feet flying forward and his head plummeting backward.

She catches him under his shoulders. "Careful, cowboy." She rights him with surprising strength. He glides onto the immaculate ice. She moves in front of him with the ease of a bird soaring across the sky, her coat like wings.

He follows her over several laps of the rink before she slows to skate beside him. "What's your story?" she asks.

"What do you mean?"

"Who are you? What do you want to be when you grow up? What's your favorite sin?" She laughs as if she isn't serious. But then she gazes at him as if she is.

He edits his answers so he'll sound cool, adventurous. But she follows up with more questions, and he ends up telling her the truth: His name is Walt Taylor. He is fifteen years old. His best sport is swimming. His favorite class is geography. (He wouldn't have said this before today, but he is convinced of it now.) He doesn't have a girlfriend. He last kissed a girl when he was in the sixth grade. When he was younger, he sometimes practiced kissing on his dog. He doesn't know what his favorite sin is because he feels guilty even when he doesn't sin. He wants to be in the movies. He'd settle for being a newscaster in Cleveland.

"All right," he says, "now you."

Her name is the Rink Girl. No, of course it isn't. But she knows people call her the Rink Girl. She doesn't mind. She loves skating rinks. She loves how they smell. She loves how the Zamboni mows them clean, leaving tiny, shimmering puddles. Her parents, who won a bronze medal in pairs skating at the World Championships a hundred years ago, moved to the United States from Russia when they were in their early twenties in order to join the Skating Sensations tour. This lasted two and a half years. They have been the managers of six rinks, the last outside of Omaha.

"What happened in Omaha?" he asks.

"The city couldn't afford to operate the rink anymore. It's a ghost building now."

"That won't happen here."

She shrugs. "Let's hope."

They skate a loop around the rink in silence. "Are you bored yet?" she asks.

"What?" he says.

"Boys tend to get bored with ice skating."

"So you've skated with a lot of boys."

"My brother," she says. "If he doesn't have a stick, a puck, and a net, he doesn't want to be anywhere near a rink."

"What grade is he in?"

"He's in the army."

"In the war?"

She nods. She is silent as she skates.

"I'm not bored," he says.

She says, "You know what my favorite sin is? Disobedience."

"Oh," he says. "So your parents don't know you're here?" He looks around, as if they might be hiding in the shadows.

"They do," she says. "But they don't know *you're* here." She smiles and dashes in front of him. "Catch me," she says.

It's impossible. After they have done a dozen laps, she calls across the rink: "You don't have to go the same direction I'm going." In a louder voice, she says, "Catch me any way you can."

But even when he turns around, she is too skilled and swift for him. He fails even to touch her. Cramping from exhaustion, he leaves the ice. She joins him in the second row of the three-tiered bleachers. Panting, he says, "Trying to . . . catch you . . . is like . . . trying to . . . catch light."

She touches his knee. He looks at her hand, then at her face. Her dazzling hazel eyes. Her pimples like small pink jewels. Her lips.

Her hand meets his. He squeezes it and she squeezes back.

"This doesn't mean I'm going to kiss you," she says.

She says they ought to leave. "I could probably teach you to be the world's greatest figure skater in the next couple of hours," she says. "But then neither of us would have a reason to come back. You would be on a Wheaties box and I would be the Annie Sullivan of skating teachers."

"Who's Annie Sullivan?" he asks.

"She coached Helen Keller to gold at the '24 Olympics."

Outside, the sky is as luminous as he's ever seen it. She walks up steps to the street and is about to cross. "What about a kiss?" he asks, surprised by his boldness.

She turns around. "Maybe when you catch me," she says. There is a pause. "Hell, that will never happen." She skips down the stairs and plants an ice-cool kiss on his lips. The sensation is like winter's first snowfall. "Goodnight."

On Monday morning in the third-floor hallway at Sherman High School, she doesn't acknowledge his wave. At the door to the geography classroom at the fifth-period bell, he touches her shoulder. She looks at him as if he's a stanger.

At the end of the school day, he walks home, disconsolate. As soon as he steps into the alley off Lye Street, she leaps from behind a green garbage can. He is too happy to be startled. But remembering how she treated him today, he narrows his eyes. "What's up?" he says.

"I know I ignored you at school," she says. "But I did it for your own good."

"What do you mean?"

"If your friends knew you liked the Rink Girl, you wouldn't hear the end of their teasing."

"I can handle them," he says, although without confidence.

"Besides, it's easier this way," she says. "We can concentrate on school when we're at school."

"And after school, we can do what we want."

"No, we have to do our homework."

"Are you serious?" The disappointment in his voice is as evident as a tuba in an orchestra of harps.

Softly, she says, "My parents don't want me to grow up to be the Rink Woman. And they don't want me to join the army like my brother. They're thinking doctor, lawyer, CEO of the world. So they want me to spend every afternoon and evening between Sunday and Friday in the company of books, calculators, and computers."

"I see," Walt says.

"So Saturday night is all we have." She pauses. "Saturday night and now."

She pulls him toward her. Squatting behind the green garbage can, they touch each other's ears and tangle tongues.

At the rink on Saturday night, she dazzles him with what she can do.

"What was that?" he asks. "A double axel?"

"Is that an official jump?" she says.

"I think so."

"I never had a lesson in my life—my parents were always too busy to teach me—so I don't know any of the real jumps or spins or moves. I've made up my own. I'll teach them all to you. This one I call the Floating Phantom."

She dives into the air, her body—he swears—horizontal to the ice before she rolls over as if on an invisible bed and, with her arms in front of her like a sleepwalker, returns to the cold surface.

"This one I call the Sit Up." She jumps into the air, kicks both legs straight in front of her, and curls up to touch her toes before sticking her legs back on the ice.

"And this I just call Crazy." She leaps into the air, summersaults, and lands without falling, without even trembling.

"Wow," he says. "Wow."

"Which one do you want to learn first?"

He considers. "How about we begin with you teaching me how to skate backwards?"

She taps her lips. "Boring," she says. "But all right." She steps in front of him, facing him. "Put your hands up like you're touching a wall."

When he does, she puts her hands in his. Neither of them is wearing gloves. But if his hands were cold, they are no longer. For years when he sees a couple standing like this, facing each other, palms pressed together, fingers interlocked, he will remember her, and he will feel sweetly disoriented, as if he had time-traveled.

Gently, she pushes into him, instructing him how to move his skates like he's using them to draw ovals in the ice.

After several minutes, she says, "I think you have it," and she gives him a push and he glides backward, as if on air, to the end of the rink.

The Rink Girl does not insist he practice his skating, but if he is to become as good as she is, or even half as good as she is—if he is to impress her at all—he must practice. So he comes to the public sessions on Wednesday and Thursday nights, fighting past mad-dashing eight-year-olds in hockey masks and trios of linked-armed twelve-year-old girls and divorced men and women on first dates as awkward as their skating.

On occasion, he glimpses the Rink Girl at a desk in the small office behind the rental skates, a textbook spread in front of her, a pen or pencil in her hand. Always, he lingers, wanting her to see him and beam, wanting to leap over the counter, slide up beside her, whisper into her brown hair.

During a school assembly in mid-March, he finds himself, by luck of the way homeroom classes occupy the rows of seats in the auditorium, sitting beside her. Police officers occupy the stage, railing against drugs or graffiti or something else subversive. She won't look at him, won't acknowledge him with anything even so small as a smile. He is terrified of making such a move himself, worried she will respond in a manner as cold as the ice on which she thrills him.

"Say no to temptation," he hears a police officer say. "Say no to impulsiveness, to wildness, to irrational behavior. Say no, no, no."

He feels his hand fill, remarkably, with hers. She leans over to him, kisses his ear, whispers, "Say yes, yes, yes."

As a skater, he isn't improving as quickly as he wants. He skates backward now, but he is far from mastering even the move she calls the Semi-Sane, which is a leap, a landing on two feet, and a spin into a backward skate. "Watch," she says. When she does it, it seems as simple as playing hopscotch. But when he tries to imitate her, he falls.

"Again," she says.

He falls.

"Again."

He falls.

"Again."

He falls. He falls. He falls. He falls. He falls. He falls.

He succeeds.

"Again."

He falls.

"Again."

He is in love, but no one knows it. He confides in no one. Not his parents. Not his older brother. Not Brian and Ben. To tell, he thinks, might be to awaken him from his dream or to have it trivialized with "Isn't that sweet" or with teasing or with (in Ben's and Brian's case) rude remarks about her pimples or her oily hair or the way she smells of old skates.

"Again."

He falls.

"Again."

He falls.

"Again."

He falls.

"I'll show you something special if you do it right."

He succeeds.

In the center of the ice, she lifts her blue sweater slowly. Thinking she is going to show him her breasts, his heart chugs like a manic choo-choo train. But she stops short, the bottom of the sweater a barricade. Now he sees her revelation: a red scar beginning at her navel and shooting like an angry bolt toward her breastbone.

"What happened?" he asks.

"I was doing a combination of the Buddha and the Ballerina. My blades had just been sharpened. They might as well have been ninja knives."

"It's amazing."

"You were probably hoping I'd show you my tits."

"I mean, it's amazing that you made a mistake. I've never seen you—."

"Who said anything about making a mistake? I tried to do a mash up of two irreconcilable moves. It's like dancing over the canyon of a paradox."

"Excuse me?"

"You did want to see my tits, didn't you?"

God yes, he thinks.

"Well, it's your lucky night."

In the beginning of June, he turns sixteen. This is good fortune. He needs an automobile because his summer job, to which he applied nine months earlier, is at a YMCA overnight camp in Bellefontaine, Ohio, four hours from Sherman. The automobile wasn't originally a necessity. He'd planned to spend his entire summer on the campgrounds. But if he wants to see the Rink Girl, which is akin to asking if he wants to live, he'll need to drive back from Bellefontaine every Saturday.

Each employee of Camp Belle is allowed one night off a week. Naturally, everyone wants Saturday night. Seniority dictates who is assigned what day, however. As a junior counselor, Walt sees he will be stuck with Tuesdays and Thursdays. On his first day at camp, he thinks about quitting. But his parents—his accursed parents—have opted to trade houses over the summer with a couple from Vallebona, Italy. He has nowhere to stay in Sherman.

In exchange for their Saturday nights, he surrenders to his fellow counselors his baseball glove, his fishing rod, his iPod. He doesn't miss any of it, except, perhaps, his baseball glove when, playing leftfield during the camper-counselor softball game, he catches a fly ball with his bare palm.

Because he is permitted to leave camp after dinner on Saturday, he has no problem arriving at the rink by midnight. The return trip's timeline proves tighter. He leaves the rink as the sun slips its first light over the horizon like a lover sliding a letter under a door. He crushes the gas pedal to make it back by Sunday breakfast, which, fortunately, begins only at nine-thirty.

Over the succeeding days, he catnaps when he can in order to recuperate the sleep he lost in staying up all night. By the time Saturday comes again, he is fully rested. He doesn't tell the Rink Girl about the lengths he goes to see her. He doesn't want her to think he's as lovesick as he is.

The Rink Girl spends her summer weekdays at a series of science and math camps. Sometimes he hears her mumbling what sound like formulas or Latin mottos. *Supra glaciem stemus, cum corde ignis.*

She teaches him the Slam, which is a series of short jumps followed by a high jump. She teaches him the Slow Mirror, in which one side of his body repeats the movements of the other. She teaches him the Backward Peek-a-Boo, in which he skates backward and pokes his head between his legs to see where he's going.

Despite the scoreboard above the east end of the rink with its red-numbered clock, dawn always surprises them. At first light, they kiss with the fury of hummingbirds stealing dew from the flowers of a butterfly bush.

On the Saturday night before the beginning of school, when he is back from camp, she isn't at the rink. In her place is a note with his name: *Had to leave town. Left the door open. The ice is yours.*

But without her, the ice feels—and he realizes how odd it is to think this way—cold. The rink feels cavernous and lonely, like a ship abandoned at sea. He drifts around the ice like a shipwrecked sailor hoping to find an island. He leaves after less than an hour, then stays up all night, wondering where she is and what might be wrong.

On the first day of school, he stands beside the main entrance to Sherman

High like a soldier. He doesn't care if she doesn't speak to him. He only wants to see her. For the past twenty-four hours, he has done nothing but worry—irrationally, he knows—that she is gone forever, off to bless another rink in another town, to turn another boy's Saturday nights into magic. The last bell rings, and he slinks inside the building and slouches to his homeroom.

But at the change of classes before third period, he sees her at the end of the hall. He is so relieved he fails to realize they are approaching each other with the speed of speed skaters. They collide, and she is sobbing a hurricane. "What's wrong?"

"My brother," she says.

"What happened? He didn't . . . Is he . . .?"

He feels her nod against his shoulder. Her tears are ferocious.

There is an audience around them. But the bell rings, and the hallway empties.

"We had to meet the body," she says. "We buried him in the National Cemetery, in Virginia."

"I'm sorry," he says. After a moment, he adds, "I wish I had more to say."

"There isn't more to say."

At school, it is impossible to pretend they aren't boyfriend and girlfriend. But perhaps owing to her brother's death, news of which everyone seems to have heard, they are left alone. They eat their lunches at the far end of the football field, in a corner where the grass is softest. They walk home together every day. In the wake of her brother's death, there is a solemnity to their conversations. Even their Saturday nights on the ice assume a mournful aura, the jumps, spins, and moves she teaches him bearing such names as "Cerement" ("a shroud," she explains helpfully), "Heaven's Door," and, defiantly, "Death Be Not Proud."

One Saturday night, she gives him a pair of ice skates, black with red eyelets. She doesn't say to whom they belonged, but he knows. They fit perfectly.

"I think it's time," she says at the beginning of October.

"Time?"

"To do a duet."

His role is simple. He skates forward, from one end of the rink to the other. She moves around him like water moves around rocks in a rippling stream. "Now backward," she says. He skates backward, and she flies around him, a predator about to devour him. No, only a butterfly looking to land.

Which she does, in his arms. "I feel better," she says.

In the middle of October, she invites him to have dinner at her house. From outside, her house looks ordinary: faded brick, ornamental wooden shutters with chipping white paint, a covered front porch with a pair of rocking chairs. Inside, he discovers a long hallway whose walls, top to bottom, are lined with photographs of her brother. "My parents say if the photos went halfway around the world," the Rink Girl whispers, "it would be too short a distance by half."

Presently, her parents come to meet him. Her father is tall and burly, with a beard that could hide a small child. Her mother is short and thin, with dyed orange hair in the style of a broom end. "I see you've met our son," she says. Walt looks around, as if there might be someone else in the room. But of course there is: the walls are alive.

"I'm sorry for your loss," he says.

But they appear not to have heard him. "Handsome, isn't he?" her mother says.

Her father adds, "And smart as a scientist."

Her parents have already eaten—or perhaps they aren't hungry—because after a minute more of polite talk, they excuse themselves and disappear. The Rink Girl waves him deeper into the house, into the kitchen, where she pulls pots and pans from cabinets. "What would you like to eat?" she asks. "Name anything."

"Anything?"

"Anything."

You, he wants to say.

"I don't know. Well." *Right now I'd like to taste the right corner of your mouth.* "Sea bass with rice pilaf, carrots au gratin, and a Caesar salad."

"Excellent," she says. "Next time, I'll know. Tonight we'll have peanut butter and jelly sandwiches. Any objections?"

He has none.

As they eat their sandwiches with a side of apple sauce in lunch-sized containers, he says, "Where did your parents go?"

She shrugs. "They haven't been here in anything more than body since my brother died. If I were a different kind of daughter, I would take advantage of the situation by, I don't know, hauling you upstairs and losing my virginity to you under the poster of Amelia Earhart on my ceiling."

"You have a poster of Amelia Earhart on your ceiling?"

She looks at him askance. "That's what you found interesting about what I just said?"

On the ice, he learns, or half learns, or watches her demonstrate, the Rabbit, the Monkey, the Horse, and the other nine signs of the Chinese zodiac.

"Someday," she says, "I'll teach you the Big O."

"What's the Big O?"

She only smiles.

Several times she tries to sneak him into her house—"to introduce you to Amelia Earhart," in her winking words—when she thinks her parents aren't home, but one or both is always present. One time, her parents are entertaining the Medev family from Moscow. If the Rink Girl's father was ursine, Lev Medev—tall, bearded, and with a girth so large he might have eaten a bear— is doubly so. He is the owner of the Moscow Circus on Ice, which is in town to do a one-night show in Sherman. The Medevs have a son, whom the Rink Girl's parents have been encouraging her to spend time with.

"I hope he's twice as ugly as his old man," Walt tells her, feeling jealousy burn so hot in him he could cook a four-course meal on his chest.

"I thought he would be" is all the Rink Girl says in reply.

She likes him. Damn it all. Could she like him more than she likes me? Please, God, no. Now Walt's chest blazes like the center of the sun.

The next Saturday night, the Rink Girl brings a pair of blankets onto the ice.

"Don't pretend you don't know what these are for," she says.

"Oh," he says.

"Close," she says. "The Big O." She laughs and pulls him down toward the unforgettable.

"This is it," he says afterwards—or after the third afterwards. "This is the summit of my existence on earth."

"Time to move to Mars," she says, kissing him again.

But it is she who might be moving. The Medevs have offered her parents the chance to manage their five rinks in Moscow as well as the amusement park next door to a prison that briefly housed Alexandr Solzhenitsyn. "There's a ride called One Minute in the Life of Ivan Denisovich," she says. She looks him over. "You don't think I'm funny?"

"I know you're funny," says Walt. "But I don't know who Ivan Denisovich is. And I can't stand the thought of you moving to Moscow."

"My parents haven't been happy since Leo died," she says. "They might see this as a chance to start over—to be reborn where they were born."

They live as if she might leave tomorrow. Saturday nights at the rink become every night at the rink. Some mornings, Walt doesn't know how he manages to rise from his bed. He is deliciously, deliriously exhausted. The holidays come. Halloween. Thanksgiving, Christmas. At midnight on each, he is at the rink.

On New Year's Eve, she tells him her parents have decided they won't be moving to Moscow after all. They celebrate by skating the New Year's Toast, the New Year's Resolution, and Auld Lang Syne. The latter is the easiest. They stand next to each other, wrap their arms around each other's shoulders, and sway.

The next night when Walt arrives at the rink, he sees a pair of two-by-fours nailed across the front entrance. Something awful must have happened inside, he thinks. A gas leak. A burst pipe. A hockey player gone berserk with his stick. But the Rink Girl, behind him now, says, "The rink is closed. The owner is tearing it down to build condos."

Walt turns to her. Her tone tells him she is serious. But he cannot refrain from asking, as if out of an obligation to hope, "Are you joking?"

"The owner told my parents the rink is too expensive to maintain," she says. "He blames it on global warming and sixty-degree winter days."

"But he's creating global warming with his coal. If he would shut down his coal mines, he could keep his rink." The world suddenly seems sinister and doomed. "What happens now?"

She shakes her head. "Moscow," she says. "We leave in three days."

Global warming has taken the evening off. Walt's breath pours out of him as thick as smoke from a coal-fired power plant. What world will he be living in when the Rink Girl is gone? "What? You can't be serious. Are you serious?"

"I would love to be joking."

"You don't have to move," he says. "You can stay here. You can finish high school in Sherman. I'll talk to my parents. You can live with us."

She smiles softly, and he knows it's a prelude to words he doesn't want to hear. "I thought of this," she says. "I thought of a hundred solutions." Her breath fills the air between them. "My parents would miss me too much. Because of what happened to my brother, they want me close."

They walk around the rink, checking windows, checking doors. But nothing gives, nothing opens. They come to the last door, on the edge of the forest at the back of the rink. He kicks it with his black winter boots. He punches it with his bare hands. Bang. Bang. Bang. He finds a brick behind him and smashes it against the wood. Bang. Bang. Bang. He tries his boots again, the brick again. Bang. Bang. Bang. Bang-bang-bang. He drops to his knees.

"I guess no one's home," she says.

He turns. She is at the edge of the woods. A step backwards, and she would be swallowed whole by the oak and maple trees. "Fate isn't our friend," she says with a resignation he has never heard from her. "But who marries her high-school sweetheart nowadays, anyway?"

"Half the people in this town," he says, sweeping his hands over the dark wood.

"How happy are they?"

"A thousand times happier than I'll be when you're gone."

On their last night together, the Rink Girl proposes they go with their skates to Murderer's Cove on Sky Lake, where the ice is frozen solid. In the twenties and thirties, Murderer's Cove hosted criminal activity ranging from bootlegging to assassination. Or so local legend goes. Now it's a refuge for teenage lovers who lack a private place to crawl into each other's bodies.

The sky is full of stars, as if, from Acamar to Zubeneschamali, they had thrown back the curtain of night to spy on love's last ice dance. He watches the Rink Girl skate across the cove. When she is at the far end, barely visible against a background of pine trees, he skates toward her with a rage he wouldn't have imagined himself capable of. She is facing the trees, her back to him, when he slices to a stop behind her. "Why aren't you furious at the world?" His voice is half accusatory, half perplexed. "Why aren't you as sad as I am?"

But when she turns to him, he sees she is crying, and not gently. "Oh," he says, embarrassed and strangely relieved. They fall into each other. He slides his arms into her coat and around her waist. He pulls her toward him.

"What are we going to do?" she asks.

"Run away with me," he says.

"I wish I could."

"What would it take to convince you?" he asks. "I'll do anything. I'll walk home on my skates. I'll sing all night to the stars." He pauses. "Wait," he says. "I know. I'll show you I can do the most difficult jump you ever tried to teach me." He pushes back from her, onto the starlit cove. "No, I'll do an even harder jump. I'll do the jump you only spoke to me about. What did you call it? The End of the World, right?"

"It's impossible to do an End of the World," she says. "Even I can't do it. You haven't even done a Mini Apocalypse."

"You'll see," he says. "If you say you'll run away with me, I'll do it." The energy of superheroes flows in his veins; he feels he could leap and grab hold of a star. He isn't going to lose her. He's going to do the impossible and they are going to live together forever, their lives always sweet, always delicious.

"If I do it, will you run away with me?"

She nods, a nearly invisible gesture.

"Promise?"

This time there is conviction: "I promise."

"All right," he says. He skates up to her, cups her cheeks, kisses her. "Here goes."

He skates to the center of the cove, fifty feet from her, before halting and swirling around. She is gray against a black background, but she is all the color of his life. He skates toward her with a power he has never possessed. His skates feel like they are barely touching the ice. He moves fast, faster. Ten feet from her, he soars, streaking toward the stars. He does a complete twist and a half, and he is still climbing, like a roaring rocket. He dips his head toward the ice and curls his skates toward the sky. Presently, his skates fall and his head rises, a delirious somersault—and another! Now he is coming down clean. He anticipates her joy, and his, and how their happiness will see them past hardship and doubt, will outburn the stars.

His skates strike the ice straight and perfect. He lifts his arms in triumph, but at the same time he feels the ice give and open around him. He plummets like a stone.

Years pass, and every breath without her is like ice water in his lungs.

Joy Castro

THE DREAM OF THE FATHER

———

Angela Cardenas was not only a liar and a bitch but also a boyfriend-stealer, which didn't keep me from being best friends with her the last three years of high school. I'm not sure what that says about me, considering even my own boyfriends weren't off-limits.

For instance like the time she and Rick Piscatelli made out in my driveway after my seventeenth birthday party while I busted ass inside, scrambling to collect all the bottles before my folks got home from the Steelers game. I didn't even know about it for almost a week until Tanya Rodebecker told me, in this surprised way like she thought for *sure* me and Rick must've broken up. But Tanya was like that, acting like she didn't mean anything; Angela would just rob you blind. Which in a way, you had to respect.

I mean, you couldn't blame her, at least I couldn't, what with me being the original wallflower of the universe. I figured she couldn't help herself, and neither could the guys, with her looking like she did. She was so pretty you couldn't even envy her, she was in such a different league. When a certain black-haired, pouty-lipped, big-bosomed actress made it big, about the time me and Angie were seniors, people started coming up to her all the time: "Has anybody ever told you that you look just like so-and-so?"

"No—really?" she'd say, all sweet and surprised-like, sucking it in like honey, although I swear I must have seen it happen at least thirty times at the mall or up at Colassessano's. If you've ever hung out with a truly beautiful girl then you know how it is, how you're not really even jealous. You just drink up the excitement of it, proud to be standing next to her. I mean maybe I wouldn't have handled it so well if she hadn't been so great. Not that she really was so great, at least if you look at it in a surface kind of way. It was more complicated than that, and I've always been enticed by complications.

Being the less pretty one, I always played the straight man when we hung around in public together, and she was the one laughing and bouncing from lap to lap, squeezing biceps, me saying *come on, Angie, we're gonna be late.* I remember her writing me notes in Chemistry class about how it was like swallowing six raw eggs one after the other until you think you're going to throw up or die and not to start up unless I was into total gaggery because once they'd had it they wouldn't quit asking. And me taking the notes and copying the equations that pulled us through exams.

I know this is making me sound like a fool, but if you've ever been there, then you know that there are times you don't mind being taken for one. I guess I was suffering Angela to teach me something. And I learned real well, even the details, sneaking into the basement girls' room with her during lunch hour to puke our cafeteria meals into the toilets, her having to keep her weight down for cheerleading and me along for the ride. *Shit, sweetie, you got some in your hair,* she'd say. *This apple crumble shit's a bitch.*

She could eat a half-gallon of ice cream at a sitting, something I could never do, and then rush to the bathroom, a smooth chocolate gush swirling into the toilet bowl. She'd go through three half-gallons in an evening—her mom worked nightshift at McCrory's so I'd go over there and we'd watch comedies on the VCR until we were too tired to see. *Put the blusher across your nose a little bit too, honey,* she'd say in the bathroom the next morning. *It looks more natural if you glow all over.*

I never heard anybody call her a slut, exactly, but she did have a certain kind of reputation, and I guess you could say it was earned. I remember driving her car back from Kennywood Park, two hours south to home, me and Tommy Larsen in the front seat talking about him opening up his own shop someday—which he did: Larsen's Auto Body—but that was years after. And Angela with her twenty-nine-year-old in the backseat (him with an ex-wife and little girl payments) screwing all the way down I-79.

So, how much capital would you need? I ask Tommy, because my dad says stuff like that on the phone all the time. They're real quiet but her knee or something keeps pushing on the back of the seat.

Probably around five thousand to start, he says, and I say I think that's a real fine idea, because Tommy after all knows his stuff and he's a real nice guy and patient too. The twenty-nine-year-old does something that sounds like clearing his throat and the pushing stops.

He was just one of a whole bunch during the three years me and Angie were friends—older ones, married ones, even our own East Fairmont assistant football coach—but in private she was a real nice girl and would talk seriously about things, like what she wanted to do and how scared she got sometimes thinking about nuclear war and stuff like that. Sometimes we'd drive around for hours in her little car listening to The Police and not saying anything. And she wasn't a dumb girl at all.

It's taken me a lot of years of not seeing her to wonder why somebody who was secretly smart and had dreams for herself would go to such lengths to hide that away from everybody. Why she would take me so serious in private, like we were the best friends in the world, but treat me so bad when it suited her. Making out with my boyfriends and such. We talked about a lot of things, me and Angie, but there are things I still wonder about when I think of her. And it's a true story that her dad shot himself on her bed when she was twelve years old, before I knew her, but she wouldn't talk about him to save her life.

If a dead man's face can really look out of an upper-story window, if a dead man's elbow can prop itself on the sill and his shoulder can wedge against the casement. If a dead man can light a cigarette and throw the match down into the street. If a dead man's match can land in the street where his daughter waits, if it can land at the feet of his living daughter, his daughter who is alive and asleep watching the match burn at her feet. If she can see the way his eyes drink in the orange pinpoints when he pulls on the cigarette. If she can see him seeing her in the darkness. The way his eyes suck the light out of the air and swallow it, the way when she looks at his eyes she is shrinking, she feels the shrinking of her body into a tiny flicker, how she starts to float, billowing toward him across the warm dark air. If she can see him seeing her in the darkness. If he can see her in the darkness, see her in her bed with the covers pulled around. If he can see her no matter which way she moves, if he can see her in the light. If he can see her during the day, during cheerleading practice, during those times when suddenly her smile muscles grow rigid and her eyes stare back, her teeth bared in a rictus grin. And Mrs. McManus yells at her to get with the other girls! and she does, she gets with the other girls, she matches her movements to theirs, her arms to their flashing arms, her legs to their leaps, her chant to their pumping voices go boys go.

Jonathan Corcoran

THROUGH THE STILL HOURS

It's Saturday. I wake up early, and after having a cup of coffee alone in the kitchen, I cook and bring him breakfast in bed. French toast and eggs. This, in my head, seems the simplest way to make romance. It's our fourth anniversary—four years since we met each other in that parking lot. I think I might catch him off guard this morning, before he has time to think of all the ways to keep me at arm's length. Food, I reason, is something that still motivates us to make nice with each other. The promise of taste and smell and drink still stirs something inside of us in the most primal ways. Sad, I know, for someone not yet thirty years of age to act fifty, but this is where I'm at—where we're at.

At first, in the bedroom, it seems I might trick him into submission. He awakens with a smile—his ash-blond hair a mess from the static of the pillow. I think, this is how it should be, two lovers naked, all proverbial walls down. I kiss him on the neck and use the stubble on my chin to trace patterns on his back. His pale white skin turns red in abstract hearts and figure eights. His initial complacency, his unmoving body, surprises me, given the defensive posturing that usually greets my attempts at sex. His lack of a defense is enough to arouse me, and I try not to overthink things. I let the smell of his night sweat pull me into his body. "I want to make love to you all day long," I say. "And then I want to make love to you some more, until the sun sets and rises again."

I wonder if I really mean these words. I try not to think about how making love, in the few times that it ever happens with us anymore, has become an almost selfish act, driven more by basic needs and less by a desire to revel in the other's pleasure. It's a letting of blood for us. A release of tension. But I don't dwell on the usual way of things. I convince myself that anniversaries can act as a reset button. In bed, as I'm blowing hot air onto his neck, he's the Gerry of day one, with a lust inducing shyness, his falsely innocent eyes beckoning.

But this doesn't last. As he awakens and recognizes my intent, his smile melts away. His eyes harden. It's as if I've stirred him from the most sexual dream, only for him to realize that the man who's been fucking him in the clouds is not the man in his bed—is not me. "I'm tired, love. Maybe later?" He finishes with a peck of a kiss, quick and dry. He sits up and sticks his fork into the eggs. He eats with zeal.

———

How we found each other goes something like this: Four years ago, we message each other on one of those Web sites whose sexually punny names I prefer not to pronounce aloud. We settle on a spot in the next town over for the sake of discretion. We decide to meet just off the highway in a McDonald's parking lot. I remember seeing his face for the first time. I think of that electric sensation when I'm alone in the shower.

On that first day, we are two anonymous Internet profiles taking a chance on explicit pictures from the chest down. His car is just as he said it would be: a 1991 silver Toyota hatchback with a belt of rust along the bottom. He rolls down the window, wanting to speak, but scared. Before he can say a word, I utter, "Yes. It's me."

He leans over the gearshift and throws open the passenger door. It groans. I make him take his car, because I don't want to run the risk of anyone recognizing me, even here, twenty miles from home. I'm no fool—I know that people talk. Some people drive twenty miles to do their shopping, looking for a change of scenery. Others drive that far because they're tired of being seen. Like the preacher said at church when I was growing up, "Someone's always watching you." God, or that old woman who lives next door.

In his car, the smells wafting from the vents of the fast food restaurant mix with the scent of his cologne. This combination—salty, florid, cheap— makes him seem younger than the age that was on his online profile. We take one long, deep look at each other, and then we both lock our vision straight ahead through the windshield. His face burns into my mind in that look, exists still in my memory: frightened blue eyes, nervous lips. I prefer that face. Even his blond hair, back then, seemed to suggest *soiled*. In my dreams, I see that face, and he says, "I'm holding back, but only for a moment."

In the car that evening, he says, "Where are we going?"

"I don't care." My heart beats too quickly. My hands clench down on the sides of the vinyl seats. "Just drive."

So we do. We drive down back roads, past rolling farms at the edge of mountains. We drive past abandoned gas stations, the victims of four-lane highways. He knows the roads by heart, as we all do, because that's where our fathers took us on joyrides to tell the dirty stories of their youth. My instinct is to recount these stories, to tell him where my father brawled with drunken men. To tell him where my father took an easy girl under a tree and asserted himself. I bite my lip, though, and say nothing. Somehow these stories feel too shocking, as if I'm not actually driving down a back road with a stranger intent on doing things that seem too embarrassing to speak of.

Gerry steals sideways glances when he takes sharp turns. I notice, then look away. We fumble. We shimmy in our seats. We become braver, in fits and starts, make eye contact, breathe heavily to fill the silence. He moves his lips, but no words come out. He put his hand onto mine, after switching gears. He waits for me to meet him halfway, to curl my fingers into his own. It's such a teenage gesture, but for us, there's a newness to it.

"Are you a murderer?" I say, only half-joking, when his skin touches mine. "Why haven't I seen you around town? I've seen everyone."

"I'm from the next county over," he says, naming the town. It's a place I know well, not much more than a pit stop on the way down from the mountain. He looks the part, with his Sunday best on: the checkered shirt, the khaki pants, and the schoolboy cut. He sang in the church choir no doubt, bringing old women to tears with his honey baritone and startled eyes. I judge him for these things, as if being from my town of eight thousand is any better than being from his town of five hundred.

"I just moved here for work," he says.

"You look, well, normal," I say. "What do you do?"

"High school teacher."

"Are you out?"

"Define out."

"Do people know that you're into men?"

"They suspect. I don't talk about it. Why does anybody need to know?"

We drive for miles, lay down the basics, or at least as much as we feel safe revealing to a stranger who suddenly knows too many of our secrets. It's fall and everything is red—the dropping leaves, the setting sun, the fire of our cigarettes, blazing brighter as they catch the wind from the cracked windows. I see the blood in the back of my eyes with each throat-clenching heartbeat.

We pull over onto a secluded lookout: a meandering river and hay bales in the fields below. We are far from any named town: existence incognito out here. We watch the day disappear. The sky fades like a rotting peach. We sit in silence and pass a flask of whiskey to cut the tension.

At a farmhouse in the distance, a porch light shines like a nightlight or a warning. I understand this darkness. I revel in the feeling of it. One can't avoid it growing up underneath the mountains. The darkness never fails to frighten and to thrill me, to conjure ghosts and campfire stories. We get out of the car and lay back on the warm hood. Thousands of stars circle slowly above, clustered and thick, hanging over the non-forms of trees along the hillsides, the black on blacker horizon.

"Do you do this often?" I ask.

"More than I'd like," he says, his voice quiet but sultry. His admission, which I can also claim as my own, both shames and turns me on. We're pushed by the world to dark spaces, filthy bathrooms, and secret lookouts. We feel dirty always, but then at a certain point, when we become familiar with these dark terrains, we begin to like the feeling. We claim the dark spaces and the secret corridors as our own. These acts become at first an outlet, and then an addiction: an instant erection upon pulling into a highway rest stop.

Because of all this, we know what's coming without prompting. We knew what was coming before we sent the first message online. We get back into the car. We touch lips. We feel the contours of the other's body and delight in the mystery of what exists under our clothing. We recline our seats.

But just as we're beginning, the headlights of a vehicle break the darkness. It's a half mile down the road, lumbering toward us.

"What if someone catches us?" he says.

I don't stop, though. I can't stop. The fear of getting caught is also part of the game, part of the turn-on.

"And what if?" I say, challenging him with my hand as I squeeze his inner thigh.

"Don't you . . . aren't you . . .? Oh, fuck it."

The headlights grow brighter and closer. I kiss him deeply. My hands stop touching and start pushing, forcing their way, fueled by some exhibitionist tendency. I dare the night to interfere, to trespass on this scene.

And then the lights arrive. The truck slows to a halt just outside our car.

Bright white pierces the glass, blinding us. Gerry pushes me off of him, looks to the steam on the windows. His shoulders shrink inward. We are guilty and scared. I roll down the window—decipher the face of an old man in a dented pickup. The brim of his ball cap hangs down to the edge of his eyes. He nods his head at us, firm and quick. His face is clean-shaven. He looks nervously over his shoulder. Clears his throat. "You boys be careful out here," he says and drives off.

We don't finish what we started. Gerry drives me back to my car, through the night, in silence.

———

I watch Gerry finish his breakfast. He smiles as he eats. He tells me the food is good, raises his fork, nods his head with approval. When he finishes, he hands me his plate. I get up to walk to the kitchen.

"Happy anniversary," he calls after me.

I take his dish to the sink. I drink a glass of water. I look out the kitchen window. I see the solitary willow tree that takes up a full half of our fenced-in backyard. The willow's thin branches flutter with the breeze, caress the grass like fingers. I imagine my body as the grass. I want to be touched.

I come back to the bedroom to get dressed. Gerry plays on his laptop, as I put on jeans. When I look at him, my neck tenses. I breathe in. The air feels thick.

"Ariana just texted," he says, not looking up from his computer. "She said she really wants margaritas before we go out tonight. We have tequila, but would you mind going to pick up the mixers?"

"You know I didn't want to do this tonight," I say. I want to hit him. I want to grab him by the wrists and squeeze so hard that I leave a bruise. "I still don't understand why we can't celebrate by ourselves. It's our anniversary—not theirs."

"Because what we have is so special," he says, in his high, whiny voice. "I want them to know what we have."

I don't respond. I walk into the living room and put my shoes on. I grab my car keys. He yells goodbye as I walk out the front door.

———

I drive to Walmart, and as I pull into the parking lot, I think maybe I should find a secluded place in the back lot to finish alone what I had attempted to start with Gerry. But the back of the lot is too busy. Saturdays are always madness here, with every last troll and ogre lining up to do their weekend shopping. I decide to save my solo joy for a later time. I clench my teeth and walk inside.

I'm treated to a vision of every person I don't care to see. We all know each other—by face or name. If not, we could surmise enough, by the type of clothes we wear, by the way we carry ourselves. I left the house in a hurry, throwing on whatever I could find, but here, I'm a snobbish prince. I hold my head low, so as not to attract any unneeded attention.

I stop into the bathroom before I begin shopping. In the bathroom, as I'm in the middle of pissing, a wrinkly old man with a high school letterman jacket begins to jerk his dick at me two urinals down. He swings it around like he's offering me gold or a diamond or both. His all-knowing glance sizes me up, perhaps by my clothes or the way I return his eye contact. He thinks: queer, horny queer, likes to suck queer, takes-whatever-he-can-get queer. That's the standard around here, be it in a bathroom or on the Internet. When I refuse his ilk, I'm never sure if they're going to burst into tears or pummel me.

I've stopped trying to make sense of it. It happens once a week at least. The same old men you hear trash-talking outside the redneck bars—faggot this, faggot that. Gerry doesn't believe me when I tell him this—doesn't trust my face when I emerge red and angry from a piss at the movie theater. It's because he doesn't look at people—at least not directly. He's head-forward everywhere, bulldozing through air—all *excuse me* and *pardon me*. Knows his place.

Before Gerry and I started dating, I'd never kissed the same man more than once. Half of the men I met—on the Internet, in the stalls of bathrooms like this—didn't even kiss me on the mouth. I thought that was the way life worked: a series of shady encounters with men I'd never see again. Gerry gave me something I'd never felt before. It was love, I thought, or something like it.

In the restroom, with the Walmart radio blaring upbeat country music designed to push this week's camouflage coat, my eyes settle not on the old man's dick but on the golden band on his left ring finger. Though I'm not attracted to this man, I feel myself getting hard. I smile. I laugh. I proffer him a look at my penis. "Relationships are tough, huh? I'm sorry I can't help you out."

And what does he say, in response to my gesture at civility? "Fuck you, faggot."

I leave the bathroom and continue on with my shopping, unfazed.

———

I return home with the mixers, and Gerry avoids me for the duration of the day. He lesson-plans for school and then putzes around on the Internet while I read a book. He pulls me aside before our friends arrive. "This means a lot to them," he says. "We're the only gay couple they know."

"And we're the new paradigm," I say. "We're the hope for the future."

"You can be a real dick," he says. "Don't be that way tonight. Be happy. For me."

That's the end of our conversation until evening comes and our friends arrive, couple by couple, taking seats in our living room. There's Ariana and Chris, and Karen and Michael—two pretty and talkative women who Gerry met through teaching, and their blissfully silent husbands, who are really just quiet because they're unsure of what to say to us: the nice little homos that mix such delectable drinks. There's no harm in their silence. I take no offense. It's as awkward for me as it is for them.

It's just another Saturday, slightly altered subjects: the politics du jour and the strange old man who showed up this week outside the grocery store and greets customers with cat noises. He meows if he likes you, hisses if he doesn't. Gerry receives purrs, while I receive claws. I think there must be something in that, some larger comment about the quality of my soul, but I can't quite put my finger on it.

Gerry and I sit on opposite sides of the living room in two hardback chairs. The two couples sit on the loveseat and the big sofa, hands on knees, and close enough to advertise that they still feel something for each other.

We sit and the chatter rolls on. Karen regales us with the politically incorrect things that her high school students say. Ariana talks about taking a trip to Pittsburgh to go shopping for some "real" clothes. As they blather on, the room grows darkly golden with the sunset. The light always disappears sooner than expected here: the end-of-summer shrinking sun falling behind the mountains, gnawing at my psyche. A breeze blows against the trees and rocks the neighbors' wind chimes as if to say *take cover!* So I close the windows and the curtains. I switch on lamps and light tapers in brass holders on the coffee table. Our shadow figures gesture on the walls, and I wonder, how is it that the shadows seem more animated than we do?

"I always feel so comfortable here, guys," Ariana says. "You have the coziest apartment in town."

Once, I would have been flattered. Once, I would have proudly agreed with her. I remember back when Gerry and I first moved in together. We tried to create beauty and warmth in the way that we draped a curtain just so, in how we painted the walls of the living room an inviting burnt orange. We thought we were so smart in that choice, building our refuge. We wrapped ourselves in blankets on Sunday mornings and held each other until the dusk. I look back on the conversations we had, back when we thought that the burnt orange walls were a symbol of our life to come, not a marker of stasis. "Imagine," I said then, "a world—this very world, same place, same town—where two men could go walking down the street arm and arm and the neighbors would just smile and wave." And then we'd hold each other some more, and think that maybe that future was a real possibility. We watched the television, the promise of a president. Obama, we thought, a man who would change everything. Childish optimism, I know, to think that the outside world would somehow find its way here, to our small world. But in those moments, there was a forward movement with us: a connection through hope and a sharing of secrets.

And at some point after those moments had played out, something quiet happened. After all our secrets were revealed, our fantasies confessed aloud, we began to pretend that we were just like everyone else. We played at husband and wife, though we knew it was forbidden for people like us. Or maybe we just didn't understand the game, or the rules. Or maybe, most importantly, we tried to be something that we weren't. We became like apes wearing human costumes. We could play the part, and though we were different at the core, we were close enough in kind to fool the onlookers.

Ariana moves her gaze from Gerry to me. She extends her arm and her margarita glass for emphasis. "I'll fucking kill the both of you if you ever break up."

———

We drink until we're all sure of our insobriety. Then we prepare to head off to the bar to go dancing, the second leg of our Saturday night group anniversary celebration. Gerry collects everyone's margarita glasses, and as he takes mine, he kisses me on the cheek. I feel like shivering, but I catch a warning in his eye. I reach out and touch his arm. I feel disgusted with myself for playing at this game.

"You guys are just adorable," Karen says, as if on cue, another hint of what will be an evening of excessive drunken flattery. And I know that he loves this idea: that we're the porcelain figurines missing from their otherwise perfect shadowboxes. He throws an extra shimmy into his hip as he walks. He spouts sassy one-liners stolen from bad reality television. Of course, he won't touch me once we leave the safety of our apartment.

As we walk out the door, I imagine what it would be like to fuck him, right in front of their faces. To show them what a dick looks like going into an ass. To show them that we're capable of lust and aggression and messiness. I picture tying my sweater right around his mouth, jerking his head back as I push into him. Would they remain seated? Would they drop their cocktails?

And what would Gerry do if I grabbed him by the balls and squeezed? Would he moan in pleasure? Would he call my name?

No. I think he would slap my face.

———

We approach the steps of our destination, which is just a short walk from our apartment. The bar is called "The Commander's Pub," and it sits on a residential street, off the main drag of the quiet downtown. It's an old Victorian house with a big wraparound porch where we escape the crowds and smoke cigarettes. The neighbors complain about the hippies and write to the newspaper about the strange music that blasts until two in the morning. It's our sanctuary, and sometimes I wish I could climb up the old wooden stairs and claim one of the Commander's extra bedrooms as my own.

We hear a trumpet and drums as we walk up to the screen door. It's salsa night. Ariana turns to us. "Chris and I've been practicing at home. We've been watching videos online. I think he's finally ready to spin me."

Gerry and I used to dance alone with the blinds pulled. We taught ourselves salsa and swing. I led him with strong arms, and he followed, turning once, twice, dipping low. I would pick him up and toss him around my body and under my legs, as I'd seen on television. We're different, the two of us. His body is light, featherlike. Skin and bones, but not fragile. Easy to push around. Easy to hold.

"I can't wait to see, honey," Gerry says to Ariana.

There's something about the way he speaks to her that makes me want to run away. I'm embarrassed to be a part of this. Sometimes I feel he's like a talking doll with a cord in his back. A jester. Their toy.

The owner of the bar, the namesake, the Commander himself, greets us as we walk inside. He's the town's favorite eccentric, with his bald head and white beard down to his hips. He hugs the girls and shakes the boys' hands. Karen stands on her tiptoes and whispers something into his ear.

"Esmé," the Commander says to his pretty, young wife standing behind the bar. "Drinks on the house for Cliff and Gerry."

She pours us two whiskeys on the rocks—our regular drink. "What's the occasion?"

"Our anniversary," Gerry whispers and winks. The words roll from his mouth so easily that I feel guilty. "Four years."

"Congratulations," she says. "Drink up, lovebirds."

Gerry forces a toast, clanks his glass against mine and bottoms out the whiskey. I can't even bring myself to sip—I just swish it in a circle.

"I'll have another," he says.

I know this is the beginning of many more drinks for him, which means when we go home he'll crawl into the bed and fall asleep in minutes. I used to try to kiss him after nights like these. I would kiss his neck and touch his back, and he'd say he was too tired. He'd roll over, mumbling about how there'd be time in the morning. When the morning came, he'd say he was too hung over.

A half-dozen couples have started dancing in front of the band. We watch the band for a moment: a trumpeter, drummer, and a piano player. Gerry is tapping his feet and his fingers to the rhythm. I lean over to his ear and whisper: "If you love me, then dance with me."

He looks shocked, then angry, then hurt. "You know we can't do that here," he says.

I recognize all the faces: the same ones who have been coming to this bar for years. Every one of them knows about us, though I can't think of a single person who has ever brought it up without prompting. They never ask questions—as if that would be some sort of transgression. They don't need qualifications. Or really, they don't want to know the details. We're just us: Gerry and Cliff, those boys, two names that go together.

———

A few drinks in, and our friends are all out on the dance floor. We sit alone, Gerry looks away, and I look at him.

"We haven't fucked in a month," I say. "Happy anniversary."

"Why are you acting like this?" he asks, and then turns away.

We sip the whiskeys and watch the dancing couples: carefree, ridiculous, completely wrong but right. I swallow the last of my drink, and feel an anger-fueled intoxication streaming through me.

"Just fucking dance with me," I say. I reach for his hand, but he pulls away. He reaches for his cigarettes, takes his glass, and heads to the porch.

I follow him out the door. From the porch, the music bends into something different, creates a tunnel-like dream world. There's the life inside and the quiet reality of the streets just down the steps.

Gerry sits in a rusty metal chair around the corner, out of the light, almost invisible. I go to him. I get down on my knees so that we're face to face.

"I'm sorry," I say. "But what do you expect me to do?"

He seems to consider my words, as he looks into my eyes. His face fades in and out of the shadows, picks up a bit of fire from the cherry of his cigarette. "Why don't we dance together, Cliff? Why don't we hold hands? Do you need me to explain it to you? Do you need me to tell you, step by step, about what happens to men like us in towns like this? Are we really going to go over this right now?" His eyes look like glaciers: reflective and uninviting. "If you don't want to be with me," he says, "then go."

"I can only try so much," I say. "This isn't my fault."

"It's no one's fault," he says. "No. It's everyone's fault."

He's crying now. I want to comfort him, but I can't. We've done this one too many times. I walk off the porch and leave.

———

I weave through the side streets to avoid the main drag. The night is mostly quiet, but with sudden bursts of sound. Yips and yells, and tire squeals that smash the stillness unexpectedly and send chills through my body. The sounds fade just long enough to surprise again when they return.

I walk by the rows of old houses. Brick and clapboard. The lights are mostly off, but television screens flicker blue and white and beckon. The windows sit framed by low-hanging sycamore and maple trees. I want to be home. I want to go into my bedroom and curl under the blankets, pull them over my head, and seal off the world. But I continue to walk along because the home I'm thinking of is not the home in which I live. I'm not sure where that home is.

As I'm walking, I sometimes stop and close my eyes—the sidewalk curves, familiar as a recurring dream. I imagine Gerry taking my arm, and I jump a little, surprised by the vividness of this thought. In my mind, he holds me tightly and leans his head on my shoulder as we walk. People smile when they see us. And then their smiles make us want to take off our clothes. Then we're making love on the streets, and the audience is cheering.

I walk past the homes of the people I've known all of my life. I can assign names to most doors. I meander down sidewalks and look at the moon, and try to imagine what life would be like there, on the bright side, when a shadow is always a shadow, never shifting with the position of the sun.

I take a turn and pick up the pace. Now I'm rushing through the main street of the downtown, past the rough-and-tumble pool halls that I'm afraid to enter. The handful of gruff men who smoke outside these places utter prophecies in my direction: *broken neck, fuck your pussy.* Some of them blow kisses and lick their lips. They call me with two fingers: *here queer.* But this only fuels me. I smile back at them, with teeth. I watch them retreat, then, their heads going down, like dogs backing off from a fight.

I walk past all there is to see in the downtown, which isn't much more than the same old buildings that have been here for a hundred years. Half of them are boarded up and empty. I walk across a swinging footbridge over the town's shallow, dirty river. The river seems so much more enchanting here and now, as it reflects the moonlight and the lamplight from the windows of an adjacent apartment building. I cross the river and leave the downtown, heading back toward my apartment. I look at my watch and realize I've been walking for over an hour. I wonder if Gerry is home now. I wonder if we will apologize to each other and then cuddle, sexlessly, until we fall asleep. Or more likely, we'll say nothing at all, and then in the morning, we'll say even less.

I'm only two blocks from home. I don't see the truck at first. I hear it, sense its presence—air moving different than the wind. I turn around, watch as it drives toward me, a dark form with no headlights turned on. It appears as a living, moving thing under the street lamps: an animate beast of sorts, with instincts, on the hunt. I don't see the driver. Instead, I see the fluorescent reflection of the streetlights in the windshield.

The truck slows down as it nears me, and I look straight ahead, to show that

I have a destination. The confidence that I showed to the men earlier is gone, though, and I fear that the driver can sense it. The truck rolls along beside me. I pick up the pace, expecting the worst—though I'm ready for it, prepared to be beaten, can already feel my face against the ground, head stomped by a steel-toed boot, teeth loosened. The thought doesn't bother me—almost delights me, in fact. I can already feel the sidewalk, cold and comforting, like when you have the flu and you collapse onto the bathroom floor. I wonder if I will call out to my lover, as the attacker calls out to me, "Dirty faggot."

The truck drives away, though, and in that moment, lucidity returns. I finger my cell phone in my pocket. Should I call the police? Should I call Gerry to come meet me? I'm only a block from home now. I can see our porch light just down the street. I could run, and that seems smart, but I don't. I have the urge to test fate, or maybe just experience a thrill—anything but home, anything but Gerry.

The truck returns, as I expect. The same pattern—slowing down as if to escort me. The passenger window is rolled down. I see the man's shadow of a face—sad, hard-leather skin. This villain has a backstory, I think, full of broken hearts. His own heart included.

"What do you want with me?" I ask.

I think the man smiles, though in the obscured light I cannot tell. There is some movement in the truck. I can hear the shifting of the man's weight, and his breathing.

"Do you wanna go for a ride?" he asks.

We have stopped moving: two parallel souls in the dark night. There are stars out, and televisions flickering. There are people dancing in bars, and the thought enters my mind that there are children writing wishes in diaries by the light of the moon shining through their bedroom windows.

I wonder if Gerry can see us—if he has hitched a ride home, feeling lonely and raw, and now sits at the kitchen window, watching for moving shadows, my body hulking through the dark streetscape.

I take one step toward the man and pause, waiting for his reaction. He leans across the seat and opens the door. "You don't have to be afraid," he says.

And in this man's voice, in his face, in the darkness of the night, and the still intact body I inhabit, I know I can trust him, this man who wanders alone through the still hours of the earliest morning, looking for people like me, offering comfort in a familiar phrase: "You have nothing to fear."

"Where are we going?" I ask.

"Wherever you want," he says, as if he were sucking in the words, not speaking them.

He is me four years ago. He is Gerry four years ago. His aged face is unimportant. What matters is the tone of his voice.

"I know a few places," I say, and get into his truck, settling into the seat as if I've always belonged there.

As he drives off, without asking any directions, a surge of feeling emanates from my gut and into my throat. And it's in that feeling that I know this is both exactly where I should and shouldn't be.

Ed Davis

THE BOYS OF BRADLEYTOWN

––––––––

Just when I'd begun to wonder if my uncles knew where they were going, they pulled off the road in front of me. A state route, it was only a lane and a half through the heart of the West Virginia coalfields where my father, their brother, Benjamin James Bradford, was to be buried in the cemetery of Redeeming Blood Baptist on Wolford Mountain, my mother's church.

After parking the Jetta off the road, I walked up beside Elm's pickup. Three o'clock on a grim November afternoon, the day was already fading, and I saw he and Frank had on the dome light, illuminating their friarish balding grey-fringed heads. The window was down, allowing their cigar smoke to curl around me as I leaned inside to peer over Elm's shoulder. Pointing with the gnarly hand that held the stogie, Frank said, "There it is, Route 23, as plain as day going south."

"Too far south," Elm said. "We shoulda been there already. It's getting late."

I retracted my head, turned around and leaned against the cab. My eyes bored into the bare-limbed forest across the road. Not only was Frank wearing Elm's bifocals—always a bad sign—but the map was clearly upside down.

I thought I detected motion among the trees, as if someone were waving from the top of one of the old white oaks. But when I stared harder: nothing. Then I heard Dad, clear as Digital Dolby inside my head, tell Mom one more time, *That's the way them boys are.*

I walked back to my car. Mom and I'd traded shifts until the final forty-eight-hour round-the-clock vigil. Then the arrangements, then the wake. I hadn't eaten much, nor wanted to. Thank God for hospital coffee. We drank gallons of it. I glanced across the road one last time before getting behind the wheel. We'd get there when we got there. If they didn't hold the service for us, then I wouldn't have to deliver the eulogy.

The day was headed for bed when we finally pulled into the parking lot an hour late. I couldn't tell if the aura around the sun was real or the product of my own road-induced double vision. Sure enough, they'd waited for us, everyone's worried looks turning to big grins when both Frank and Elm accused the other of getting us lost. Mom, bless her heart, had ridden with her cousin Ella. Now she just gripped my arm, kissed my cheek and whispered, "Thank you for getting the boys here." I didn't tell her that my father had waved from the upper limbs of an oak, in death still treating his brothers like headstrong kids.

The sanctuary overflowed. Everyone within a twenty-five-mile radius had turned out for the local hero, who'd never left the place of his birth. Though there were black and white action shots and yellowed newspaper clippings borrowed from Bradleytown High's trophy case, it was the shoes that nearly did me in.

Atop the bronze casket sat a pair of high-topped black and white Converses, probably the very shoes he'd worn in the last tournament he'd taken the Blackhawks to. Hard shoes to fill. Elm and Frank had discovered that, when they'd tried to play triple-A ball at the same school where their big brother had broken all the records. Forget that Ben Bradford had always been able to resurrect any gasoline-powered engine, had been school board president and mayor twice and had almost made it to the statehouse; Benny "The Bullet" was forever frozen in mid-jump-shot above the warped boards of Bradleytown High, circa 1961. Head bowed in the pew beside my mother, I turned my face toward the stained glass shepherd and wiped the stray tear. He'd want me dry-eyed for this job.

The service seemed fine, but all I heard was the constant clamor from the front of the church where Frank and Elm were moaning like holy rollers and attracting attention, as usual. *Grow up,* I wanted to stand and holler—me, the boy who'd fled West Virginia, unlike the man in the box, unlike my uncles, unlike everyone else in the room. I'd gotten away as soon as I could, gone to college out of state, married a girl from Cleveland, divorced three years later, and now saw my twin girls two weeks in the summer. I wouldn't be here but for what Mom said night before last when Dad lost consciousness for good.

"Billy, your daddy knew a month ago that the cancer had gone to his brain—was inoperable—and he told me then he wanted you to give his eulogy." She paused to wipe her eyes with one of her embroidered handkerchiefs. "'Bill's the best of us Bradleytown boys,' he said."

A glance left showed me the shoes were still there on top of the coffin, awash in a puddle of bloody stained-glass glow. Eyes front.

I'd hurt Mom when I moved north for good, but I'd ground her heart beneath my heel when I'd lost the grandchildren that she now never got to see. Doing this thing for her was the least I could do. My hands were sweating. I'd rehearsed a few brief sentences—what's a five-minute eulogy in a country church to a big city public defender?—but now I couldn't recall a single word. And the tingling in my belly didn't feel like the on-my-toes burst of energy before I rose to cross-examine; it felt like the descending rush of blood when Mom sighed on the phone and said, "I wish you'd fought harder for your babies." Brother Jarrett was winding down. I was up next.

"Friends and family," the reverend said, smiling through his wrinkles, hands clasped before him, "Benjamin's son William from Columbus, Ohio, will remember our dearly departed with a few words."

Looking neither left nor right, I lurched up front to the plywood and velvet lectern, keeping my eyes averted from the box and those shoes.

When I turned, the light in the room shimmered, dimmed, then went out altogether. The sound of a buzzer startled me and I saw, as if through smoke, stands full of hunkered-forward people, their mouths open, some hugging themselves, a few standing, arms raised. The old gym smelled like armpits, hairspray and mold. I followed their eyes to the floor, saw the long pass inside to the tall, dark-haired boy breaking for the basket. He faked left, spun through traffic and made the layup as the buzzer sounded. Through the stifling haze of memory and mist, I realized that once again The Bradleytown Bullet had beaten the clock to take the team from the coalfields upstate once more.

The mist dissipated and I was left staring at the grief-ravaged faces of my father's people. *Your people*, a voice echoed, as in a high-ceilinged gym.

No, not really, Dad.

"I've come here today to say . . ."

Not another word came. In my four decades, this had never happened.

Words always came. I was raised on books, the ones in my grandparents' attic; then those Dad brought home from the library in Welch; eventually the considerably better stock Mr. Holly, my speech teacher, ordered for me on interlibrary loan from WVU and Marshall. My teacher drove me to debates all over the state, was something like a father. At such times, I always felt like I was betraying Dad, whose first diagnosis came during my sophomore year. I attended as few athletic events as I could during my three years at Bradleytown and spent many hours I could've been sleeping or studying wishing my name weren't Bradford or that my mother had been able to have other sons.

Despite the chemo and radiation, Dad never missed a game and never quit asking me to go with him. My refusals always brought the same response: "Wherever you go, Billy, you'll always be a Bradleytown boy."

Dad, I was never a Bradleytown boy.

Their frozen faces stared up at me, saying, *Who are you?* I couldn't say. At the moment, my throat was soldered shut.

Elm stood up from the front pew and walked forward, careful not to stagger ("the boys want you to join 'em for a little 'shine outside," Ted Sowers had whispered to me almost as soon as we'd arrived. The last thing I thought I needed to be while eulogizing my dad was drunk; now I wasn't so sure).

Elm slowly strode up front, his old washed-out blue eyes fierce as he faced me before turning.

"This here is a good boy," he slurred. "He's honored us by coming back."

Their faces relaxed. I wanted to slug him. Was I so far removed from my father's people I needed an interpreter?

"And if he's too overcame by his feelings to talk, it don't matter. Somebody'll have something to say." He flung out his arm as if sowing seed.

Everyone in the church had a story about Benny Bradford, but in their shocked confusion, they just sat there. Uncle Elm must've thought they'd cast a secret ballot and elected him spokesman for the dead and dumbstruck. Or the 'shine told him it was time to divulge secrets.

"When he first got sick, Benny asked us to take Billy here and raise 'im . . . if he, y'know, didn't make it. He told us to make his son a man."

I longed to be anywhere but in my mother's church on this mountain; I wished I were facing the toughest prosecuting attorney in the world; to be inside that box beneath those accusing shoes.

Frank shot out of his seat, as if hurled off the bench by a coach who's seen his team blow a double-digit lead. Glaring at Elm as he had while trying to read the upside-down map, he stood on my other side. Convicted as I was, I still had to grin. How could you find anyone's final resting place with a reversed map? Yet here we stood.

"It's true that Benny said that," Frank began, "but he wasn't thinking right—this was a man with poison coursing through his brain and blood. Besides, we wasn't about to do it. His mama did the job just fine, giving this boy—our brother's son—exactly what he needed to become the man he is today, the man who came back to stand with us for Brother Ben."

Awkwardly he put his arm around my waist at the same time Elm laid a huge paw on my shoulder, squeezing their bodies so close I smelled Old Spice, alcohol, sweat, and cigar. At last I looked at Mom, her white-gloved hands laced atop her black purse, the way she always placed them in church when I was a boy beside her. Those hands had said, *Be still and listen.* I'd listened to some powerful sermons in pews like these, full of fire and fury, grace and love. Out "in the real world," as Mr. Holly called it, I'd learned to speak—to talk fast and fancy, to dazzle, crush if I could. It took Mom's hands on a black purse to remind me to pay attention. In this place, words neither convicted nor acquitted; only the grace given by blood did that.

Disengaging, I stepped away, approached the box and snatched the shoes, aware that not even an infant had uttered a sigh. Clutching those size thirteens to my chest, I detected a faint trace of rubber and sweat. Back before the gathered mourners, I offered a shoe to each uncle. Elm stepped backward and wagged his head. Frank, as always, stood his ground.

"No, Billy. Them's yours."

At last my throat opened. "Thank you," I whispered. Turning, I held my trophies aloft. "Thank you, all."

Letting my gaze wander to the casket, I saw, as if through a rain-glazed window, the polished wood above my father's body, the shrinking crimson sunset stain.

Mark DeFoe

AUGUST, WEST VIRGINIA

———

This season of sear weeds, of mornings soft
with fog; this season of fat spiders and
praying mantis and gaudy butterflies.

Of the moon like a silver platter and
the sun a blood orange gong. And each sultry
afternoon the monotonous skirl of
cicada and cricket and katydid.

Of chicory, wild carrot, golden rod,
poke berry, joe pie, iron weed and sumac
edging toward scarlet and locust turning
its late shades of ocher, of maple leaves
tinting pink and sycamore leaves crinkling,
brown in the furnace of afternoon.
This is the season of trout suspended
deep in the stream's dwindling eddies.

Season of squash like golden teardrops,
melons like striped footballs and zucchini
long as your arm, tomatoes like scarlet
Buddhas, peppers like happy green grenades.

We sit on the porch, watching the rain clouds pile,
listening as the thunder talks itself into
a downpour that will cool the asphalt
and clean the dusty roadside weeds.

Soon a million caterpillars, fated
Wooly Bears, will hump across the interstate,
in each a tiny myth of coming weather.
We drive on. This is our time of predictions
and big plans, here on the far edge
of winter, here on the cusp of hope.

Cheryl Denise

THE DIRT ROAD

That old man was nothing but good.
When he come the first night to stay with Mama and me
he brought pepperoni rolls and milk.
I called him Dad, me forty-two.

Last Tuesday he sent me for snuff
even though my truck was part run down.
When I come back I yell but don't find him
then there he is in that rotting shed, rope round his neck
legs still swinging.
It's a wonder that rafter held.

When Mama died he went crazy,
up all night, sleep all day
never once thought about our neighbor
needing help with the cows.
So I done his share too
drove posts, stapled wire.
Man could break his back throwing that maul in the heat.

Cows got out twice before I was done
spent half one night looking for 'em.
They'd went all the way to Hackers Creek,
looking slow and stupid but they ain't.

I'll borry Dad's green flannel shirt
and cowboy boots for the funeral, his Aqua Velva.
Left half a blue bottle in the bathroom.
He won't mind.

I don't remember my first dad
he was killed on Rt. 92
drove into a telephone pole
laid in the truck passed out.
It was Feb. and he was froze when they found him.

I been studying on something.
That story of Lazarus, how he got raised back up.
His family didn't have to wait for no heaven to see him again.
Martha had Mary to help pester Jesus;
me I ain't got no one no more.
Musta been nice to have them sisters looking after you,
Jesus walking down your dirt road.

WAKING TO SPRING

———————

I've been collecting words for years
for this exact day—
the sun spread thick over the land
thick as Dad butters his toast
as if butter is better than bread, than earth.

The pond quiet as an unopened story
since the red-haired boy shot wide
to shoo two beavers.

See the quaking maple leaves,
branches bobbing, *Yes, Yes, Yes.*
And the buttercups in the tall grass telling me
            Be beautiful.

My golden retriever with grey-rimmed eyes—
yesterday we sheared him with the sheep.
Feel he is softer now, younger.
And I still have a little childhood inside.
Red Rover, Red Rover, let Cheryl come over.

In the field with the fence yet unbroken
the spotted Jacob sheep walk single file
on spindly stalks, down to the spring-fed trough.

See the newest lamb
hopping straight up,
left   and   right,
as if the ground is full of coiled springs,
look, her umbilical cord
        still dangling.

Andrea Fekete

JENNIE

---

from **WATERS RUN WILD**

When is the rain gonna quit? Anna May lays beside me in bed asleep. I can't help but watch her, the way her little chest moves up and down just below her angelic face. I'm sure angels must be skinny little children with round, pasty-white faces, and half-dollar-sized blue eyes, pouty pink lips that say no evil.

I put Anna May in the only gown she owns: a small white one with long sleeves and ruffles that hug her birdlike wrists. How I wish I had something to curl her hair with, to turn her dishwater blonde hair into streaming circles of gold. I watch the purple shadows move across her face as she breathes through her tiny nose. She dreams of marbles, maybe chasing rabbits in the hills with Ezra. I hope she ain't dreaming of nothing else.

Mama always told me, "There ain't nowhere to go for girls like us, Jennie. You gotta love these hills. Love 'em, honey, 'cause if you don't, you'll be the saddest girl there ever was." But what did she mean by *girls like us*?

Ain't we tough as nails, strong as the meanest storm to hit any valley? Can't we scrub, sew and chop wood till our knuckles peel like oranges and bleed? I've seen my Mama's hands slowly twist up like the branch of a rotting tree over the years from all the planting, the packing, the canning, the digging and the cold mountain air that gets in through the cracks of our walls that she tries to keep out with torn newspapers, and blankets. Can't those hands dig through these mountains, build our own road, a road for *girls like us*? Ain't our skin as thick as a horse's hide? Our backs like the steel shovel Daddy has in the barn? What's she mean *girls like us*?

Now I don't know what to tell Anna May. Maybe I'd be happier if I loved these hills more, or maybe I'd be just the same. But I want to know what I'd see if I ever climbed to the top of the mountain bordering Blue Diamond and looked over. What I'd see if I climbed even the next one and looked, and the next, and the next. Wouldn't there be something besides valleys if I kept going? What is there besides Caney Branch, West Virginia?

In my dreams last night I imagined two crosses standing tall and white at each side of a wide, black road. The road led somewhere full of strangers, lots of handsome men. I imagined men. Lots of men. Tall men with big black eyes, silky hair and soft hands. Short men with broad shoulders and stiff-brimmed hats, flashy white teeth and gold watches. Women in new dresses and white gloves, walking with lean, straight strides, their curls shining in the sun.

Anna May grips my finger and twists it a little. Her large, soft eyes roll like eggs underneath her thin eyelids. She is dreaming. I kiss her cheek, and she slaps me away.

I almost wake her from laughing. "You're even rotten in your sleep," I whisper.

She's dreaming of the rabbits.

The rain pelts against the window like tiny rocks. Outside it looks like the ground is coughing up dust. The air sticks to my lungs. I breathe in hard, enjoying the heavy smell of honeysuckle that gets riled up when it rains, or when the wind blows. The smell of rain makes me want to be in love. Somehow, I know the man I fall in love with will smell like a rainstorm, like the raw, dirty wind.

Denise Giardina

THIN PLACES

---

from FALLAM'S SECRET: A NOVEL

Uncle John explained about thin places. A thin place, he said, is located at the boundary between heaven and earth. A place where you can ever so briefly glimpse what lies beyond, perhaps even talk to God. When Moses met Yahweh in the burning bush he was standing on a thin place. The Celtic monks who came from Ireland to pagan England identified thin places, like the island of Iona, for their monasteries.

Thin places were like any other at first glance. If one goes into such a place heedless, nothing may appear out of the ordinary. But in these places only the most delicate of membranes separates mundane reality from the Infinite. Go in with eyes and heart open and you can sense this.

"Diaphanous," Uncle John said. "I love that word. That's how to describe the membrane between dimensions. You could call the altar rail of a church a thin place, where people kneel and meet the divine as though God stretched an invisible hand through a curtain. Or the New River cutting its old, old way through ancient mountains, God's finger tracing a jagged path. And the thinnest of all places, where the jagged crests of those old mountains touch the sky. Stand on such a place and you're close to true reality. Destroy it and you rip a hole in the fabric of creation."

"Hold on!" Lydde held up her hand. "You're talking like a mystic or something."

"You're here and confused," he said. "That should be enough to make you listen to me."

"Yeah. Well, I'm tired of the weirdness. You're a scientist. I want a scientific explanation."

He smiled. "Okay. You don't want thin places. How about a combination of relativity and quantum theory that posits ten or more dimensions including more than one dimension of time? Each dimension separated from the other by the thinnest of membranes pierced by wormholes too small to be detected. How about spacetime so elastic that you can't even get an agreed-upon sequence of events? Time not as a straight line but like—like a handful of shaving cream. How about universes that continually split off one from another into an infinite number of universes that proceed in infinite parallels?"

She sat back against the bench. "You're not making any sense!"

"You of all people should understand," he said. "What's a well-told story but a parallel universe? When you step onto a stage and become another person, you pass into another dimension. The book, the play, that's the wormhole."

"That's not real."

"Yes, it is. You certainly believe it at the time, or you wouldn't read the book or play the part." He rubbed his head in an old familiar gesture. "Look. There's not a physicist in the world who understands how this works. I can barely begin to grasp it. All I understand really is what I'm working with here, and that mostly because I'm living it."

"Then start with that," Lydde said.

"All I know," Uncle John repeated, "is the math I'm working with to plot the dimensions of the New River Gorge. Because the Gorge is a place where the membrane between universes has been ruptured. We've known about wormholes for a while, but the technology doesn't exist to pass through them. Now, back home in the Gorge, you don't need any kind of futuristic technology. At least one of the wormholes has been enlarged."

"The one you and I passed through?"

The one Uncle John inadvertently discovered back in 1950. He explained to Lydde how he'd been looking for runes in caves and fallen into the seventeenth century by mistake.

"Same as you," he reminded Lydde.

"Okay," she said. "So how did the wormhole become large enough to pass through?"

Instead of answering, he asked, "Have you ever been to a battlefield? One time Lavinia and I were on vacation up in the Eastern Panhandle at Shepherdstown and we decided to drive across the river to Antietam. It was

October, a cold blustery day, and there weren't any other tourists around. We got out of the car and I took a few steps and stopped. I saw that Lavinia had stopped too. And she said, 'Do you feel something?' And I said, 'Yeah, I sure do. Want to go back?' And we got back in the car and drove back to Shepherdstown."

"What was it you felt?"

"A heaviness. A dread. The atmosphere trying to bear the weight of thousands dying in agony, was how I thought of it later. The departure of all those souls at once, even if you don't believe in an afterlife, even if they were just extinguished, it would have to scratch the thin membrane between dimensions. Though not tear it completely. And if you went in summer in the heat with cars and buses and people everywhere yakking about this and that, taking pictures just to say they were there, wondering where to buy souvenirs, kids crying—you'd feel nothing then. Do you understand? It takes silence to sense the closeness of another dimension. And a battle may not be enough to tear the fabric in a place that was ordinary otherwise, but a battle in a thin place might do it."

"What's happened in the Gorge that could do that?"

"I don't know for certain. But I think it may have started with the blasting of the tunnel under Gauley Mountain back in 1931."

"You think the blasting shook something loose?"

"Maybe. The unprecedented blasting combined with something else. The inhumanity. What you had was a company sending hundreds of poor men, mostly black men, to their deaths. Knowingly. They were blasting through pure silica without protection, going in and breathing ground glass every day."

"It's not the only place people have been treated inhumanely."

"No. But thin places are by their nature recognized as special, even holy. They're usually protected, a focus of pilgrimage, not atrocities. It's so seldom that terrible evil is committed in a thin place. You know how special the Gorge is. You know you can stand and look down along the river and it's like a force that tries to draw you in. The entire Gorge seems to exist in another dimension. A thin place. Yet we've killed people there, and since then there's the strip-mining nearby, blowing apart the mountains. So much blasted earth you can see it from outer space. And all this in a place already thin, with the divine already pressing in like an aneurysm ready to burst."

"In which case you end up here."

"Or somewhere. Where you end depends on who you are, I think, and who you're connected to."

The light was fading so she could no longer see his face. "Are you trying to find my brothers and sisters? Do you think they ended up here?"

He shook his head. "Not here. I don't think they would have found that particular wormhole. It's too far down the hollow from Montefalco. But I think there might be other wormholes. That's what I've been trying to calculate. I've done a lot of the math already. I've superimposed a Chartres labyrinth on the Gorge and tried to plot out my calculations."

"So that's what the red notebook in your desk is all about. Why a labyrinth?"

"It's a geometrical figure," he said, "but with spiritual implications. I've tried other things, squares, trapezoids, rectangles, but didn't see much of a pattern. With a labyrinth, with its entrance superimposed over the Mystery Hole, some interesting things show up."

"Like what?"

"It doesn't totally work yet. But how about a potential wormhole across the river on Gauley Mountain where there are other cliffs? Or in the town of Lafayette? And near Montefalco, although that one is covered by a valley fill now."

Lydde leaned back. "My God," she whispered. . . .

Maggie Glover

ON FINALLY BLAMING MYSELF A LITTLE FINALLY

My porch upon the cliff, my house upon the mountain—
I push my sneaker between the roots of the maple,
remembering the gypsy moths, their wormy threats waving
from its branches, the low-flying planes that followed
with their heavy smoke dipping into us (my mouth, his mouth)
until, cotton-eyed and ragged, we circled each other in the dirt.
This is how I got him back: I bled myself against the tree,
I dressed in pink, I let someone else have him.
From the other side of the valley, cows peek through
the bare trees: a little moo shapes the forest, just for me.

Crystal Good

ALMOST HEAVEN, ALMOST FAMOUS

———

—For the girls who never made it anywhere, but home.

For the coulda.
the shoulda,
and the wouldas,
I tried.

Regrets like shot gun pellets
missing the can,
ambition shooting up
landscapes or stuck in
the well

Well—I was.
Well—I did.
Well—I met.
Well but

But, what?
But, you didn't.

No better, no worse
you went that route
only to return and turn those

Shouldas
Couldas
Wouldas

into a life, a poem of sorts
where almost
is good enough.

James Harms

KENNEDY WINS WEST VIRGINIA!

He started out
a friend of Kennedy's,
though he started out
a Texan. Today
he swings
on the porch next
door and sings "Someone
to Watch Over Me"
as dusk thickens
in the street and
grays the day
down to shouts
and TVs mumbling
through open windows.
Twice he's talked
of Texas as all
horizon, the sort of
promise that slips
as evening wears away
the light, of coming here
to mountains so old
they ache and drift
beneath the weight
of sky, the way day
ends in hill shadow
and dust, smell of slag,
of water. He delivered

Hancock County
in a locked box, shook
JFK's hand, and
went home. But home
is an accident
of grace or birth,
is where you run out
of money or luck or find
yourself standing still
too long. LBJ sent him
back to West Virginia
and his wife Elaine
came with him; she liked
the virgin hemlocks,
the rhododendrons,
so they stayed.
He watches swallows
smoke from the glass
factory's cold chimney
and waits. Maybe home
is where purpose falls
in love with the light
settling in the trees
at dusk. LBJ called
once more to say
thanks, to say
Come on home. But Elaine
liked the chances
of her garden better here
than Texas, and there's
no horizon in these
mountains to remind him
of what's out of reach.
He likes to hear the roar

on Saturdays
from the stadium
across town, the crowd
noise bending in the silver
autumn air like
a train whistle entering
a tunnel. He likes
the way the river implies
an ending. So maybe
home is where we don't
mind ending, or don't
reach to flick on
the porch light
when evening falls
too early, the sun
surprised by the hills.
How easily
the hills surprise us.

Marc Harshman

SHED

―――――――

Ten times he pounded the nail head, ten times spoke her smoky name into the mist. With the mountains all gathered, mumbling their dark enchantments, he abandoned prayer and tethered himself to the skulls of his ancestors, those buried below the knoll where the cedars gossip. It was as much as he could do, that, and build this shed: board and batten, poplar and oak, pound and curse. The nail apron had been his dad's and the hammer his uncle's. Out beyond the slope of the hill, he heard the redtail scream as it fell from the sky onto vole or rabbit or squirrel. He accepted the blame for losing the farm, for the drinking, for debt, and the chains that had drug the family through a circus of courtrooms. He opened his mouth to drink the rain. Blessings were unaccountable. He could not keep up forever, but right now he knew this was a thing done well. This shed. It would keep dry a man, or hides, or those three bushels of potatoes he'd dug. He couldn't keep her, though, and so he planted the nails with curses. Strange. A war somewhere in the world. Laid off on a Thursday. Rent due day after. Predator and prey, pound and curse, pray and despair. Strange. Years. A man comes to believe almost anything when he lives on the inside of himself long enough. A dozen sheds now. At dusk he patrols them, nails clenched in his teeth.

WITH NO QUESTIONS

———————

A steady sheet of rain is slipping through the woods,
    apple blossoms plastering the ground, the last snow, our first sorrow.
The gentle rush of the creek will be both dirge and lullaby.
A barred owl stutters deep within the beech grove.
My tea is cooling where it sits on the windowsill.
The rain lifts its last skirts over the ridge and leaves a dripping quiet in its
    wake.

Suddenly, a tableau of four deer within the settling fog.
My dog barks now, belatedly, once, twice
    to let me know they're there—none of us very excited
    though the beauty of it, of them, still slows
    the reach of my hand for that solitary cup.

Meadow grass is dangling from one of their mouths, a damp, green bouquet.
When I stumble, drawing closer, their match-stick legs
    ferry them effortlessly down the rocky bank,
    their taupe velvet flanks soft as kisses, tough as weathered callous,
    their black eyes, their black noses, every part marvelously balanced.

They've stopped now inside some pocket of quiet below me.
We are all listening, each to the other,
    waiting for the next move in the universe.
And just here becomes the only place
    I know where time surrenders to itself
    and reverses what I think I know.

My tea is cold. The dog asleep. The rain gone.
And somewhere the owl is sliding the silence into the hidden trees
    of a deeper night with no questions about philosophy,
    with no questions at all.

Rajia Hassib

QUILTING

———

Mr. Henderson is making a quilt. He is the only man in the quilting bee where Hala just started taking quilting lessons. Hala is the only Egyptian there, the only foreigner, as a matter of fact, and she sits across from Mr. Henderson at the large, rectangular table that takes up the brightly lit backroom of the quilting store. The quilt she is working on is her first; it is small, made out of four blocks, and she is working on one block at a time, so she does not take up too much space on the table, which works out well because Mr. Henderson's quilt is huge.

Hala is working on sewing the long sides of two triangles together to make one square. One triangle is red and the other is white, and she likes the way the colors contrast. She works by hand, even though most of the other women prefer the sewing machine. Nancy, who owns the store and runs the quilting classes, had given her the option to try hand piecing or machine piecing, and Hala had preferred hand piecing because she liked the way the thread felt as she pulled it through the fabric and the way the small needle balanced between her fingers, and because hand sewing reminded her of her grandmother, who used to embroider every evening back when Hala had lived with her parents at home.

Hala and Mr. Henderson are the quietest ones in the room. Nancy and the other eight ladies who sit around the table every Monday and Thursday evening are always loud. One or more of the sewing machines is constantly humming in the background, and the women, perhaps because they can sense the table vibrate with the motions of the running machines, feel a need to yell even though the machines are not that loud. Hala appreciates the noise. She listens to what they say while they work and, sometimes, she even looks up and ventures a short comment. They are all very nice to her; they smile and nod and try to get her to talk more, but she does not. She has only been in the US for five months and is very self-conscious about her accent, even though all the ladies have assured her they can understand her perfectly and they find her accent very sweet.

Every now and then Hala looks up and watches Mr. Henderson work. He is a large man, with long, gray hair that he ties in a ponytail at the nape of his neck. His arms are muscular and covered in tattoos, and Hala believes he must like to show them off since he is never in long sleeves, even though it is not quite summer yet. The first time Hala arrived at the quilting store to attend the lessons she saw him get off his Harley and walk into the store ahead of her and she was scared of him. His Harley was black with shining silver accents and a red, orange, and yellow flame drawn on its body. His helmet also had red, orange, and yellow flames on it. The first time Hala sat across from him she spent more time looking at him than she did paying attention to her work. She could not believe that such a man could be sitting there, quietly sewing, occasionally shooting some remark back at one or other of the ladies who teased him and flirted with him. He was very witty but he never smiled or looked up when he spoke, even when his remarks caused an uproar of laughter around him.

After that first lesson Nancy told Hala Mr. Henderson's story. His late wife, Jenny, had been a member of the quilting bee for over a decade. She stayed even after she had her cancer, attending every single meeting up to only a week or so before she died. When she died, she was working on a large bed quilt, a queen-size Dresden Star with a cream background and five rows of stars, four stars in each row, their tips in shades of lavender and yellow. Mr. Henderson had shown up at the meeting a couple of weeks after she died with the unfinished quilt top. He did not know what to do with it. He wanted one of the ladies to finish it because he knew how much Jenny had liked that quilt. So he sat in the corner and watched as the ladies each took an unfinished block from the wicker basket where Jenny had cut the pieces and sorted them, each block in one little zip-lock bag. The ladies had expected him to leave but he did not. So they challenged him. They teased him and said he wouldn't know how to handle the tiny needle with his stout man's fingers. Mr. Henderson said nothing, but he pulled out a stool, sat at the table, and picked up a bag with its pieces of cut-up fabric. The ladies cheered and helped him out. They threaded a needle for him, showed him how to hold it, and pinned the pieces together and prepared them for him. That first day they all stayed late but the only block that was finished was the one Mr. Henderson had worked on. Afterwards, he attended every meeting. He started working on miniature quilts, and made enough of them to set up his own show at the town's hall. He sold the quilts for charity. Quilting, he said, was a form of meditation. He liked it because, while he was quilting, he did not have to think of anything at all.

The new quilt Mr. Henderson is working on is a wall hanging six feet square. He has drawn the design for it on a twelve-inch square piece of sketch paper and then photocopied it to get the actual-sized templates. Hala likes to look at the original sketch. It is not a traditional patchwork quilt made out of repeated blocks, but rather an appliqué showing an organic form that grows from the center and then multiplies and expands until it fills the entire quilt, leaving room around it for only a narrow border. The form is made out of leaf-like shapes that overlap and intersect in shades of reds and oranges with sporadic darker pieces of earthly browns. Occasionally, smaller pieces peek out from under the larger ones in a yellowish gold. The whole design looks like a large, exploding flower, or like fire. When the ladies asked Mr. Henderson what he was going to call the quilt, he said, "Jenny."

Hala's quilt is a wall hanging, too. It's made out of four pinwheel blocks inside a simple running border. Hala is making it out of red, white, and black prints, but mostly red. She chose the colors because she wanted something red to hang on the wall in the living room. The small apartment where Ashraf, her husband, has lived for five years is all black and white. The living room has white walls, and the sofa and recliner are black leather. The coffee table has a circular glass top sitting on a silver base shaped like a hollow cube. The walls are bare. Hala wants to hang something red on the walls, at least for now. Ashraf has promised he will let her furnish the new house they are planning on buying in the next year or so, some time before they have their first child.

Mr. Henderson is cutting a large, orange-colored, leaf-shaped piece. He has spread the quilt top as far as he could on the large table and is pinning the pieces he is cutting in place so that he can start sewing them in. The table is large but still part of the quilt top is hanging off his side. Hala pulls her things together, puts them in her small sewing basket, and then, smiling at him and saying nothing, she pulls the edge of his quilt all the way to her side of the table, giving him more room. Mr. Henderson looks up at her and smiles back. For the rest of the evening, Hala places her sewing basket on a stool next to her and, taking out only the pieces she needs, sews with her hands in her lap.

———

Ashraf is sitting in the large leather recliner and surfing the Internet on his laptop, as he does every evening after dinner. Hala is standing on the sofa, taping the fabric blocks to the wall. She has finally finished the four blocks and, even though she still has not pieced them together and to the border, she wants to know how the wall hanging will look. Around the blocks she tapes the red border. Then she steps down from the sofa, steps all the way back till she stands with her back to the large TV, and looks at the wall hanging.

"What do you think?" she asks Ashraf. He looks up from his laptop and looks at the taped quilt blocks. He is resting his feet, in white socks, on the glass top of the coffee table.

"Is it finished?" he asks.

"No, of course not," Hala laughs. "I still have to piece it together, then I have to sew it to a backing, as well. That will probably take more time than the actual piecing, because you can sew it in all kinds of ways, using the stitches to draw patterns, like embroidery." Ashraf has already looked back down at his laptop screen.

"So, what do you think?" she asks again.

"Oh, I like it," he says without looking up. "It's very nice."

"Do you like the colors?"

"Yes, sure."

"Do you think I should add more black?"

"Huh?"

"More black. Do you think I should add more black? You know, to tie it in more to the furniture."

Ashraf looks back up. "You have some black here, around the center," he says, pointing with his hand and drawing a square in the air.

"Yes, that's the inner border. And then I'll have a wider border in a red print, and then the outer border in black again. But I don't have any black in the blocks themselves, they're all red and white. Do you think it looks OK?"

"I think it's fine just as it is," Ashraf says. He is looking at his computer screen and typing something.

Hala steps up to the breakfast table in the open kitchen, pulls out a chair, and sits down. From where she is sitting she can see the living room, her unfinished quilt hanging on the wall, and Ashraf. Rather, she sees Ashraf's feet in their white socks, his legs in blue jeans, and the top of his head showing from behind the laptop screen. Behind him, a large window shows a line of trees on one side and some lights in the distance. Hala looks at the lights glowing in the dark. They are familiar, more familiar than the rest of the apartment because, for the year and a half she was engaged to Ashraf, these lights glowed behind him every time he called her online to chat. They talked via the Internet every night, he sitting in the same black leather armchair he is now sitting in, she halfway around the world, in Egypt. Because of the time difference, he would always call at midnight and she would wake up at six or seven in the morning to talk to him before she went to class. During the year and a half they were engaged, they met face to face only twenty-six times. The twenty-seventh was on their wedding day, when Hala stood in the lobby of the Alexandria Sheraton in her white wedding gown, the drums of the wedding band beating in deafening rhythms. Five days later they landed in JFK. He spent the following week taking her around New York and New Jersey, where he had lived for eight years, five of which in that same apartment, and then he went back to work.

She met him on one of his vacations, when he went to Egypt to visit his family and try to find a wife. She had never imagined she would consent to going on a blind date with a man, a date attended by both their mothers and reminiscent of the old arranged marriages. But her mother had insisted she go meet him and had told her she could always turn him down, if she did not like him. When she finally agreed and they met at the apartment of a friend of her mother's, Hala found she liked his face, calm and dark with greenish-brown eyes that met hers and did not look away. He told her he had gone to America on his own and put himself through college, and she respected him for that. He worked in hospital administration. One day, he could be the CEO of a hospital. She told him of her studies at the Faculty of Fine Arts, where she was majoring in Interior Design. He listened to her when she spoke and asked about her work. They spent over four hours talking, that day, such a long time that, when they finally headed out of the apartment, Hala's mother kept apologizing to their host, though Hala knew both women were perfectly happy the date had lasted as long as it did. Ashraf walked Hala and her mother all the way down to their car, held the car's door open for Hala and helped her get in, and then, holding her hand in his, looked her in the eye and asked if he may call her tomorrow. She said yes.

They met every day for the rest of his vacation. Hala's sisters liked him, her parents liked him, and her cousin, Hala could tell, had almost died of envy when she first saw him that time when his parents had invited all of Hala's family to spend a week with them in Marina, the famous resort by the Mediterranean. Ashraf stood tall and had thick, black hair. He wore blue and black Polo shirts and dark jeans and loafers with no socks, in the summer. At thirty-four he was eleven years her senior but did not look a day older than twenty-five. He spoke English with a perfect American accent, and could talk to Hala's father about everything from politics to the environment to religion. Hala's father knew more about religion than Ashraf did, but Ashraf knew more about the environment. He was courteous, held the door open for her every time they passed through one, and held her hand when they crossed the street. They got engaged on the following vacation, when he had gone to Egypt specifically for the celebration, and got married a year and two vacations later. Whenever he went back to the US, they spoke online every day. For the first few weeks after they got married, Hala found it strange, almost surprising, that they could spend so much time together. She was used to his two-dimensional image on the monitor, not to his three-dimensional, live presence. Every time he would walk suddenly into a room or if she turned in bed and found him lying next to her, the first thing that would flash into her mind's eye would be the image of the Skype logo.

"Are you going to leave this hanging up there?" he asks.

"What?"

"Are you going to leave this hanging like this, with Scotch tape?" He is bent to the side, looking past the computer screen and at her. "The Scotch tape can ruin the paint."

"It won't ruin the paint in only a few minutes!" she says.

He says nothing. Instead, he goes back to browsing the Internet. Hala looks at the lights flickering in the window behind him. When she had seen the lights on her screen as she chatted with him, she had imagined they were the lights of Manhattan, glowing in the dark. She thought that just because he lived in New Jersey and New Jersey was close to New York he would be able to see the city from his living room window. New York, it turned out, was two hours away, in the other direction.

Hala looks at Ashraf's feet. She spent a year and a half speaking to him every day but still she did not know so much about him. The last five months have been months of exploration. She liked the intimacy of learning he had size twelve feet, and learning he liked to sleep in his boxers, even in the winter. She also learned other things. She learned the lights flickering out the windows were those of a small factory that manufactures shoelaces. The lights were kept on at night to keep the vandals and the homeless away. And she learned that Ashraf, who spoke to her or listened to her talk for a full hour every day when they were half a world apart, was a quiet, calm, and serious man. In the five months they spent together, he had not once raised his voice. Silently, Hala gets up, walks to the sofa, and, standing on the soft, black cushions, peels the pieces of Scotch tape off the wall.

———

"You're complaining because he doesn't fight?" her mother says over the phone. Hala is standing in the small kitchen, holding the phone with one hand as she unloads the dishwasher with the other.

"No, of course not. That's not what I meant."

"Then what did you mean?"

"I just meant that he's . . . he's so quiet. He doesn't get . . . upset, you know, over anything."

"And that's a bad thing? You'd rather he got upset and started flinging things at you?" her mother says. Her voice is sharp and she speaks in bursts of small, short sentences. Hala knows she is struggling to keep from yelling at her.

"No, of course not, Mama, that's not what I meant," Hala says. The image of her father in his fits of anger flashes in front of her eyes.

"Then what's your problem?" her mother asks.

"I don't have a problem. I'm just talking, that's all."

"You're just complaining, that's all. And, frankly, you have nothing to complain about. Nothing. Is he a good man, or not?"

"Yes, of course he is."

"Does he ever beat you up? Is he mean to you?"

"No, no, of course not."

"Is he a miser?"

"No, Mama, you know he's not."

"Does he drink? Is he a womanizer? A gambler?"

"No, Mama, no. Please, just listen . . ."

"Listen to what?" her mother yells. "Listen to you complain and make yourself all miserable over nothing? Listen to you throw what God has given you to the floor? Discard what others would have died to have? What any of your sisters would be lucky to ever see?"

"Mama, I don't . . ."

"You don't thank God, that's what it is. I know you, Hala, you're my daughter and I know you. I know how it is with you. You start getting these ideas and then you work yourself up and end up with your head up in the clouds. Instead of complaining that your husband 'doesn't get upset,'" her mother imitates her in a sing-song, whining voice, "you should thank God you have all the stuff you have. You have a good husband, a respectable man who has a good career and who can provide for you. You won't have to work a day in your life, if you don't want to. You won't have to spend your life holed up in a small apartment that's kept from crumbling down on you only by the power of God's mercy and grace. You won't have to look at your children and wonder how on earth you'll provide for them when they grow up."

"Don't yell at me, Mama," Hala says, her voice breaking. "Don't do that. I just needed to talk to you, that's all. I'm just . . . I'm just . . ." she starts sobbing.

"You're just what?" her mother asks.

"I'm lonely," Hala says, sobbing quietly, now. "I'm so, so lonely. I miss you all and I'm so lonely."

Her mother is quiet. Hala walks up to the sofa, sits down, and stares out the window, looking at the shoelace factory. In the morning light, the brick building looks old and battered. One of the windows is broken and the missing panel is covered with a white vinyl sheet that looks like a shower curtain.

"Listen, Hala," her mother says, calmer now. "Nobody said this is easy. But you have to remember how lucky you are even to be there, in America, and to have such a good husband. I know it's hard now but it'll get easier, once you have kids. They'll keep you busy, trust me. It's just that now you have too much time on your hands, that's all."

Hala listens and says nothing. On the glass coffee table lie the quilt blocks she has taken off the wall the evening before. She stares at them.

"It's just that I'm afraid for you," her mother says, slowly. "I'm afraid that you'll forget just how blessed you are to have what you have. I'm afraid that, the more you'll have, the more you'll want. And then you can lose everything."

Hala is quiet and waits. Her mother does not talk and Hala, listening closely, can hear the noise in the background. Her sisters are watching a soap opera on TV. She can hear their voices talk. One of them is laughing. All three of them had shared a room. Hala had slept on the upper level of the bunk beds, while her younger sister occupied the lower level and the youngest the trundle bed. She wonders which one of them now slept in her bed, in the upper level, but does not ask. Outside, she sees the white vinyl sheet covering the broken panel flap in the wind but hears nothing.

———

Hala's first quilt is done. Mr. Henderson helps her hold it up while the ladies at the quilting bee hover around it and let a torrent of praise and admiration rain on her. Hala smiles, her face flushed. When they are done admiring her quilt she carefully folds it and puts it in her basket. Nancy gives her two quilt hangers shaped like daisies and shows her how to nail them to the wall to hang the quilt. For the rest of the evening Hala walks around the store, picking out new fabrics for her next project. Mr. Henderson's Harley is parked at the front, and Hala sees it through the glass storefront and hears the ladies chatter in the background, their sewing machines quietly humming. Hala picks out a couple of bundles of fat quarters, quarter yards folded in neat triangles and stacked up on top of each other to form small stars and then tied with satin ribbon. She wants to do what Mr. Henderson does; she wants to make a quilt and call it Ashraf, but she does not know how to do so. She feels she is not experienced enough to come up with her own design. The fabrics she has chosen are in shades of blue and gold, and, after she sets them aside, she sits down with a sketchpad and some color pencils and tries to draw something. She draws squares and stars with intersecting lines, but it does not feel right. She uses up half the sketchpad and still nothing works. Walking up to the stand at the front of the store, she picks out a few magazines and walks back to her seat, flips through them looking for inspiration. She does not find anything that she feels can represent Ashraf—or, rather, she feels that anything can represent Ashraf. She does not know. At the back of one magazine, she sees two projects she likes: a baby quilt and a set of four placemats and a table runner. Ashraf wants to wait a year or so before they have their first baby, and she doesn't want to start on the crib-sized quilt now because she thinks it's bad luck to work on anything related to a baby before the baby is born. The table runner and placemats are simple enough, and she can see how the new fabrics she has chosen can work with the design.

Mr. Henderson's quilt top is almost finished. He is working on the border, now, which has a running vine of flame-red flowers appliquéd to it. Nancy walks up to him and looks at the almost finished work. She pulls the corner of quilt top to get a better look at it and knocks down a small cardboard box Mr. Henderson has set to the side. The box has all the discarded bits and pieces of fabric left over from his appliquéd motifs, narrow strips of red, gold, and yellow with frayed edges that look like small fringes. The box falls to the floor and Nancy, bending down to pick up the pieces, holds a handful of them up and shows them to the ladies, commenting on how beautiful the colors are. Everyone looks at the strips of fabric in her hand. Then, in one slow upward motion, Nancy throws the bundle of strips up in the air and over the large table. The strips rise up then slowly fall, and Hala watches them swirling and turning in the bright white light like strings of confetti that have been lit on fire.

John Hoppenthaler

A JAR OF RAIN

———————

Wrapped in threadbare & faded
cotton towels, snuggled
between the hub & Beth Ann's
sneakered feet, the faint
sloshing of jarred rainwater
too muffled to hear
above road whine & Rolling
Stones on the tape deck.
But like some rare & fragile
egg, she nestled it
there all four hundred long miles
east to Manhattan.
When her brother left Wheeling,
it had been springtime.
He allowed how he'd miss it—
yearning green mountains,
misty Ohio River,
& mostly the rain,
how it sluiced off mom's rooftop
to collect & brim
in an old metal oil drum,
how when he would thwack
its steel side with his finger,
rings would shiver toward
dark water's chilly center.
He would miss the rain,

& they would miss him,
gone to the city, dream job
among skyscrapers
the "big break" of his young life.
They'd sung the theme from
The Mary Tyler Moore Show
together that night
he first heard he'd been hired
& flung cloth napkins
high at the kitchen ceiling,
"You're gonna make it
after all" deflecting off
walls & rising like
hymnal passages till dawn.
Alvin hit a bump.
Careful, she hissed, her left leg
swiveling on raised
toes, hard up against the jar.
It was what she could
still do, the only thing more:
to wash what ashes
were left of his—gutter
to river to sea—
with West Virginia rainfall
dipped up from a drum
whose surface October had
started to freeze over.
Mick Jagger was belting out
"Paint It Black." She saw
the brimming hole in a sky-
line she'd never seen
before begin to unfold.

Ron Houchin

PHANTOM FLESH

My great aunt's great arms
were seismic slabs I feared.
Passing near their cetaceous wobble,

I smelled bleach and sea breeze.
When she lifted them to hang
wet sheets on her clothesline,

I expected to see loose droops ooze
to fleshy drops. Bewitched, I
stared in moonlight at chicken

necks lined up on her chopping
stump. I saw those arms go down
where crawdads rattle claws in clear

or murky shore. I tear up now
remembering her and what comes
from the wear and the blue of time's pull.

FAMILY PORTRAIT WITH SPIDER WEB

———————

I can't remember why we gathered
around the giant web out by the well

house and rose trellis that afternoon,
but it is about to storm. Cousin Ginny

fears a lightning flash will spoil her shot.
There's more than one uncle I don't know.

At the height of web and belt buckles,
I hear pieces of voice falling. In the inner

tube air, we all have the same fuzzy hair
and gray eyes that squint disavowing

cataracts to come. The spider's yellow-
speckled legs match Aunt Ruth's leotard.

The air feels numb. I barely know these
people light and lightning turned into ghosts.

Norman Jordan

APPALACHIAN GHOST

———————

As a boy
I remember men
Coming up the mountain
From working
In the Hawks Nest tunnel
Covered with white silicon dust and
Men going down the mountain
From working
In the coal mines
Covered with black amorphous carbon dust
All of them carrying in their lungs
Industrial diseases
Slowly and painfully
Killing them and their dreams.

Laura Long

DARK EARLY

———

One November evening, Billie tasted onion soup in her kitchen and remembered her honeymoon two years ago. She and Sam had flown—her first plane ride—to Mexico and jounced on an old blue bus to Isla de las Mujeres. There they drank milk from coconuts that fell with soft thuds in the sand, and strolled under clicking palms beside a sea that lapped turquoise over their toes. When Sam floated in the salt-heavy water, eyes closed above a dreamy smile, Billie thought, *I don't know him.* The next day they giggled in bed and waltzed naked around their room, perched on stilts above the Caribbean. Sharp-winged terns dropped like stones into the sea and rose flapping, spraying light into light.

Now they lived in Morgantown, West Virginia. The old house where they had an apartment was part of an enormous maze of old homes stubbornly dug into a steep mountainside. Billie had graduated from a little college in Ohio, and afterwards, when she was visiting Morgantown, she fell for Sam. She hadn't planned to move here; she wanted to live somewhere out of West Virginia. "Of course you do," her grandma Essie had laughed. "Wanting to leave is part of being a West-by-god Virginian. Even our state song is about leaving and pining to come back: 'If o'er sea or land I roam, still I think of happy home, and my friends among those West Virginia hills.' Honey, you'll move to a city or some flat land, and wind up homesick."

Still. She was twenty-four and ought to get somewhere with her life. Today she had surfed the websites of restaurants in Los Angeles, Miami, and the Bahamas. She was a waitress, so she could get a job almost anywhere, right? Sam didn't want to leave. He was mired in writing his master's thesis on the Battle of Waterloo. That or his day job was scrambling his brain. All day he drove a taxi through these crooked streets and up into the hills.

"It's ready," Billie called to Sam and she carried bowls of soup into the dining room. Something was odd, was off, as if a piece of furniture had been moved. She looked down the open room that ran the length of the house. In the middle of this length was a black fireplace they couldn't use because the landlord had said the chimney might catch fire. The fireplace gazed at her with disappointment, remembering fires it used to have, was meant to have.

No, nothing was awry but something was different: the huge old windows were black instead of soft with evening light. "Look," Billie said when Sam walked in and kissed her neck. She pointed to the nearest window. The merged shape of the two of them glinted there, ghost-pale yet definite.

"The time changed. It's dark early now," Sam said. They sat down, bowls of soup, plates of spaghetti, and a basket of bread between them. "We're supposed to get a killing frost tomorrow." He ate with the concentration of a weary man. He rhythmically ate the soup, then dug into the spaghetti, plummy with tomatoes.

She twirled her fork. "I took this sauce out of the freezer today. Remember, I made it in August?"

He nodded.

She had picked up a crate of tomatoes cheap from a roadside stand. The ripe tomatoes were bruised and cracking, oozing with sweet juice, and needed to be cut and cooked right away. She'd simmered them all the next day in two big pots. That seemed far away now, a day when she knew exactly what life was asking of her.

"I've got to find another job. I don't want to drive a taxi in the ice and snow." Sam's eyes skittered into hers and away. His left forearm was still slightly tanned from being angled out the taxi window all summer and fall. He used to spend every evening in his study, a tiny back room off the kitchen. His stacks of books went straight up to the low, angled ceiling, the spines spilling letters in prim little banners. For the last few weeks, his thesis had sat in several heaps on the desk, untouched.

Billie twirled and untwirled her spaghetti. One afternoon this past summer she had ridden downtown on her bike and seen Sam parked in front of the courthouse, where he waited for dispatches. It seemed he wasn't her twenty-six-year-old husband, or a grad student stranded within a thesis on the Battle of Waterloo. He was an anonymous taxi driver submerged in the shadow of a big yellow taxi.

He hadn't seen her. He ignored the coal trucks that heaved by, the pigeons flapping above the courthouse square, and the old men on benches who played dominoes and talked about the good war and the new mayor in rumpled old-men voices. Unlike the other two taxi drivers parked there, Sam didn't read a newspaper. He read a thick, hardbound book propped on the steering wheel.

She knew the book was *War and Peace*, and then he was her Sam again. He saw wars as terrible events, usually bumbled into by power-crazed rulers. But Sam was intrigued, even obsessed, by Napoleon and the thousands of lives he had commanded into death. "A lot of those men," he once told Billie, "died for love. Real loyalty is the same thing as love."

Did some of the men following Napoleon die for love? She couldn't agree. Surely loyalty wasn't the same thing as love. Love had to be more, somehow. But every time she tried to figure out if loyalty could rise to the level of love (loyalty was generous, hopeful, idealistic, blind), her mind went doodling down paths that weren't argument or answer, till finally there was no path at all.

———

After supper Billie climbed on the bed to write a card to a college buddy who had just gotten married. Sam washed the dishes. Billie began, "I hope . . ." What should she hope for her newlywed friend? Health and wealth? Moony-spoony nights? Adorable puppies and drooling babies?

Billie's mother had wanted her to be beautiful and ladylike (Billie refused to make an effort), major in business (not history), become a manager and rise in the ranks of one company or another (not graduate from a fine little college only to rise from part-time to full-time waitress), and find an excellent husband. At twenty-two, Billie had married a poor man without ambition—so her mother described Sam, after which mother and daughter didn't speak for several months. "Money doesn't matter now, but it will later," her mother had warned. Now her mother visited twice a year, called Sam "Bob," and bought Billie shoes and a haircut. Afterwards, Billie and Sam vied with each other for the best imitation of the mother's dismay. "Darling, let's measure these windows for curtains so you can take down those tacked-up bedspreads."

Sam stretched out on the couch that served as most of their living room furniture and unfolded the Sunday paper. The "Help Wanted" pages crackled as he shook them open. He murmured, "Doctor, lawyer, Indian chief."

Billie scrawled on the card, "Wishing you everything—". She paused and chewed on the pen tip, then finished "you want." She signed the card for her and Sam, hurried it into an envelope, then sprawled on the bed.

She knew Sam's recurring dreams about a black dog with blood on its teeth, and he knew about her childhood rage at her mother's strict diets and constant irritation that Billie was plump. Billie trimmed the hair that curled behind Sam's ears, and he rubbed her legs with almond oil. Every week the limbs of their clothes became mysteriously entangled in the laundry and clung together with a dim-witted insistence.

A moth flittered against the window beside the bed. Havoc, their cat, batted her claws against the glass, frantic. Billie stroked her spine to soothe her. But the cat meowed and darted her paws up toward the lone, light-ditzy moth. In summer, moths by the dozens twirled around the porch lights. Soon snow flakes would twirl down, melt against the window. Billie thought again of palm fronds and tern wings splintering the light.

Sam came over and lifted Havoc into his arms, chanted into her eyes, "Butcher, baker, candlestick maker." Havoc purred with instant enthusiasm.

Billie pressed her face to the pane, brightly chill as water. Leaves covered the garden. In the steam of summer, she and Sam had picked frilled lettuces and fat bell peppers. *This is an odd cathedral*, Billie thought once when she cut the top off a pepper. *The air inside is so still.*

Billie clenched her fists. She wanted to move to a place where all year round cantaloupe swelled into splendid balls. Surely a tropic of cornucopia existed. People were living there right this minute, humming to themselves. The sun heated the backs of their necks. Sweat trickled into their eyelashes, and they headed toward the house to pump water up out of the earth's cool depths. Frost was a rumor, as remote as the rings of Saturn.

With Havoc curled up on the couch next to his head, Sam turned back to the want ads, found the first page. "Accountant, advertising, auto mechanic . . ."

Billie wondered when she would tell him. Maybe he already suspected? And how could she convince him it wasn't his fault?

She had to tell him: she was going away though she couldn't explain why. She would go somewhere else, find out who she was besides someone married to a kind man. But she would not be a coward who left a note.

Sam folded the newspaper, got up, and opened the closet. He heaved her large suitcase down. It thumped on the bare floor. "What?" She gasped and sat up.

He opened the suitcase. "I reckon it's time to procure our winter provisions." He lifted out lumpy sweaters, floppy turtlenecks, and flannel sheets scattered with silhouettes of dancing bears. She sorted the socks from the mittens. He pulled t-shirts and shorts from the dresser's deep drawers and fitted them into the suitcase. A bikini she'd worn on their honeymoon slipped to the floor and she picked up the two pieces, splashes of scarlet and gold. She expected them to burn her fingers but they were cool, like fish.

Sam refolded the winter clothes and stacked them in the drawers. He had been the oldest of four kids, and took care of them all while his single mom worked two jobs. He didn't think twice about folding clothes.

The suitcase loudly snapped shut. Sam sat back on his heels. Billie felt his eyes resting on her. "I'm leaving you," she wanted to blurt. And then she'd explain: "Loyalty isn't the same thing as love—not that I know what either one is." But that was no explanation at all.

She saw herself in his mind in the future. The word "Billie" would translate into a blot, a fool, a heartbreaker. She would call him at midnight crying and get his voice mail. There was no right road for her, no battle to follow, only a crooked path. She opened her mouth. The room grew quiet, as if the killing frost had come and was long forgotten, because now the world was full of snow.

Marie Manilla

BELLE FLEUR

Belle Fleur was there on opening night thirty years ago, 1895. She doubts anyone remembers the skinny girl in the ill-fitting wig—a replacement for one of the hoochie coochie dancers who missed the train in Cincinnati.

"You can do it, Mavie," her mother had said, slipping her into the gypsy costume. Mavie tugged the bodice up to cover more skin; Mother yanked it down. "You've seen their act a thousand times." Her parents were The Fire-Eating Royales. That night, Mavie adopted the stage name she'd been crafting her whole life, Belle Fleur, and posed with a dozen dancers while Mr. Waller mumbled his speech. Nobody booed, since he owned The Burlesque and paid for the acts that had arrived by train that afternoon. Belle and The Lovely Sisters and The Brothers Grimelda carried trunks two blocks to the theater. Mr. Peels, the chimpanzee wearing a suit, tipped his bowler hat to women and children as he'd been taught. Kids and drunks followed him all the way to the theater where the marquee read: "Suitable for the Entire Family!" The hoochie coochies would have to clean up their act.

Directly across the street was the hotel still under construction, but they likely wouldn't have taken in the performers anyway. *Not the right clientele,* they'd been told in town after town. After setting up the stage and unpacking costumes in the basement dressing rooms, the thirty-odd performers settled in the boardinghouse run by Mama T, with a backyard, thankfully, for the dancing pony and jump-roping dogs, but not Mr. Peels, who refused to sleep outdoors.

Opening night, before the theater doors opened, the performers scattered like ants around the rococo-style house, caressing the orange drapes and seats, ogling the gold-rimmed balcony and gas wall sconces. The manager shooed them backstage when carriages arrived with the Waller family and other notables who lived in that stretch of stately homes Belle had walked by earlier with the knife thrower's kids.

101

From the stage, Belle saw those fine ladies on the front row with their ascotted husbands, all of them decorated with more diamonds than Belle had ever seen, sparkling more brightly than the pounds of fake stuff the performers wore. Even Belle understood this crude display was a sign of new wealth.

Though the performers had been told it would be an integrated audience, she was surprised to see negroes sitting on the main floor right next to white folks, not just tucked in the balcony or peering in from the lobby. This didn't bother most of the Northern performers, a mixed lot themselves: Jews, Germans, Irish, and Italians all sharing the same train car and toilets.

After the first dance number Belle's heart pounded not just from choreography, but from the way the men ogled her that made her feel chosen. Mr. Waller bumbled on stage as skittish as Butter, the elephant that had been banned from the show. Waller talked to his feet, fidgeting in his ill-fitting tux, applauding the theater's craftsmanship and promising only the best entertainment for his hard-working townsfolk. And then he finally did speak up. "I know you've all been anxiously awaiting the name of my new hotel, which will open this spring. Only one name will do: The Dorinda, offering the grandest accommodations for miles, suitable for statesmen and queens."

Mr. Waller bowed to his wife, Dorinda, perched in the front-most box seat. "Now your name will forever be linked with opulence!"

Mrs. Waller leaned forward; the only things glistening on her were tears.

Thirty years later Belle was back in the theater—even if it was showing its age, but so was Belle, no longer chosen. Last fall she'd been so thoroughly booed in Peoria for her botched dancing that she'd been reduced to getting spritzed in the face with seltzer and playing baseball with a goat.

Tonight there was only a smattering of men in the audience drinking bathtub gin from flasks. Belle kept missing her cues. Several men hooted: "Bring on the fan dancer! We want the fan dancer!"

But Chéri wasn't for three more acts and at that moment was in the dressing room tending the baby.

Belle rushed offstage and downstairs to collect the infant who, like Waller's hotel so many years ago, still had no name. The baby lay sleeping in an open trunk.

Chéri rouged her cheeks and fluffed her ostrich feathers. "Do I look all right?"

"You look just like—" Chéri blustered off before Belle finished. "—Irene Castle before she cut her hair."

Belle changed into street clothes and scooped up the six-week-old whose lips pursed as it dream suckled. The thought made Belle's milk seep, a sensation she never thought she'd experience again, especially this late in life. She clamped the baby tighter to her chest and went into the hall, pressing herself against the wall to make way for an usher carrying a laundry basket, hidden bottles clanking beneath the sheets. He darted into the tunnel that had been gouged out after Prohibition to sneak liquor under Front Street to the hotel. Without forethought Belle followed him, her shoulders scraping the whitewashed walls, electric light bulbs dangling sporadically to guide the way.

The tunnel ended at a stone stairwell. Belle ascended and found herself in The Dorinda's kitchen. Chefs piled silver-domed plates onto trays for waiters to serve to diners. Someone hollered: "Baked Alaska for the mayor!"

The baby cooed and a black dishwasher looked up, unperturbed, as if he were used to Madonna with Child rising from the pits. He nodded to a plate beside him loaded with scraps. Belle scooped up bread and a pork chop with a napkin and tucked it into her purse.

Belle followed a waiter into the dining room. The maître d' spotted her and headed her way. She went in the opposite direction, but he expertly navigated around tables to reach her. Before he opened his mouth Belle said: "I just wanted the mayor to meet his new baby." Maître d' swiveled toward a table where sat the mayor and his stout wife.

"Absolutely not," sputtered the maître d', whisking her and the baby through the main doors.

The lobby's orange and gold décor matched The Burlesque's with the grandest chandelier Belle had ever seen. If the mayor really were the baby's father, Belle would be eating flaming desserts and wearing a beaded gown. But the father was a Baltimore wharfie who'd waited at the stage door with daisies, then disappeared with Belle's pocket watch. She skirted the lobby, peeking in the Gentlemen's Club where men drank tea and smoked cigars, and the Ladies' Parlor where women sipped tea and gossiped. One wall by the front door was crowded with autographed photos of Buster Keaton, Mary Pickford, John Barrymore, entertainers famous enough to earn a room in The Dorinda. A sinking in Belle's chest at what she had already seen coming.

Just that afternoon she had tried to quiet the baby by walking it around the theater. She paused at the Wurlitzer organ that had been installed several years prior and signaled vaudeville's death, even here in Wallers Ferry, by moving pictures.

In The Dorinda, Belle faced a stairwell that begged to be ascended, but there was also an elevator car descending inside an ornate shaft. It hummed down, the uniformed operator opening the accordion gate and letting out two men who tucked coins in his hand.

Belle stood before the car, debating, until the operator, Jeb, one of Mama T's boarders, leaned out. "Like a ride?"

Belle entered and Jeb worked the levers with more skill than she thought he was capable of, felt the jolt as they made their way to the top floor.

Jeb opened the door, graciously not extending his tip hand. "Have a look around."

Belle read suite names as she passed, each with engraved illustrations on the metal plates: Blood Fruit, Sleeping Bear Rocks, Ferryboat, little works of art, much nicer than the hand-painted numbers at Mama T's.

A young couple exited one of the suites and Belle froze, embarrassed to be caught with the baby. They probably assumed she was the nanny. Or grand-mother. The man bowed and forgot to lock the door. When they were out of sight Belle slipped inside and bolted the latch, awed by the high ceiling rimmed with crown molding, gleaming parquet floor, separate dressing rooms for the man and woman. A basket filled with fresh blood fruit and caviar and familiar blue bottles, except now the labels read: Sparkling Juice—the factory having been converted.

Belle laid the baby on the bed and rifled through the woman's dresses and jewelry. The pearl ring fit perfectly and she felt entitled to it. She also bundled a mink stole inside a kimono and set it by the door. She'd always wanted a fur. The baby cried and Belle sat in the chair by the front window to feed it, not the least bit afraid the couple might return. This was her town, a place she'd visited every year for decades. This was her room. To prove it she gouged a B in the wooden arm of the chair with a diaper pin. The streetcar clanged and Belle looked below at Front Street where couples promenaded beneath streetlamps as if they were in Boston or New York.

"The Great White Way."

The theater manager was already taking down the poster for the vaudeville that would leave by the midnight train, just hours away. He unrolled the newest poster and even from this height Belle could see it was for *The Gold Rush*. A crowd gathered around the poster, their excitement already predicting the movie's success. The Dorinda would certainly accommodate Chaplin. Belle switched the baby to her other breast. "I should have gone into pictures."

A whistle sounded and Belle felt the ka*thunk*athunk-ka*thunk*athunk as the train passed. She would miss Wallers Ferry even if it was harsher now that old Mr. Waller was dead. Last year, she and several of the performers had taken the streetcar to pay their respects.

The cemetery was on an acre of land surrounded by blood fruit trees. The Wallers' obelisk was the most prominent, Mrs. Waller buried years before her husband, and now they rested side by side. After laying flowers on Waller's stone the performers walked to the farthest corner to place a bunch of bananas on the grave of Mr. Peels, who had died in his sleep in Wallers Ferry two years before at the ripe age of forty-five.

The baby mewled and Belle looked down at it. She had thought she was beyond fertility, but several months earlier her body had begun blooming the way it had twenty years ago. Back then her parents were still working and it was her mother who noticed even before Belle. "You're carrying," Mother had said so matter-of-factly when Belle's costume no longer fit. Mother lectured her not about morality, but about lost wages and one more mouth to feed. When she neared full-term Mother left Belle in Wallers Ferry with Mama T who later delivered the thing. For weeks after, Belle gritted her teeth every time a train rumbled past carrying people not stuck in a boarding house with a baby. Belle was not like other vaudeville girls who'd found themselves similarly encumbered and happy to give up nomadic lives. They either married the real father, or some unsuspecting yokel who would never know he was raising another man's child.

A month after the delivery Belle was at the train station to meet her family just passing through. Mother wanted to see the baby boy whom the boarders called Little Man.

Belle had waited on a bench inside the station letting him suck on a slice of blood fruit to keep him quiet. Beside her was a family speaking Russian, the mother handing peppermint sticks to her children. By her feet was her valise, wide open, filled with clothes and something wrapped in linen. Belle wondered what it was, if the woman had brought it in steerage across the Atlantic. Something valuable that they could sell to begin their new lives. It was a baffling tableau, the concept so foreign, this family heading for a home where they would put down roots, the children salved by candy until the dream arrived.

A whistle had sounded. The train carrying Belle's family approached. She moved faster than she thought possible so that no one would see her reach in and grab that linen-wrapped treasure. She was on her feet before the family noticed, dashing to the door, then outside where the train was slowing down. She raced along the platform looking in windows until she spotted The Daring Palenkas and Teacup Lil. Belle hugged the thing to her and jumped on board, her mother heading her way, but Belle said, "Go back to your seat!"

When they we safely nestled Mother looked at the bundle in Belle's hand, her face a puzzle as Belle unwrapped it to expose, not a baby, but a Matryoshka doll. A couple of vaudeville kids leaned over their seatbacks. "What is it?" Belle picked the thing up and opened it to find another doll inside, and another, and another, all the way down to a baby no bigger than a lima bean.

Mother held the littlest one in her hand. "Where's your baby?"

Belle looked out onto the platform and into the station, but she could not see the family.

"It died." She wondered if at that moment the mother was looking inside her valise to find Little Man surrounded by three blood fruit that might salve him too. Belle considered it a good trade.

Mother's head dropped. She looked at all the nesting dolls on her daughter's lap. "Maybe it's for the best."

The train lurched forward and as Belle reassembled the dolls her mouth opened but no sound came out.

Belle often thought about Little Man, a tiny crack in her sternum that not even being chosen could fill—when she was still chosen. She wondered if he spoke only Russian. If he learned his father's trade. If they even kept him or turned him over to the station agent. Maybe Little Man was still living in Wallers Ferry, and every time Belle came to town she looked into the faces of little boys, then bigger boys, big ones, men, wondering if it was him. Or if the Russians had taken him, but he ran away time after time, always heading to Wallers Ferry for reasons he couldn't explain. *I belong here.* Maybe he even loved vaudeville. She already knew he loved blood fruit.

And now here was a daughter asleep in Belle's arms. She could leave her here with this couple just beginning their lives, and what a rich life it would be. Tuck her in an open drawer and surround her with blood fruit in this town where her half-brother perhaps lived. Belle could board the midnight train with just her trunk, which still held those nesting dolls. *The baby died*, she would say if anyone asked. Or maybe she would board a different train bound for San Francisco, a city she'd always dreamed of visiting. Maybe open her own boarding house with the nest egg she'd accumulated. She'd make a good Mama T.

Ten minutes later Belle darted out onto the street, bundle clutched to her chest. She walked briskly to Mama T's intending to hide in her room and rub the mink across her cheek, but Jeb sat in the parlor playing his Jew's harp. He stopped when he saw her. "I beat you home." He eyed the loot in her arms, but didn't say a word. Belle started to leave when one of the salesmen playing checkers said: "King me." Mrs. Oswald imbibed in her nightly sherry. Mama T mended linens in a rocker by the fire, hands so gnarled from arthritis she could barely hold the needle. She lifted one of the sheets. "Why don't you help me with these, dear?"

Belle considered the request. She'd helped Mama T with a thousand chores. Mama T had helped Belle with her own labor. Tonight there was more than just sheet mending in Mama T's request.

"I'm awful tired," Mama T said.

The parlor was more familiar to Belle than the thousands of train cars she'd ridden in over the years. And it would never go anywhere, ever, nor would this town where she had carved her initial as if to claim it as her own.

"Let me set this down." Belle carried the bundle to the divan and unwrapped the kimono that held the mink.

Mama T reached out to touch it. "Gift from an admirer?"

"Yes." Belle felt the fur too, then caressed the baby she'd nestled inside.

"You'll spoil that child," said Mama T, a woman who had acted more like a mother to Belle than her own.

If Mama T could act, maybe Belle could too. Who needed moving pictures? She could pretend to be a good mother, could dote and fawn, and maybe in a few years she would be one. And tomorrow, she would walk to Harbinger's, buy three blood fruit, and line them on the wall in the back alley behind the boarding house where her son was born, a gift for Little Man in case he walked by.

Jeff Mann

A HISTORY OF BARBED WIRE

———

It itches as I write this, my new tattoo, first tattoo. Black barbed wire wrapped tight around my right biceps and triceps, a desire which took decades to distill. Four times a day I dutifully rub lotion on it, study the design in the mirror, watch it peel and heal, try to discern its history.

———

First, a boy in southern West Virginia, a drizzly March day. I'm helping my father run barbed wire along a new pasture fence, from locust post to locust post, then about a corner oak. We tug the thorny wire carefully off its roll, pull it tight, and staple it to the wood. Always there's the knowledge, the dread, the slightest chance that a tautly stretched length of wire might snap. I remember stories: the farmer in an adjoining hamlet, the sudden accident, the way the wire, too tense, turned on him just as a rattler abruptly betrays the snake handler's confident piety. In my imagination, this man I never met is naked, lying in the meadow grass, his beard the thick copper of August light. The barbed wire's wrapped about his torso, the dark hair on his chest is rilling with rain and scarlet, a March drizzle such as this is lapping away the blood. "Pull it tighter," orders my father. I start nervously, and one of the barbs pierces my thumb. Wincing, I lift the wound to my mouth, lick off the red stain, the taste of rust, waiting for the sound of a whip in the rain.

High-school loner, I'm reading my first gay novel, Patricia Nell Warren's *The Front Runner,* trying to imagine the track star and his coach making love. Finally I must face what I am. The local mountain men have always frightened me, but now I realize that I also desire them, though I know my lust, if expressed, would be met only with contempt and violence. Brought up

on stories of courage—Confederate soldiers, Greek and Roman heroes—
I'm trying to decide what manhood means in light of this problematic and
uninvited homosexuality. I want to become the sort of man I desire, I want
somehow to absorb the apparently effortless masculinity of country boys.
Boots, beards, chest hair. Denim jackets, pickup trucks. Tattoos.

———

In my early twenties now, I'm escaping into university anonymity, buying my
first leather jacket, swaggering self-consciously into my first leather bar, cul-
tivating roughness, learning how to drink bourbon straight. That red-mous-
tached bartender, veins cresting the pale ridges of his biceps—his eyes meet
mine. Back in Steve's apartment, he lights a votive candle, slowly strips for
me, pulls lengths of rope from beneath the bed. I tie his hands to the head-
board, knot a bandana between his teeth, and take a doubled-over belt to
his perfect ass. He groans when I enter him. In the candlelight, his eyes are
moist, his eyes are bright.

A decade later, I take my turn in Richmond. The cock gag's buckled in
tight, the rope cuts into my arms, wrists and ankles. I'm a martyr drunk on
too much Mezcal, seduced by a leather couple who've been looking for a sac-
rifice. Drew, black-bearded, his shoulders dense with muscles and tattoos,
holds me down. Tom, pony-tailed, ruthless, expressionless, drips hot wax
over my nipples. I sweat, buck, shake my head, bite down on rubber, a muffled
beggary, wrestling against them. They force me back against the mattress,
their tongues and moustaches ranging over my body, and then they arch
together above me, their kiss a keystone. Drained saint, exhausted, replete,
I fall trembling against Drew's big tattooed shoulder. Gently he smooths my
thinning hair, runs a finger through the sticky opal puddling on my chest.

———

In St. Mel's Church in Longford, Ireland, I sit in the pew, watching locals pray,
wondering what tragedies they are wrestling with. Somewhere near are the
graves of my ancestors, blood two hundred years removed. My youth's almost
over, my temples are slowly silvering. Before me, Christ opens his robe to
reveal his heart, which is tightly wrapped in thorns. Suddenly I remember

the corner oak, at the angle where two fences meet, back home on the farm. Barbed wire again, its intermittent fangs my father and I wrapped around the tree's expanding girth (the wood widening within like concentric circles a skipped stone sings across pond water). Over the years, into rough bark that tight barbed wire will slowly sink, then be swallowed up, a sharp suffering disappearing beneath the skin.

Ireland still, Sligo now. Above the door of the Cathedral of the Immaculate Conception, Christ is stretched in gleaming marble upon his cross. Drunk on pub Guinness, I want to ascend somehow—ladder or levitation—run my fingers across the painful arch of that carved chest, stroke the long hair and beard. My last lover still arches beneath me so, at least in memory, summer afternoons stolen together, his husband safely ensconced at work. A rainstorm rips the white oak leaves, rival gods wrestle within our bones. To the bed, to this crucifix of sheets, I tie him tight—the way we both like it—then hurt him gently, hairy savior, gym-pumped imp. I run my mouth over soft black moss, hard curves of chest, shoulders, biceps, cock, till our skins are splashed with magma. I bury my face in the sweaty fur between his pecs, wishing time would cease on this spot. I know what nothing surpasses, the world's beauty held entirely in my arms.

———

All my lonely youth I dreamed of marriage, and now the domesticity I dreamed of seizes me fast. Television evenings, cookbooks, monogamy. Conversations about lawn, house, and car. Hum of the dishwasher, the air-conditioner. Days spent behind a desk. I want some reckless, irrevocable gesture, some proof that a little youth, a little edge is left.

Context can eroticize almost anything. In gay porno I buy, magazines like *Drummer, Bear, Bound and Gagged*, tattooed men are tied and tying, sucking, fucking, flexing, posing. In the campus gym, I study athletic college-boys as they sweat and strain. Tattoos dark against pale skin and muscle-bulge. Designs delicately drilled into shoulders, biceps, calves. Sophisticated body art, long ago superseding the trashy, primitive tattoos I remember on hillbilly boys of my hometown. Even middle-aged, it's instinctual: incorporate what you find desirable, make it your own.

My mother, my sister, now my lover—how they've tried to keep out my wilderness, my warrior, my extremes. The first tattoo I wore was temporary, a rose wrapped around a dagger. Then the henna flirtations: a thin black armband in Rehoboth Beach, a few tribal swirls across one shoulder. No drunken adolescent spontaneity here. Now I take years to contemplate consequences, to make decisions that are permanent. For months, sadly dick-whipped, I'm wheedling my dubious spouse for his approval. Meanwhile, I carry around designs in my backpack, pull them out in the evenings, stand before the mirror, roll up my right sleeve and hold them up to my arm. I wonder how badly it will hurt.

———

It's a snowy Spring Equinox. Into Ancient Art I step for my long-postponed appointment. Pulling off my coat, sweater, and shirt, I stretch out bare-chested in the padded chair. Patrick is one of the best tattoo artists in the region. He's young and handsome, with blue eyes and a scruffy blond goatee, colorful Celtic designs swirling along his thick forearms. I wish he'd tie me down and stuff a rag into my mouth before he begins. Instead, he pulls on rubber gloves, sets out tiny pots of ink, and then the needles begin to hum and bite.

A small proud pain, almost a pleasure: nails, honeybees, wild rose thorns. A minor test of strength, sweat rolling down my sides like spring thaw. When Patrick bandages me up, a little over an hour later, I'm sorry that it's over. Now barbed wire's tied about my arm. Appetite's inscribed, flesh is emblematic. I shake his hand, pull on my clothes and my respectability, and step out into the snowstorm, flakes coming down thickly now in slate-gray dusk.

———

What we want's indelible, unlike so much we know, those transitory passions that wash over us and trickle away into meaninglessness. Something like a scar, but chosen, freed of accident or random circumstance. Here art's eternity and body's ephemera reach some compromise. As if ink might redeem the page, might lend meaning. It's scrimshaw, rope burn, rough touch that does not evaporate. Thorns wrapped around the heart of the Sacrificed God. A naked man bound tight, strength in restraint, learning to submit, letting go, learning the pedagogy of suffering. A message which will not erode away, like epitaphs in rain, which will perish only when its medium smoulders reluctantly at the edges, like wet paper, then takes to flame.

Mesha Maren

CHOKEDAMP

In the blue dawn light my brother paced, his boots pounding loud and the smoke from his cigarette curling into my bedroom.

"Hey, Billy," he said, pushing my door open. "You coming?"

John had Mom's beauty made manly, sharp features, long bones and straight teeth. I stared at him but said nothing. Under the blankets, I was dressed already, Realtree vest over my brown sweatshirt, Carhartt boots laced tight. I'd woke at five and drank three glasses of milk in the dark kitchen but when John's snores didn't stop I'd climbed back in bed. The baseboard heat in Mom's apartment couldn't cut the cold, not like a woodstove would have.

"Look what I found." John stretched his arms out, showing off his faded denim jacket, spray-painted with the stencil of a car and the words Death Devil—the name we'd given to the Oldsmobile we'd raced in the demolition derbies three summers back.

"You ready?" he asked, turning away towards the living room.

I followed, my muscles stiff with sleep, and grabbed Daddy's Winchester M70 out of the gun cabinet. Up until yesterday, I hadn't seen John in six months, not since the afternoon of his twenty-first birthday when he'd announced he was joining the Marines, handed me the keys to his Chevelle, and got on a bus to Parris Island.

"I've been looking forward to this for weeks," John said, taking the stairs two at a time.

We passed all the other numbered apartment doors, each one the same, with boots and trash bags set outside, smelling of coal oil, baby diapers, and damp tobacco.

"I tried to go duck hunting with this guy down in Carolina." John pushed open the front door and moved out into the sharp morning. "Dumbest shit I ever seen. The dude couldn't shut up for a second. We're sitting out there in the duck blind and all he wants to do is talk about how his girlfriend, back in Oklahoma or wherever, loves to suck dick."

John kicked at the door to his Chevelle, loosening the thick ice and pulling at the handle, his shoulders rippling under the Death Devil jacket.

The afternoon John had left for South Carolina, I'd gone into his room. The air had changed already, thickened with dust, as if he'd left long before. I'd rifled through a pile of letters from his ex-girlfriend but they were boring notes full of hearts and flowers and baby-making propositions. In the closet, I'd found the United Mine Workers belt buckle Daddy gave to John when he turned thirteen, and that jacket we'd stenciled and painted together. I'd tried to wear it, but though I was only four years younger than him, the coat hung huge on me, the sleeves almost reaching my fingertips.

"Last night Mom was talking to me." John eased the Chevelle out of the driveway and onto the dark stretch of Polk Road.

"Mom's always talking," I said.

John laughed. "Well, last night she was telling me about this idea she's got of moving down to South Carolina."

Turning onto Front Street, John cut the wheel too sharp and had to slam on the brakes as the car skimmed to a stop just shy of the wooden railroad-crossing arm. I rocked forward and braced myself, palms flat against the dashboard, as a coal train shuddered past, the yellow cone of engine light piercing the morning air and spreading across the hillside of pokeweed and nettle. I glanced over at John. He drove too fast. He did everything too fast, too showy. Jack-ass-backwards, our daddy would have said.

"She said she tried to talk to you but you just fussed at her."

Through the snow encrusted window the red crossing-signal blinked on-off-on.

"Billy," John said, "this ain't easy for Mom either, but she deserves something like this. A new start, a little apartment down by the beach."

The last train car shivered by and disappeared behind the bend, following Milk River and Highway 64 out towards the Piedmont.

Mom's plan wasn't nothing new. I could see she'd been plotting for the past five years, pretty much since the day Daddy died. When the Frazier mine collapsed all the oxygen sucked out, left the shaft an unlivable lockbox of carbon dioxidized air. A week later Mom started talking about how she couldn't keep the farm going, even with two full-grown boys to help her. She started talking about how much she hated the cold up on the mountain and having to keep the woodstove going. Said it was lonely up there and the land was mean and hard. She kept the farm but used Daddy's whole pension to move me and John and her down off Bethlehem Mountain and into a tiny apartment above the laundromat in Render. Now she wanted to sell the farm and move to the beach. It was nothing new. She'd just been waiting till John established himself out there, waiting till I was almost done with high school.

"I promised her I'd talk some sense into you." John drove up over the tracks and onto Snake Run Road.

"It ain't sense she's talking," I mumbled.

"What the fuck's wrong with you? Huh? Why the hell do you like it around here so much?" John brought his lighter up to the tip of his Pall Mall. "First you whine and cry about us moving off the mountain and now you'd rather rot here than move to the fucking beach."

Out the window bare trees whipped by. We passed the gravel road that wound around to the Yarborough and Layner cemetery. When Daddy died, they'd tried to say there wasn't room for new graves in the family plot. But Uncle Bud was sheriff of Monongah County and so they found space in there somehow. Mom and John and I'd gone up to see his grave yesterday. We put a handful of plastic junk-store flowers in a vase and mumbled some words. I wanted to tell Daddy I was sorry for the whole pitiful scene: Mom fixing the flowers just so and making a fuss, rubbing her dry eyes, John not even looking at the grave, just scraping the mud off his brand new boots, and me not doing nothing, just watching the whole thing. The flowers probably blew away before the afternoon had passed. It didn't matter; it was all fake anyways.

John and I'd gone down to the cemetery by ourselves when we were kids. The day after Daddy was laid to rest, we walked there through the fields behind the old home place. John carried Daddy's bottle of Jim Beam. He took big swigs and then screwed the top closed and walked ahead, swinging the bottle through the waist-high yellow grass. I'd always known where Daddy hid the bottle, in the corner of the woodshed, but before he died I'd never tasted it. I was only twelve but John'd shared the bottle with me anyways.

"Half and half," he said, pouring part of the bottle into a mason jar. "Toast." He raised his bottle high. "To Daddy, the old asshole."

Daddy's grave had been mounded, a pile of raw red clay. John kicked at the loose dirt.

"Why the fuck'd you have to die?" he shouted and, spinning around, he'd slammed his fist into the tall poplar that shaded the grave.

"Fuck you, fuck you, fuck you." He'd kept punching, pounding at the bark until I grabbed onto his arm and pulled us both to the ground. John's hand swole up all purple and bleeding. My face was a mess of tears and snot. Pulling his handkerchief out, John'd tore it down the middle with his teeth. Half for my face, and the other half for his fist.

On the home road John slowed the car to a crawl. The path was choked with multi-flora rose bushes and greenbrier vines. Through the empty winter branches the farmhouse rose up before us, a two-story hulk of a structure covered in yellow tarpaper. John parked the car in the yard and stepped out, stretching his arms and wandering down towards the chicken coop, overrun now with blackberry vines. I opened the passenger door but didn't move.

"Man, I ain't been up here in so long," John hollered, "must be two, three years now. I betcha there's some fat little deers out here, been munching in the apple orchard all fall."

I came up to the old place as often as I could. I brought my girl Regina up about two weeks back; told her how my great-granddaddy built the house in 1903. I'd made a fire in the belly of the woodstove to chase out the cold. Bending close, I lit twigs and paper, coaxing them into a crackling heat that could sustain a larger log. My muscles had relaxed and my mind focused as the yellow flames licked with the promise of warmth. I led Regina upstairs to my parents' old double bed and burrowed my hands through her layers of sweaters and blue jeans to reach the soft mounds of her hips. Afterwards we lay under the mouse-eaten blankets and stared out the window, but Regina had complained that it still felt cold. The gray-blue evening light stole across the frozen fields while the neighbor's Herefords moved like patches of rust against the windblown hillside, their breath billowing in great white clouds as they cried out for feed.

"It's spooky in here," Regina whispered. "Come on, let's go."

"Aw, shut up, you sound just like my mom," I'd said, kissing her neck in that soft spot just below her little white ear.

"Hey," John hollered. "Watcha waiting for? The deer ain't gonna come and climb in the trunk."

I reached into the backseat for the rifle and followed John along by the old garden plot where the fence sagged over the rotten posts. In my daydreams I set new posts and rolled out wire to protect the plot where Regina would plant her tomatoes, okra, and string beans.

We skirted around the house and took the path past the garbage pile out towards the cliff, John walking in front, head high, rifle slung over his right shoulder.

"Watcha thinking about, huh?" His voice came out in a nasal whine. "Cat got your tongue?"

I shook my head. "I was just thinking about Regina," I said. "I was thinking about asking her, after we graduate and I get a job and all, if, you know, she'd wanna move up here with me. Fix the place up again. But now Mom's talking all this foolishness."

John's laugh erupted in a snort. "Two things I got to say to you, Billy. First off, no matter how well you're hung or how much money you planning on making, you ain't gonna be able to convince a girl to move up here with you. The place is falling apart man, wasn't all that well built to begin with. Besides, you don't wanna marry the first girl you fuck, there's a whole lot more pussy out there in the world. Move to South Carolina with Mom, you'll see what I mean."

Out in the pasture the wind had sculpted the snow into miniature glaciers and knee-high mountains. I stuffed my toboggan in my coat pocket and freed my ears to catch the slightest rustle.

We chose a grove of tulip poplars and settled ourselves there, crouched low against the trunk of a mid-size tree, training our gaze along the edge of the crystalized pasture. A plump rabbit bounded from between tuffets of gypsum weed, its fat body bouncing across the snow-ice. I raised my rifle but John slapped my arm down.

"You do that," he hissed, "and you'll scare off every damn deer from here to Kingdom Come."

I slumped against the poplar, reaching for the thermos of coffee. My fingers ached and I wished I'd come up here alone. Off the edge of the cliff at the far side of the field I could see the raw open earth at the mouth of the Frazier mine. I always figured I would work there, even after Daddy got killed I still thought of it as a good, steady job. But the tipple burned down in '97 and they closed the whole operation, said slope mining wasn't profitable anymore.

"Lookie there," John whispered.

I followed the barrel of his rifle where it pointed to the slender legs and white tail of a doe, half-hidden beside the trunk of a black oak. She broke from behind the tree and disappeared too quickly into the deeper woods.

"Shit," John said.

I leaned forward, my own rifle raised.

"Now don't get all trigger happy," John whispered. "We'll get her, that's for damn sure, we just gotta wait her out. She'll be back. She's been stuffing herself on them acorns and she ain't gonna be able to resist long."

We sat there a full twenty minutes before either of us spoke again. In the branches above my head a woodpecker tapped. The first heavy snowflakes began to fall, sifting down like feathers and clinging to the dry grass. The deer did not reappear and the excitement ebbed out of me, leaving a cold anxiety. Running my hand along the barrel of my rifle, I felt its smoothness against my palm, and there on the stock, my fingers found the carving of Daddy's initials.

When I was eight Daddy'd placed that same rifle in my hands, set me down by the trunk of a locust and told me not to come home without at least one squirrel. I sat at the base of the tree for hours without managing to kill anything. I needed to pee bad but was afraid to move for fear of scaring away the few squirrels I'd seen. So I sat stock still till warm piss spilled down the inseam of my jeans and even then I didn't move, picturing my empty hands and the anger rippling across Daddy's face. After a long while John'd come upon me and pulled me to my feet, laughing. He opened his thermos of lukewarm coffee and poured it down my leg to cover the urine, then handed me a squirrel out of his own bag and sent me home.

"I'm gonna circle around," John announced, "see if I can't get her, if nothing else maybe I can scare her out and you can shoot her in the field. We can't stick around here all day if it's gonna snow like this." He turned his face up, and squinted into the whirling flakes. "We're likely to get stuck."

I nodded as John rose and started off in the direction the doe had fled.

"Now be ready," he called to me. "I might scare her out soon as I walk over thata way."

I stood and lifted the rifle to my shoulder. The woods were silent except for the crunch of John's footsteps in the dry leaves and the echo-whistle of a coal train down in the valley. As I scanned the tree line for movement, my right finger rested lightly on the safety, my left hand steady on the forestock. If I could be the one to shoot the doe, to dress her there in the field and carry her back to town, then maybe John would quit acting like he was the cock of the walk. Maybe then Mom would listen to *me* for just one second.

The snowfall thickened and I lost sight of my brother among the bare branches. My eyes swam fast up and down the edge of the trees and just as my arms began to cramp a slight rustle and blur of movement pulled my attention to the far end of the clearing. I narrowed my focus, squinted and pulled the trigger and as the recoil shuddered into my shoulder, my brother's scream split the silence.

"John?" I called, my heart slamming.

No sound came. I dropped the rifle and ran. Snowflakes spun before me, my breath booming loud. I moved towards the shadowed woods, searching the trees for the shape of my brother but snow sealed the line between earth and sky. A world of white.

"John," I screamed again.

Something darted. The doe. She moved fast, flickering back into the trees, dripping a red trail.

"Shit balls." John stepped out from behind an oak. "Look what you fuckin' done." He walked across the clearing towards me.

My body vibrated with the ebb of adrenaline. "I . . . I . . . thought . . . "

"What? Thought you hit me? Surprised you didn't with what a fucking lousy shot you are." He kicked at the red drops in the snow. "I could of had her easy."

I breathed deep. "We'll find her," I said, my voice steadying.

"Naw." John shook his head. "Not in this kind of blizzard we won't. You barely wounded her." He waved his hands in the thickening flakes. "Besides, I gotta get my car outa here before we get stuck."

John walked tall, with his shoulders all thrown back, and I thought of how his face must of looked while he hid, smiling behind that oak, watching me run all frantic and screaming across the field.

"I ain't lettin' her die and rot out there," I said. "Our people ain't like that, to waste like that. I'm gonna find her and dress her even if it is snowing."

John shook his head. "Man, you do whatever the fuck you want. Me, I'm going home, get warmed up and go shoot some pool. You can track that damn deer to hell and back if that's what you want."

"Fuck you," I screamed at him.

John picked up his backpack and walked towards the woods. I didn't move and when he reached the edge of the trees he glanced back over his shoulder at me.

"Hey, Billy," he hollered. "Come on, man. I'll buy you a beer."

"Fuck you," I screamed again but my voice sounded small, sucked up by the dense snow-clouds and then John disappeared into the leafless trees.

The blood-path grew faint in the woods where the snow did not pile as deep and I lost it at times among the browns and grays of the forest floor. I kicked at the piles of damp leaves, shaking my hands to keep the cold out. When I found it again, the blood ran thicker, slick pools dotted across the snow at regular intervals like morse code messages. Bleeding like that, she couldn't of got far. I walked with my head down, pausing now and then to listen for her rustling and when I emerged from the trees and looked up, the dark outline of the old house loomed on the far side of the clearing, and there she was, splayed out below a gnarled apple tree. Following her path, I'd come full circle, round the back way to the house without even realizing it.

She lay there, on her side, eyes liquid and frantic, thick blood spilling across her brown coat. I knew I should shoot her right away, finish her off and begin dressing her before the storm got much worse, but I'd never been so close to something that was dying. Her eyes followed my movements as I dropped to my knees, still clutching the rifle. I hovered close and smelled blood and wet soil. The doe's breath slowed, the light brown coat over her barrel of ribs barely rising. Her muscles relaxed as her body grew slack and her eyes emptied and in the silence, I heard the delicate spattering of snow-flakes against the dead leaves.

I let my own breath out and pulled my Buck knife from the sheath on my belt and rolled the doe onto her back. Just below the breastbone I made a slit and pulled the blade down straight between her legs as the purple-red organs spilled out, slick, warm and shimmery wet. I sliced the diaphragm and reached blindly up inside, her body heat thick on my arms. The flow of dark blood melted the snow around us, soaking through the knees of my jeans and steaming in the cold air. I cut loose the heart and severed the windpipe, but stopped then, sat back on my heels and looked up to the clouds. The snowfall had quickened, fat flakes dissolving on my skin but piling deep on the ground all around me. There was no way I could carry her carcass all the way out to the road in a storm like this. Though my hands knew each movement by memory, it was pointless to go on dressing her, to keep spreading the quantity of this waste out around me.

The spilled blood turned chill and as the cold crept into my body, anger surged up through me. I thought of John punching his fist into that poplar beside Daddy's grave. *Fuck you, fuck you, fuck you.* After that day John never really seemed to grieve, as if the power of that moment had slammed the sadness right out of him.

Footsteps rustled and I glanced up but saw nothing aside from the spindly winter trees and fat clouds, and then there, by the house, the smooth brown back of another doe. She stood beside the front porch, her slender legs meeting the earth precisely where an eight-year-old me had dug two holes for the red and yellow rosebushes Mom always fussed over.

But the bushes were long gone and the house itself leaned to the left, the roof hanging soft with rot under the wet weight of the storm. Looking closer I could see that the living room windows were shattered, the door hung off its hinges. And though she stood frozen in fear, I knew the doe was only waiting. The place was hers now. Come spring, sharp green grass would push up through the rib cage of the deer that lay before me and the house too would slump just as she had. It would fall under the winds and the rains until locust saplings sprang up between the floorboards and twisting oaks climbed through the window frames.

Lee Maynard

from **THE PALE LIGHT OF SUNSET: SCATTERSHOTS AND HALLUCINATIONS IN AN IMAGINED LIFE**

1936

The Parlor

I am born in the parlor of my grandmother's house. I come screaming into the world among the only valuable things my grandmother owns. There is a small settee on which no one is allowed to sit; a tiny table of unknown origin; a pump organ, which no one plays. A strange polka-dot vase with a string of white glass coiling around it. Doilies on everything. And me, pulled into the world by a midwife I would never know and would never meet again.

I am born in West Virginia. I am a West Virginian. And, as are all of us, I am a child only of West Virginia. And of no where, of no one, else.

As I grow older and my mother brings me in from the mountains to visit my grandmother, I realize in my child-mind that my grandmother's house is the only place in my world where I feel safe, where I feel comfortable.

Each time, before I even go inside, I can smell the biscuits my grandmother bakes, larger than any biscuits I have ever seen, larger than my hand. My grandmother feeds me biscuits and homemade jelly and then I go back outside to play.

There is a cherry tree in the front yard and a small grape arbor stands sagging in the sunlight at the side of the house. There is a small garage, a shed, and a chicken house. And a vegetable garden, where my grandmother grows what her family eats. I love to play in the tall grass just beyond the garden, spending hours scratching in the dirt, digging trenches, building forts of sticks and twine, moving imaginary cowboys, Indians, and soldiers through cataclysmic battles.

Fifty years go by before I learn that one of my mother's sisters, a twin, had been stillborn in the same parlor. A stillborn twin, a sure sign of a curse on my grandmother's family. It was too much for my grandmother, and her family, to bear. No one must know.

And there was another reason. There was no money for tiny burials.

In the stillness and quiet of a black summer night, with waves of heat pouring down the valley and out across the rivers in the distance, with the heavy scent of honeysuckle hanging in the night air, the tiny body was named, wrapped in my grandmother's prized quilt, and buried in a hand-dug grave beneath the tall grass just beyond the vegetable garden. Beneath the tall grass where I played.

But I do not grow up in my grandmother's house. I only visit there.

And then I do not visit at all.

And far away on the down side of my life, my grandmother a long time gone, I find the house gone, too. There is nothing but a shallow imprint upon the earth, faintly marking were the house once stood. There is no garage, no shed, no chicken coop, no vegetable garden.

But the grass beyond the old garden stands knee high.

I lie down in the grass and stare upward into a pale steel sky. And I realize that, had I, too, been stillborn, I would lie here, too, forever, next to an aunt whose name I never knew. Under the grass.

I close my eyes, and smell the faint aroma of biscuits baking in a wood burning stove.

1941

The Shotgun

It is the first memory I have.

I hear the old shotgun go off and I fall over backwards and roll down the side of a steep ridge through layers of leaves autumn-dropped from the hardwood trees. The gun makes a noise beyond all imagination, beyond all reason. When the gun goes off, time stops, the breeze does not blow, birds freeze in mid-flight. Bits of leaves are in my eyes and mouth and my ears ring from the terrible thunder of the 12-gauge. I try to cover my ears with my hands as I slide to a stop somewhere down the hill, my shirt full of dirt and twigs, my mind spinning. As the booming fades into the woods and across the far ridges, I can hear only the small crashing of something plowing through the leaves.

Me.

I am five years old.

I have been following my father through the dense West Virginia forest, early sunlight dripping through the gnarled trees in broken blobs of gold and yellow. Trees, the smell of leaves on the forest floor, warm sunlight, the huge gun, hunting with my father.

It is terribly hard to move quietly when you are five years old, and my father constantly glances over his shoulder at me, both, I know, to make sure I am there and as admonishment to hunt as he has told me—quietly, trying to move only when he moves, trying to stay behind him and not too close, scanning the ground and the trees in front of us. Looking, always looking.

I try to keep looking but, usually, my eyes are glued to my father, especially to his right arm, where I can see the worn and shiny stock of the gun pressed lightly between his elbow and his body. I walk in fear of the gun going off, of the noise it will make. Surely, I think, I will see his arm move and have plenty of time to put my hands over my ears.

We are squirrel hunting, and it is the first time he has allowed me to go with him. We do not hunt for sport. If he kills a squirrel, we will take it home to the tiny cabin on the side of the hill, and we will eat it.

There is a flicker of motion high on a tree limb, a gray instant of fur.

And then, for the first time, I am with him when he fires the gun.

His arms come up in a liquid, flowing movement and the barrel of the gun washes a thin blue arc against the gray of the tree trunks, a blur, a painted still life of frozen motion before my eyes. Before the blur can fade there is an explosion that shakes the limbs of the trees and makes the ground shudder and sends me over backwards and down the hill.

The shotgun is a pump-action with an outside hammer. Strangely, as I am falling over backwards, I hear him work the slide and I know there is another shell in the chamber of the gun, even before I, or the squirrel, hit the ground.

In all the times I hunt with him, I am never able to anticipate the shooting of the gun, the blur across my eyes always there before I am ready. As a child,

I think it is because I am a child, and children are slow. Later, I know it is because my father is fast, faster with his hands, and with a shotgun, than any man I will ever know. And, finally, I know it is because the old shotgun fits my father as the hands of two good friends fit together in warm greeting.

2003
Where I'm From

All my life, no matter where I am, people know I am not *from* there. Know, perhaps, that I do not belong there. As I know.

I wrote once, long ago . . .

> Everything I have ever done,
> every place I have ever been,
> has seemed no more than a temporary stop
> on the way to someplace else.
> And something always tries
> to hold me back.
> Just let me be gone
> and be done with it.

I always want to be gone, to be someplace else, to be done with it.

And in that wanting, I never quite know where I'm from, never quite figure out what forms me, hardens me.

And when I think about it, all I get are images . . .

Images . . .

. . . mountains that seem to form us and send us tearing along their sides and down across the ridges to run staring-eyed out into the world like mythical beings charging out of the forests of Valhalla.

. . . hollows, those dark, pungent, quiet places that instill in us a way of moving, a way of seeing, a way of being. Hollows capped with smoke and mist, bottling us up, aging us, keeping us still, our lives clear and silent, like Mason jars of crystal moonshine gathering dust on a wooden shelf in a shed long forgotten on the back side of an abandoned ridge-top farm.

... hickory trees and chestnut split-rail fences and walnuts that fall in their soft and bursting black husks, rolling near-silently down the sides of hills.

... blackberry brambles woven into masses of thorn-guarded stands too thick to allow my arm inside, and rambling rose tangled so tightly against the leaning fences that, when the fences have long since disappeared, no one notices.

... paw-paw bushes.

... spike-hard stands of rhododendron.

... the smell of the hardwood forests in autumn, a smell so thick and rich that it can flow through your veins like blood—and indeed it is. Blood. Enough blood from the bodies of mountaineers to raise forests from hard desert and then lie in wait for us to come and breathe it in, again. It is not by accident, that color of old maple leaves.

... thin, wispy strands of acrid smoke escaping softly from the ends of long guns held by men, and sometimes women, who could hold those long guns for hours, days, years, generations.

... creeks, with their slow moving water the color of green eternity, glistening softly in the tiny shards of sunlight that manage to penetrate the overhanging limbs of trees that finger down into the softly moving clouds of dragonflies.

... sounds of banjo music played on front porches that have rails just high enough to put your foot on—if you're sitting in a rocking chair. The music ... hard, ringing notes of pure, clear transcendence that maybe only front porch string pickers can ever really achieve.

... "kin," kinfolk, who sometimes, only sometimes, only forever sometimes ... forgive, but who never, ever, forget. Kin. Old men and older women who lived lives that we will never know, can never be recorded, but lives that have become part of the evolutionary threads of which our lives are woven, lives of many colors, spread across the earth.

Images.

They are always with me, no matter where I am.

And when I think about it, I know where I'm from.

There has never really been any question.

There is only one such place.

But what does it matter now, near the end of it all?

Scott McClanahan

PICKING BLACKBERRIES

---

from **HILL WILLIAM**

I didn't want my mom to find out about anything. One day we stopped at the Handy Place after school and I saw this Bill Elliot ball cap. It was one of those fake hats you see at gas stations that cost like $15 and I wanted this ball cap bad. I asked her for it everyday when we stopped, but each time I asked for it she would never get it for me. For some reason though I saw that today was different. So I asked her if I could. At first she said no but then she grabbed it and put it up on the counter with our pop bottles and beef jerky and bubble-gum. The cashier rang it up but I guess it was more expensive than we thought.

My mom searched through her big purse, but she didn't have enough money. So mom put back her pop, and even then she had to go looking through her purse for a couple of extra nickels to pay for it all. We finally got it, and on the way home I felt so bad for making her get me a crappy old ball cap that I didn't even want really.

When we got home I felt even worse because she was acting strange like walking in and out of all the rooms in the house and then walking into the living room. Then she went walking into the kitchen. Then she went walking from the kitchen and the living room into all of the other rooms in the house. Then just a couple of minutes later she was going through these little orange pill bottles she took sometimes (she knew something was wrong). She held one of the orange pill bottles in her hands and looked down at the label.

She kept staring at it and then she turned to me and pointed to her Diet Coke and said, "Hey, Scott. Is diet pop alcohol?"

I looked at her and giggled, thinking she was joking, but then I saw that her eyes were just wired and she was looking at the pill bottle now and she wasn't joking.

I told her. "No, pop's not alcohol."

She said, "That's what I thought. I thought pop wasn't alcohol."

I shook my head thinking, "Good God, what a weird world."

Fifteen minutes later she lay down on the couch and closed her eyes.

I said, "It's going to be all right. It's going to be all right."

I sat and watched her on the couch and I said again, "It's going to be all right."

I decided to go outside and do something to cheer her up. There were all kinds of blackberry bushes on the side of the mountain where we lived. Sometimes I looked up at the mountains and I felt trapped in a mountain grave. I felt myself being consumed by a mountain mouth. I walked to the top of the hill where the blackberry bushes were and I thought, "I can pick some blackberries and that will make her feel better." I was wearing my Morris the Cat T-shirt that I bought with 10 proofs of purchase from cans of Nine Lives cat food. I was wearing Velcro tennis shoes that I bought at Shoe World. It might not seem like it now, but you weren't anything in the mountains back then if you didn't wear Velcro tennis shoes. I was fast without my Velcro tennis shoes on but I was especially fast when I was wearing them.

I stood eating the blackberries and putting the blackberries into my Morris the Cat T-shirt to take back home to my mom. I was using my T-shirt like a container to hold them together. But I was also eating more of the blackberries than I was keeping. I ate the blackberries and I whispered the poem my mother always whispered to me . . .

> The little toy dog is covered with dust,
> But sturdy and staunch he stands;
> And the little toy solider is red with rust,
> And his musket moulds in his hands.
> Time was when the little toy dog was new,

And the soldier was passing fair;
And that was the time when our Little Boy Blue
Kissed them and put them there.

I put a blackberry in my shirt, then I ate a blackberry.

"Now don't you go till I come," he said,
"And don't you make no noise!"
So, toddling off to his trundle bed,
He dreamt of the pretty toys;
And, as he was dreaming, an angel song
Awakened our Little Boy Blue—
Oh! The years are many, the years are long,
But the little toy friends are true!

I ate another blackberry.
I decided to save one.
I ate one.
I saved one.
I finally had enough. I thought inside my head, "It's going to be all right now. It's going to be all right."
I took off back down the mountain to take the blackberries back to my mom. As I was walking back home, my shirt all full of blackberries, I got excited and started walking faster. I was coming down a mountain, so as I started walking faster I felt myself picking up speed, and then picking up more speed, and before I knew it I was running, and before I knew it again I was running even faster, and then I was running so fast that I couldn't slow down. The mountain was running me.
I couldn't stop.
My legs were kicking out wild beside me.
They were going everywhichway and I couldn't stop. I tried to stop but I couldn't stop. I fell face flat forward against the ground.

I sat up and looked down at the ground. There were blackberries all broken and bruised on the dark dirt stained purple. There were blackberries resting against the rocks too. I looked down at my chest and there were blackberries mashed against my chest. They were sticking to my shirt like loogies.

I held up my arms and I went, "O, god."

I knew the world was so full of shit sometimes.

I was only ten years old but I knew it.

I started to cry a little baby cry.

I walked back home and I cried even more. By the time I got all the way back home to my mom you couldn't even understand what I was trying to say. It was one of those cries where all of the words start blending together and all you can hear is some crazy crying sentence. It was,

"Iwasgoingtopickblackberries(sniff)foryoubutthenfelldown(sniff)and theywentallover." I wanted to tell her I hoped to make her feel better.

I wanted to tell her I spent all of this time picking them just for her. I started babbling and my mother tried calming me down. Then she did something beautiful.

My mother was always someone who believed in miracles and now here she was making a miracle just for me.

She picked the smashed blackberries off my Morris the Cat T-shirt and tried eating them.

The blackberries were all caked in dirt, but my mom ate them and ground the grainy berries between her teeth and said, "No, they're good. They're really good. Thank you for picking them for me."

My mom ate the dirty blackberries and whispered, "It's going to be all right. Why are you crying? It's going to be all right."

She gave me a dirty blackberry and I ate it too. I felt the little pieces of dirt crunching between my teeth like diamonds. I whispered like I whisper sometimes now, "Yeah, it's going to be all right. It's going to be all right."

And here I am years later and I'm still saying it to myself.

I'm saying, "It's going to be all right now. It's going to be all right."

And sometimes I believe it to be true.

John McKernan

I HAVE SLEPT IN BEDS AND IN GUTTERS

———

On trains and cars and buses
In planes and cranes and bridges

On golf courses
Once in a sand trap
Twice on the ninth green

In front of a class
In the back of a classroom and on many roofs
In libraries and police cruisers
In study halls

In caves and jails
In tents bars barns parks
In chairs on stairs at parties and weddings
On rocks and docks and dorms and beaches
In my mother's womb for nine months

Watching movies plays opera ballet tennis baseball golf chess
While driving walking talking
While riding a horse or a power mower
In lectures churches stadiums courts offices stores
On a bale of hay and in a pile of rags
At many rock concerts

And one night
In Huntington
After a bet
On blue silk cushions
On a white pillow
With the lid closed
In a bronze coffin Drunk

Llewellyn McKernan

HELEN, SOVEREIGN

---

as the month
of May, when the iron
of winter rises to
the lip of a flower. Even

now, your bald head
knows beyond its hairless
symmetry, its memory
bank of scarlet-feathered

pain. What lies
outside it
is the hospital bed where your
anecdotal body floats, the

white flanks
of the sheet searching and
finding the diminished sculpture
of your bones. The twilight

of your body
darkens, the black bubbles
of your eyes open and
close like a doll's, the

red wafer of your heart
goes on bleeding. I curse
the sullen scavenger
scraping away now

at your belly and bowels, the
slow torture the IV drip becomes
in your veins. I
can guess how much

your breathing is like the waves
that dimple the surface
of a river before they
vanish, how your crossed arms

mimic a dove's folded wings,
but I'll never know how you went
beyond the silver mockery
of your marriage or

your dirt-poor youth, some
music you tongued like gulps of fresh
sweet milk, perhaps, some defiant
stance that startled even

your parents' cold lapidary poses.
Sovereign Helen, you know
so much now, but you're
not telling, like the Holy

of Holies in the Jewish Temple when
Pompey invaded it, only to
remark. "It's empty. There
is no God." But I am

patient. I can wait my turn
for the kind of knowledge
that makes one deaf and
blind. In the mean-

time, I study
the white discs of your lids and
clouds flying like wild
blue geese outside the window:

how they shape the sky,
its ripple of sun, how
they stun each slow breath
that keeps you alive.

Irene McKinney

HOMAGE TO HAZEL DICKENS

———————

Neither the house nor the barn can keep me, now I'm moving on.
Whether I go or stay the pain will be the same, so now I'm picking up

my suitcase with the leather handle that my Uncle Brack brought
home from France, and now I'm waving to you all.

After this nothing can ever hurt me because my heart is wrung
like a wet towel here, and my lips are swollen and red.

By way of Gerrit's Gap and then by way of Deep Creek Road
I've come to the turning, and turning away from air

fog-soaked and shining, away from the suckhole in the river.
The sewing factory closes and I've got to have a paycheck.

Since I was twelve I knew I'd have to turn my back
on the smoky kitchen, on the tow-headed boys fighting at the well,

on my mother's peaceable face. The faces I will meet later
will never measure up, you know that. Nothing will.

Both me and you have got to go sometime. Come on, let's tear
the heartstrings loose and head for the station.

Whether we go or stay, we've lost it.
The porch, the cold crocks of cream in the cellar,

the redbone hound in the yard, the wild azalea all orange
and sweet, we've lost it standing here looking at it

this way. So we should turn our faces outward
from this place, string our guitars, and go.

Devon McNamara

ZACH SPEAKS

My love,
it is sunset,
this is our walk after rain,
scarlet in muck, azure
in cow prints, horse tracks,
the skyey stream where I dunk
my muzzle, shake out my
blaze of splash.
       You, in your coat,
your redolent boots, call
my name, and I hear but attend
to the thrill of the smells of
the evening, sea wrack heaving
away out there, hare scut in nettles,
the byre beyond, wild pee on
this stone, chips in their papery
slick and a beer, the dark rich stink in
the ditch. Then I look back,
waiting, spangled in mist, to
raise my head to your hand.

What? You think I'm past
speech and don't love
how you lie on the floor
by me talking and stroking?
Even now, my big, ambery paws

reach your shoulders, I
open my breath in your face.

Oh my love, how your hair, wet
with sky, is my color. Don't cry.
Our lost words are shining. Turning
and turning for home, how they glisten
and sing.
      See how I lift my head golden
and breathing beside you, the way I will
always, and you will, deep in your hands
feel my voice, hear our listening touch.

Kelly McQuain

CAMPING AS BOYS IN THE COW FIELD

———

Summer and the pureness of a wooded hillside,
the far dark of evening come to meet our fire smoke
on the old farm, our tent up and the cows away,
rabbits in the grass as the first slow sweep
of the light tower above the little landing strip comes to life.
Feel the vibration of the cows and how even now
the dew still collects, and the insects and crickets blur to song.
Our minds were the sky and the sky was our minds;
what we knew of brotherhood was shared not with brothers
        but friends.
Our legs shook as we climbed the tower,
hand then foot, rung after rung, minds drunk with dizziness
as our eyes translated the stars from dots of light to wonder.
As the light circled, we stumbled upon a first high
and let go of our solid selves, hearts radiant and red
as stamped tin trinkets in some future Mexico.
Later there would be cheap wine and girls,
the light of those nights diffuse by now and a part
of all space. Did we know then how everything in the world
is connected, like the wounds of Christ eternally exposed?
And you with a finger in the wound. And you with salt.

RITUAL

My mother and I find a bat
reeling above our heads the evening we arrive
with light bulbs
to screw into the ceiling sockets of the half-
finished home
my father began building before he died:
the bat startled
by our flung door and blithe conversation,
my mother and I frozen
among dusty paint rollers and push brooms,
equally shaken
at the veering path of such sudden
unexpected flight—like a black scarf
let loose in a stiff, chill wind.
Hearts calming,
we follow the bat. We formulate a plan:
a plastic bowl and a small piece
of cardboard to use as a makeshift lid
so I can trap the tiny body
when, exhausted, it finally alights
against the ceiling
in the recess of another lightless
light. A stepladder,
a careful climb. The bat no longer nimble
but trembling

and looking not so terrible: dustbin fur;
   a faint twitch
among his folded wings' leathery creases—
   strange architecture
I bury beneath my white plastic bowl.
    I slip in
my cardboard lid, press it tight,
   carry the bones and skin
I could break so easily apart
    to the open door my mother holds
and release him. Our bat disappears
   into a sky embroidered
with the first faint stitches
   of the coming night.
My bag's already packed
   and in the car; my mother
will have to finish building
   this house herself.
In these ways, we rescue ourselves.

Rahul Mehta

QUARANTINE

"You will only see him the way he is, not the way he was."

Jeremy and I have rented a car and are driving to my parents' house. He has never been to West Virginia. All week he has been looking forward to seeing the house where I grew up, my yearbooks, the wood paneling in the living room where I chipped my tooth, the place by the river where I drank with friends. He is annoyed that I am talking about Bapuji again.

"Don't you think I know by now how you feel about your grandfather?" he asks.

"Yes, but I am warning you. When you see him, you will feel sorry for him. You will forget all the stories I've told you."

"I won't forget."

"You won't believe me."

It is late by the time we reach the house. My parents hug me at the door. They tell Jeremy how much they enjoyed meeting him in New York last year. They are awkward. They half hug him, half shake his hand. They are still not used to their son dating men.

"Make yourself at home," my mom says to Jeremy.

"Bapuji is in the living room," my dad says to me.

We remove our shoes and go inside. Bapuji is sitting in a swivel chair. The lamp next to the chair is off. In the dim light it is difficult to see him, but when he stands up and comes closer, I see how loose his face is, the deep dark eye sockets and sharp cheekbones, the thin lips oval and open, as if it is too much effort to close them or smile.

I bend down to touch his feet. The seams on his slippers are fraying, and his bare ankles are crinkled like brown paper bags. He lays his palm on my head and says, "Jay shree Krishna." Then I stand and he hugs me, my body limp.

"This is my friend Jeremy," I say. Jeremy nods and Bapuji nods back.

Last week when I called my mom to discuss plans for our trip, she said it was better not to tell Bapuji that Jeremy is my boyfriend. "There is no way he could understand," she said.

My mother warms up some food and, even though they are leftovers, Jeremy and I are happy to have home-cooked Indian food, to be eating something other than spaghetti and microwave burritos. After dinner, my mom tells us we can make our beds in the basement. She and I spoke about this on the phone, too. She said we shouldn't sleep in the guest room because there is only a double bed there, and it will be obvious we are sleeping together. Better we set up camp in the basement where there is a double bed and a single bed and a couch. She said "camp" like we are children and it is summer vacation. She hands us pillows and several sheets of all different sizes and says she is going to sleep.

I make the double bed for Jeremy and the single bed for myself. Jeremy suggests we both sleep in the double bed and that we can mess up the single bed to make it look like one of us slept there. "I don't think it's a good idea," I say. "What if we sleep late and someone comes down and sees us?"

As we are falling asleep, Jeremy asks, "Why did you touch your grandfather's feet?"

"It's a sign of respect."

"I know, but you don't respect him."

"I respect my father."

"You didn't touch *his* feet."

"Don't be funny," I say. "He is Americanized, he doesn't expect such formalities. But if I didn't do pranaam, it would hurt my grandfather's feelings, and that would hurt my father's feelings." A few seconds later I add, "It's tradition. It doesn't really mean anything."

"Yeah, tradition," Jeremy says, sighing, sleepy-voiced. A few minutes later, I hear him snoring from across the room.

Whenever I see my grandfather, I have to touch his feet twice, once when I first arrive and again as I am leaving. Each time I hold my breath and pretend I am bending over for some other reason, like to pick up something or to stretch my hamstrings. He always gives me money when I leave, just after I touch his feet. I never know what to do with it. I don't want to accept it, but I can't refuse. Once I burned the money over my kitchen sink. Another time I bought drinks for my friends. Once I actually needed it to pay rent. But it didn't feel right. It was dirty, like a bribe.

Now, as I try to sleep, I toss and readjust, trying to get comfortable. I am not used to sleeping alone. I don't know what to do with my body without Jeremy's arms around me.

————

The basement where we are sleeping is where my grandfather lived when he first came to America. I was ten then, and Asha was eight. Bapuji came a few months after his wife, Motiba, died. At first he tried to live on his own in India, but he found it too difficult. He couldn't take care of himself, didn't even know how to make tea. He shouted so much that whenever he hired new servants they would quit within a couple days. In the end, my father took it upon himself to bring Bapuji to America. As the eldest of five brothers and sisters, he thought it was his responsibility to take care of Bapuji, which, I quickly learned, really meant it was my mother's responsibility.

My mom says Bapuji wanted to live in the basement because the spare bedroom upstairs was too small and he needed more room. After I left for college he moved upstairs into my old bedroom, which was bigger than the small spare.

When Asha and I were young, we'd hardly ever go all the way into the basement. We'd only go part-way down the stairs and hang on the railing like monkeys and spy. The basement smelled of Indian spices and Ben-Gay. Bapuji made my mom hand wash all his clothes, because he said the washing machine was too hard on Indian cloth and stitching. He didn't like the smell of American detergents. He made her scrub his clothes in a plastic bucket with sandalwood soap and hang them to dry on clotheslines he strung across the room. He tacked posters of Krishna and Srinaji to the walls, and he played religious bhajans on a cheap black cassette recorder that distorted the sound, making it tinny and hollow, as though it were coming from far away. Asha and I called the basement Little India and my grandfather the Little Indian.

Those early years in a new country were difficult for him. He barely spoke English, and there were no other Indian families in our community. He couldn't drive, and our housing development wasn't within walking distance of anything. He wasn't used to the cold. Even in the house, he would have to bundle up with layers of sweaters and blankets and sit in front of a space heater. Now and then my parents would try to take him to the mall or the park, but there was nothing he wanted to buy and he claimed the Americans looked at him funny in is his dhoti and Nehru hat.

But if it was hard for him, he made it equally hard for everyone else, especially my mom. She took a couple months' leave from her job in order to help Bapuji settle in. He made demands, and as far as he was concerned she couldn't do anything right. He wanted her to make special meals according to a menu he would dictate to her each morning. He insisted my parents add a bathtub to the basement bathroom, even though they couldn't afford it and there was already a standing shower. He would call my father's brothers and sisters and tell them his daughter-in-law was abusing him, that she was lazy and disrespectful and a bad housekeeper. He would say his son shouldn't have married her. When my mother was cooking in the kitchen, he would sit at the table and say, "This isn't how Motiba made it."

Years later, my grandfather even claimed my mother was trying to kill him. Bapuji was a hypochondriac, always complaining about his health, aches in his joints, a bad back, difficulty breathing. He had started complaining about chest pains. My mom was sure it was heartburn. She said she had seen him sneaking cookies and potato chips from the kitchen cupboard late at night. She said he should stop eating junk food and then see how he feels in a couple weeks. But Bapuji called everyone, my aunts and uncles, even relatives in India, saying his daughter-in-law was refusing to let him see a doctor because she wanted him dead.

When my mother told Asha and me Bapuji claimed she was trying to kill him through neglect, I said, "If only it were so easy."

"You shouldn't joke like that," my mom said. But then I looked at Asha and Asha looked at me and we both started laughing, and my mother laughed, too.

My mother and father often argued about Bapuji, never in front of us, but we could hear them shouting in their bedroom. Sometimes they'd go for a drive, or sit in the car in the driveway. Once after a tense dinner during which my mother served Bapuji rice and dhal and Bapuji looked at the plate, dumped all the food in the garbage, and went to the basement, my mother took my father onto the back porch. Asha and I peeked through the window blinds. It was winter, and my parents hadn't put on coats. We couldn't hear what they were saying, but they were pointing and pacing and when they spoke their words materialized as clouds.

―――――

On the Saturday evening after Jeremy and I arrive, Asha visits us with her husband, Eric. They live a couple of hours away and are both in med school. Jeremy and I spend the morning in the kitchen helping my mom roll and fry poori.

After dinner we play Pictionary as couples: Dad and Mom on one team, Asha and Eric on another, and Jeremy and me on the third. Bapuji sits in a corner while we play.

Asha and Eric are winning, mostly because Asha is so good at drawing. When we were kids, she drew the most beautiful pictures, mostly horses. She loved horses. They were so good my mother framed a couple and hung them in the living room. My drawings were terrible. I threw them away without showing them to anyone.

It is Asha and Eric's turn, and the word is "snatch." Asha guesses it quickly, but when I look at Eric's drawing I am horrified. He has drawn something vulgar. I hold up the picture and show it to my parents and say, "This from a future doctor." My mother giggles and blushes as though she is twelve. I tell Eric and Asha that they should be disqualified from the round because the category is "action" and he drew a noun. Eric says he can draw whatever he wants, as long as the person guesses the right word.

"Uh-uh," I say. "Look it up. It's in the rules. Plus, your drawing was rude, so you should lose two turns." Everyone is laughing and arguing. My grandfather comes over to see what's going on.

"Do you want to play?" Jeremy asks him. I look at Jeremy like he shouldn't have done that, and he shrugs.

Bapuji shakes his head no.

"Then you should go sit down," my mother says. "Otherwise, it's too crowded around the table."

Bapuji goes back to his chair. Two rounds later, we are all racing to see which team guesses "diminish" first. It's in the "difficult" category. My mom is frustrated because it *is* difficult, and it is her turn to draw for her team and my father is guessing all wrong. "Look!" she says, pointing emphatically at her paper. "Just look what I've drawn. Look what's here. Can't you see?" Bapuji comes over again, and he is leaning over my mother's shoulder looking at her drawings. He starts to guess "little" and "smaller" and my mother says, "Please go sit down." She continues drawing and he continues guessing "tiny" and "shrink," hovering over her, leaning closer and closer until his chest is touching her back. My mother slams her pencil down on the table. "Bapuji," she shouts. "Please, just quit it!"

We all stop. Bapuji looks around at us. Then he walks over to the swivel chair and sits down. After a couple minutes, he collects his shawl and goes upstairs without saying goodnight.

No one wants to play Pictionary anymore. Asha suggests we watch one of the movies my father rented. It is a big-budget comedy, one that I would never rent, about a man and a woman who don't like each other at first, but end up falling in love. The movie is formulaic, the dialogue horrible, but the actress has such a stellar smile and the actor is so goofy and good-looking, we are all charmed. We laugh loudly at the bad jokes. We guess the ending, but the predictability is comforting, and we are all smiling as we tidy the living room and prepare for bed.

The next morning Asha and Eric leave. My father challenges Jeremy to a tennis match. He is eager to show off the fancy country club with the indoor courts that he joined last year. He's always wanted to join, ever since he came to this town.

My mom and I go to a café by the river for bagels and coffee.

"I'm sorry I made a scene in front of Jeremy," she says.

"It's no big deal," I say. "It seems like things are getting better, though. For you, anyway. I've noticed Bapuji mostly spends time in his room now. Not like when Asha and I were kids and he followed you around the house, barking orders."

My mother takes a sip from her coffee. "I don't like who I am when he's around. I don't like how I behave. I know I am mean sometimes."

"You're not mean."

"Do you know what it is like to have someone living in your own house who hates you?"

"He doesn't hate you," I say.

"It would be easier if your dad would take my side. When we're alone he says yes he understands, yes Bapuji is difficult, yes he disrespects me, but he doesn't say it to Bapuji. He doesn't stand up to him."

"How can he?" I say. "Bapuji is his father."

"I am his wife."

I finish my bagel and coffee and my mother pays at the cash register. When we get in the car in the parking lot she says, "Forget it. I'm sorry for bringing it up. I want to have fun with you and Jeremy before you leave." She puts her hand on my knee for a minute, then starts the car.

———

I was sixteen the year my mother's father died. She hadn't seen him in years. She got a call from Bombay that he was ill, and left the very next day. By the time she arrived, he was dead.

When she returned, she was different, quiet. She didn't go back to her job right away. She stopped cooking. She spent most of the time in her room with the drapes closed.

My father tried to keep house. I helped, too. We took turns cooking dinner: burned rice, over-cooked vegetables with too much chili pepper and salt. After ten days Bapuji said to my father, "How long is this going to last?"

"I don't know," my father said. He was rummaging in the fridge.

"It is her duty to take care of us. You must tell her."

"Her father died."

"My Motiba died. You didn't see me behaving like this. She is selfish. She has always been selfish. Why must we suffer because of her?"

My father picked up the phone and ordered pizza.

I went upstairs to my parents' bedroom. The door was slightly ajar, and I wondered if my mother had heard them talking. I knocked twice and she didn't answer. I opened the door fully. It took several seconds for my eyes to adjust to the darkness. My mother was lying in bed on one side, the covers pulled over her head.

"Are you OK, Mom?" I asked, still standing in the doorway. She didn't answer. "I'm worried. Please, Mom. Do you want to go out? I can take you for a drive. Maybe some fresh air. We can get buckwheat pancakes at IHOP."

My mother was silent. I walked toward the bed, and as I approached I could hear her crying beneath the covers. I stopped, not sure what to do. I wanted to put my hand on her shoulder, sit on the edge of the bed stroking her the way she would stroke me when I was a kid and I was sick or upset. But I didn't. Instead, I turned around and left, pausing for a moment in the doorway. "I love you, Mom. Please get better."

A couple days later, my mother returned to work. She started cooking again, but she still didn't talk much, and she didn't smile. I saw her standing at the stove one evening, stirring the dhal. My grandfather was sitting at the kitchen table, watching her.

———

I want to take Jeremy on a road trip. There is a town seventy miles up the Ohio River, famous for three things: ancient Indian burial mounds, after which the town is named; a state penitentiary; and a large Hare Krishna commune.

When I was young, my family visited the commune often. It is beautiful, set atop a hill with views of the river valley. There is a temple and a Palace of Gold. My family went a couple of times a year to worship. In those days, there were no Hindu temples nearby, and my father figured the Hare Krishnas were the next best thing. But my mom was wary. She thought they were weird.

"This isn't our religion," my mother said.

"Krishna is our god," my father said.

"These people aren't our people," my mother said.

When we had visitors from India, my father always took them to the Palace of Gold, which the Hare Krishnas called "the Taj Mahal of the West."

One summer, he tried to send Asha and me to summer camp at the commune. He showed us a brochure. He said he wanted us to learn something of our culture, to understand where we came from. But looking at the children in the brochure, their white faces blank as they sat in the temple while a white man in a saffron robe read from a book, I couldn't understand what my dad meant. Asha, on the other hand, was lured by the pictures of kids riding horses. In the end, my mom refused to let us go. Even Asha, who had seemed so excited, was relieved. She was nervous the Hare Krishnas would shave her head.

Now, as Jeremy and I plan our trip, my father warns us the commune isn't what it used to be. He says there was a murder a couple of years ago, and the head of the commune was arrested for tax fraud and embezzlement. Still, I insist on showing Jeremy.

It is my father's idea to invite Bapuji.

"He'll get in the way," I say. "We'll have to stop every five seconds so he can pee."

"C'mon," my dad says. "He hasn't been to temple in years. Besides, he can use an outing."

I tell my dad I'll think about it. Later, Jeremy says to me, "If we stay late it will give your mother a break from your grandfather. Think of it as a favor to her."

————

The three of us drive up the valley on the two-lane road. We drive through one-light towns with old church steeples and county general stores, and picturesque hills broken only by the spitting smokestacks of the chemical plants that have proliferated along the river.

When we reach the town, it is even more depressed than I remember. The penitentiary was shut down a couple of years earlier when the state ruled that the prisoners' cells were too small, that keeping inmates in such cramped quarters was cruel and unusual punishment. Many people lost their jobs. The town is still suffering.

To get to the commune, we have to take a narrow road that snakes up a large hill. It is separated from the rest of the town. Both the Hare Krishnas and the town's residents prefer it that way.

The Hare Krishnas own the whole hill, including the road. It is in such bad condition, I have to drive extra slowly. The sign for the temple is so faded I almost miss it. Once there were cows on the green hills and white men with shaved heads wearing necklaces made of tulsi beads, and women in saris with hiking boots and heavy coats in the winter. Now the hills are empty. Many of the houses are boarded up. The cows are gone.

Our tour guide at the Palace of Gold speaks with a Russian accent and explains how, in Moscow, under the Communists, he had to practice his religion in hiding, at secret prayer meetings. He is lucky to be in America, he says.

The palace isn't heated, and Bapuji shivers beneath his layers—two flannel shirts that don't match, two crew neck sweaters, a heavy jacket that once belonged to my dad. He pulls the coat collar closer to his neck.

Outside, much of the gold leaf has flaked off the structure, and inside there are cracks in the ceiling. The marble and wood need polishing. One stained-glass window is broken. The tour guide tells us we should come back in summer when the rose garden is in bloom. "It's really beautiful," he says.

After the tour we eat a late lunch with the devotees. There are only a dozen of them, and we all sit silently in rows on the floor eating off stainless steel thalis. The food is modeled after Indian food, but it is nothing like my mother's. It is bland and tasteless—beige and brown and gray.

When we go to the temple, the alcoves with the statues of gods are all covered with velvet curtains. A devotee tells us they won't open them until the aarti at five o'clock. He says we should stay. Jeremy and I decide to take a walk around the commune, and Bapuji says he'll wait in the temple. He is talking to the devotees when we leave him.

Jeremy and I find a pond flanked by fifty-foot-high statues of Radha and Krishna dancing. Their hands are joined in the sky, forming an archway. Small cottages, modern-looking with large windows, surround the pond. I tell Jeremy that one year my father wanted to rent one so we could visit on weekends, but my mom refused. I tell him there used to be peacocks. We walk around searching for them. We find deer and swans and rabbits, but no peacocks. Not even a feather.

When we return to the temple, the aarti has already begun. The curtains have been lifted, revealing a gold statue of Krishna in the center and Hunuman and Ganesh on either side. They are layered with garlands and surrounded by candles. My grandfather is standing in the front of the room before the statue of Krishna. To our surprise, he is leading the aarti, chanting "Hare Krishna, Hare Ram." He is holding a large silver platter with coconuts and flowers and a flame and burning incense, and he moves the offering in clockwise circles. He seems too weak to carry such a heavy platter. I wonder how he is managing. Everyone is watching him, following him, echoing his chanting. Jeremy and I sit in the back silently.

Afterwards, several devotees talk to my grandfather. They want to know about India. Are the temples beautiful? Has he been to Varanasi or to Mathura, birthplace of Krishna? He is smiling and gesturing and he has more energy than I have ever seen. It is only with great difficulty that we are able to pull him away.

When we return to the car, it is almost dark. Bapuji is quiet again, moving slowly. I ask if he wants to sit in the front seat. He shakes his head no.

After twenty minutes in the car my grandfather says, "I want to go back."

"We are going back," I say.

"No," he says. "To the Hare Krishnas."

"Did you forget something?"

"I want to stay there," he says.

"You can't," I say.

He taps Jeremy on the shoulder so that Jeremy turns around, and then he whispers, "I am not happy."

Jeremy looks at me.

"Don't talk nonsense," I say.

The road winds around a corner and I can see the moon reflected on the river up ahead. After a couple of minutes, Bapuji says again, "I want to go back."

I grip the steering wheel tightly, and my shoulders tense. "Be quiet, Bapuji."

"Your friend understands me," he says, tapping Jeremy on the shoulder again.

"He's not my friend," I say. "We are a couple, like you and Motiba were."

Bapuji is silent for a few minutes. Then he says, "Your mother is a bad person."

"Do you want to talk about bad people?" I say. My hands are shaking. "You are a bad person. You are the worst person I know. You have caused nothing but pain in my family."

"Be careful," Jeremy says. "Watch the road."

"Your life is nothing anymore. Look at you. Pathetic. Let my mother be happy."

I look in the rearview mirror and see my grandfather's face in shadows. It catches the light from a streetlamp, and through his glasses I can see his eyes and cheeks are wet and he is trembling.

Jeremy screams and grabs the wheel. I hear a horn and look forward and see flashes of light.

When we finally come to a stop, our car is in the grass beside the road facing in the wrong direction. A car honks loud and long as it passes us, and the sound disappears in the distance.

I flip on the overhead light and look over at the passenger seat. Jeremy is OK. He is staring at me, trying to catch his breath. I look in the backseat. I can see my grandfather's seat belt is fastened, but his head is down, his chin on his chest. "Bapuji?" He doesn't respond. "Bapuji?"

I get out of the car and open the back door. I put my hand on his shoulder, shaking him gently. Even with all the layers of clothes, his shoulder is thin and narrow. My grandfather looks up. His glasses have fallen on the floor and the lenses are cracked.

"Are you OK?" I ask. He nods.

I walk around the car a couple of times to see if there is any damage. We try the engine, and it starts. Jeremy drives the rest of the way home.

When we reach the house, Bapuji goes straight to his room.

"Is something wrong?" my dad asks.

"He's probably tired," I say.

My mother asks us if we are hungry, and we say we already ate. I tell them I am tired and we have to leave early the next morning so we should go to sleep. Even though it is early and it is our last day, my parents don't argue. My mother says she is tired, too.

———

A few years ago, while I was away at college, Bapuji contracted tuberculosis. At first, we couldn't figure out how he got it. We had never heard of anyone getting TB in America. Then my father remembered that Bapuji's younger brother had died from it when they were both children. The doctors said Bapuji must have been exposed to the bacteria then, and that it had been dormant in his system all these years, waiting for his body to weaken, waiting to attack.

For the first few days of his illness, Bapuji was quarantined in the house. He wasn't allowed to leave his room except to take a bath and use the toilet. The doctors said he could be dangerous to others. They advised my parents to limit their contact with him, and not to let anyone else enter the house. Later, when his health got worse, he was admitted to the hospital and isolated in a room with special ventilation. Whenever anyone visited, they had to rub antibacterial liquid on their hands and forearms and wear masks and gloves before entering the room, and they could only stay for a short time.

My mother visited the most. She brought him homemade food during lunchtime and sat with him every evening. My father came less frequently. My mother said it was too difficult for him.

One weekend, I flew home to visit my grandfather. Just before going to the hospital, I gulped coffee and ate nachos. When I put the mask on, I couldn't believe how vile my breath was. I couldn't escape it. I thought, *This is what's inside of me.*

Bapuji seemed disoriented and didn't recognize me at first. He was tired. The mask must have made me look strange.

In the car, on the way to the hospital, my mother had told me that when

Bapuji's brother was dying of tuberculosis, and he was miserable and in pain, Bapuji would let him rest his head on his chest, and sing to him until he fell asleep. This is how Bapuji got exposed to TB. I couldn't quite picture the scene. Such tenderness didn't fit with the grandfather I knew.

Bapuji said he needed to use the toilet. My mother helped him to the bathroom. When he got up, I noticed a brown stain on his bed sheet. His gown was open in the back, and I could see a bit of dried excrement on his backside and his skin peeling like birch bark. I remembered my parents telling me the TB medication made his skin dry.

When Bapuji was finished, he called for my mother, and she went into the bathroom and helped him clean up. I buzzed for the nurse to change the bed.

Watching my mother, I realized this could be her future: he could fall seriously ill, and she could spend many years taking care of him. My mother also knew this. I could tell by the matter-of-fact way she went about her tasks—cleaning him, rinsing his drinking cup, flipping his pillows—the blank look on her face while she did them, as though she were the one fading away.

———

Jeremy and I wake early the morning we are leaving my parents' house. We eat cereal while my mom makes sandwiches for our car ride. She has cooked some extra Indian food for us to take with us, and she puts the curries and subjis and rotis in a small cooler and sets them in the foyer next to our luggage. "Everything is cooked. All you have to do is heat it up when you're hungry."

We are all standing in the foyer.

"I'm glad you guys came," she says.

"Me too," my dad says. "Bapuji!" he shouts up the stairs. "The boys are leaving."

It is silent upstairs. My father shouts again, "Bapuji!" Still nothing.

"He is tired," I say. "Let him stay in his room. I'll go up."

His bedroom door is shut. I knock, but he doesn't answer. I open it. The room is dark. Bapuji is in bed. His broken eyeglasses are on the bedside table, on top of the Bhagavad Gita. He has the covers pulled over his head.

"Bapuji," I say, quietly, "I am leaving." He doesn't answer. He is either asleep or ignoring me.

I remember so many years ago, my mother in bed after her father died, the covers pulled over her head, me approaching, hearing her cry, not sure how to comfort her.

I remember also my grandfather's story about comforting his brother as he was dying.

Now, I don't approach my grandfather. I don't know whether he is crying under the covers. I stand in the doorway another minute, watching him, and then I leave.

When I go downstairs, my father asks if I did pranaam, and I say yes.

Jeremy drives most of the way home. We don't talk much. I fiddle with the radio, which usually annoys him, but today he doesn't say anything.

Back in New York, our apartment smells terrible, like we forgot to take the garbage out, or something died between the walls. Even though it is cold out, we open a couple of windows.

I walk into the living room to open another window, and I see the answering machine is blinking the number eight. I figure some of the messages are from my friends or from Jeremy's friends, but I'm sure some are from my family. Probably my mom or dad. They'll want to know we arrived safely. Maybe one is from Asha. Maybe there is one from my grandfather. I don't play the messages.

I go into the kitchen, take my mom's food from the cooler, and put it in the freezer. Jeremy is in the bedroom unpacking, and I can hear him opening and closing dresser drawers.

"Are you hungry?" I ask.

"Starving," he says.

Jeremy wants some of my mom's Indian food, so I take out a couple of Tupperware containers and pop them in the microwave.

As for me, I can't stomach it. I reach for a box of spaghetti and set a pot of water on the stove to boil.

Sheryl Monks

ROBBING PILLARS

Maiden Estep leads the Red Hat into Number Six at Bear Town, where the mine starts. They walk at first, back to the crawl, miles deep inside, under the town of Grundy. Already, they have cut a strip in both directions, and soon they'll be coming back through the middle, robbing pillars it's called, the most danger any of them have been exposed to except the old guys, the robbing line and the dynamite guys. Maiden runs the scoop, loading what they dig and blast loose onto the conveyor that carries it out through the mountain and into the yard. A couple times a night, he climbs off the scoop and crawls along the belt throwing pieces back on that have fallen over, up and down the narrow gangway.

The Red Hat's name is Charlie Hawkins, barely out of high school. Most of the men know him already. Got a little girl pregnant his junior year. Who hadn't gotten a little girl pregnant at some point?

The kid's tall, six-five or -six, there abouts, and carries it all through the legs, not the trunk of his body as some men do. From the knee to his hip, he is nearly as tall as the mine is deep in this section, so the crawl behind Maiden is cumbersome.

"Don't bow your back," Maiden warns. "4160 running overhead."

Maiden is only a White Hat himself. This is the first time he's been part of robbing pillars, and he is uneasy, even though the actual pillar robbing is not his job. Once they've humped out the vein they're working on, the robbers will come behind and start pulling the pillars, the mountain collapsing at their heels.

There is water standing in ruts along the crawl, which dampens the knees of their work pants. Occasionally they hear a drip, but once they travel deeper inside, the floor of the shaft becomes dry again. Visibility is only possible by the dim lights of their miners' caps, powered by wet-cell batteries. Overhead, the 4160 hums in Maiden's ears.

The only other thing so far that has spooked him is the blasting. When the dynamite men come in, the others hunker down where they are and protect themselves as best they can. The only real thing between them and fire-in-the-hole is prayer. Not even the unbelievers chance it.

"Faith can move mountains," the miners say. "Just pray like hell it don't have to."

A case of the nerves makes the Red Hat natter on about something or other behind Maiden. Baseball. Goose Gossage. Maiden has never watched a game of professional baseball or any other sport, on television or anywhere else, but he can't imagine pulling for a player from New York City. He likes only westerns and war movies, though he doesn't mention it to the Red Hat. Maiden lets him blather on, respectfully saying nothing, only occasionally issuing a calm reminder now and again about the current running overhead.

The Red Hat is having trouble, though, and somewhere deep in the pit of Maiden's stomach he knows something's going to happen. Something bad. It's as if a ghost has suddenly whispered in his ear. His flesh crawls all over and he throws another piece of slab up onto the conveyor. Then he turns to look at the Red Hat, low-crawling for every penny he's worth.

Maiden thinks of learning to low-crawl himself at the boy's age, nineteen or there abouts, in the army, basic training, under concertina wire, fake rounds fired overhead and only sporadically. Nothing nearly so dangerous at 4160. The Red Hat hasn't thrown the first chunk of coal up onto the belt, but Maiden does not reprimand. The boy is scared. Maiden lets him prattle on.

"Got an aunt over here in Grundy," the kid says. "Reckon we might be up under her house?"

Maiden doesn't answer. Says only again, "Watch it there now."

"Hard to say, I guess. Never know though. Could be we are. Right up under Jimmy's old room. Jimmy's gone off to Beckley. We got people there. Know anybody in Beckley? I knew this one girl from War, nearby you know, and buddy I'm telling you she was abou—."

And then, just like that, Maiden sees things happen twice before his eyes. One version takes place quick. In an instant, he sees the Red Hat stretch forward with one arm, his head buried into the earth. Then he bows up for leverage to push off again. And just as he pitches back on one knee, he arches his spine and the wet strap of his mining belt draws too near the 4160 and sparks.

"Oh, Lord!" the boy cries. "Oh, Lord! Oh, Lord! Oh, Lord! Oh, Lord!" Over and over and over while Maiden screams back down through the shaft that a man has gotten tangled up in the wire.

"Kill the switch!" Maiden screams. "Cut the goddamn juice! A man's hit! A man's hit! Good Jesus, a man's hit!"

"Oh, Lord! Oh, Lord! Oh, Lord!" the Red Hat seems to say, even though he is a puddle of flesh, melting like cheese in the damp but smelling of meat. Maiden knows he's dead, but the kid keeps talking and Maiden just lies there, waiting helplessly as he was taught to do in miners' school. He does not extend a hand. He doesn't rush to the boy's side, though the urge to is over-powering and Maiden just screams his guts out and cries for God in heaven to have mercy. He's just a kid. Nineteen. Twenty at most. A big, gangly-legged kid whose knee caps have been blown off. "Jesus! Oh, Jesus! Hurry the fuck up down there!" Maiden calls again and again before the power is thrown and the Red Hat stops chattering.

In the other version, Maiden had seen a ghost behind the Red Hat. Some kind of phantom. A wisp or something. It was blurry but distinct enough that Maiden had fixed his gaze upon it while the kid had talked on and on about his cousin Jimmy going off to Beckley.

Maiden's wife begs him every night to quit. Number Six is about to shut down soon anyway, she tells him. When Maiden dons his carbide light and packs his dinner bucket with water and leftovers, she resorts to threats, name-calling. Maiden, you son of a bitch! Maiden! Maiden! He lets her speak her peace. Goes on to work. Someone has to run the scoop.

Today they are coming back up the middle, robbing all the pillars. Number Six will chase them tunnel by tunnel as they pull timbers and wait for the roof to collapse one room at a time so they can mine the fall. That's money standing there, supporting the roof, and the company wants every square inch.

The Red Hat is not the first man Maiden has known about dying, nor the only one he's witnessed firsthand. Parmelai Cline was caught between two cars on the tipple of a breaker. Clarence Price was killed by a rush of slush when water forced it out the gangway. Julius Reed was tamping a hole when powder in the tunnel exploded. During miners' training, Maiden heard about men suffocating when they walked into pockets of gas, being struck by frozen slags of culm or being smothered by a rush of dirt working at the culm bank. Men had been run over by loaders, crushed by cave-ins when ribs gave way. They'd been burned, mangled by machinery, and electrocuted like Charlie, the young Red Hat.

When Maiden runs the scoop back through the shaft where the boy died, he wonders about the aunt's house in Grundy and whether or not they had indeed been somewhere under it when the kid had gotten caught up in the wire. It's risky, thinking about the dead so soon, if old wives' tales are to be believed. Bad luck. Better if he thinks of something else, just in case, but the Red Hat consumes his thoughts. Goose What-was-his-name? And then the boy melting like a Popsicle before him. He wonders where the boy's aunt might've been standing. Had she felt something, deep in the earth, some pull on her like a dowsing stick drawn by a vein of ground water?

The robbers begin taking out a few of the timbers as Maiden waits near the other room with the scoop and watches. Those remaining start to buckle under the weight of the roof, but the process isn't as fast as he expects. The roof does not cave in immediately in order for them to load the fallen coal onto Maiden's scoop and send it out into the yard. The robbers go one timber at a time, striking with their hammers, prying and shoving on each one until it kicks loose from the floor and the weight of the rock above their heads is redistributed to the others still standing. It's a game of Russian roulette, no telling when the roof will fall, so they work slowly, pulling one timber and then watching, listening as the other supports begin to splinter and crack in the dark around them. There is nervous energy between the robbers. They talk casually together, laugh loudly, estimating if they should maybe pull another one. Watching by the dim torch of his carbide light becomes unbearable for Maiden. He can feel the weight pressing down on them, inch by inch, timbers slowly splintering and buckling all around, but still the roof is content to hold.

"Son of a bitch," one of the robbers says. "She ain't budging. Run the scoop up here, hoss, and let's see if we can shake this bitch loose."

Maiden realizes he is being addressed, but still he hesitates. "What's that?"

"Run the scoop this a'way and see if it don't shake the ground just enough."

All four of the men, including Maiden, are working on their stomachs.

Whenever the roof does decide to fall, they won't be able to run. The robbers can't risk pulling out another timber. Maiden watches as they make their way toward him to the other room, a safe distance away from the shattering timbers. At least he has the scoop, which might be fast enough.

He wedges himself into the machine and drives forward cautiously as the robbers tell him how to proceed.

"Tap on that one right there," says Arbury Massey. "Easy ought to do it, and then hightail it back."

Goose Gossage was the ball player's name, Maiden remembers. And then he is caught by a feeling of being drawn upward. He hears a low growl of thunder and looks around to see that the cap boards have begun to twist and rip. The watery contents of his stomach seem to rise like a wave in his diaphragm. But it's not only that; the blood in his heart and veins pools at the top of his head, in both arms and legs.

The Red Hat's aunt is standing directly over him, he realizes. Maiden closes his eyelids, lifts his face, and as the tears well in his eyes, they too are drawn up in streaks that wash the coal dust from his temples and over his forehead. The woman kneels to the floor and places her hand, just there, on his cheek. And then the earth rains down.

Mary B. Moore

DOGWOOD, CARDINAL

The cardinal, an ungodly red, elongates
his throat to call. He's perched on our barn
singing dogwood into bloom, the gate
to its hinge, the neighbor's blue hound
to her doghouse door. He sings the land to itself,
even the four rust-red stains to dogwood's
four-petalled blooms. They're covenants, stigmata,
an Appalachian folktale says. Used to build
the cross, dogwood prayed and God vowed
to make it too small, gnarled, and knotted
to hang another wounded son. The blood-
spotted petals incarnate memory, awe.
Now dogwood flowers in humility and grist,
Christ's blood its gist. The red bird praises it.

Renée K. Nicholson

BOY KILLED ON THE GRAFTON ROAD

Drive-in closed for years,
blank screen shrouded by dusk
pushed against hills, tucked in the crook
of a valley.

Fifty-five miles per hour,
turns, thirty-five, and it's all turns
the way roads wind through West Virginia.
Signs only remind us how safe
we'll never be.

His middle school didn't close.
In ten years, who will remember
one boy's favorite color, what
book he was reading? Dim stars
illuminate that dingy screen, wind-
flickered ghost boys, scenes we'll never know,
just shadows across that gray-matter expanse.
Empathy is all we got, and never

enough. Fall showers, cold rain
collecting in steel barrels, pooling
in clogged gutters, damp earth,
night sweats, moon dipping into the black
pavement, the black sky, that impenetrable quiet.

Valerie Nieman

APOCRYPHA

———

Summer: Long days athwart the wooden arms
of the grammar school year—lightning
coiled in the westerly clouds,
smell of corn swashing toward tassel.
I was stretching out, then, too,
scraggly as a rose-of-sharon before
the flowers unfurl, common as those million
gray broken stones in the tar road.
In the five-acre field I lay down
with Grandmother's carry-to-meeting Bible,
lining my way through John's gospel
'til a swallowtail fluttered past and
I followed, turning, turning, leaving
no crumb of path through the standing hay
to wind me back to where the Book
must be.
Oh God
let me find it let me find it,
the sun of no help sliding down
toward the hills and shadows
boiling out of thunderheads
black-eyed susans a crazy pattern
daisies amidst the grass that grows
to burn in the bellies of the neighbors'
cows to make milk and meat
lilies chewed in the furnace
and the Bible a pearl

a silver coin a sheep a lost
child in that green waving
until my hands tingled
with answered prayer.

Matthew Neill Null

NATURAL RESOURCES

———

Bears had been seen on the road. Black bears, young males thrown out the den, nipped at by their mothers, romping over the green drop cloth of spring. They tore up the last worm fences in that county—those relics of another life, 1860, 1870—and raked the wood for termites. They scared cows and old men picking up trash along the road. Too early, the young males tried mounting sow bears, to make more of their perfect selves. When bitten hard and warned back, they looked joyous even then. So happy to be alive. After two hundred years of decline, they were managing an upswing. A new era had come.

———

When the population dropped to less than five hundred statewide, the legislature had responded. It closed entire counties to bear hunting, over the protests of farmers and sportsmen; voided the bounty system; banned hounds; tripled the number of game wardens. It established the Cranberry Wilderness—a fifty-thousand-acre swatch of mountains—and made it a sanctuary. This was public land, bought back from timber companies when it was nothing but fire-scarred leavings. No vehicles allowed. No guns.

Two decades passed. Black bears took to this stony land and, to everyone's surprise, other ruined places. They found the first-generation strip mines, exhausted of coal, the mountains carved down to nubs and benches and abandoned like botched pieces of pottery. The strip mines grew lush with exotic plants the coal companies seeded there to stop the entire county from sloughing downhill in wet plates. By the time the legislature made it law to use native plants for mine reclamation, there was little left to reclaim. Autumn olive and Japanese rose overwhelmed everything, so tough and spry the worst winds couldn't bend them. Tartar honeysuckle matted the slopes in a rich, unnavigable pelt, an otherworldly green, something out of a movie set.

In hindsight, a good place for shy things to lose themselves. When the strip mines filled up like hotels, the bears spilled into an old quarry, then hillside farms gone to briar, to sapling, to forest. They needed just *this much* rock.

They suckled cubs, owned the ridgelines, and toppled apiary boxes in singing clouds of bees. In consternation, in awe, you gazed out the window.

————

Tuscarora County wasn't used to seeing bears. Many would deny their existence for years to come. Once something had been taken away, it wasn't given back: elk and wolves, mining jobs and cheap gasoline, even a village where the Army Corps of Engineers flooded a valley. So it took a while to believe these visions:

A black cape cracking itself across a midnight road.

Or what looks like a dog, then emphatically is not a dog.

Cubs rolling down a hillside like cannonballs.

Near nightfall on Fridays and Saturdays, a caravan of trucks and cars made its snaking way to the county dump. People lined up at a distance you couldn't call safe. When the natural light turned soft and blue, bears eased off the mountain and sifted through trash. Soft human cries went up. A bear gripped a bowling pin in its mouth. Another savaged a washing machine, rocking it back and forth. Metal cringed. A wealthy store of rotten cabbage was uncovered in all its septic glory.

The show attracted a democratic swath: coal miners and lawyers, nurses and accountants, old and young. This went on for months. If you leaned out the window, a bear would delicately take a lollipop from your pinkly offered palm. Snap, snap, snap! went the cameras. You could smell its hide like sour milk.

They called it the poor man's safari. A woman drove there with her children. She wanted a picture of her youngest with a bear; she wanted the child to graze the mystery, as people lift babies from the throng and lean to the president's drifting touch. She took the boy, smeared his hand in honey, and put him out there so sweetness could be licked from his fingers. Moans and nervous laughter from the cars. She had her camera ready. Two bears came loping.

The Department of Health and Human Resources absorbed three children, the county fenced off the dump, the good times were over. And they say this was once home to the happiest bears on earth. *Not only are they giving us their toddlers, they're dipping them in honey first.*

Winter on the way, the bears sequestered themselves deep in the earth. The mountain filled. You thought about them. You had to. You nursed their absence like a missing tooth. Imagine the molasses drip of their sleeping blood, their idling hearts. They're safe from the razor wire winds that flay you, safe from the leaden days, the country loneliness, the cold stars in the sky. What if the earth shrugs and crushes them in their beds? They won't even know. Which may be the name of bliss.

Far away, the bear question was discussed under flickering fluorescent lights. Time had come for the Department of Natural Resources to draft the new management plan, as it did on the decade. Pens lifted. Legal pads recorded notes, outbursts, muttered asides.

The bear in a cave, its black eye as deep as a well, endless, plunging in blackness deeper than night. Suspecting and unsuspecting of all designs. The pupil focuses, the point of a knife.

———

Living with them is such a risk. Something must be done. The incident at the dump just goes to show. Can we call a vote? Raise your hands. Higher. The population peaked at twelve thousand. Time to thin them out. A yearly kill of 10% is sustainable. A bear stamp was designed and meted out for tax purposes; estimates of economic impact slavered over. The legislature opened Tuscarora to bear hunting—except for the Cranberry Wilderness, that lone green corner.

You started seeing trucks with bristles of CB antennas and raucous dog-boxes in the back. The first day was a circus. Sound split the quiet places of winter: Cranberry Glades, Hell-for-Certain, Shades-of-Death, Pigeon Mountain. Hounds, reports, radio crackle.

A record harvest. Near the village of Canvas, crowds gathered at the gas station, which had invested in a big tackle scale, the kind harbors use to hoist dead sharks. They had a Hall of Fame, photographs on a corkboard.

Men with arms dipped in blood, and the Chinese merchants there to buy gallbladders, three hundred dollars apiece, green greasy aphrodisiac, casting looks over their shoulders for the warden.

People dug out curling photographs of great-grandpa posing over a dead, darkish thing—a rug maybe? a tarpaulin?—and blew off the dust, taped them to refrigerators. The generations in between were considered—what? a little cowardly?—ones who had forsaken the hunt. The bloodlines of Plott hounds were traced with a care once accorded kings.

You looked forward to December. Walking the ridge, gun in hand, the cold air blooming in your lungs like a tree of ice. Out there among them. One more reason to love this place.

And the biologists were right. In a year, the population recovered.

———

The Bear Hunters Association called for changes. They proposed an open season in spring and summer. No, they wouldn't shoot the bears, just run their hounds in all that green, for practice. After treeing a bear, they'd let it go free. No harm. Play. God, the sweltering boredom of June. In the country you make your own fun.

The biologists thought the proposal was a joke—with a sinking sensation, they realized the truth. Voters were polled, and thought it a good idea. The legislature responded. The reform was approved 31-3. The DNR director resigned. The governor appointed a new one that day.

Chased three seasons through, the bears couldn't store enough fat for hibernation. They were skinny, mean animals, not the wobbling clowns of seasons past. You got used to seeing hunters out in warm months and muttering into handsets. On the mountain, hounds sang that clean bawling treble, clear as a movie soundtrack. Bears lifted their purpled muzzles from the blackberries, knowing again it was time to run.

Winter mortality on the rise. Cubs aborted in the womb. Old sows crawled back in caves and never came out. The population dropped 65%. Biologists pleaded. A response was called for.

The Cranberry Wilderness—the last sanctuary—was opened for business. It had served its purpose. A new era had come.

———

It took a few malingering years, but that was the end of black bears in Tuscarora. Teased endlessly by the dogs, they seemed to fling themselves in front of the guns. Everyone had one of those bleached skulls on the mantel. The orbits were huge. That long, daft grin. You traced it with your thumb. Bone gathered a sleek film of dust and yellowed. Finally, the skulls were stowed away in trunks and drawers among old chattering crockery.

(People cherished the odd sighting and would brag on one for months, for years. A midsized black dog, running, was called a bear. An interesting, dark rock glimpsed from a passing car was called a bear.)

But earth turns, and old ways are reexamined. The insurance companies say there are so many deer, so many wrecks. They have algorithms on their side. Kill more deer. Let all the predators live.

Ann Pancake

ME AND MY DADDY LISTEN TO BOB MARLEY

———

In the good Granma smells Mish stands—nighttime powder and church perfume—his fingers tumbling the man in his pocket. His daddy peels the foil from the tiny package he has taken from Gran's dressing table drawer. Daddy, hand tremoring, fishes in the package's dropper of water, snares the lens on a finger and daubs it at his eye as Mish watches. It's not out of curiosity for the contacts—those he has seen his whole life, whenever Daddy can get them, Mish is used to that, looking on from the low single bed at Daddy's house, bedtime, get-up time, Daddy picking plastic in and out of his eyes. Mish watches for the funniness of Daddy at the same dressing table where Granma combs her hair and puts on her makeup, for the strangeness in Gran's mirror of Daddy's raggedy-brimmed Stihl cap, his penny-colored beard. With the effort to keep his eye open, Daddy's top lip is raised, and in the mirror, Mish can see the two big front teeth browning from the middle out. Then the lens pops in, and as though having the thing in his eye grants him the gift of seeing behind, Daddy speaks.

"I told you, wait for me downstairs."

Daddy's right eye streams, and the man somersaults in Mish's pocket.

"Well." Daddy is whispering. "Be very, very quiet. We can't wake Pappy up."

Mish feels around him his coat.

Daddy presses the other contact at the other eye, his hand quivering, the lens falling onto the table top, and he quiet-cusses. They are very tear-able, very expensive. The contact goes in, and Daddy is stepping away from the mirror, blinking hard, then he turns back, sweeps the little packages into the pockets of his coat, and as he passes Mish, he hisses, "You wait right here, Mish. You hear me? I'll be right back."

Mish follows Daddy. Daddy doesn't hear the rustle-roar of his coat, just like he didn't hear it when Mish walked into Gran's room to watch. Arms held away from his body, his feet in slow motion, Daddy wobbles down the hallway like a cartoon wolf, Mish swishing behind, them passing the bathroom, the closet, to the open door of Pappy's room, where Mish stops. The smells of this room are the inside-out of the Gran room smells—unflushed toilet smells, dead thing in the ditch smells, smells of crusted laundry—and Mish does not go in, he never does.

A floorboard shrieks. Daddy's outsplayed elbow hooks Pappy's hat rack, the rack bobs, but Daddy teeters on, balancing on the toes of his boots until he can reach into the clutter on Pappy's high chest of drawers. From the door, Mish can see only the standing-up things on the dresser. He knows there is a picture of old-timey people, of Uncle David as a grown-up, another of Daddy as a little boy, looking exactly like a Mish with blond hair. Daddy is unfolding Pappy's hip-worn wallet, and Mish flicks his eyes to the caterpillar shape under the rusty knit blanket on the bed, Pappy's head on its end. The spooky pink of Pappy's shut eyelids without his glasses over them. Mish looks back to Daddy, one hand replacing the wallet, the other tucking bills into his jeans pocket, then back to Pappy. Mish sucks a quick breath. Pappy's blue eyes are open. They hold Mish's there.

Then Daddy is hurrying through the door, scooping up Mish as he does, and they are down the stairs and into the kitchen where Daddy sets Mish on his feet. "Shhhh." He grabs a block of cheese from the refrigerator, a package of lunchmeat, reaches across to the breadbox and snags one of Gran's mini doughnuts for Mish—Mish crams it in his mouth right there—and Daddy swings Mish up again, Daddy grunting, staggering back a step, the enormous coat, the cheese and lunch meat, Mish's lengthening legs, then he finds his footing and they slam out the back door.

It is late afternoon, the land winter-hard and unsnowed, the air hard also, Christmas three weeks past. Gran's car is gone, her at Walmart in Renfield a long drive away, exchanging one of Daddy's Christmas presents. Daddy is strapping Mish into his carseat in the old car of Pappy's that Daddy has been driving since he had his wreck in Pappy's newer one—Mish was at Mommy's during that—then they are tearing out of Gran's driveway, gravel splattering, and the Cavalier leaps onto the highway.

Daddy leans into the gas. They swallow Route 30, fast, faster, spewing it spent behind, and as Gran's house vanishes and the woods close in, them alone except for the cars passing in the other lane, Mish feels the man who lives in Daddy ease down. The Cavalier insides are sealed, invisible to the other cars, just *whush* and gone, and by the time they swing onto the county back road that goes to Daddy's house, Daddy has loosened enough to scrabble in the mess on the front seat floor. "Listen, Mish," he calls over his shoulder. "Tater made me this for Christmas." He thrusts a cassette into the deck and begins to sing, a high, chokey string. It is not Bob. Mish reaches into his coat pockets and pulls out the Silver Surfer in one hand, a red Power Ranger in the other.

He'd waited until lunch on the couch at Mommy's in his new coat, a Dallas Cowboys coat given him for Christmas by Gran, the coat reaching almost to his knees on one end and almost to his ears on the other, *Now I got it a couple sizes too big so you can grow into it*, a Ninja Turtle shell, Ranger armor, the Dallas Cowboys coat *is* football pads. The Dallas Cowboys are his daddy's favorite team, and the noise of its nylon, the "I'm here!" crash, the blue star on its back with a white border around it, and sometimes Mish can feel the star there behind him, lit up and hot. Him on the couch and Mommy on the phone, her face bearing down as she made the fourth call to Daddy, then fifth. She sucked a breath and blew it out. "Take off that coat, Mish. You're gonna burn up."

Carlin sat cross-legged in front of the TV, thumbing the iPod his own daddy got him for Christmas, while Kenzie, whose daddy got her nothing, perched at the kitchen bar where Mommy'd put her because she couldn't keep her hands to herself. Kenzie pitched at Mish pizza coupons folded tight and hard when Mommy couldn't see—"You look like you're a hole with your head sticking out!"—but Mish heard her voice only at a distance, didn't hear her words at all. He was watching Carlin. "Wet me wissen," Mish said it again, low, conspiratorial, his tone simultaneously pleading and leaden with respect. "Wet *me* wissen, Cawwin," because Carlin, thirteen, sometimes gave up a kindness if it cost him nothing (Kenzie, nine, a deer fly, poison ivy, never gave anything at all). But Carlin, bent in concentration, his mouth slightly open, two juicy scabs under his lip, the thumb scrolling, pretended not to hear even though the buds weren't in his ears. "Pwease, Cawwin, wet me wissen," Mish tried again. "Wet we wissen. Wet we wissen," Kenzie simpered, and Mommy yelled, "Lay off, Kenzie! Mish, Steve's pulling in." Kenzie threw a refrigerator magnet at Mish. "Just three hours late. I guess that's not bad, a busy man like he is. Mish, let's get that coat zipped up—"

Now they are looping down Bonehaul Ridge, the last hill before the last curve before Daddy's house. Daddy's singing trickles to a hush. He brakes, and as they creep up on the curve, Mish slips his men back into his pockets. The car comes to a stop, the man who lives in Daddy back on his feet, finger to his lips, and Mish watches, too. Late afternoon, just this side of dark, Mish holds his breath. But the road in front of Daddy's house is vacant. No tail-lights of waiting cars. No figure slumped on the crumbly steps. They lurch forward, turn into the dirt tracks by the side porch, and pull around back where they park right up against the chimney. The yard brown waves of high winter weeds, dogless doghouse coughing bright garbage. Mish strokes with his thumb the Power Ranger's chest.

Their breaths steam around them while Daddy quivers the key in the side door padlock. Mish encases himself deeper in the coat, higher in it, his hands in his pockets to his forearms, his shoulders hackled to his ears. The man in Daddy is full raised now, Mish can see him, behind Daddy's bones. The man is flat and black, out of heavy construction paper snipped, a shape only, and only recently has Mish learned, from a Marvel Comics coloring book, the man's name: Quickshiver. The lock unslots, and Mish trails Daddy through the dim, stale kitchen, into the window-blanketed front room, dark as a groundhog burrow, and Mish, coat whispering, feels right away with his feet for the men he left on the floor last Sunday. Daddy squats to prime the kerosene heater, a stubborn cast-off of Gran and Pappy's, and all around Mish, as ever-present and familiar as the house's sour smell, presses the house's black burring, a static not ear-heard in the way Quickshiver is not eye-seen. Mish finds a man, then two, with his toes, and then he stands still, careful not to smash. With the men safe, he can let down a little, take his hands from the coat. He can feel Bob Marley behind him on the wall, tracing warm the rim of the star on his coat. The heater finally flares, Daddy scrambles upright, and in the pink-orange glow, Mish does his quick accounting: the Blue Power Ranger, Spiderman, the Hulk, Dash Incredible, Luke Skywalker, and a swarm of tiny knights. Mish's shoulders ease.

Then he turns around, and out of the dark Bob soars. Bob a beam through the static, radiant and still, and although the heater lights only Bob's chest, chin, and mouth, Mish sees the rest clear. Bob has made his face the colors he likes, red, yellow, and green, something Mish'd like to do, something even Jesus cannot, and under the toboggan hat-thing, Mish knows, three little birds nest in Bob's blacksnake hair. Bob does not worry, you see it in his smile, smoke curling it like Santa Claus's in Gran's *Night Before Christmas* book, only Bob is real. When Mish turns away, he feels the heat again on his back, and he starts to kneel to his men, to reach, when a hand closes over his shoulder.

"C'mon, buddy. Let's eat."

Mish sits cross-legged on the kitchen table with a bowl between his legs, gulping Froot Loops as fast as he can. Daddy is watching the window, dipping into a mustard jar pickle loaf slices he's rolled into tubes, a Budweiser humming in his other hand. Quickshiver crouches. Between bites, Daddy rubs his eyes, pulls now and again on their lids. Mish blinks. Daddy's opened the oven door for heat. They eat in the red U of its element and in a disk of light from a small, goose-necked desk lamp. The room is off the road, but from the side window where Daddy sits, you can see a car's headlights glint off the aluminum "No Hunting" sign tacked to the fence before the car pulls up by the house. Mish hits the bottom of his bowl and slides off the table.

"Keep that overhead off," Daddy says. He watches the window.

Mish stands in the dark doorway. From the floor, the men pull, invisible. To see them at all, he'll have to sit very near the hot cylinder of heater, but right after he thinks that, it doesn't matter anymore. Kneeling, he draws the Silver Surfer and the Power Ranger from his pockets and sets them among the others in their scattered circle. The air over the men is static-less, Mish can feel, and glassy. The black burring pushed up and away. For the first time since this morning, he wriggles out of his coat and lets it drop behind him. Bob has his back. He picks up The Hulk.

The calm almost instantly comes, like a vein from The Hulk into Mish's palm, then up his arm to his heart. The other men begin pulling, showing Mish, and Mish knows what to do. He divides them into the sides they ask for, setting them up for their fight, and as he does, the glassy dome settles, Mish barely notices it with his mind, but the rest of him knows. The dome cupping over, embracing, and inside, only Mish and the men. And soon, Mish hears the murmur, the quiet telling, it comes from his mouth and at the same time from outside of him—

"Mish! C'mere!"

Mish stops.

"Mish!" An amplified hiss. "C'mere!"

Mish leans back. He looks at his men. Then, pulling on his coat, he climbs to his feet and rustles to the kitchen.

Daddy's face is squashed against the window glass. "Look out here." Daddy reaches behind him and snaps off the lamp. Mish rests his chin on the sill and circles his face with his hands like Daddy is doing.

"Look hard. Let your eyes adjust."

Mish stretches big his eyes.

"Do you see something? There by the sycamore?"

Mish strains.

"Somebody moving?"

"I jush see a buncha weedj."

"You're sure?"

Mish looks a little longer, for the sake of Quickshiver. "Nuh-uh. Nuttin dere, Daddy."

Daddy angles his hands around his face, desperate to confirm it. When Mish turns back to his men, Daddy gives up and follows to his own front room spot, the straight chair with the stained pillow drawn up to a crack between blanket-drape and window-frame. He lights his nerve medicine. Mish strips off his coat and studies his men. Half of them sleep in the roofless Lincoln Log house, the other half in the Hot Wheels garage. It is Spiderman wants to be picked up first. Mish does.

Again, the immediate grounding, the vein from man to heart. Whoever Mish holds in his hand, he enters, the man pulling, a speaking way under words, Mish simultaneously following the man and directing him. The men strap on their weapons, pump their muscles, toss back their heads—The Hulk, Luke, Spidey, Knight—Mish both Mish and men and more, the dome settling good now, the block of the black burr. The further he sinks, the calmer he deeps, the good real weight of the men's real world, anchor weight, ballast weight, so different from the daddy weight. Mish speaking not only the men's parts, but the story in-between, and always, every word of the murmur understood. Now the men are shouting challenges to each other, girding for the fight, Mish and the men completely endomed, Bob unworrying overhead like a tricolor moon. The first man dies, the second one, the first man resurrects, the dome holding away—

"Mish! Do you have to pee?"

Mish's mouth crackles, two knights crashing.

"Mish, I said, do you have to pee?"

Mish blows out a breath and sits back on his thighs. While one hand has been moving the men, the other has been holding his crotch. "Uh-uh," he mutters, almost to himself.

"Yeah, you do. Do you want me to come up with you?"

He's let go of his pants and picked up Spiderman, trying to follow him back.

"Mish, do you want me to come?" The voice sharpens. "I'm not cleaning up another mess, I'll tell you that."

"Nooo," Mish groans.

"Well, watch that hole. Hear me?"

Up the dark narrow steps, Mish climbs. The hole in the bathroom floor finally opened all the way through a month ago. The hole's right in front of the toilet, so to pee, you have to straddle it, which Daddy can do, or you have to sidle around and pee from the side, which Mish has to do. Many a time, in daylight, Mish has squatted over the hole and peered down to the stove. Its black coils, its scaly, unwashed pans, the streaked dishtowels borrowed from Gran. Once he dropped a man through to see what would happen, one of the faceless olive army men—he wouldn't have done it to most of the others. When it hit the stovetop, Daddy jumped and cussed. Sometimes, looking through, Mish imagines the what if? of falling himself and frying on a burner. Sometimes, in the night, the bathroom lit, the downstairs dark, like now, Mish sees the hole as not dropping into Daddy's kitchen at all. Mish sees it leading right out of the house to someplace else.

———

The day after Christmas Mish stood on the footstool in the bathroom off Gran's kitchen, his men battling in the sink. Through the dome arched over them, the shut bathroom door, Mish heard Gran and Uncle David walk into the kitchen and their chairs scrape. Then the grown-up talk, of no more import than the toilet running, as Rescue Hatchet dove off the faucet to save Dash from Darth—when, suddenly, Mish heard his real name. He stopped.

It was Uncle David, of course, who said it. Uncle David, who only came twice a year, *at most*, twice a year, *if that*. And now he was saying it again, in a string of words Mish couldn't reverse and unscramble.

"Steve is thirty-eight years old, Mom. Thirty-eight years old. And has never held a job longer than, what? Three months?"

"Well, he looks better than he has in years. And just happier than he's ever been—"

"Looks better than he has in years with his two front teeth rotted out."

Through Mish, a coldness was unrolling. Starting in his chest, uncurling even into his arms and his legs.

"You know what I mean. Good color in his face. And not all skinny like he has been."

Mish hunched back over the sink, his mouth moving. Rescue Hatchet hacked at Spiderman now.

"...don't understand why nothing's come of what happened last summer."

"Well, I'll tell you, David, the court system in this county, it's unbelievable how busy they are. At the magistrate's, I heard they're backed up for six months...."

Mish made his murmur louder.

"Did you and Dad really press those charges? Or did you just say you did?"

"He's doing better than he has in so, so long. Why, he walked in here yesterday morning with a wrapped present in his hand—"

"Mom, did you press those charges?" Uncle David asked.

Mish threw open the bathroom door and leapt into the kitchen, "Boo!" He landed with a smack on both feet. Uncle David's and Gran's faces snapped toward him like they were fixed on the same pivot. "Ba-ha-ha-ha-ha-ha!" Mish bellowed his best villain laugh. After a couple seconds, Uncle David laughed, too.

"C'mere, Matthew. C'mon. Give me a hug. I'm leaving this afternoon."

"Don't pay any attention to Uncle David," Daddy tells him every time. "He thinks he's better than us."

Mish grinned, shook his head, and ran.

———

Downstairs, the phone rings. Mish freezes. The insides of his ears stand up like a dog's. He lowers himself closer to the floor hole, head tilted. Hears only a wordless rumble spiked here and there by a snicker. He tiptoes to the top of the stairs, but he can tell nothing from there either. He waits.

"Hey, Mish," Daddy calls. "Get down here get your coat on. We gotta take a quick ride."

Mish's chest clenches. He backs up a few steps and leans into the dark wall, the plaster cold against his cheek.

"It's not a big deal. You can sleep while we're there. And Tater should be around."

Mish breathes deep and blows it loud enough for Daddy to hear, his lips flapping like a horse's.

"C'mon, Mish, it's not a big deal. I'm not gonna stay long."

"Can I sleep in da car?"

"No, it's too cold for you to sleep in the car."

"Daaa-deee."

"Listen, it'll be a nice ride. We'll listen to Bob. And afterwards, we'll stop at Burger King to get you that new toy."

"Wha new toy?"

"I can't remember, I saw it on TV at Gran's. Some kind of man. Now come on down."

"I din see it on teebee at Mommysh."

"Well, I saw it. Get your coat on."

Mish stops on each step, brings his feet together, sighs. When he shuffles into the front room, he sees that Daddy has already swapped the threadbare Stihl cap for the newer one with the Nike swoosh. He's pulling on the canvas coat he got when the Salvation Army came in for the flood victims over in Maddox last year. His usual coat, the one with the tape over the holes to hold in the stuffing, lies on the floor, worryingly close to the men. When Daddy tugs Mish to him, Mish droops, his arms limp, head sagging, and while Daddy threads him into the Dallas Cowboys sleeves, Mish wrinkles his nose against the reek of spilled kerosene in Daddy's coat. Then Daddy is duelling with the zipper, hands buzzing, the cussing a steady grit, but over his shoulder, Mish notices Bob, heaterlit on the wall. Daddy glares at his hands, stiffens and shakes them. Tries the zipper again. Mish watches Bob, tall and easy on his wall, the smoke from his smile, Mish knows—happiness. Bob can make the feeling seen. The star on Mish's back starts to heat, then to ray, and finally the anticipation of Bob in the car overrides what waits at the end. "Your zipper's broke," Daddy says. Mish stoops quick, snatches the two nearest men, and stuffs one in each pocket.

They hurtle past the "No Hunting" sign. They hairpin back up Bonehaul Ridge. With each yard of asphalt collapsing behind, Quickshiver inside Daddy lies a little more down, the safety of being between place and place, Mish knows this without knowing whose knowing it is. They chute through trees, the house static receding, then burst out into a star-gray field, closer, closer, closer drawing to Bob, and when Mish pulls out the men and sees they are Luke Skywalker and Dash Incredible, he smiles. The Cavalier cuts loose on the first of the road's few straights, and Mish can't help but bounce in his seat, this is where Daddy always asks. And then Daddy does, he calls over his shoulder, Quickshiver nothing but a black puddle at his bottom, "What do you want to listen to, Mish?"

And Mish says, "Bob!"

And Daddy says, "Me, too!"

And Daddy steers with his thigh while he respools the cassette on his pinky, the men warming up in acrobatic leaps, until, finally, Daddy jabs the tape in the deck. And instantly, they are swallowed—Mish, men, Daddy—in the belly of Bob.

Rhythm of reggae, happy heartbeat and a half, Mish reeling it into the cave of his ribs, his pulse recalibrated, the soothe, the joy. The throb patterning, echoing, the loops of the curves, the hills' nods and lifts, Mish swaying, the men flying, the car, Mish knows, if seen from outside, red green and yellow glow, colors of Bob. The Cavalier dances the bends, the banks, and Daddy stringy-sings, *This is my message to you - ou - ou*. And Mish's happiness rides on a pillar of memory, sedimented, three years old. Last week, last month, yes, but down, back, further than that, to when Mish stayed at Daddy's half the week, further back still to when Daddy lived at Mommy's house. So much in those layers dark, dangly, shivery, loud, but all that vanishes in the happiness of Bob. The Bob memory constant, soaking up through the sediment and richening each level—memory, memory, memory—whenever Mish was fussy or inconsolable or too tired to sleep, Daddy strapping him in the car, punching the cassette, and they ride in the cradle car to Rockabye Bob.

And three weeks ago, on Christmas night, Carlin stretched out on the bottom bunk with his iPod in his ears, his eyes as blank as if he lay in his coffin, Mish standing behind him, Mish straining with marvel, straining with want, all that glorybig music held in a wafer no thicker than ten Pokemon cards. "Wet me wissen," Mish outright begged, too desperate even to calculate, manipulate, "Wet me wissen," while Carlin paid him no more mind than he did the fluffs of crud under the bed. "Pweeeese, Caw-win, wet me wissen," Mish peering now directly into his face, poking him gently on the shoulder. Until Carlin, his eyes still dead, reached out, planted a hand on Mish's chest, and pushed. Once.

Mish staggered backwards, the tears geysering behind his face. He grabbed the nearest object, a Transformers sticker book, and swung at Carlin. As he did, he yelled, "Me and *my* daddy wissen to Bob Maw-wee." And the tears weren't anymore.

Daddy turns the volume halfway down. "Now, Mish."

"Yeah?"

"Don't say anything to anybody about us taking this ride, okay?"

"Okay."

"It'll just be between you and me."

"Okay."

"Don't say anything to Mommy. Or Gran. Even if they ask."

"Yeah."

Daddy cranks the music back up, even louder than before. It is the Bob beat that propels Mish's blood through his veins. Bob is heart. The car tremors, Mish feels the speaker thrumming against his legs, his hips—beat; beat; beat, beat-beat—and he settles back in his seat, the men catching their breaths in his lap, *everything's gonna be*, music carrying rhythm carry, the car a rocker. Lullabye Bob.

The loss of motion wakes him. He flexes his fingers. One man is still there. One he has dropped. Daddy's unstrapping him—Mish tucks the man in his pocket—lifting him out, and Mish buries his face for a second in Daddy's jacket against the cold, which has shocked him full awake, immediate and blunt. The cold has blacked the night darker, crisped the stars whiter, but over Daddy's shoulder, Mish can see clouds like a dirty blanket pulling over distant sky. They are parked just off the hardtop in the mouth of a dirt road leading into a broad field, and Daddy sets him on his feet on the hood of the car. Mish can feel its heat through his tennis shoes. "See the house, Mish?"

Mish looks past the winter grass, bowed and brittle-humped in the three-quarter moon. The house is the only thing rising off the flat of the field until the mountains start again. Mish nods.

"Can you see cars around it?"

Mish nods. Quickshiver is taut on his toes, his hands splayed, head cocked. Mish pulls his coat sleeve against his side, a muted crackle. Daddy is standing on the ground right next to Mish on the hood, one arm around his waist, and Mish thinks of the apples. "Can you start this for me, buddy?" Mish, bearing down with his small front teeth, breaking the peel and gnawing around in the white to give Daddy a good opening.

Daddy takes a finger and stretches the corner of his eye, his lip lifting. "Do you see Tater's truck?"

Mish squints. "Yeah." Tater's truck is easy. A big white Ford extended cab.

"Okay, good." Daddy pulls the corner of his eye again. "Now this is important. This is important, Mish. Look at all of them."

Mish is looking.

"Do you see a blue Toyota Four-Runner?"

Mish wiggles out of the arm around his waist and lifts onto his toes. A heaviness has come into him. One that makes him bigger and tireder. He knew his cars before he knew his colors, that's what Daddy always says, and Mish squints again, drawing on the stingy moon, to untangle the snarl of vehicles around the house. He can't tell blue in the dark, but the shape of a Four-Runner he can.

"Nuh-uh," he says.

"You're sure?"

Mish nods sharp, twice. "Only Toyoda's a Tacoma."

Daddy slaps the star on his back. "Okay. Good. Good job, Mish."

They roll through the field, the house swelling in the windshield. Bob is gone. Daddy drives to the right to straddle the road ruts, the wash of grass against metal, the car cold now because Daddy left the door open while they were looking for the Four Runner. As the house grows larger, clearer, the heaviness drains out of Mish, leaving something worse. When it's summer, Daddy lets him sleep in the carseat, he leaves the door open for air, and sometimes Mish doesn't even wake up. But in the winter, he has to go inside. The car pitches into a deep hole and Mish is thrown forward, and he thinks to reach behind him, to the star, but the carseat straps bind him. Then Daddy's carrying him, crunching through frozen mud to planks across cinderblocks that climb to the front door, and when the planks wobble, Daddy stumbles to the side, Mish scissors his legs around Daddy's waist, Daddy finds his balance, and the door opens.

The party explodes in Mish's face. Laughter without fun, heat without warmth, smoke without smile, every party he's ever entered, and the grownup bodies packed upright and reeling, an October cornfield, rattle and wind. "Hey, Steve!" somebody yells, then somebody else calls it, too, and Daddy grins and yells back. The top half of Tater swims out of the crowd, him brandishing a quart-sized Sheetz cup. "Mish! How you doing?" He strips Mish from Daddy and squashes him to his soft chest, Tater in a T-shirt odored of cigarettes and mildew, and the cup's straw pokes Mish's head and whatever is in it splashes a little on Mish. "Ricky's got it," Tater says, and Daddy says, "Where's he at?" and Tater says, "He'll be here." Past Tater, Mish sees a silver Christmas tree on a table, listing to one side, drooped with brassy, teardrop ornaments, each exactly the same.

He is set on his feet into the cornfield of legs. No, not corn. Brush, thicket, thorn, briar, the legs pressing, posting, buckling, shifting, and Mish clings to Daddy's jeans pocket to avoid being swept down. "Who's this?" The lady stoops to Mish, and her face reminds Mish of the file Daddy uses to sharpen the chainsaw.

"This is my son, Mish."

"Mish?" This is what they always say.

"That's what I call him. He's named after me, my initials smashed together."

"Oh, isn't he handsome?" They always say that, too, unless they say "cute."

"Yeah, looks just like me when I was little."

"What did Santa Claus bring you, Mish?"

"He can't talk very good, I'm the only one who understands him." Daddy ruffles Mish's hair. Mish ducks. "You got some place he can sleep?"

Then Daddy is steering him by his shoulders through more legs. There's not even room enough for Daddy to pick him back up. Mish stumbles around mud-splattered workboots, plasticky high heels, tennis shoes with mismatched shoestrings, Christmas gift clogs. He watches the feet, his head lowered, to save him from belts and butts, zippers and belly fat. Hands reach down to pet him—"Ahhh, cute!"—Mish fighting the urge to bite Daddy's fingers, until they're in a skinny hall, passing a vibrating washing machine, and finally entering a back room where Daddy swings Mish onto a coat-heaped bed. He pulls Mish out of the Dallas Cowboys coat and wraps the coat around him like a blanket. Then he sheds his own coat and spreads that over Mish, too.

"Will he fall off?" the file lady asks.

"Nah, nah. He's three years old."

Daddy leans in as if to kiss Mish goodnight. Mish snakes an arm out of the coats, snatches Daddy's Nike cap, and flings it as hard as he can. One of Daddy's hands flies to his head, the other tomahawks out to intercept the cap. It misses. And there is Daddy's head, naked. The smashed wads of his balding hair like damp caterpillars crawling his scalp, the patchy bare places in between. The file lady giggles at Mish, and Daddy sweeps his cap off the floor, jams it on his head, and shoots Mish a scarlet look. Mish shoots the look right back.

"Sleep tight, cutie." The file lady's voice.

The door shuts, ugly music damps by a third. Mish slings Daddy's reeking coat off himself. He rolls out of the Dallas Cowboys one. Then, his brow hard, his teeth steeled, him holding tight to the Cowboys coat, he windmills his arms and his legs to make a clearing for himself. Furious snow-angel, the foreign coats rolling and bunching away, some of them tumbling onto the floor. Mish's breath comes hard and coarse, and he picks up Daddy's coat and heaves it over the bed edge, too. Then he seizes the Cowboys coat in both hands and clashes it together, nylon on nylon, drowning the horrible music, the coat louder, louder, the coat hollering, screaming. And then Mish stops. His breath comes more quietly. He turns on his side and hugs the coat towards him. He opens his eyes and there's the label where Granma inked his name. M-I-S-H. Matthew Steven Halliday, Junior.

It wasn't long after he began Head Start the fall before that Kenzie started the game. "Let's play school!" She'd grab Mish and push him onto the couch. "I'm the speech therapist! You're the kid!" Her hands pinning his shoulders, one knee on his thigh, Mish squirming, while Kenzie swooped in and out of his face. "Repeat!" in-swoop, "After!" out-swoop, "Me!" in. Then she would hover, inches from his nose, her breath odored of cold, boiled potatoes. "Ma!" she'd bleat. Then, her tongue tipping out and sucking back, thick. "Thew! Ma-Thew!" Mish wiggling, grunting, shoving her away. "Ma! Thew!" Twisting his head to the side, clamping tight his eyes. "Thew! Thew! Repeat!"

Mish reaches into his Dallas Cowboys pocket and touches the man there. It is Dash Incredible. Luke he dropped in the car. He holds Dash quietly in the pocket. He doesn't bring him out into the room.

Suddenly, Mish is being arranged in the carseat again. He recognizes this from deep in a hole of sleep, and after the recognition, he sinks back, but then a knowing pricks him. He blinks, half-opens his eyes, closes them, reopens. And begins clambering up to awake. As he does, he reaches for the man in his pocket. But the man is not there. Daddy is blundering his seat straps, his hands revved to their highest, bumblebees, propellers, the buckles clacking, missing. His face so close to Mish's Mish can feel the heat off it, smell the salt of sweat. Then Mish feels that it's not just the man who's not there, the pocket isn't there, either, and then Mish understands: the Dallas Cowboys coat is not there.

"Wheresh? Wheresh?"

He is swaddled in Daddy's stinky jacket again. He sees Daddy's flannel is gone too, him in only his long-john shirt, the yellowed armpits ripped, the sleeves pushed up, and Mish hears himself say, "Wheresh my Dawash Cowboysh coat?"

Daddy is slamming Mish's door and reeling around the front of the Cavalier, one hand scratching vicious the back of his neck, then he drops in the driver's seat. Mish shakes his way out of Daddy's coat and throws his head around, sweeps his arms, hunting the dark car insides for his own coat, and he asks again, panic sparking his voice, "Wheresh my Dawash Cowboysh coat?"

Daddy taps a close-parked car, then another, cusses, pulls forward, tries again. Now he's gaping over his shoulder so he can see behind him better, showing his face to Mish, but Daddy doesn't look at him. "Calm down, Mish. I had to loan it to Ricky for a few days. Then you'll get it right back."

"Wicky? Who Wicky?"

Daddy escapes the mess of cars and throws it into Drive. "Ricky needed it for a few days. Then you'll get it back." They are bouncing down the dirt road, and Mish twists in his seat, the house, little, littler, littler behind them, and then, Mish remembers. Dash is in the coat pocket.

"Go ba ge i! Go ba ge i!"

He is shrieking, his words unravelled to how he talked a year ago, two years ago, Mish hears it but cannot help it. The dirt road levels and they plunge even faster, and Mish smacks the seat beside him, searching for the fallen Luke Skywalker, but hits only Dorito crumbs. Then Mish feels the pressing in his chest. The cave begins to creak. The black to leak. Mish grabs hard, pushes back, and when he shouts next, it is a command, no whine in it. "Take me back to Mommysh!"

At the hard top, Daddy jets left without braking.

"Take me back to Mommysh!"

"Mish," Daddy says. "Are you a baby or a man?"

"Take me!"

"I can't, Mish." One front tire drifts onto the shoulder, snags on the pavement lip, the ripping sound of asphalt against rubber, and Daddy jerks it back up, the car swerving into the left lane, then sailing back right. "This is how the judge did it. I've told you a thousand times." He talks the after-party talk, each word deliberate, an egg laid. "It's not my decision. You're with me from Saturday morning to Sunday evening. We have to do what the judge says."

"I doan care wha da judge saysh!"

"Well, I do. It's the law." Now Daddy does look at Mish, his I'm-a-grown-up-and-you're-not look. He turns back to the windshield, his forefinger massaging the corner of his eye. "C'mon, Mish." Now he's lightened his tone, a phony breeze in it. "We'll go in to Burger King tomorrow and get you that man."

Mish's lips are sucked tight in his mouth. His fists are clenched, his arms, too, his stomach, all of him seizing against it, pushing back. But the cave—gradually, excruciatingly—opens. Mish's chest slow-cleaving, the stones cracking, the walls unsealing, until, like always, the first part can't help but spill out. The first part not even plain pain, but the warm wave of pity, and not even for himself, pity for the coat and for Dash, left behind. But once the pity's free, nothing can stop what it's blocked. The grief batter-rams Mish's chest and leaps torrenting out.

The G.I. Joe left at Ponderosa, the Superman shoes outgrown, Kingy run away and the monstrous stench from the ditch, Mommy breaking up with Aaron who liked to play Spiderman, Daddy gone a long time away so the doctors could help him. Daddy gone a long time away. The loss is a tidal wave and Mish strains against it, shoulder to boulder, leaning, gasping, his fingertips shredding from the rough of the rock (*Crybaby. Stop that right now (no woman, no cry. No woman, no cry)*). Until, finally, Mish feels it. The breach swings back. The cave, heavily, slowly, closing its walls. The rift shrinking from yawn, to gap, to slit to, finally, nothing at all. Mish breathes. As his heart shuts, all that black loss is anvilled, smelted. Into a tower of flame-colored mad. And the right words come.

"I'm gonna tell," Mish says. His voice is even. Only he can feel the buzz underneath.

Daddy hesitates. It's less than a second, but Mish hears it.

"You're gonna tell what?"

"Dat you sto dat money fom Pappy." On "you stole," Mish feels a spurt of fear, exhilarating. Not of Daddy, but himself.

Daddy watches the road. Mish watches Daddy. "Pappy owed me that money, Mish. For that wood I cut. I just didn't want to interrupt his nap."

"Dat you sto Gransh contacsh." The cave is sealed completely now, and Mish feels himself growing bigger, even without the coat.

Daddy is quiet. Then, "I'm not going to argue with you, Mish."

"Dat you sto my Dawash Cowboysh coat."

Daddy whips his head around, and the bare anger in his face pumps Mish even bigger. Mish almost smiles, and Daddy sputters, in the tone of the wrongly accused that works so well on Gran. "Mish, I did not steal the coat. I loaned it to Ricky. I'll get it back when I get paid at the end of the week."

"You doan eben hab a job!"

Daddy is watching the road again, each hand clamped on its side of the wheel, his shoulders squared. The model of the safe driver. Trees along the road scroll up gray then disappear. When Daddy speaks this time, his voice is flat again.

"This is between you and me, Mish. It's between men. Babies tell Mommy and Granma." Daddy glances over his shoulder. "You keep our secret . . . I'll get you an iPod." He nods. "Yeah, how about that, buddy? Like Carlin's."

Mish sits motionless in his carseat. It has begun to snow, the flakes driving against the windshield haphazard, bewildered. Then Mish feels, there in the front seat, Quickshiver inside Daddy ease down. Quickshiver drops his shoulders, unkinks his neck, loosens his knees, and lies down. And with each step Quickshiver unwinds, Mish flares a notch tigher. Breath to Mish's ember, gas to his blaze. Now both Quickshiver and Daddy think it is over, Mish bought off by a lie, and the cave again bulges, Mish squeezing with all his power back. Daddy is ejecting the Bob tape, jabbing in his new one, and right when he is lifting his finger to PLAY, Mish says, "I'm gonna tell Uncle Dabid."

Daddy's hand freezes, finger extended. For one cold moment, everything hangs in air.

Then Daddy is slamming on the brakes, Mish shot through with gratification and fear, a hah! and *uh-oh,* all at once, the car yanked onto the shoulder. With a thud-crunch Daddy throws the gear into Park and twists all the way around, his knee against the back of the front seat, in his eyes a full white circle around each iris, Mish sees them clear. Daddy squeezes the front seat back.

"Mish, listen." He speaks from between the rotted teeth, the others gritted. "You listen." He moistens his lips. "Even if you tell Uncle David, let's say you sit right down and tell him." Daddy's eyes grip Mish's. "Do you think he'd understand anything you said?"

Daddy's eyes hold Mish's. The dry screek of the windshield wipers on too fast, the snow too thin. Behind Daddy, the snow spins, scattershot, eddying, like it's not even down it's falling, not even sky it comes from. Finally Daddy turns. Inside Mish, a hundred things scutter away into dark. Daddy drives.

———

Daddy carries Mish, wound in the canvas coat, through the black kitchen and into the blacker front room, tripping over Mish's men. He totes him up the stairs. He sets Mish down in the cold bedroom, switches on the bedside lamp, and clatters over a stack of CD's. Mish lets the coat spill off him and onto the floor, then, like every Saturday night, he follows Daddy to the bathroom. Both of them wary around the floor hole, Mish pees first, as he always does, Daddy waiting, then Mish waits for Daddy. Back in the bedroom, Daddy shakes out the old Gran covers on the unmade bed, tugs off Mish's shoes, and scoots him under. He drops his cap on the floor and strips off his jeans, his heel catching in the folds and almost bringing him down. Then he crawls under and pulls Mish to him.

"I love you, Mish," he mumbles. He kisses Mish, hard, on his forehead. He reaches over and snaps off the lamp.

Mish lies still, not touching Daddy. He tries to turn himself into a stick on the very edge of the bed. But it is cold in the bedroom, the bed a twin, the blankets thin, Daddy warm. Mish draws a little closer, still careful not to touch him.

"Shit," Daddy says.

He flops over, clicks the lamp, and swings his bare legs over the side of the bed. Rummaging in the junk on the bedside stand, he comes up with a grubby contact case. He pinches the contacts from his eyes and slides them into the case. Then he worms back under the covers and after a single blast of outbreath, begins to snore. The lamp blares on.

Mish squeezes his eyes shut. The light bleeds through. He opens them. The lamp's plastic body is shaped like a lamb. It was Daddy and Uncle David's when they were little boys. Mish watches it. Then he widens his gaze to the photos curling on their tacks on the wall. Various Mishes from baby on up. Daddy snores louder.

Mish slips out of bed. He pads into the hall, the floor numbing his feet. He stops at the top of the steps, where the bedroom lamp throws light before the staircase diminishes into dark. "Ma," he whispers. Then he concentrates, his brow hard. "Yew."

Mish sighs. He licks the roof of his mouth. "Ma," he says again, full-voiced. Then he lifts his tongue, positions it between his teeth like Kenzie does, and sucks it back. "Foo," it says.

Mish drops down one step. He tries again. "Ma. Foo." One more step, and he tries it quick, all run together, a little spit flying, "Ma-foo."

He blows out his breath, knocks his head gently against the wall, and descends another step. And this time he doesn't even try. He just opens his mouth. *Matthew.*

He stops. Not quite believing, he tries again. *Matthew.* Although his ear still doubts, his mind hears it clear. *Matthew,* he practices in his head. *Matthew. Matthew,* once for each cold stair, until he steps into the room where all his men wait.

Jayne Anne Phillips

from **LARK AND TERMITE**

Winfield, West Virginia
JULY 26, 1959

Lark

I move his chair into the yard under the tree and then Nonie carries him out. The tree is getting all full of seeds and the pods hang down. Soon enough the seeds will fly through the air and Nonie will have hay fever and want all the windows shut to keep the white puffs out. Termite will want to be outside in the chair all the time then, and he'll go on and on at me if I try to keep him indoors so I can do the ironing or clean up the dishes. Sun or rain, he wants to be out, early mornings especially. "OK, you're out," Nonie will say, and he starts his sounds, quiet and satisfied, before she even puts him down. She has on her white uniform to go to work at Charlie's and she holds Termite out from her a ways, not to get her stockings run with his long toenails or her skirt stained with his fingers because he always has jam on them after breakfast.

"There's Termite." Nonie puts him in the chair with his legs under him like he always sits. Anybody else's legs would go to sleep, all day like that. "You keep an eye on him, Lark," Nonie tells me, "and give him some lemonade when it gets warmer. You can put the radio in the kitchen window. That way he can hear it from out here too." Nonie straightens Termite. "Get him one of those cleaner-bag ribbons from inside. I got to go, Charlie will have my ass."

A car horn blares in the alley. Termite blares too then, trying to sound like the horn. "Elise is here," Nonie says. "Don't forget to wash the dishes, and wipe off his hands." She's already walking off across the grass, but Termite is outside so he doesn't mind her going. Elise waves at me from inside her Ford. She's a little shape in the shine of glare on the window, then the gravel crunches and they're moving off fast, like they're going somewhere important.

"Termite," I say to him, and he says it back to me. He always gets the notes right, without saying the words. His sounds are like a one-toned song, and the day is still and flat. It's seven in the morning and here and there a little bit of air moves, in pieces, like a tease, like things are getting full so slow no one notices. On the kitchen wall we have one of those glass vials with blue water in it, and the water rises if it's going to storm. The water is all the way to the top and it's like a test now to wait and see if the thing works, or if it's so cheap it's already broken. "Termite," I tell him, "I'll fix the radio. Don't worry." He's got to have something to listen to. He moves his fingers the way he does, with his hands up and all his fingers pointing, then curving, each in a separate motion, fast or careful. He never looks at his fingers but I always think he hears or knows something through them, like he does it for some reason. Charlie says he's just spastic, that's a spastic motion; Nonie says he's fidgety, with whatever he has that he can't put to anything. His fingers never stop moving unless we give him something to hold, then he holds on so tight we have to pry whatever it is away from him. Nonie says that's just cussedness. I think when he holds something his fingers rest. He doesn't always want to keep hearing things.

My nightgown is so thin I shouldn't be standing out here, though it's not like it matters. Houses on both sides of the alley have seen about everything of one another from their second-floor windows. No one drives back here but the people who live here, who park their cars in the gravel driveways that run off the alley. We don't have a car, but the others do, and the Tuccis have three—two that run and one that doesn't. It's early summer and the alley has a berm of plush grass straight up the center. All us kids—Joey and Solly and Zeke and me—walked the grass barefoot in summer, back and forth to one another's houses. I pulled Termite in the wagon and the wheels fit perfectly in the narrow tire tracks of the alley. Nick Tucci still calls his boys thugs, proud they're quick and tough. He credits Nonie with being the only mother his kids really remember, back when we were small.

Today is Sunday. Nick Tucci will run his push mower along the berm of the alley, to keep the weeds down. He does it after dusk, when he gets home from weekend overtime at the factory and he's had supper and beer, and the grass smells like one sharp green thread sliced open. I bring Termite out. He loves the sound of that mower and he listens for it, once all the way down, once back. He makes a low murmur like *r*'s strung together, and he has to listen hard over the sounds of other things, electric fans in windows, radio sounds, and he sits still and I give him my sandals to hold. He looks to the side like he does, his hands fit into my shoes. His eyes stay still, and he hears. If I stand behind his chair I can feel the blade of the mower too; I feel it roll and turn way down low in me, making a whirl and a cutting.

Sundays seem as long as a year. Sundays I don't walk up Kanawha Hill to Main Street to Barker Secretarial. I'm nearly through second semester, Typing and Basic Skills, but I'm First of Class and Miss Barker lets me sit in on Steno with the second-year girls. Miss Barker is not young. She's a never-married lady who lives in her dead father's house and took over the school for him when he died of a heart attack about ten years ago. The school is up above the Five & Ten, on the second floor of the long building with the long red sign that says in gold letters MURPHY'S FIVE AND TEN CENT STORE. It's a really old sign, Nonie says, it was there when she and my mother were growing up, but the store was both floors then. Now Barker Secretarial has filled the big upstairs room with lines of Formica-topped desks, each with a pullout shelf where we keep our typing books (*Look to the right, not to the keyboard, look to the right—*). We have to be on time because the drills are timed and we turn on our machines all at once; there's a ratchety click and a rumble, like the whole room surges, then it hums. The typewriters hum one note: it's a note Termite could do, but what would he do with the sound of us typing. We all work at one speed for practice drills. We're like a chorus and the clacking of the keys sounds measured, all together. Then at personal best we go for speed and all the rates are different. The machines explode with noise, running over themselves. Up near the big windows, for half the room, there's a lowered fake ceiling with long fluorescent lights. The tops of the windows disappear in that ceiling and I hate it and I sit in the back. Barker Secretarial stopped with the ceiling halfway when they realized they didn't have the money for air-conditioning, and they brought in big fans that roll on wheels like the wheels on Termite's chair. Miss Barker gets those fans going and we all have to wear scarves to keep our hair from flying around. With the noise and the motion I can think I'm high up, moving fast above the town and the trees and the river and the bridges, and as long as I'm typing I won't crash.

I tell Termite, "It's not going to rain yet. He'll still mow the alley. There's not going to be stars though. It's going to be hot and white, and the white sky will go gray. Then really late we might have that big storm they talk about."

Big storm they talk about, Termite says back to me, in sounds like my words.

"That's right," I tell him. "But you'll have to watch from the window. Don't think you're going to sit out here in the rain with lightning flashing all around you."

He doesn't say anything to that. He might be thinking how great it would be, wind and rain, real hard rain, not like the summer rain we let him sit out in sometimes. He likes motion. He likes things on his skin. He's alive all over that way. Nonie says I put thoughts in his head, he might not be thinking anything. Maybe he doesn't have to think, I tell her. Just don't you be thinking a lot of things about him that aren't true, she'll say.

But no one can tell what's true about him.

Termite was pretty when he was a baby. People would coo over him when we walked him in the big carriage. His forehead was real broad and he had blond curls and those blue eyes that move more than normal, like he's watching something we don't see. He was so small for his age that Nonie called him a mite, then Termite, because even then he moved his fingers, feeling the air. I think he's in himself like a termite's in a wall.

I remember when Termite came. Nonie is his guardian and his aunt, but I'm his sister. In a way he's more mine than anyone else's. He'll be mine for longer, is what Nonie says. Nonie isn't old but she always says to me about when she'll be gone. She looks so strong, like a block or a rectangle, strong in her shoulders and her back and her wide hips, even in her legs and their blue veins that she covers up with her stockings. Your mother didn't bring him, is what Nonie told me, someone brought him for her. Not his father. Nonie says Termite's father was only married to my mother for a year. He was a baby, Nonie says, twenty-one when my mother was nearly thirty, and those bastards left him over there in Korea. No one even got his body back and they had to have the service around a flag that was folded up. Nonie says it was wrong and it will never be right. But I don't know how Termite got here because Nonie sent me away that week to church camp. I was nine and had my birthday at camp, and when I came home Termite was here. He was nearly a year old but he couldn't sit up by himself, and Nonie had him a baby bed and clothes and a high chair with cushions and straps, and she had papers that were signed. She never got a birth certificate though, so we count the day he came his birthday, but I make him a birthday whenever it suits me.

"Today could be a birthday," I tell him. "One with a blue cake, yellow inside, and a lemon taste. You like that kind, with whipped cream in the center, to celebrate the storm coming, and Nick Tucci will get some with his ice tea tonight, and I'll help you put the candles in. You come inside with me while I mix it and you can hold the radio. You can turn the dials around, OK?"

Dials around OK. I can almost answer for him. But I don't. And he doesn't, because he doesn't want to come inside. I can feel him holding still; he wants to sit here. He puts his hand up to his face, to his forehead, as though he's holding one of the strips of blue plastic Nonie calls ribbons: that's what he wants. "There's no wind, Termite, no air at all," I tell him. He blows with his lips, short sighs.

So I move his chair back from the alley a bit and I go inside and get the ribbon, a strip of a blue plastic dry-cleaner bag about four inches wide and two feet long. It's too small to get tangled and anyway we watch him; I take it out to him and wrap it around his hand twice and he holds it with his fingers curled, up to his forehead. "I'll get dressed and clean up the kitchen," I tell him, "but when I make the cake you're going to have to come inside, OK?"

He casts his eyes sideways at me. That means he agrees, but he's thinking about the blue, that strip of space he can move.

"You ring the bell if you want anything," I say.

The bell on his chair was my idea; it's really a bell for a hotel desk, flat, and he can press the knob with his wrist. That bell was mounted on a piece of metal with holes, maybe so no one would steal it once upon a time, or so it wouldn't get misplaced. A lot of years ago, I sewed it to the arm of Termite's chair with thick linen cord. His bell has a high, nice sound, not a bad sound. He presses it twice if he has to go to the bathroom, or a lot if something is wrong, or sometimes just once, now and then in the quiet, like a thought.

"Termite," I tell him, "I'm going back in."

Back in, back in, back in. I hear him as I walk away, and now he'll be silent as a breather, quiet as long as I let him be.

I stand at the kitchen sink where I can see him, put the stopper in the sink, run the water as hot as it can get. The smell of the heat comes up at my face. The dishes sink into suds, and I watch Termite. His chair is turned a little to the side, and I can see him blowing on the ribbon, blowing and blowing it, not too fast. The little bit of air that stirs in the yard catches the length of that scrap and moves it. Termite likes the blue of the plastic and he likes to see through it. He blows it out from his face and he watches it move, and it barely touches him, and he blows it away. He'll do that for thirty minutes, for an hour, till you take it away from him. In my dreams he does it for days, for years, like he's keeping time, like he's a clock or a watch. I draw him that way, fast, with pencil in my notebook. Head up like he holds himself then, wrist raised, moving blue with his breath.

People who see him from their second-story windows see a boy in a chair across the alley. They know his name and who he is. They know Noreen and how she's worked at Charlie Fitzgibbon's all these years, running the restaurant with Charlie while Gladdy Fitzgibbon owns it all and parcels out the money. How Nonie is raising kids alone that aren't hers because Charlie has never told his mother to shove it, never walked off and made himself some other work and gone ahead and married a twice-divorced woman with a daughter and another kid who can't walk and doesn't talk.

Nonie is like my mother. When she introduces me, she says, "This is my daughter, Lark."

Nonie would be raising us anyway, whether Charlie ever did the right thing or not. And I don't know if she even wants him to, anymore. It's just Nonie should own part of that restaurant, hard as she works. Charlie does the cooking and runs the kitchen, and Nonie does everything else, always has, ever since she came back here when she left the second husband. She came back and there was Charlie right where she'd left him, living with his mother and going to Mass, and they fell right back into their old ways, and Gladdy fell into hers. Except the Fitzgibbons had just about nothing after the Depression. When Nonie came back, they'd barely held on to their house and the business. They would have lost the restaurant if Nonie hadn't saved it for them, doing the books and the buying and waiting tables herself.

Nonie can do about anything, but she says she doesn't do what makes money in this world.

Dish washing doesn't make money but I like it at home when I'm alone. I'm so used to being with Termite, he feels like alone to me. He's like a hum that always hums so the edge of where I am is blunt and softened. And when I push the dishes under I don't even look at them; I keep my eyes on him, out the window. He moves that clear blue ribbon with his breath, ripples it slow in front of his eyes, lips pursed. Pulls air out of air in such still heat. Sees through blue, if he sees. Or just feels it touching him, then flying out. I can hear the air at his open lips. I hear the air conditioner down at the restaurant too. Nonie is taking orders in the breakfast rush and it's already crowded and hot, tables and stools at the counter filled, and the big box over the door is grinding its firm noise. Charlie calls it the system. Later, in the afternoon when most everyone has cleared out and Nonie is getting ready to come home, the system will be catching and pulling like it can't quite breathe, saying *sip, sip sip*. All wounded. Nonie leaves while it's sighing, when they're setting up for dinner. Charlie wanted me to take the dinner shift after I graduated, but Nonie said I wasn't graduating high school to be a seventeen-year-old waitress. Barely seventeen, she pointed out. I finished school early because she sent me early. No reason not to, she said, I could read, and school had to be as interesting as sitting at Charlie's all day on a lunch stool with a pile of Golden Books. She says I don't need a job. Termite's my job, and Barker Secretarial, when she can be home nights to stay with Termite. The point is to make things better, Nonie says, have a future. I'm looking at Termite and the alley past his chair, and it's funny how that piece of see-through blue he holds to his face looks how I think a future would, waving like that, moving start to finish, leading off into space.

I'll let him go on a few more minutes. Nonie says it's strange how I'm satisfied to let him be, and it's a damn good thing, because life is long.

Life feels big to me but I'm not sure it's long. I rub cereal off the hard curved lips of the breakfast bowls, and life feels broad and flat, like a sand beach rolling into desert, miles and miles. Like pictures of Australia I've seen, with a sapphire sky pressing down and water at one edge. That edge is where things change all at once. You might see the edge coming, but you can't tell how close or far away it is, how fast it might come up. I can feel it coming. Like a sound, like a wind, like a far-off train. . . .

Termite

He sees through the blue and it goes away, he sees through the blue and it goes away again. He breathes, blowing just high. The blue moves but not too much, the blue moves and stays blue and moves. He can see into the sky where there are no shapes. The shapes that move around him are big, colliding and joining and going apart. They're the warm feel of what he hears and smells next to him, of those who hold and move and touch and lift him, saying these curls get so tangled, wipe off his hands, Lark, there's Termite. He sings back to keep them away or draw them near. That's all he'll say, he won't tell and tell. Lark bends over him and her hair falls along his neck and shoulders, her hair moves and breathes over his back and chest in a dark curtain that falls and falls. Her hair smells of flowers that have dried, like the handful of rose petals he grasped until they were soft and damp. Lark names the flowers and he says the sounds but the sounds are not the flowers. The flower is the shape so close he sees it still enough to look, blue like that, long and tall, each flared tongue with its own dark eye. Then the shape moves and the flower is too close or too far. The shape becomes its colors but he feels Lark touch it to his face and lips like a weightless velvet scrap. The flower moves and blurs and smears, he looks away to stop it disappearing. Pictures that touch him move and change, they lift and turn, stutter their edges and blur into one another. Their colors fall apart and are never still long enough for him to see, but the pictures inside him hold still. Their gray shades are sharp and clear and let him see, flat as the pages of books Lark holds near his eyes. The books are colors that run and shine but the pictures inside him stay and never blur. They might say one color or two, bright colors that shine in the gray like jewels. He sees them when the sounds of the train or the pounding of rain flies all around him. The pictures move, revealed as though a curtain slowly lifts, moving as Lark's hair might move, parting and falling away until the picture is still and complete. The pictures tell their story that repeats and repeats again and stays inside him until it ends. He sees them without trying. It's how Lark sees everything, everywhere they go. She couldn't walk and run so fast and be so sure through his moving colors, his dark that blurs. But she can't hear what he hears. He listens hard to tell. She never knows what's coming but he can't say and say.

Lark gives him the glass moon man that smells of soap. Inside the hole behind the face there's a trapped sweet smell no one can wash. Lark's fingers are long and smooth. They come and go.

Lark says feel your soft blue shirt want to wear this? She says hold the crayon it's green as grass is green. She says listen to the radio even if it's not so loud as you like. She says eat your toast while it's hot and she gives him toast, thick and warm and buttery in his hand with the blue jam on the knife like the farmer's wife. The knife comes and goes across the plates. The table holds the pouring and crashing and banging while Nonie walks hard and fast in and out of the kitchen in her white shoes. Her legs swish every step and he can feel her stepping room to room to room. No matter where she is he can hear and he puts his head on the table to hear the sound alone through the wood without all the other sounds. But she picks him up, one strong arm around his chest and the other bent for the seat under him she calls his throne. They move fast, thudding across the floor out the door onto the ground where the sound goes hollow and deep.

The porch door bangs.

Sudden morning air floats low to the ground amid the small houses like fragrant evaporating mist, a cool bath of dew and shadow and damp honeysuckle scent. He gasps and hears the sharp grass under them move its fibrous roots. Lark has brought his chair but he leans far back in Nonie's arms to look and look into the dense white sky. Heat will climb down in wisps and drifts, losing itself in pieces until it falls in gathered folds, pressing and pressing to hold the river still. Far up the heat turns and moves like a big animal trying to rouse. All the while he can hear Elise's car roll its big wheels closer until it turns roaring into the alley but Nonie puts him in his chair. She brushes his hair back with her two broad hands while the car throbs in the narrow tracks of the alley, crushing gravel to rattles and slides and bleating loud. He calls and calls and he wants to go but Nonie goes. Under the motor sound he hears the car take her weight, a sigh before the door slams. The car roars away down the stones onto the smooth pavement and goes until it's gone. There's a shape in the air where the car was. He feels the shape hold still before it begins to end. Slowly the air comes back. The grass begins small sounds. *The ground under the wheels goes hard and soft. Lark pulls him to the trains in the wagon and the rail yard is silent. Each stopped train is a deep still weight. Water trickles in the ditch where the dogs drink. They snap their jaws in the heat and Lark throws stones to make them run. They skim their shadows across weeds and broken pavement, loping the slant to the tipple where they slink and watch. Lark gives him his ribbon to hold. She knows which train will clank and rumble, jerking back before it smashes loud. He blows on the ribbon, moving the blue, and the train begins to move. Lark is quick and strong and she pulls the wagon fast, running beside the roar that clacks and smashes and races smooth. A dark rush spreads and moves and holds them, rattling inside them and tunneling deep, leaving and roaring, pushing them back and back. The boxcars go faster and begin to flash, moving their heavy shapes. The closed doors glint and the open ones are moving holes, dark in the rattling noise. Lark runs closer, harder, and the roar begins to make the shape, long and deep like the roll of the river, shaking round and wide. The picture inside him opens in gray shades, closer and sharper until each still line and curve has its own pale sound and the lines and shapes can turn and move. He lets go of the blue to tell and say and the train takes and takes it, whistling loud, bleating and disappearing into the trees. The train shrieks and the narrow bitter smoke is a scar that whispers and falls, pouring away across the railroad bridge, over the river and on.*

Lark stops running and sits on the ground. She leans against the wagon and her breath moves the wooden slats. He listens until she's quiet. The hot rails hum and each cinder thrown into the wagon is a small rock spark. The little rocks are warm.

Termite, Lark says. I'll fix the radio. Don't worry.

Here's your ribbon, Lark says.

She wraps the blue around his wrist. He moves it to his face, just above his eyes, but he doesn't look.

Mow the grass, Lark says. Big storm they talk about.

He waits. Soon she'll go.

She says, don't think you're going to sit out here in the rain with lightning flashing all around you.

He holds still, listening. Far down the alley where the gravel meets the street, he hears the orange cat paw forward on its ragged paws. Away down the alley across from Tuccis' house the ragged orange cat is stepping careful, dragging its belly along the stones under the lilacs. The cat waits then for Lark to go. The cat waits low and long where no one sees and the growl in its belly thrums deeper. The cat knows Lark will throw a stick or a handful of gravel that lands like stinging rain.

Termite, Lark says.

She puts her face close to his, her eyes against his eyes. Lark's brown eyes are stirred like the river when the river is milky with rain. She knows he can see if she's very close but he doesn't look now, he doesn't try, he doesn't want her to stay.

She says, you ring the bell if you want anything.

He wants to hear the train. Far off the train's bell sound is long and wide and dark as the shade under the railroad bridge. The bridge goes over the river and the trains pour over top. He wants to feel the roar. *Lark and the Tuccis take him through the rail yard on the way to the river, between the Polish boys and the ditch. The boys have got a snarling something in the ditch with their sticks and Lark says they're worse than the dogs, cornering one thing or another, beating and hitting until a dog sounds like a cat and a farmer's wife with a carving knife. Joey and Solly fight the boys and Zeke stays in the wagon. Lark is never scared. Joey and Solly roll in the dirt punching and grunting with the Polish boys from Lumber Street and Zeke throws stones behind.*

Zeke, hold Termite tight. Here's a faster ride.

And they're riding faster into the cool where the arched tunnel walls are furry. The leaves move up and down the rock and the ivy is shadows on the curve above. No sky it's a stone sky Termite that's why it's gray. Beside them the river is the only sound until Joey and Solly burst out yelling from the bushes.

So you've got a bloody lip no call to yell like a banshee. Look Termite, a scrape like a star on his chest. Solly, wash off in the water and cover that up with your shirt. If Noreen sees it she'll know you've been fighting. You cold, Termite? Look, we'll make a fire on the dirt where no weeds can catch. Zeke, no more telling about fires or fights and you can have marshmallows. We only need some sticks for Joey to sharpen, he loves his knife so much.

Termite, look how the fire leaps up, see how warm?

Doesn't matter if it rains the river is full of rain. We could ride the river all the way through Winfield past Parkersburg to Sophia and Shady Spring, past Pulaski and Mount Airy. We could ride the train to Charleston straight through to Charlotte and Jacksonville, clear to Florida, Termite, to the ocean. Like our seashells I show you, like that water sound inside them, all spread out for miles, bigger than a country, bigger than the air you watch through your ribbons. Nonie cuts ribbons from the blue plastic bags that cover her uniforms three at a time. Sometimes her uniforms hang in Elise's car in the sun and the blue is warm. Nonie works at Charlie's and she doesn't go to the river. She says the rail yard is near deserted now and no place for them to be. But there are no boys anymore at the rail yard, no sounds in the ditch, only empty trains passing south and sometimes a man in a boxcar throwing bottles out. Not at you Termite, tramps ride the trains and sometimes they clean house. Lark takes him close to the empty boxcars on the overgrown sidings and lets him touch the hard broad sides of the cars from the wagon. Blocks of silence shift behind the huge doors, trapped inside, too big to turn or rest. The sides of the metal cars are grainy with rust and warm with banked heat even in the morning. Termite feels their low steel drone in his fingertips, a drunken stir like hundreds of stunned insects warmed and beginning to move. But the cars don't move; they're hot and cold and day and night and he stays still to hear them. Lark says there were coal cars, long flatbed cars filled at the tipple no one uses anymore, now the mines have closed. The wooden boxcars breathe, she says. They carried animals and have skinny windows too high for cattle and pigs to see out. Loud wind poured through, cooling chickens in cages so small the hens couldn't move and so they went to sleep. That was a long time ago. Now the boxcars only wait or move empty to bigger towns. The freights pour through without stopping and Lark moves him far back to watch. Once a bottle thrown from a train smashed at his feet, brief as bells in the roar. A mean drunk, Lark said, not like most of them, old men riding and drinking. They don't bother us, Lark says. It's the trains that are fierce, rumbling their rattling music to shake the ground, crossing the river and leaving the town, leaving and leaving. At night the long low whistles sound like windy cries, moist with dew and darkness. Nonie doesn't know, she doesn't hear. She comes home and takes off her shoes and says she'd give anything. *At the special school the teacher tells him to hold still. She holds his hands tight shut and says to nod his head to the music. The farmer in the dell. She puts the straps around him in the chair with wheels, across his front and his chest.*

There. You're nice and safe and sitting as straight as you can.

The Victrola scratches out the song and the song comes to the end.

There that's once.

She starts it again. It's Lark's song not her song. He moves his wrist to sound the bell on his chair but there's no bell and this is not his chair. The bus will come a long time after lunch to take him home. He likes the bus and its big noise even if he's the only one the driver carries up the steps. The driver belts him into his seat and he can lean his head on the window. Footsteps pound heavy while the other kids climb on and the voices go high and low. The driver starts the engine and says Quiet, quiet now, while the special bus gets quiet. The long low growl of the bus can start then, and the thrum and shaking. The whole floor trembles like an animal under its skin and the sound is warm and deep, pouring into him through the vibrating frame of his seat and the silver rim of the window. The bus stops at railroad crossings and shudders, swings the big doors open on their giant hinges. There's a whoosh and flap like metal wings slapping out, then in. He sits still to feel it all at once, breathing when the bus breathes. The bus is a long hard shape like the tunnel under the railroad bridge, but the bus is from the school. The bus goes to the school and comes from the school where the woman holds on to his hands.

Did you listen close that time? Now we're going to clap.

She reaches for him and he pulls away. The lights on the ceiling are tubes that flicker when he blinks. She grabs his hands hard and pulls his face to hers. She smells hard and clean but there's another smell, small and curled and crumbling in her mouth where her words come out.

I'm here in front of you, see? Look at me. People? I need an aide. You, please assist. Stand behind him and keep his head stationary. Both hands. Gentle but firm.

The music goes again and the hands beside his eyes are fat and damp, his head held fast in the cleft of a pillowy white chest. He can't move and his breath gets fast and hard. He reaches, trying to go, his fingers going fast. The teacher holds his arms and jerks them once twice three times and smashes his hands together. The sound stings and cuts and she grasps him hard, counting. His fingers race and his heart pounds and he hears the dull alarmed thud of a heartbeat in the back of his head. A sound keens out of him, a sound to push her back, and he goes into the sound. Then there are cold cloths on his head and his stinging wrists and his chair is pushed to the window. The needle of the Victrola bumps and bumps in air.

Stronger than he looks. Let him sit quiet if he will. Let him sit.

The smashed air swirls all around him and the straps of the chair let him lean forward just enough to touch the window with his forehead. Colors and shapes surface through the pocked glass. The yellow form of the bus sits like a loaf-shaped blob on pulsing blacktop. The black tilts toward him in a sidelong square and the hot tar surface seethes in the heat, whining deep in his head like an insect he hears through a pin. He breathes Lark's name inside himself where only she can hear and the hard black shape lies down. Now he stays still and waits for the bus to move.

Termite, Lark says.

I'm going back in, Lark says.

The ragged cat drags its belly across where the grass is short and the stones are sharp, under the lilacs that have no flowers. The flower smell is gone and the white falls off the trees. Seeds, Lark says, little seeds with para-chutes to fly them, Termite, all in your hair, and she runs her fingers through his hair, saying how long and how pretty. He wants the grass long and strong, sounding whispers when it moves, but the mower cuts it. The mower cuts and cuts like a yowling knife. He hears the mower cutting and smells the grass pouring out all over the ground, the green stain so sharp and wet it spills and spills. The mower cuts everything away and Nick Tucci follows the mower, cutting and cutting while the orange cat growls low to move its soft parts across the chipped sharp stones. Deep under the lilacs where no one sees, the orange cat waits for the roar to stop.

Sara Pritchard

WHAT'S LEFT OF THE JAMIE ARCHER BAND

———

Many, many, many, many years had passed since the man with the black beard and the black ponytail and the black eyes—the man from another planet—had asked Nina to be his wife, but now that Julius was dead and buried and Nina was widowed and so alone, save for the little wire-haired fox terrier, Ponce de León, the man from another planet appeared out of nowhere—skating out of the slippery past like Chekhov's black monk—dominating Nina's imagination day in and day out in an embarrassing and some would say lascivious manner.

Nina had met the man from another planet when she was a young graduate student pursuing a master's degree in English literature and hell-bent on resurrecting from what she would eventually understand to be well-deserved obscurity a twentieth-century southern writer with whom her mentor had had a tumultuous, illicit, all-consuming love affair in the 1950s (so he claimed) and had in his possession (so he claimed) a cache of banded letters, which he promised would rival the correspondence of Eloise and Abelard; the correspondence of Mariana Alcoforado and her French cavalry officer, Captain Noel Bouton; the correspondence of Napoleon and Josephine. These letters, the distinguished professor would share, he promised, with Nina and Nina alone if Nina would agree to base her thesis on the topic and (somewhat understood) pull down her pants.

Nina was seduced not by her thesis chairman, Dr. Chops, who was still passably handsome with grizzled hair, glinting gold crowns, a cigarette cough, and an aura of general academic debauchery, but by a postscript, the famous postscript Napoleon had added to one of his love letters to Josephine.

"I'll be there in a fortnight, my love," Napoleon scribbled as an afterthought in an 1810 letter to his beloved. "Don't bathe."

Who could decline an invitation to base their master's thesis on genuine, secret, handwritten, probably steamy and lyrical, probably perfumed love letters penned by intellectuals, instead of spending dreary hours in a musty library carrel trying to prove that Jim and Huck were up to no good on that raft or that Virginia Woolf's lighthouse symbolized penis envy, or that all of Shakespeare's plays were written by Francis Bacon's first wife?

And, as for the pants part, Nina figured, *Hell, she could get around that.* She would see the love letters first, that was certain.

"*Semper ubi sub ubi*," Nina said to herself, leaving the professor's dingy Stansbury Hall office. Latin for "Always Wear Underwear." It was her high school Latin club's motto, proposed by Peter Humphries, a silly, buck-toothed egghead who often wore a boy scout uniform to school and grew up to be a cost engineer.

———

After the letter-underpants proposition, Nina, full of agitated hope and promise, bids the English professor adieu and starts walking home. She walks down North High Street, past Nick's Cantina, where a greasy whiff of cheese steak makes her salivate. She crosses Wiley and continues down High, where the neon Dairy Queen sign winks and beckons to her. Nina stops, rummages in her fringed rawhide purse for loose change. Does she have enough for a small hot fudge sundae with sprinkles? Yes!

She stands in line, waits, orders.

And just as she's at the counter window, leaning down and placing her order, directly to her left a commotion ensues. Someone—a man—has thrown something into the large trash container beside the Dairy Queen stand, and *something* inside the can has apparently grabbed the man and pulled him in! Is it possible? The man's head and torso from the waist up are entirely inside the weighted receptacle, just his legs and Chuck Taylors protrude, kicking. A great thumping and muffled screaming resounds from inside the can.

"Help! Help!" the voice inside the trashcan screams. "It's got me! It's got my arm! Let go! Let go! Help! Ohmygod, No! Noooooooooo!"

A crowd gathers. Nina drops her hot fudge sundae. Two hippies run up to the trashcan, each grab a leg, and pull. Flustered and shaking, the man who was inside the trash container thanks his saviors, wipes his brow, and brushes off his tattered cutaway swallowtail tuxedo jacket. The crowd disperses, buzzing. A clump of bystanders congregates around the trashcan, poking its maw with an umbrella.

The rescued man takes a step toward Nina, removes his watch cap, and bows—a deep, chivalrous, theatrical-encore bow, bending from the waist, his head touching his knees, the knit cap brushing the sidewalk with the graceful swoop of his right arm. He has a black beard and long black hair pulled back in a ponytail, and he looks a little bit like Jesus, a lot like Rasputin, and sort of like—Nina pushes the comparison out of her mind in spite of the fact the comparison is right on: he looks a little like Charles Manson. On the sidewalk between Nina and the man who was trapped in the trashcan lay the hot fudge sundae oozing from its pink dessert cup. Rising up to full height and clicking his heels, the young man with the sparkly black eyes winks at Nina and smiles. He points to the sidewalk sundae.

"My apologies," he says, motioning toward the counter. "May I . . . "

In a ginkgo tree nearby, a shiny crow with its eye on the soft-serve prize caws and flaps its wings and shifts its weight from one leg to the other and caws again, louder this time.

And so the great love affair between Nina and the man who was swallowed by the trash can—the man from another planet—begins.

———

When Nina first met the old woman, she was startled by her eyes: clouded over with cataracts, white as milk glass. Nina had a dish, a nesting hen made of milk glass, which her mother always said was very old and worth something. The dish belonged to Nina now, and she placed it on the Hoosier cabinet in the new garage apartment. In the hen's nest she kept the beaded hippie earrings she'd developed a weakness for.

Nina stepped on the porch and before she could knock, the screen door was pushed open by the rubber tip of a thick black cane. Had the cane been white, Nina would have put two and two together right away and realized that the old woman with her hand on the cane was blind, or nearly so. But because the cane was black, the door opening so swift, the timing so perfect—a split second before Nina's index finger pressed the doorbell—Nina did not register the cloudy eyes with anything but alarm.

Nina's grandmother had suffered from the same affliction: cataracts. Her eyes also had turned white as Orphan Annie's, but she wore glasses with smoked lenses. After some time, she'd had the operation to remove the cataracts along with the lenses the cataracts had attached themselves to like barnacles. The recovery was lengthy and involved being strapped into bed with small sandbags placed on the eyes so that the patient could not move even an angstrom in sleep, could not loll the head, roll over and jar the irises during the convalescence. The room was kept dark as a coal bin, and Nina was not allowed to enter. After the irises healed from removal of the lens, eye glasses had to mimic the missing lenses and were thick as paperweights. This was a common sight back then before soft contact lenses thin as cellophane, before laser surgery: old people with thick, heavy glasses that left raw sores like little heel marks on the bridges of their noses.

This all was coming back to Nina, coming down the years, as the old woman spoke.

"Come in," the old woman said. "I've been expecting you. You must be Nina."

The old woman's name was Mrs. Stella Majally, and Nina had come to Stella Majally's house to pay her deposit on the garage apartment she had rented over the phone. Stella wore a dark wool suit with a long skirt and a jacket with a large collar and covered buttons the size of nonpareils. The jacket was of good quality and tailoring, but it was probably at least a half-century out of style, what with its gathered shoulders, three-quarter length puff sleeves, ribbon soutache, and empire waist. Underneath the neckline of the jacket, a few luminescent pearls peeked out like the Hawkline Monster.

It did not immediately register with Nina that the ensemble was totally inappropriate for this August morning, which already promised to live up to its Dog Days' reputation, this ordinary encounter, this time—the early 1970s—this neighborhood—a student ghetto—with its rows of run-down houses built of bricks once red as strawberry jam but blackened now by time and grime, encrusted with a patina of coal dust that had turned them the color of charbroiled hamburger.

The porches of these houses, high up off the street and once flirting white gingerbread, were propped up now with unsightly, precariously leaning cinderblocks. At nearly every house a mongrel dog staked near the steps had in its restrained frenzy rendered the front yard a patch of dirt in the dry spells, mud after rain. And the lovely, decorative gingerbread, testimony to some Victorian fancy? Rotted. Peeling. Gone. And the porch steps tumbling, unsightly, tilting, descending as irrevocably as double chins.

These houses had once been the pride of immigrants—mostly eastern European—who had come to America and found work here, in West Virginia, in the glass factories along the rivers. The original houses were once neat and modest, with polished floors and woodwork, chestnut kitchen cabinets, big clawfoot bathtubs worthy of nursery rhymes and staged productions of "The Miller's Tale," and each house with an ample garden plot that extended from the back porch to the alley. Now these once-fertile gardens, planted with plum tomatoes and new potatoes and a dozen varieties of peppers, camellias, and roses—so many roses!—were thinly graveled parking lots, and most of the houses had been chopped up and converted into mean little apartments with shiny paneled walls, home to poor graduate students like Nina.

A few of the houses were still intact, inhabited by elderly people like Stella Majally, who—for one reason or another: stubbornness or economics, mostly—were holding out, refusing to sell to the absentee landlords who owned this neighborhood now, known as Sunnyside, adjacent to the university campus.

Nina had rented the garage apartment behind Stella Majally's house sight unseen, assured of its appropriateness by its classified ad description.

VERY CLEAN, ONE-BEDROOM GARAGE APARTMENT. AIRY. WALK TO CAMPUS. $40/MONTH, INCL. UTILITIES. 292-1374. FEMALES ONLY.

"Yes or No?" Stella Majally said over the phone when Nina called to inquire. "I must know immediately: Do you want it? Yes or No?"

Nina hesitated. Should she commit to renting an apartment without even seeing it?

"Yes or No?" the uninflected voice asked again.

"Yes," Nina said. "Yes, yes, I'll take it." The price was, after all, right.

"Good, then," Stella Majally said. "I like your voice, and I'm tired of answering the goddamn phone."

⸻

The garage apartment wasn't exactly what Nina had in mind. What she had imagined was a small, furnished efficiency built on top of a garage. She'd been in a few such apartments about town. A creaky wooden staircase creeping up the side of a Virginia creeper–covered block wall. One moderately good-sized room with a daybed along one wall, a gas stove, small sink, an apartment-size refrigerator squatting along the opposite wall. A few small windows. A gas heater. A tiny bathroom. A chrome dinette set, the formica-top table serving as a desk. A plank and brick bookshelf. A moribund Swedish ivy weeping from a crude macramé plant hanger. A lumpy, overstuffed chair. A floor lamp with a scorched and lopsided pleated shade.

Not so. The apartment behind Stella Majally's house is not the second story of a garage at all. It *is* the garage, and a one-car garage at that. One entire wall is a heavy wooden garage door with a horizontal row of four little windows. The door can be opened to expose the entire living quarters and presto-change-o, drawn down again with a rope-pull. And although a hint of motor oil permeates the space, the odor is not pronounced, only suggested, and the apartment is clean, with new wall-to-wall indoor-outdoor carpet the color of Easter egg grass and plasterboard walls the color of leftover deviled eggs. A cot, Hoosier cabinet painted white and decorated with decals of cornucopias laden with colorful fruit and flowers, a sturdy but swaybacked pine table with one long drawer warped shut. Two pressed-back chairs and a round tufted ottoman. A large wicker floor lamp with an enormous woven shade like an inverted basket. A little Warm Morning gas heater. The bathroom occupies the back of the garage and is equipped with the requisite clawfoot tub, a new commode, and a sink wearing a polished-cotton skirt with Bing cherries. A freshly painted white, three-legged stool.

Along the side of the garage, Nina will plant Russian Giant sunflowers, she decides, four-o'-clocks, phlox, Heavenly Blue morning glories, and hollyhocks.

It is *perfect*.

———

And so it is here that Nina lives and here that Nina and the man from another planet—Jamie Archer is his name—spend the night after their Dairy Queen encounter. The garage door is wide open, crickets are singing. A fog thick as cotton candy rolls in off the river, and lightning bugs prick it "like Braille," Jamie says, looking out, smiling, tickled with his simile. Coal barges moan, tugboat bells clang. Dogs bark their evensong call-and-response down the alley—WOOF! Woof! woof! —and now and then bursts of sparks from the enormous round chimneys of the glass factory kilns along the river splatter the night sky with spectacular, transient stars.

———

They were young then, Nina and Jamie, and their pasts were still interesting to them because the past had not yet become huge and incomprehensible, alien, and unmanageable, and they could dwell on the past and talk about it in the present as something logical, something cause-and-effect adding up to something that seemed to make sense. And so they reconstructed the past with ease (and embellishment, on Jamie's part), getting to know each other, eating jars of Gerber's baby food—strained apricots and split pea-and-ham junior dinners—what Nina lived off of those days—establishing each other's claim on being, pouring out the kettle of who they were, where they'd come from, what they'd done, where they'd been.

Jamie was younger than Nina, a boy really. Only nineteen. An orphan, he said.

"Sort of like a free radical," he said, laughing.

Jamie had finished school, he told Nina that first night.

"Oh, when did you graduate?" Nina asked, wondering if he meant high school or college.

"Oh, I didn't graduate," Jamie replied. "I just finished."

"Oh."

"I'm in a band now," Jamie continued. "Got my own band. The Jamie Archer Band. Got a kind of ring to it, don't you think?" Jamie said, laughing again, smiling his toothy smile.

"Close your eyes," Jamie said, and Nina heard him banging about in the kitchen corner, doing something with the oven.

"Keep them closed," Jamie said, unlacing his high-top Chuck Taylors and removing the laces.

"Okay, open your eyes," Jamie said, and Nina did, and there was Jamie standing in front of her, holding the oven rack, his shoe laces tied around the top corners. "Now, stand up," Jamie said, "and wrap the shoe laces around your index fingers and stick your fingers in your ears, and just lean forward a little bit and let the oven rack hang there, not touching your body."

"What?" Nina said, laughing, but she did as Jamie instructed. And then Jamie sat in front of her on the green Naugahyde ottoman and played the oven rack dangling from Nina's ears, played it with a spoon and a fork and a little whisk broom that he'd taken down from its hook where it hung by the door, nestled in its tin dustpan. It sounded sometimes like a dulcimer, sometimes like a xylophone, sometimes like a wind chime. And while he played the oven rack, Jamie sang, *I once had a girl / Or should I say . . .*

What a strange, strange boy, Nina thought, her head ringing with oven-rack harmonics.

And then Jamie turned out the light and pulled from his army-issue knapsack a Fall 1970 Sears & Roebuck catalog and a red flashlight and began reading Nina random catalog descriptions: HOME IMPROVEMENTS (aluminum down-spouts, chain-link fencing); CRAFTSMAN POWER TOOLS (band saws, chain saws, circular saws, drill presses, routers); WOMEN'S FOUNDATIONS (girdles, bras, panties); this from the Sears Figure Control Shop, page 347:

INFLATABLE SHORTS: Make exercise a part of your daily routine when you wear these vinyl shorts to do housework, simple exercises, or just walk! Inflated squares give pneumatic support at waist, hips, thighs, buttocks. Helps you shed body moisture, gives gentle massage. Pump and suggested exercises included. One size fits most. Weight 2 lbs. . . . $6.88.

Jamie closed the catalog and clicked off the flashlight. The garage door was wide open. The fog moved forward, the lightning bugs like infantry, some of them coming right up to Jamie's face and blinking their Morse code, as if trying to communicate, to get a better look. It was like the Battle of Cape St. Vincent, Jamie mused, when thirty-five ships passed silently within a stone's throw of the Spanish armada on St. Valentine's Day, 1797, obscured by a heavy curtain of dense, propitious fog. And Jamie lay down beside Nina and curled up against her like an inverted question mark.

––––––

Days pass. Weeks pass. Leaves fall. Jamie stays. How quickly things can change. It is that "twinkling of an eye" thing, Nina thinks. "In the twinkling of an eye we all are changed," she repeats to herself over and over. One day Nina is a serious graduate student, unattached, and then suddenly, over a spilt hot-fudge sundae, she is in love, cohabitating, staying up into all hours of the night reading *A Coney Island of the Mind* and *Reality Sandwiches* aloud and listening to *Tea for the Tillerman* and *The Dark Side of the Moon*, over and over and over again, dancing in her underpants, making love, not war.

Eventually, the sunflowers droop but the stalks remain standing along the garage wall like a long row of locker room showers. Jack Frost scribbles his crazy poetry on the four little garage windows, the blue flames on the gas stove dance, the Warm Morning heater glows rosy red, and Jamie and Nina stay under the covers, cuddling while the wind whistles through the joints in the wooden garage door, and snow piles up in big, elegant swoops and drifts along the alley.

They are in love, Jamie and Nina—so Nina thinks—but after awhile, things are not going well. One day Nina trudges home through the snow after teaching (she has a graduate teaching assistantship and teaches two sections of a freshman-level writing class called Composition & Rhetoric, even though, if pressed for a definition, she's not really sure she could tell you what rhetoric really is) and Jamie and two of his friends are sitting in the garage apartment, huddled around the Warm Morning heater, smoking pot.

"You don't mind if they stay, do you, Nina?" Jamie whispers to Nina. He is referring to Trapper Bill and Simon Magus, his two band members who have been living in tents along the river, in an old hobo camp known as The Cottonwoods and who have begun to appear at Nina's garage apartment more and more often. Every day, to be exact. The temperature is supposed to drop that night into the low teens, and what can Nina say? Trapper Bill has already pitched his pup tent outside the bathroom, and under the table, Simon Magus has unrolled his sleeping bag, a tattered olive-green affair lined with a flannel of mallard ducks frozen in flight.

Even though Jamie talks often of his band and their big break, Nina has no idea what kind of band it is, and they never have had any gigs, as far as Nina can tell. And there seem to be no instruments save a tambourine, which Simon Magus always carries, tapping it against his thigh, and a plastic fluto-phone that Jamie plays. Finally, Nina asks.

"Madrigal," Jamie says. "Madrigal singers."

Simon Magus's real name is Henry, Jamie tells Nina, confidentially, "but don't ever call him that." Jamie whispers. "Call him Simon. Or Merlin."

Simon is a sweet, elfish character with curly ash blond hair and burning eyes, who claims he can fly and levitate objects. Once he convinces Nina to be levitated. They light candles and strawberry incense and Nina lies on the wooden table in a flannel nightgown, and Simon dances around the table, chanting and shaking his tambourine and waving a sage smudge stick, while Jamie plays his flutophone and Trapper Bill strums the oven rack with Nina's whisk broom. Nina feels a strange twitching and tingling along her spine and a little breeze tickling its way up under her nightgown, and according to Jamie and Trapper Bill and Simon Magus, her body hovers a few inches above the table and glows. Simon declares that Nina is a reincarnation of Helen of Troy, and from then on, whenever Jamie or Simon or Trapper Bill greet her, they say, laughing, "Is this the face that launched a thousand ships?"

Nina begins to spend more and more time at the library and in her "office" in Stansbury Hall: a dank, windowless basement space she shares with five other graduate teaching assistants. She leaves the garage apartment early in the morning while Jamie and Simon and Trapper Bill are still sleeping and comes home after dark, usually to find the three musketeers (which is what she calls them) sitting on the floor, in front of the Warm Morning heater, stoned, and discussing Nostradamus or Zarathustra or reading aloud random passages from *Finnegan's Wake* or "The Wasteland" and playing "Revolution Number 9" backward on Nina's record player.

Paul is dead. Paul is dead, a spooky, scratchy voice intones.

Often, they have prepared a meal: one time, squirrel, which Trapper Bill has trapped in the university's arboretum, and another time, stone soup: a murky broth with carrots and gravel that Simon explains he has rinsed and boiled to sterilize and which contains rich trace minerals and one-hundred percent of the recommended daily allowance for calcium. You are supposed to suck on the gravel and spit it out, of course, Simon Magus instructs. Nina eats nothing those nights.

And on top of that, progress on Nina's thesis is going slowly. Actually, not at all. She's gotten the letters from Dr. Chops, and they are nothing like she had hoped. They do not illuminate one single interesting thing about the quasi-famous southern writer, and furthermore, they reveal the quasi-famous Southern writer to be rather trite and affected, a very poor speller, and ignorant of the proper use of semicolons. The letters are boring, full of smarmy endearments, their very existence an embarrassment. Nina begins to feel pity for Dr. Chops, who has saved this banal correspondence for so many years and put so much stock in it. Slowly, Dr. Chops takes on an old and weary appearance, and Nina is mortified to see him. She writes nothing that semester—not a single word on her thesis—and she cancels every appointment with Dr. Chops, leaving vague notes in his mailbox, claiming fever, impacted wisdom teeth, migraine headache, mono, food poisoning, hives, female problems, and a death in the family.

One bitter February morning—Valentine's Day, to be exact—leaving the garage apartment for school, Nina steps out into the alley, and Stella Majally calls to her from her back porch. Stella is wearing a large fur hat like a Cossack and a heavy fur coat, which upon closer inspection, appears to be ancient seal or ratty sheared beaver.

"Nina! Nina!" she calls, "I must speak with you."

Nina has only twenty minutes to get to Armstrong Hall before her class begins, but she hurries up the walk and climbs the slippery stairs to Stella Majally's back porch.

Mrs. Majally ushers her inside.

"Who are they?" Stella wants to know, and, "Where did they come from?" and, "Are they living with you?" She is stern with Nina. She reminds Nina that the lease she signed stipulates *females only* and that there is a provision that no overnight guests are allowed. Nina bursts into tears. It is all too much. She wants them gone, too, but how will she tell them?

"You just tell them to leave, dear," Stella instructs, "or I'll call the police."

All that day, Nina frets over the inevitable confrontation with Jamie and his band members. If only Simon Magus and Trapper Bill would leave, and she and Jamie could be alone again, but even then, Stella Majally would not approve. And lately, Jamie seems agitated and hyperactive. He talks endlessly, long into the night, espousing all kinds of crackpot theories and wild ideas. He believes in spontaneous generation and is going to get a government grant for $50,000 to prove it, he says, and his only investment will be a box of Rice Krispies. And he says that in a lucid dream the true location of the Fountain of Youth has been revealed to him by heavenly beings—he alone has been given the coordinates and has written them in indelible ink on his ankle; the Fountain of Youth is buried 797 feet under N41° 14.6281', W075° 53.558', a building infested with fleas and bats.

And he says that the philosopher's stone is not a stone at all but a medium: Jell-O pudding and pie filling. The garage apartment is full of boxes of Jell-O, which Jamie simmers day and night, adding coins and nuts and bolts and flatware, trying to convert base metals into gold. It is the aluminum stew pot, Jamie declares, that is inhibiting the transmutation, and so they save S&H green stamps, pasting them in their flimsy little books, saving up for a enameled graniteware canning contraption, which Jamie is certain will do the trick. Jamie's beard grows longer, his eyes brighter. He has stopped bathing and washing his hair and insists that they sleep with the garage door open, even though the night temperatures drop to well below freezing.

For a Valentine's Day present, Nina has bought Jamie a wooden recorder, which he has often admired in the window of DeVincent's music store. The recorder is a beautiful dark cherry with its own small velveteen-lined cedar box and a soft piece of blue cotton flannel and a rod for cleaning and a rolled paper displaying a fingering chart and the music to "Sailor's Hornpipe" and "Greensleeves." Nina bought it on layaway for $35, paying $5 per week, and has kept it in her office, hidden in a desk drawer, wrapped in aluminum foil and tied with a satin hair ribbon. They have arranged to meet in Sunnyside at a bar called the Bon Ton Roulette, which is decorated with hats. Nina has saved sixteen dollars, more than enough to buy them one cheeseburger and French fries platter and two mugs of beer each. Provided that Trapper Bill and Simon Magus don't show up, that is.

The Bon Ton Roulette is a dark, semi-subterranean tavern in an alley, two blocks up from the river, down a flight of stone steps, with a heavy plank door and a sticky, slate floor. Wooden booths line the knotty pine walls, and small candles flicker on the tables. The room is crowded and noisy, full of college students, young lovers. Bob Dylan is singing "Visions of Johanna," and Nina spots Jamie in a booth in the corner near the door, under a mobile of men's fedoras, a stained glass window depicting Adam and Eve behind him. Nina's heart flutters. Thank god, Simon Magus and Trapper Bill aren't with him. But how will she tell Jamie that even though she loves him, she's kind of afraid of him, and she wants her old life and her garage apartment back?

Jamie jumps up and embraces her and pulls her down beside him. "Is this the face that launched a thousand ships?" he says and kisses her forehead. Nina pulls off her velvet beret.

In his hand, Jamie conceals a tiny box, a midnight blue sueded box, and inside it, swaddled in white satin, is a ring. A mood ring. And Jamie proposes.

"Nina," he says, "Nina, I love you. Nina, will you be my wife?"

Nina is dumbfounded.

And Jamie continues his declaration of love. He will honor Nina and adore her, he says. "For rich or for poor," Jamie says. "In sickness and in health," Jamie says. "From this day forth, even forevermore." And then he adds that there is one thing he must tell her. He will mention it now, Jamie says, but it will never have to come up again, never be an issue, but he must tell her. He must be honest and up-front as they embark on their life of marital bliss.

"I'm from another planet," Jamie tells Nina, "but in this life I am just like you. I am *exactly* like you. I, too, am a spiritual being on a human journey. And my origins will make no difference to our life together. I am human incarnate just like you, do you understand, Nina?" Jamie says, his eyes blazing. "But when I die, my spirit will return to my planet. I just wanted you to know, Nina, my love."

————

That was long ago. Nearly forty years ago when Nina ran out of the Bon Ton Roulette alone and stayed in her office for five days, afraid to go home. And when she did go, accompanied by a friend, no sign of Jamie and his band remained. Even the Jell-O pudding and pie filling boxes were gone. The only evidence of Jamie having been there was a flimsy book of S&H green stamps, all but two rows of the last page full, laid atop her American Heritage dictionary, which always sat on the Hoosier cabinet, next to the milk glass nesting hen.

And the oven rack was gone.

Nina never saw Jamie Archer or Simon Magus or Trapper Bill—or her oven rack, for that matter—again.

————

Time passes, and Nina gives up on her love-letter thesis chaired by Dr. Chops and drops out of graduate school and takes a job as a technical writer for a contractor to the Department of Energy and at age thirty-three marries a dull but responsible cost engineer, who is known in the workplace and their social circle for his puns, and after every pun he says, "No pun intended, ha-ha-ha-ha." But Julius is a good man, a good husband, a good father, a good provider, and Nina raises three dull and responsible children, punsters all, and Nina has always hated puns, and over the years, she forgets all about Jamie Archer and his mood ring and his band and Simon Magus and Trapper Bill, and settles into her ordinary life, except for now and then when she reaches for her 1970 *American Heritage* dictionary and out falls a book of S&H green stamps.

The little garage apartment is gone now, along with the Russian Giant sunflowers, the four o'clocks, phlox, Heavenly Blue morning glories, and hollyhocks, as well as Stella Majally and her butter-brick house and pretty much the entire neighborhood.

Where Nina's garage apartment once stood are stacked row upon row upon row of cheap, prefabricated townhouses. "The Kennels," Nina calls them. She drives along Beechurst Avenue, shaking her head in disapproval, Ponce de León riding shotgun, his front feet on the dashboard, yipping at everything that moves or appears to be moving, which is, of course, everything. The glass factories, too, are gone, and the immigrants who worked in them. One factory—Bailey Glass—is a honeycomb of chichi shops that sell Birkenstock shoes and Crabtree & Evelyn soaps, Ruffoni and Le Creuset cookware, expensive wines, and Swarovski crystals, antique glass-blowing instruments decorating the brick walls.

One day Nina is out driving with Ponce de León, headed for her monthly oncology check-up, and she stops at a stoplight in Sunnyside, and there, right beyond her car is a poster stapled to a utility pole. WHAT'S LEFT OF THE JAMIE ARCHER BAND, the poster says, Saturday, August 4, 10:00 p.m., 123 Pleasant Street. Nina throws her Mini Cooper into park, jumps out and rips down the sign, Ponce de León barking wildly.

It's only Tuesday, and Nina looks at the torn poster day and night. She is sixty-two years old and has osteoporosis, hypothyroidism, hypertension, low blood sugar, high cholesterol, a weak heart, free-floating anxiety, plantar fasciitis, osteoarthritis, and only one breast. Julius has been dead for seven years. Nina had been to 123 Pleasant Street many years ago, when it was a hippie bar called The Underground Railroad and Bo Diddley played there and it was operated by a woman named Marsha Mudd, who disappeared in 1988. Some people say Marsha Mudd was murdered, some people say she had ties to the Chicago Seven and has gone underground; some people say she was a drug informant and now lives under an assumed identity in a foreign country but had been spotted dancing wildly at a Grateful Dead concert years later in Golden Gate Park. Some people say Marsha Mudd has gone to the planet where Jimi Hendrix, Janis Joplin, and Jim Morrison were really from and have returned to.

Tuesday, Wednesday, Thursday, Friday. Saturday, August 4, 2010. All day and every night since she came upon the poster, Nina thinks of Jamie. In bed at night, she dreams of the garage apartment and the little army cot, and she can almost feel Jamie curled against her, his breath on her neck. But it is only Ponce de León. Maybe Jamie has found it: the Fountain of Youth. Maybe he has transmuted base metal to gold. Maybe he has gone back to his planet? Will Jamie be there at 123 Pleasant Street with his flutophone or Nina's oven rack and a Sears catalog or the recorder still wrapped in its tinfoil and tied with its satin bow, which Nina left on the seat of the booth at The Bon Ton Roulette so many years ago? Will Simon Magus be there? Trapper Bill? Would she recognize any of them? Would they recognize Helen of Troy at age sixty-two? The face that sunk a thousand ships?

Six o'clock. Seven o'clock. Eight o'clock. Nine. Ten o'clock. Eleven. Nina is parking her car under a halogen light in the municipal parking garage across from 123 Pleasant Street. A bunch of terribly young, terribly dangerous-looking people with tattoos and dreadlocks and Mohawks and pierced lips and noses, and earlobes stretched down to their shoulders, wearing torn clothing and studded dog collars and sneers are standing outside smoking, and Nina walks in, wearing her Eva Gabor wig and her lavender polyester slacks and penny loafers and her navy blue L.L. Bean all-weather parka. It's dark inside and a deafening-loud band is playing, the lead singer shouting words Nina can't understand and flicking his head like his neck is broken. The bass vibrates through the floor and rattles the bottles and glasses behind the bar.

In her coat pocket, Nina has the tattered poster advertising WHAT'S LEFT OF THE JAMIE ARCHER BAND. She hands it to a person with a shaved head and tattooed face—is it male or female?—standing inside the door, collecting the cover charge. She-he looks at it, expressionless, and hands it back to Nina, never making eye contact but pointing to a chalk board on the wall that says $10 cover and the names of five bands:

1. Jerry Falwell and The Panty Liners
2. Urban Couch
3. Gene Pool
4. 63 Eyes
5. Non-Dairy Creamer

"But what about this?" Nina shouts above the noise, pointing to her poster. Queequeg doesn't acknowledge that Nina has spoken. Nina waits, invisible, and when all the punk-rock patrons have entered, she pays her $10 and stands against the wall, by the door, in her thin jacket, feeling like an alien, until last call.

————

Now it is late, after 3:00 a.m., and the streets of Morgantown are deserted and slick-shiny from a sudden rain, but the storm is over and the sky is pocked with stars. Nina's car is the only car in the parking garage, which smells like piss. Nina walks toward the car, her ears ringing, feeling sick with the cling of cigarette smoke. At least her car is under a security light. In the lee of the garage, in a dark corner, something shifts, something moves, and Nina, startled, fumbles for her keys, her heart pounding. Safe inside her little Mini Cooper, she quickly locks the doors and turns the key in the ignition. She backs out, and heading toward the exit, her headlights illuminate the dark corner. It is a human form, a man. Someone pulling a bright green tarp over his head. He must be wearing a backpack because underneath the tarp, it looks like he has wings, and Nina is reminded of the famous gargoyle perched atop Notre Dame Cathedral. It is probably the street person everyone refers to as the Green Man, a man with a long grizzled beard, always dressed in green, who is usually stationed downtown, outside the Salvation Army, staring blankly at the traffic or reading.

Something about seeing the Green Man makes Nina feel strangely, buoyantly happy. As if he is a tiny flag, push-pinned on a wall map, something familiar and reliable. Something that says YOU ARE HERE or YOU ARE NOT ALONE.

How silly of her, she thinks now, to have thought that Jamie and some of his band members might be there tonight. But where did that poster come from? Was it some kind of sign Jamie was trying to send her? Was he really from another planet? And why not? She has read Carl Sagan. She knows about SETI, the Search for Extra-Terrestrial Intelligence. Life is random, the possibility of intelligent life existing *only* on planet Earth, ridiculous. And, furthermore, is this life form really so intelligent? Think about it.

What does it mean to be human? Nina asks herself, driving the few blocks home. Is it being a biped with opposable thumbs and a big brain? Is it membership in a certain class and phylum/order/family/genus/species? Is it something a saliva test can ascertain? Is it some set of attributes and attendant behaviors: ten of these, two of those, one of that? Is it something you can draw a box around? Who are we, anyway, and where did we all come from, and just what . . . what . . . what on earth are we doing here?

As always when Nina's been gone, Ponce de León has been standing on his hind legs, his front feet on the windowsill, keeping vigil, watching out the kitchen window, guarding the den and listening for Nina's little car to swing into the alley. In the beam of the porch's amber bug light, his sweet little face looks sad and tired, wizened and jaundiced, and oh so old. He'll be ten come spring, seventy in human years. In a few years, he'll be dead. And what about Nina? What will be the measure of her days, her inch or two of time? It's way past Ponce de León's bedtime, but he's still awake, waiting faithfully for Nina to return. He is all she has, really. She is everything to him. He paws at the window and smiles and jumps for joy. A catbird meows from the yews as Nina swings open the garden gate and one errant shooting star rips through the lining of the moth-eaten night.

Mary Ann Samyn

WEST VIRGINIA, OR

WHAT DO YOU WANT ME TO SAY?

———————

The intelligence of sorrow, like any natural thing, isn't mean.
The green dress, too, looked better untried; I was simply lost.
I study your face, which I love. And my own, less symmetrical,
though more heartbreaking. It takes time to speak to clarity;
I'm at the perfect age. The forsythia, the color of *now*:
I get used to its comings and goings. The river bend, too,
winds its own way, and your house beyond, your heart of hearts,
as the saying goes, where everything must be imagined.

Elizabeth Savage

PATH

Everywhere there is a cushion
a spacing invitation

an arm's breadth exit ramp
caution thrown wide to race

Anywhere there is an angle
measuring a sheet of sky

Somewhere a limit, elsewhere
fine strokes

denote a wind of suspension
of trespassing intention

Thorns will climb stems
thorns will throne leaves

acre over acre of elegy
Elsewhere there is a fastening

a note pinned to your coat
another cyclone centering

suitable for wandering

UNINSURED

———

Held tight as empty scales
      widows & orphans
tip
      what's gone is gone
money burns a hole in its own
      wild song

Steve Scafidi

THE HILLBILLY BREAK-DANCE
AND THE TALKING CROW

———

So the school bus skids around the mountain and kills
my friend's dog almost instantly and Lester in the back seat
sticks his face out the window to say "Don't eat that dog,
he's dead meat" and laughs and that was long ago and Lester

lives in the mountain ghetto where the rich have not yet
ruined the land with their paper mansions and he is hillbilly
wild as a teenager and learns to break-dance and locks
and pops and turns and rocks like a robot on summer nights

drunk under the Christmas lights of his back porch where
we watch as Lester works through his routine and once
he moon-walked right off the edge and dropped down
hard into the honeysuckle and the blue rocks of the place

and sprung back to his feet and said I'm all right god dammit
and shinnied back up to move some more and so it is not
hard to believe Lester banged out of his house last week
bored on a Sunday afternoon in August and wandered in

the woods of the mountain as if through some cathedral
so dark with leaves and fiddlehead ferns that light only
reaches the ground through a thousand little tunnels and
suddenly at his feet hop-hop-hopping along comes a crow

who says *all right then, all right, how are you?* and Lester
stops. *All right then, how are you?* says the crow again and
cocks its head and looks up with its beady eye at Lester
who looks away. Trucks rumble down the mountain hard

in the distance and an airplane starts to make a sharp curve
a mile above but they don't know anymore about the world
for a minute, Lester and the crow talking a while, he says just
shooting the breeze. He says that crow knew the names of his

father and his grandfather and "all kinds of personal shit"
and it said *Lester, look at you. You've grown middle-aged
and fat but I like you anyways* and flew back into the trees
just to let him think about it. And six other people have

talked to this crow and now it is legend and that is why
I am sitting in the Mount Hebron cemetery with a picnic
lunch and waiting while the story does its thing I guess
flying from tree to tree chasing owls maybe looking

for something shiny which is why I have lined up ten
dimes and a safety pin on the stone wall. To attract some
magic, to call down the blessing of an impossible thing.
All right then. It is getting darker. Let the new life begin.

THE WEST VIRGINIA COPPER-WING

An apple falls through the branches of the tree
   and a green snake rises up flying
      with little wings iridescent

as the evening begins in the orchard
   on the edge of town. Three deer
      whisper grazing in the lane.

You could be eleven or twelve
   standing with a stillness you have
      never before known, a halo

of gnats around your head and this
   could be any year in recorded history
      of human life. No one

ever exactly remembers this moment
   or the next. We find ourselves
      in a royal pause and then we go on

asking what's next. We fall
   toward sorrow and we forget.
      Someone captures the miraculous

green snake with a net—
   pins it to a board. Someone
      sharpens a knife at the center

of the earth and it sounds like a wheel.
  Houses appear. Thousands
    of windows twinkle suddenly in

the settling dark. Stillness,
  which was the god of being
    eleven or twelve on the edge of town

just before someone you love
  calls you home and home being
    the god of this place, disappears.

All of it disappears and you are left
  lost in the majestic green clockwork
    that is next.

Angela Shaw

CREPUSCULE

―――――

Yellows cast their spells: the evening primrose
shudders unclosed, sells itself to the sphinx
moth's length of tongue. Again a lackluster
husband doesn't show. A little missus

eases the burnt suffering of a cat-
fish supper, undresses, slowly lowers
into a lukewarm tub. In her honeymoon
nightgown she rolls her own from the blue

can of Bugler, her lust a lamp the wick
of which is dipped in sloe gin. Hands
wander to her hangdog breasts, jaded Friday night
underpants, hackneyed nylon in heat.

Now his black taxidermy out-stares her, the stern
heads of squirrel and deer. Now the house confesses,
discloses her like a rumor, vague and misquoted.
From the porch, from the glider she spies rose-

pink twilight flyers—sphinx moths drinking
the calyx, the corolla, the stamen
dry. The stuttering wings, the spread petals
suggest an interlingual breathing, a beating

back of all false tongues. She thinks of the chaw
lodged in his lip when he talks or her husband's

middle finger in the snuff box and rubbed
along his gum. She walks, wanting him, into the latter-

math, into the primrose, the parched field itching
with critters. She walks, wanting and unwanting
him while birds miss curfew into the thick of the thigh-
high grass, craven and dangerous, in the heavy red.

WEST VIRGINIA SPRING

Ramps *stink worse than what wild*
onion does, but what is merely
unearthed is not

dirty. A wild leek, a lily. A furtive
girlhood spent tramping
through woods, unwinding

the skein of the heart like stolen
evidence. A pink
lipstick driven to its quick, in time,

nylons, the wayward
names of town boys, swollen
on the tongue and scarred

across catalpa bark. *They ain't*
for ladies or for those
who court them. The outer skin

around the bulb peeled back, the last
of delicate April
lifted like a fingerprint.

Kent Shaw

DON'T THINK LIKE THE MOUNTAINS, THEY'RE
NOTHING LIKE THE FUTURE

————

If only our children were colts, and sensible enough to be good at one thing.
Running. Jumping some. Looking adorable.
They would deserve our devotion.
Think crepe myrtle, nudged after a brief rain. Think zealots. Think ocean
    waves, if we'd enough sense
to give them unique personalities.
Everywhere you look, willfulness. Bountiful willfulness.
And these days it's the children you see playing along.

As though the world were a carousel teeming with one kind of horse.
What's a child supposed to do against odds like that?
Civilization is a long story. It concerns a lot of people.
When I was a child I was told there was one option: success.
Now I am an adult tired of my long life as a child.

Like the story of Adam and Eve.
Two children, who the Lord had to dress so we'd think they were adults.
I love you, Adam, said the Lord.
And you can love Eve. That is good.
Then the Lord made a museum, and He put Adam inside.
He said, Eve, you follow Adam, I like it that way.

And Eve cried out, Adam, I think that is good.
The boy fell in love. The museum was so beautiful.
And all the whole world opened then. The air. The spaces between air.

The other little airs we could see if the regular air held its breath.

The Lord made a skylight, and it was an Age of Suns.

The Lord touched their blood, and they shimmered. They contagioned. Wasps swarmed inside them.

That is good, the Lord said.

But how would He know?

In the beginning was the Word. And of course it was good. But what if that's all He had.

A human emotion is frailer than words, more subversive. It's more than one thing.

Adam took Eve. He knew her with a knowledge the Lord couldn't give him.

Everything almost was breathing.

That's what it felt like. Like a garden that isn't sure exactly how it should bloom.

Anita Skeen

LETTER TO AN UNKNOWN,
AND PROBABLY DECEASED, PHOTOGRAPHER

———

It must have been seventy years ago
you took that shot, my grandmother standing
in front of the front of a car, whitewall tire
practically up to her waist, running board
streamlining the side. A log house
backgrounds the car, square
logs, good chinking, grounded
and going nowhere. My grandmother
wears a dress dotted as the Milky Way,
a Sunday dress, and a wide straw hat
circles her head like the rings of Saturn.
She is looking at you with a difficult
smile, this woman who by now
has had a husband drown
and three daughters arrive, all
before her twenty-fifth year.
I was told she never stood for photos,
covering her face with her hands
or a scarf, taking the scissors
to any shot that took her by surprise,
excising her face. How did you do it,
you must have been kin, though back then
who could afford a Kodak, who that she knew
would have owned such a car, such a home?
Was this the one time she let you snap

the shutter, stood with her anxious
hands locked behind her back?
Would you remember her now,
as she was then, if we could talk?
I want to believe you were the friend
no one believed she had, someone
lost to family history. I want you
to be the secret she shares
only with me.

IN THE CHEMICAL VALLEY

———

*The nine-county environmental catastrophe now unfolding
in West Virginia—a spill of as much as 7,500 gallons of an
industrial chemical used to wash coal, which hospitalized 169
people and left 300,000 more without drinking water—is a
tragic reminder of the risks that spring from our dependence on
fossil fuels.*

— *EDF Voices: People of the Planet*

Up Elk River is what I used to say
when someone said, *Where do you live?*
Up past Knollwood and Mink Shoals,
past Elk Hills, all threaded together
by Route 119. On the right, Elk River
shadowed the highway, visible
at times between maple and pine.
Here was the launch pad for baptisms,
another mile up, the spot where the plane
overshot the runway of the airport
one pilot said was like landing on the deck
of an aircraft carrier. On up, near my house,
on the river bank, the muscle-limbed oak
that lifted us above the current until
we had the guts to jump. Once
in the water, we were safe.

Don't drink the water. Don't shower.
Don't cook with it or wash your clothes.
There's half a century gone. Gone
most of us who went to Elk Grade School,
gone, too. Gone the white frame homes,
the small brick duplexes, the school
we marched to for our polio shots.
Gone the quick-tongued streams, gone
the valleys, filled with mountaintop, gone
from the fog-draped skyscape. It's licorice
scented air, not sun-dried cotton sheets,
licorice wafting from the tap. *Clean coal,*
they say, *we clean the coal.* Who cleans what
cleans the coal, what stains the water blue-green,
what seeps from slurry ponds that no one
bothers to contain? *Safe,* they say, *it's safe.*

I remember the impact, the plunge
into cold, breath held till surfacing, then
the dappled light of the world. I hold my breath
now for different reasons.

Aaron Smith

LESSONS

In my father's retirement
he's learning to play
the banjo. Two hours each day:
"runs" and "vamping"
in the back of the house.
He goes to camps
where they teach him
to play by ear:
Something has to click.
When I took piano as a kid,
he never wanted to listen, attended
recitals because Mom forced him.
Relieved when I finally quit:
Such a sissy instrument.
Now there's something innocent
in the way he talks, a gentleness
I rarely find in men:
From your last visit to this one
am I getting better?
I'm happy to lie, to say yes.
I'm not a father.
I don't have to be cruel.

Ida Stewart

POINT BLANK

———————

You can have my right arm, but you'll never get my mountain.

> —*Larry Gibson, on his stand against*
> *mountaintop removal coal mining*

This is a point: a green island in a sea
of scar, a rise not unlike his potbelly

under the neon green t-shirt—
and what with the hilltop cemetery like a belly

full of bodies resting sweetly, we could fairly
call his attachment umbilical.

And after all—his overall
pockets and pores emptied of the earth—all that's left
squirreled away

is his blood.
But back to the point

and how they're making it for him,
finer and higher and deader-

on than he ever could, waiting
here with the squat rocks waiting

to be eroded
into the holler—

the sound of their machines, he thinks,
brainless as barking:

that ceaseless ghost dog of his
filling in the blank of night.

SOIL

in your mouth, sounds like *soul*—
like the word's been oiled, all the old

consolidated, uprooted, from
this spit of overtold land.

I hear you grazing in the understory,
your mouth full of maple keys,

black walnut husks, cold
autumn dirt and rock,

bark, lichen, and broken, breaking

green: sour mash.
Your mouth's a still, a stolen

cave in
which to fold the world.

Kevin Stewart

HER

She leaned against my VW Rabbit, both hands tugging the hem of her T-shirt down between her thighs. Except for dark socks, the shirt was all she had on. Eyes wide, she watched me come closer, her face as pale as concrete. She had to be cold. It was mid-September, and nights in the mountains had already cooled, the trees tinged with yellow.

I'd just come from the Gallery of Kings, a dance club in Summit, ducked out after last call. I'd gone alone that night, without my buddies, who had dates. And I left alone, which wasn't unusual. Sometimes I'd meet someone there, but I'd be with her for only one night. Now I wondered what was going on and why this girl leaned against my car, out of all the cars along the street.

Stopping a few feet from her, I pulled my keys from my pocket. She was pretty, with black, shoulder-length hair curled the way heavy-metal chicks curled their hair then, back in '85. She had three studs in her right ear, a brace-let-sized hoop in her left. Blue eye shadow smeared her eyelids. Tears had bled thick, black eyeliner down her cheeks. She looked nineteen or twenty, going on thirty-five. Behind chain link a few houses away, a mutt barked at us.

"Is this your car?" she asked.

"Yeah," I said. She had no bra on under the shirt, a black Molly Hatchet T-shirt, which she pulled down a few millimeters lower, taut against her nipples and ribs. On her shirt spread a screen-printed Frazetta of a muscular, armored man gripping an axe with a large, rounded blade. The image was as cracked and faded as the frescoes we'd studied in my art history elective.

"Could you gimme a ride home?"

I watched her a moment longer and scanned the other cars along the street, for some reason looking for someone else who might be watching, who might be waiting, laying for me. She seemed to be alone, but something had happened to her, something I didn't want to think about. I didn't want to get involved.

"Please," she said. "I just wanna get home."

Voices rose in the distance behind me. Laughing and talking loudly, a couple of drunks were coming out of the Gallery two blocks away, headed our way. I looked at her again. Her eyes were locked onto the drunks. She might have an even worse time with them than with whoever did this to her. I'd seen those two inside, hitting on every woman in the place, grabbing the asses of some on their way to the restroom or bar. When those two saw someone leave a half-empty pitcher of beer to go dance, they filled their glasses.

"Where do you live?" I asked.

Still watching the two men, she gestured her head to her right. "Jenkins Street. Across the tracks, over the MLK Bridge." I studied Stony Ridge, the mountainside that rose above the halogen glow of the Norfolk-Southern railroad yard, which, until recently, had always served as the color line in Summit. Street lamps and yellow rectangles of light gave out about halfway up the slope. She saw me gazing across the tracks. "It's safe," she said. "Not everybody's black no more, if that's what you're worried about." Her shoulders were rounded, knees bent a little, as if she were ready to beg.

The men had seen her now and were picking up their pace, already yelling at her.

"Please," she said, watching them.

I hurried her to the passenger's side, unlocked the door, nearly shoving her in, and hopped in my side. The car seat enveloped her, and she tugged her shirttail between her legs and pressed her knees together.

After I pulled away, leaving the men standing in the middle of the street, waving their arms in my rearview, she said, "I guess you're wondering about this." Her voice broke up a little, and she cleared her throat a couple of times.

"Well, yeah."

"They raped me."

I gripped the wheel tighter. "Who did?"

"Two guys I was going to buy something off of." She paused, gave me a quick look.

"Did you know them?"

She nodded.

"You're not going to the cops?"

She didn't answer. Letting go of her shirt with one hand, she wiped her eyes. I glanced at her, my gaze drawn to her lap, which flashed light to dark as we drove under overhead street lamps. A dark bruise in the vague shape of a hand was on her left thigh. She caught me looking and tugged until her knuckles touched the seat cushion. Cutting my eyes back to the road, I fidgeted in the seat, trying to get comfortable, and swerved around a flattened dog on the street. I couldn't get to that house soon enough.

"They kept my money. And they threw my clothes out the window." Her eyes shifted toward her stretched shirt, the image elongated vertically, cracks in the silk-screened image separating like parched mud.

"You gotta watch who you get in a car with."

Glaring at me, she leaned against the passenger door, her knees squeezed together, pointed away from me, as if the door were someone she could trust. For the next mile, we rode quietly down Triple Oaks Avenue. The Stones' "Some Girls" barely murmured in the cassette player, but I could follow the words. The beer taste in my mouth had begun to sour, as had the feeling in my gut, and it was all I could do to keep from tracing that smooth line of skin between the bottom of her thigh and hip and the cloth of the seat. She smelled like pot smoke and Right Guard and men's cologne and Armor All—a vinyl seat. A Camaro, I figured, or a souped-up Nova, or something. Never before had I regretted having a naked girl in my car. The post-last-call leftovers at the Gallery never interested me the way they did my buddies, but I would pick them up sometimes, especially if I were with my buddies and they were doing the same. I didn't date much either, not even the thin, pretty ones, because they required dates and more dates and time and attention, which I didn't have in me at the time and couldn't figure out why.

Then, there *she* was.

"Turn left up here." She nodded at the steel-trussed bridge that carried Jenkins Street over the railroad yard. The bridge's once silver beams had long since been blackened with coal dust and diesel soot from years of trains dragging coal from McDowell County to Hampton Roads. The steel grate decking droned under my tires. On the other side, she said, "Turn right and go one block. You can let me off at the bottom of my street."

"I can take you to your house," I said. "No problem."

"You don't have to."

"I've come this far."

She watched me for a few seconds, shrugged, and then placed the side of her head against the glass, the sharp curve of her chin cutting into the night.

I turned up the street, which was marked by a wooden post with the street sign torn off, and climbed the steep grade. Shifting from third to second, I popped the clutch too quickly. She let go of her shirttail to catch herself, and I glimpsed her pubic hair and glanced away. "Sorry."

"Stop," she said, hiding herself again.

I slammed on the brakes, wondering whether I'd scared her.

"The lights are on," she said.

"What?"

"Turn around."

The houses on both sides were identical—two-story, nondescript but sturdy 1920s models, each with a hipped roof, a dormer in the center, and a covered front porch. The houses sat close to the street, which was lined with cars no fewer than ten years old, it seemed. "Turn around. My mom's up."

"So—"

"Please. She'll kill me."

I backed into a driveway, turned down the hill, and stopped at the intersection. Gang graffiti, spray-painted in black, was scrawled across the stop sign. A solitary two-story chimney and an empty foundation grown with weeds and saplings stood in the corner lot to the right.

"Thanks," she said.

I shrugged, wondering how long this was going to take. "What now?"

"You can let me out. I can hide out till she goes to bed."

I wanted to get rid of her, to get this over with, but when I turned to her to agree with her, I saw chill bumps had risen on her thighs and arms. The crooks of her elbows were dark. I focused on the railroad yard ahead of us. Down this far, the tracks were empty. Up near downtown, coal cars coupled all night, the metallic crash fracturing the crisp air. "It's kinda cool out," I said. "You're not hardly dressed for it." I glanced at her. "Wanna just ride around, maybe, and get some coffee or something? Hardee's drive-thru is open."

She nodded slowly, as though balancing her head on her shoulders took considerable effort.

"My jacket is in the back seat." I grabbed my suede jacket, which I didn't like to stink up in the smoky club, and handed it to her. She turned away from me, slipped into it, and zipped it all the way to her throat.

———

In Hardee's drive-thru line, a cop car pulled in behind us. I watched it in my rearview, glanced at her. She stared straight ahead. I checked the mirror again. Two cops talked back and forth, occasionally laughing. The car in front of us pulled away. I drifted forward, looking at the rearview, at her. Could they see her? She glanced in the side mirror, over her shoulder, and then at me. I checked the cops again. Should I tell them?

As I handed over three dollars, the girl working the window saw her and frowned at me. I grabbed the coffees, handed hers to her, and didn't wait for the change. Pulling away, I checked the mirror several more times, afraid the cops would follow. She sank in the seat a little, holding the warm cup to her chest. I knew then that you're only a second away from being either a criminal or a victim at any point in your life.

We ended up at the old strip mines north of Summit, where kids liked to party and mud-bog in four-wheel drives with oversized tires, where car thieves brought stolen cars and stripped them and torched them, where couples parked. I'd brought several girls here myself, after meeting them in the Gallery, and it was the closest out-of-the-way place I could think of.

I pulled over at the first wide spot. I couldn't go much farther down the dirt road, which was gashed with muddy ruts too deep for my Rabbit. I turned off the engine, sipped coffee, and focused on the half moon high in the sky, well above the trees, whose branches would soon be bare. Somewhere in the distance, coon dogs bayed, and I turned toward her. The moon vaguely whitened the high, naked sandstone bluffs, which, fifty years ago, were underground until the machines came, blasted away earth and stone, leaving the rock face scored every two feet, as regular as lines on graph paper. "Why my car?"

She lowered her gaze to her lap. "It was the only one that didn't have nothing hanging from the rearview." She blew on the coffee, sipped again, and swallowed hard. For some reason she'd removed the lid.

I noticed my eyes in my mirror and saw the moonlight glinting in them. "Why'd you get in that car with those guys?"

She stared into her coffee. "They hang out at the Gallery." Her eyes darted toward me and back to her cup, and I ran as many faces as I could remember through my mind. "You go much?"

"Too much."

"Always by yourself?"

"Usually with my roommate and another buddy, but they had dates tonight." And I was glad, for her sake and mine.

"You pick up girls in there?"

I shrugged. "Sometimes."

She watched me for several uncomfortable moments. "You go to school?"

"Summit State," I said, glad she might be changing the subject. "I'm taking computer science."

"I went for one semester. Now I work at Captain D's and help Mom out with the rent. Since my bastard of an old man won't."

We went silent. The dogs grew closer, barking, on the trail of something. Sitting here like this was awkward and futile, and I was tired, still a little buzzed and very worried about her, about being caught with her. Wondering if her old lady was in bed yet, I finished my coffee, rolled down the window and tossed the cup out.

"Don't do that."

I turned toward her. "Do what?"

"Throw that out."

Outside, fast-food bags and beer and wine bottles littered the ground, down into the edge of the woods. "It's like a landfill out there now."

"Get that back."

"It's just a cup."

"Pick it up." She paused, her eyes losing their focus on me. "Don't you see what's happened?" Looking past me at the sandstone face, her eyes glistened and her mouth was pulled tight in a severe straight line. It was the closest thing to emotion she had shown and I couldn't stand looking at it.

"Okay." I climbed out. Fifty yards away, the dogs broke across the cut, six or seven of them, running, yelping, heading straight for us. I hadn't seen anything run past, but they were after something faster than a coon. Maybe a bobcat or a fox. I watched them for several seconds longer and reached down for the cup. Beside a mashed beer can, a silver graduation cap tassel had been flattened into the dirt. I grabbed the cup, hopped back in the car, and dropped the cup on the back floorboard. She watched the windshield like television.

"What are they after?" Her arms now X-ed over her chest, her cup empty and harmless between her feet.

"Maybe a fox."

The dogs raced past and cut back down into the woods behind us. Though I was afraid of what might happen next, I reached for her and tried to pull her to me. I didn't know what else to do. She stiffened and wouldn't give. I squeezed tighter, her elbows digging into my ribs. I could feel her in my bulky jacket as if she were too small for her own skin. A strange warm sensation rose in me, and I trembled. She remained rigid. "You think I'm poison, don't you?" I asked.

She sniffled.

"It's okay." I felt her relax a little. Fifty yards down the cut, flashlight beams emerged from the woods. I released her and saw the figures of four men following the dogs. They were carrying shotguns, likely liquored up. I thought about taking her to the cops again or maybe to the hospital.

"Don't let them see us," she said. "Let's go."

"We're okay. They're not worried about us."

"You wanna keep me here?" She wiped her eyes on my jacket sleeve, the hunters close enough now that we heard their voices.

"No," I said. "I don't mean that."

"Why do you wanna keep me here?"

"I don't. I just mean we don't have to worry about them."

Staring at the men, she shook her head. "Take me home now."

"I'm not trying to do anything."

She remained quiet. I studied the men for a moment longer and started the car, my headlights now on the hunters, who stood maybe twenty yards away, watching us. I u-turned and drove away.

———

When I got to her street again, she said, "It's the next to last house on the right."

I pulled up to the curb and shut off the headlights. The windows were dark. In the street lamp's light, I could see coal dust had blackened the beige siding. The next house up the street was empty, the windows boarded with weathered plywood.

She unzipped my jacket, took it off, again with her back to me, and opened the door.

246

"I'm sorry," I said.

Staring at the dash now, she said, "You can't help it." She climbed out, dropped the jacket on the seat and slammed the door. I watched her scale the steps of her front porch, the shirt uncovering the pale skin of her bottom. At the front door, she kneeled down and lifted the corner of a welcome mat. She stood, unlocked the door. Before disappearing inside, she glanced at me.

I read the address number on the house, 214, turned around in the empty house's driveway and rolled back down the hill. The downstairs lights flashed on. Standing under the yellow glow of the porch light was a woman in a robe. She leapt down the steps, waving at me. I wanted to stop and explain everything, but before she could cut me off, I gunned the engine, killed my lights, and skidded to a stop at the base of the street. In the rearview, in a cone of street-lamp light, she stood, pressing her hands to the sides of her head. A trickle of sweat dripped from my underarm and ran down my side.

At home later, I knew I'd lie awake all night, worried a car would slow, headlights filling the windows of my bedroom, the engine stopping, the lights flashing off, and two car doors opening, a dog barking a few trailers down. How could I say it wasn't me?

But now, I turned right and spun out. Pulling my headlights back on, I made a left onto the Martin Luther King Jr. Bridge, which seemed longer and narrower than before, as if not quite wide enough for my car.

A. E. Stringer

RECOVERING BLUES

Took me forty years to get the blues
and now they've surely got me too.
Enough of loving her or her, whoever
never loved enough. Every year's a rose-
wood twelve-string locked and mute

until some song comes back so right,
lightning strike, it's got to be replayed.
Like all of a sudden you're Mr. Ledbetter
or Blind Willie, young again and waking
an ache whose name you hardly knew

until the smoky words wailed out
your mouth right past a smile. How the road
the morning after got hot before ten
and maybe another gig—twelve mile—if some
woman ain't kept you bed-bound till

you begun to think of settling in.
One song unbroken, whatever years
a body's got left, whatever color they are,
or you are, whoever's bones are lying
in the sheets tonight, rehearsing.

In some dive I've been before, I forgot
the words until a brand new verse rang out
and did no wrong. The crowd sighed through
a chord, the twelve-string's hollow body
awake again, making new arrangements.

Natalie Sypolt

LETTUCE

———

I see the sky getting dark and Matt goes out to cover the lettuce. He wants the vegetables safe and unbruised, has tarps and buckets collected in the out-building for just such an occasion. I've learned not to ask if he wants help. When I used to offer, he thought it was because I figured he couldn't do it himself. But it wasn't like that. Or maybe it was. It doesn't matter anymore.

The clouds roll in and I watch him cover his lettuce from the kitchen window, remembering the time I was ten and visiting my aunt in Illinois. We had a storm, what the news people said was a derecho, like a wall of hell. A horizontal tornado, some said, but it rolled more like a hurricane. It lasted a long time and I was crying before it was over.

When we looked at the sky, the layers of dark heavy clouds, I was sure it was the end of the world. But it finally cleared, and people picked up, cleaned up, moved on.

The rain starts falling fast and hard. I see Matt stoop, but he doesn't want to sacrifice the tender lettuce. He puts the tarp over some, weighs it down with big rocks. He places buckets over the tomato and pepper plants. Then the hail comes, pellets hitting the roof of the porch, tinny and loud. Matt tries to cover himself by holding his non-arm over his head, but he doesn't quit, because now his work is even more important. Some wives would run out, grab an umbrella or a pot or something. I stand and watch, wondering how long it will take him to give in.

Before the storm came, I'd been grating carrots for a salad. Matt is a vegetarian now. This has irritated me from the beginning, not because I care about the food, but because it seems so predictable, like something that would happen in a movie. That's what this all feels like sometimes—not our real life, but some melodramatic, made-for-TV movie. Boy goes off to war, sees unspeakable, loses left arm in an IED explosion, can't stomach the blood and flesh of meat anymore. I can't name any movie where this happens, but I'm sure it has. It's not that I don't have any compassion either. I was nothing but compassion, a giant pudding ball of compassion, until I couldn't be anymore.

When I was grating carrots, I heard a car coming up the drive. Really, it wasn't in our drive, just going slow up the bumpy dirt road, but as I jumped to look, I slipped. The carrot nub flipped out of my hand, and my knuckles went down hard and fast across those sharp teeth. It took a minute to sink in, the way it does when you hurt yourself in some stupid way and can't look down for fear of what you'll see. Pictures flashed in my head of shredded skin, white knuckle bone shining through blood and gore. I grabbed a dish-towel and pressed it to my knuckles, but when I looked down I saw that a few tiny drops of blood had dripped into the salad bowl. The red was bold and hot against the orange of the carrots, and I knew that I should throw it all out. But the big wooden bowl was full of tomatoes, lettuce, cucumbers, and peppers. Throwing it out would be wasteful, and there wasn't time to run to town for more vegetables.

This was how I told it to myself. And when I came back downstairs after washing my hand and bandaging my knuckles, I mixed the carrot shreds up good so the bloody spots were gone. That's what I did and I'm not sorry.

"Son of a bitch came on fast," Matt says when he bangs in, soaking wet and dripping all over the kitchen floor. "I think I got it in time. Hope I did."

"I'm sure you did," I say, but I don't have much in my voice to convince him. He doesn't notice, so I don't try too hard.

"I don't remember the weatherman saying it was going to rain today, do you? Is it still hailing? You know what they say about hail." Matt looks out the window, though we can hear the ice bouncing off the porch roof. They say hail is sometimes a sign a tornado is coming, but I don't know what Matt means anymore. He could mean anything.

"You're dripping," I say. "You shouldn't track that mud upstairs. Just strip your clothes here, then go put on something dry." His face goes a little funny because he doesn't like the idea. "Come on, Matt. It's a mess."

"Fine," he says. I cross my arms and watch as he pushes off his boots, then, one-handed, undoes his buckle, button, and zipper; he sloughs his wet jeans off like a snake losing his skin. His boxers are wet through, but I decide not to push it. I wonder if he'll leave the non-arm on as he tries to get his wet T-shirt off, or if he'll release this contraption I hate. I see he's also wondering which would be best.

He doesn't like for anyone to see his scars, not even me, and it's not because of vanity. Matt is a good-looking man, always has been, but doesn't try too hard. No hair gel or fancy clothes. He still wears the same brand of drug store cologne his mother bought him when he started shaving, even through the army, even still. I think he's afraid the scars and stump and machine-like parts of the non-arm make him look weaker.

He already feels weak, even after all the months in physical therapy, even though his good arm is stronger than most two put together. Some men get to hide their damage, but Matt has to wear his—artificial flesh-toned and creepy veiny—every day.

It took a while, but now he can dress and undress himself, take care of his bathroom things. He can do garden work and some of the farm work for his daddy, like drive the tractor. "Use the arm," the therapists told him. "It's not like the old prosthetics. These new pieces are incredible."

At first, they wanted to give him a hi-tech, robot-like one that could grasp cups. It was an experimental model and they tried to tell me how it worked—something about nerves being re-routed, muscles in the chest learning to twitch in a way that would make the fingers move. I didn't understand. When they showed me, I couldn't stop staring at the icy silver of it.

"Matt would be able to hold your hand," one therapist said. She was a young girl with bright eyes, a long curled ponytail, intricately applied makeup. She wasn't much younger than us, but she seemed like a kid. To her, the idea of Matt being able to hold my hand again probably sounded sweet, romantic.

I touched the robot hand and tried to imagine the cool fingers beginning to tighten. I thought I felt a twitch and jerked away.

"What good is this doing?" Matt asked the girl. "I'll never be able to feel her hand. Why would I ever do this in real life?"

My cheeks went red then, imagining real life and what he might do with his bionic arm. Images flashed in my head of our bedroom, Matt saying, "Look how my chest muscles make my fingers close. Look how I can move them on you." I felt a sick quake in my stomach and had to get up. I was outside the door quick, and slid down the wall.

The pretty girl couldn't understand. She met men like Matt and wives like me every day, but then she went home to her boyfriend who still has everything he's supposed to have. Some farm boy who still has his twinkle, who holds her and undresses her and touches her with two warm hands.

"That's the last time she's in here," I heard Matt say to the girl.

Matt has a different sort of arm now. This one fastens around his body with thick straps and is still incredible, but not quite as incredible as the robotic one. He thought that one scared me, and that I was embarrassed. He told the therapist it just didn't feel right, that maybe he wasn't strong enough for that yet. So instead he has one that looks more like "the real thing" from the elbow down. The hand is always slightly bent, ready for gripping. The doctors say that the technology is improving all the time, especially now with such demand. Matt tells me he's on a list to get a better arm permanently. I read about it on the internet—the "Luke" they call it, after Luke Skywalker's bionic arm in the Star Wars movies.

I watch Matt struggle, trying to get the wet T-shirt up and over his non-arm. Normally he could do it, but the shirt is wet and stuck to his skin. "Okay, Jenny," he says finally. "Help me."

I peel gently from the bottom, first over his good arm so he can help, then over the non-arm, then over his head. I'm close enough that I can see the little welts on his shoulders and forehead where the hail hit him. That's when I remember to listen, and hear that it's stopped.

"Just rain now," I say, and realize I'm still holding the shirt above his head and that our chests are touching. On my tiptoes I can just reach his lips because he is tall and I am not. I'm surprised that I kiss him because I didn't think I would. My hand is in his hair, long now, grown out, so that I can grab it, wrap my hand up in it like he used to in mine.

"Jen," he says around my lips, but I keep my hand in his hair, and kiss him so hard that I taste blood in my mouth, his or mine I don't know. If he would take off the arm, I would lick his scars. When he's awake, he won't let me touch them, doesn't want me to look, but sometimes when he's asleep, I kneel on the floor beside the bed and run my finger around each purple crevice, each indention. I cup the missing piece. The pills make him sleep deep and I'm glad, because if he woke to find me there, he would howl. He'd push me and my kisses away like he does every time.

I pull his hair, force his head back and kiss his throat.

"What's gotten in to you?" he says. He's trying to move away, trying to laugh me off, but I don't want to let him go. How would the movie go? If we were living out this drama on the screen, would he push me away now, again, or would this be the climax where Matt finally lets me unstrap his non-arm and lies down on the cold kitchen tiles? Would he cry? Would the hail start again, or the lightning and thunder, rolling over us?

I used to love those nights when the air got thick with electricity. The thunder rolled around the house in waves, the lightning showing Matt to me in flashes as it lit up the bedroom. When it was over, there was just the slow, soft rain. We'd lie close together. I knew everything then.

With his good hand, Matt pats my shoulder. "Isn't it about time for dinner?" he asks. "I'll go get some dry clothes on. Okay?" He's using his hand to disentangle mine from his hair. He doesn't want to hurt me. He just wants to go.

I watch him gather his wet clothes from the floor. I think I should get the mop and take care of the puddles, but I don't. Instead, I get the vegetarian lasagna from the oven. I get the salad from the refrigerator.

The storm has somehow circled us and, when we sit to eat, the rain is loud again. When the thunder comes, I can feel it in my whole body as the house shudders.

"Here it comes again," Matt says. He's wearing a blue T-shirt from high school, with the school mascot—a wildcat—on the front. His hair is in his eyes. He looks so young, so much younger than I feel. How unfair that he can look like that and I have to feel like this. His non-arm is resting on the table. He's waiting for me to serve him.

"This looks good," he says as I cut the lasagna and scoop it onto his plate. I'm not a good cook, especially when it comes to dishes where delicate vegetables are expected to pull together and make something hearty.

"Have some salad." I use the plastic tongs to fill our bowls to the top. I spear some with my fork but don't put it to my mouth until I've watched Matt take a mouthful, mostly lettuce, streaked with shreds of orange. He chews and when he sees me watching, he smiles.

"At least I can make salad," I say. I take my bite, already knowing that after he goes to sleep tonight, I'll sneak out and drive the forty-five minutes to Morgantown to get a greasy fast food cheeseburger. Maybe two.

Glenn Taylor

CORTÈGE

I was giving my man Albert Townsend a ride to the walk-in clinic when I saw the funeral procession. It had no police escort. The lead vehicle was a black Chevy Suburban flashing its hazards and flying purple and white flags for the deceased. The hearse behind it wore the same flags and flashed its hazards too, and so did all the cars behind it for as far as the eye could see. Albert and I were traveling east on Adams Avenue. The funeral procession was oncoming, traveling west. Between us was a turning lane. It was May the fourth, two days before my thirty-sixth birthday, and the big morning sun was out and Albert had his ankle propped in the open passenger window. The ankle was blown up like a water balloon—he'd wrecked it just a half hour before playing pick-up five-on-five at the university annex gym. None of us had student identification of course, but I was sleeping with the front desk card-swiper, a young woman pursuing her masters degree in athletic training who was more glorious in her various yoga pants than I could ever hope to put in words.

Albert and I were stopped at a red light by the Christian school. A mother walked her little girl up the worn porch stairs and they both had the look of the tardy. I felt bad about all the weed smoke coming through the sunroof. I turned down the music. It was a reggae playlist Albert had made. He enjoyed singing along, pronouncing all the words as if he'd been born and raised in Kingston, Jamaica. I watched the slow-moving funeral-goers proceed through the red light. They were at a crawl, and I could make out faces, expressions. Nobody was talking to one another inside the cars. It made me wonder about the human contents inside the hearse. I'd bet it was somebody young, somebody sudden.

The light turned green, but I did not accelerate. I had early noticed the practices of my father and uncle in this regard, and without fail, when faced with a funeral procession, each had customarily removed his hat and pulled off on the side of the road.

There was no side-of-the-road here, only a busted curb, but I was not going to budge. I looked in my rearview and saw that the elderly pair in the Impala behind us spoke to each other and nodded in unison. They'd no doubt understood my decision and recognized its moral rightness, its hint of the good old ways they'd once known. They were content to sit unmoving in their vehicle all damn day, and for that I admired them.

The Impala's hood was steaming from the cracks.

It was six or seven cars deep behind them.

I asked Albert, "Did you all used to pull off and stop when a funeral procession came through?"

The singer of the song remarked that sinsemilla was a gift from Jah. Albert was hitting the joint with his eyes closed and working his neck in time with the bassline. "Course we did," he said. He handed me the joint. "My Grandpa Ace took off his hat too."

I spat on my fingers and extinguished the tip, stuck the roach in my watch pocket. I cracked my window. Hot bread was faint on the air. Even a block away, I could hear the big exhaust fans at Central City Bakery.

Albert reached forward and touched gingerly at the skin above his ankle. "But ole Ace didn't call it a funeral procession," he said.

There was still no seeable end to the oncoming mourners' pack. Up ahead, a gay pride flag flew on a second-story porch. It was a tough neighborhood in which to fly such a flag. I waited for Albert to continue. It seemed that he was not planning to elaborate. "Well, what did he call it?" I asked.

"Cortège."

"Cor-what?" It sounded French, but I'd lived for two years in Strasbourg and never once heard it.

"Cortège," Albert said. "Funeral train."

The horn blast was loud and carried forth with the kind of volume that grits teeth. I had no time to comment aloud before it sounded again. To my ear, it came from three cars back. I put down my window all the way and was fixing to crane my neck when the horn blower whipped his Chevy Silverado into the middle turning lane and gunned it. The passenger, a skinny young man with his ball cap pulled low, flipped me a hard bird as they blew past. The Silverado's paint job was sparkle blue and someone had fucked up the pinstriping pretty good. It was already moving too fast to make out the license plate, but I'd have bet the house on Ohio.

I dropped the shifter into D.

"Let's go get them disrespectful bomboclats," Albert said.

To each of the funeral-goers we passed, I gave a solemn look and a nod. I could only hope they'd pieced together the events unfolding, and that they knew me as the still one who had only stirred when provoked.

You have to understand the vehicle I was piloting at the time.

An Infiniti Q50 is a fine sedan with a list price of around forty grand. I'd paid cash for mine the week prior, having sold off the last of a high grade medical cannabis my cousin Chicken had stolen and transported from Modesto, California, a hybrid strain called Sixteen-Karat Bamboozle. Only rich people bought it.

When I'd seen the last of the purple and white funeral flags, I punched the gas, and Albert pulled his bad ankle inside and hollered "Let's get to gettin!" and immediately set to finding the right song on his device. Since grade school, he'd consistently and at every chance looked to orchestrate our lives, and I will admit I truly appreciated his task and his skill. That morning, for the chase, he put on Ace Beanz.

In high school, Albert made a mix tape once called Music to Make Sweet Sweet Love To. It led off with "How Does It Feel?" by D'Angelo and followed that with "Sex Me" by R. Kelly. It was not a subtle type of mix tape.

Albert had shoved his enormous foot back into his high-tops. He winced and looked up to locate our target. He said, "There he goes!"

I'd already spotted the sparkle-blue Silverado at the dogleg by Jolly Pirate Donuts. Such a turn had required caution in my previous vehicles, but on that May morning, I never did touch the brake, and that new sedan leaned smooth, and when I got on the straight stretch of Fifth Avenue, I tucked right in behind him, nice and close. The lime green decal on his tinted rear window read AIN'T SKEERT. His plates were Ohio, the heart of it all.

The traffic light at the TV station was yellow and the road was three lanes wide. I knew he'd have to stop. I swung right and came up on his passenger side. We rolled to a halt simultaneously, and I smiled up at the crew cab, my left arm hanging out the window. If the skinny boy had not seen my tattoos when he blew past in the turning lane, he'd seen them now. And though my four left fingers read K N O X, he need not be a genius to figure my right.

For the record, Knox is my last name by birth, and my Uncle Hubert nick-named me Hard when I fell out of a dogwood tree at four years old, so I feel more entitled than most to the moniker's permanence on my fists.

Albert turned off the music.

"What exactly is it you ain't skeert of?" I asked the skinny boy.

"Fuck you wigger," he answered from on high.

I laughed. I tried to get a look at the driver, but couldn't. I saw no heads in the second row.

And just like that, the light was green and ole sparkle-job was off and roaring again.

"Oh, it's on!" Albert said, and indeed it was, though I hated to pass the Rally's drive-thru without scoring a Big Buford.

We played little lane-changing games all the way through Hal Greer Boulevard, and once we'd crossed Twentieth Street, I tucked in again behind him and both vehicles settled into that perfect pace for catching green lights just in time.

He slowed down after we crossed the bridge, then yanked a hard left down to the river's access ramp. He pulled alongside a fat cylindrical bridge pylon. Someone had spray painted on it in high-sheen black: *LaJoye Mishell Teeter took a dump right here.* There was nobody around and nothing parked down there but an old fogged Airstream and an unhitched box trailer half-full of dead green onions.

The driver was out of his elevated crew cab just as soon as he'd thrown it in park.

He was sizable—I guessed 5'11, 230—but the bulk of his meat hung loose. He'd not seen the weight room in a while. His maroon sweatshirt had the arms cut off at the shoulder and read Brown University across his fatuous pectorals.

The skinny boy stayed in the cab. I squinted to see about a rear window gun rack, but couldn't tell.

Big Boy was running his mouth as he came. I'd yet to reach the flat pad of the access ramp, but I put it in park anyway, steep-graded and nose-down, and I put my hand on Albert's arm to signal how we'd play it.

Here's what Big Boy was saying: "You're lucky I didn't mash the brake and tear up that new grill!"

One of his shower shoes was duct-taped and his toenails needed cut. He'd let his beard hair grow wild on his neck.

I asked him if he was an alumnus of Brown.

He ordered me out of the car.

I left the keys in the ignition, told Albert that every single day was a gift from Jah, and made a slow show of the whole dismounting procedure. I kept my smile on all the while.

I am a tall man and keep in good shape. I've already mentioned the tattoos.

I shut the car door. "I followed you because of your decision to disrespect that funeral cortège," I said.

Big Boy didn't know whether to shit his panties or run and hide. Still, he tried to keep up his act. "How do you know I don't have a medical emergency?" he asked.

"Well do you?"

"No, but how could you know?"

Albert was listening from the car. "Are you fucking joking me you dumb cracker?" he called. He punched the dashboard.

"Hey!" I said. "Watch the maple trim!"

Big Boy squinted at Albert. The front windshield was half inside the bridge's shadow.

I knew he was trying to figure out if Albert was white or black. Everybody always did. Albert's mother was what we used to call "half and half" and his daddy was straight white.

"Sorry, Stan," he said.

I knew he wanted to hit somebody in the face. He'd always been that way. High-tempered, like his mother ZiZi, who had drunk herself to death but was once a master theremin player. I gave him a look to remind him he was thirty-nine years old and didn't need a broken hand on top of a bad wheel.

When I looked again at Big Boy, he was swallowing the way some men do when their mouth goes dry. I watched his big round neck roll like a tiny wave beneath the stubble. "Listen," I said. "This is not a major metropolitan area. This is Mosestown."

"I know where it is," he said. "My mother was born and raised here."

"What's her name?"

"Gail."

"I meant her last name."

"Gillenwater."

"She kin to Mudge?"

"Not that I know of."

The bill of the skinny boy's ball cap peeked from the cab, and for a moment I had a terrible vision of him throwing open the door and leveling a firearm in our direction, and I could hear the short-muzzled cracks and see the beautiful convexity of my new front windshield interrupted by tiny holes, Albert dropping to the floorboards inside, his humongous ankle throbbing.

"What I mean by Mosestown not being a major metropolitan area," I continued, "is that it remains a place where people don't need to blow their horn and hijack the right-of-way in a funeral cortège situation."

He took a deep breath. I saw him looking at the inside of my wrist, where the words "Unto Thee I lift up mine eyes" were inked above my old playing number, 44. I watched Big Boy start to use his brain.

"You're Stanley Knox," he said. He looked me up and down. His eyes had gone wide. He said, "I saw you score fifty-two against Morehead State back in the day."

I nodded.

"You made fifteen threes in one game."

"I know I did."

"NCAA record."

"I know it was."

"I thought you was in France."

"Nope." It always went down this way. They registered who I was, and the rest was like a script.

"Hey, Albert!" Big Boy called over his shoulder, and for a moment, I was very confused.

The skinny boy stuck his head all the way out and looked at us, dead-eyed.

"This is Stanley Knox, the basketball player."

"I don't give a fuck."

I laughed and I could hear Albert doing the same behind me.

"Your passenger's name is Albert?" I inquired.

"Yes." He scratched at that mess of neck hair.

"Hey!" I called to the truck. I pointed back at my new ride. "His name's Albert too."

"I don't give a fuck about that neither." He put his head back inside. He was a funny one, I'll give him that. Used his profanity in a congenial sort of way.

It was then that I saw the little black hasp raise on the dark rear window of the crew cab. The middle panel slid to the side, and for a moment, I had the terrible vision and heard again the crack of gunfire and pictured poor Albert hitting the deck and sniffing at the custom dragon floormats. But the fingers that pulled the sliding glass were just little things, the size of vienna sausages, and suddenly there was a round face in the opening and a nest of brown curls, and some manner of chocolate smeared uniformly around the mouth. She was no more than three. She sneezed twice rapidly.

"Shut that window!" the skinny boy shouted.

I said to Big Boy, "You have a child in there?"

He was looking back at the truck again. "Shut it, Sansa," he said.

It wasn't a name I'd have guessed.

He looked at me again and seemed to surmise my thoughts. He said, "My wife loves *Game of Thrones*."

"I keep hearing about that show," I said.

"You ain't never seen it?" Big Boy was incredulous.

I shook my head. I told him I didn't watch much TV.

"Let's go, Stanley!" Albert called from the car.

And that's when I heard a pop and a groan from high above, and I know I flinched before I looked up to see a leaning tower of old white washing machines stacked double on a speeding flatbed, falling. A tie-down had snapped clean. There was ample sparking when the first one hit the cast-concrete sidewall of the bridge and kicked back onto the road. The sound was tremendous, a raking of metal high-pitched as a red fox fight. The second washer hit the sidewall and came off on our side, and I watched it spinning down at us, and it was as if I was living inside a dream then, every object so unstoppable and every limb so unmovable and numb. The lid of the washer swung open and slammed shut as it rotated on the air. Its black cord whip-cracked like a devil's tail, and the whole whirling mass made a line for the sparkled Silverado as if drawn there by some industrial magnet. I wished that such occurrences were not possible in life, and I wanted nothing more than to shut my eyes, but I did not, and the washing machine touched down with an absurd brand of violence, smack in the middle of the eight foot truck bed, and again the sound was tremendous, and the truck's tires appeared to bounce a foot off the ground, and all around the downed appliance, Big K soda cans no doubt meant for the Cashin Recyclerly burst upwards like a timed fountain.

It was something.

All was still, quiet as could be.

The face of the little girl was absent from the open sliding window for only a moment, and then there she was again, same expression on her face, same smear of chocolate.

The skinny boy screamed like a child and I could see him crawling over the seat to get to her.

The cans had hit the asphalt and were rolling around lazy. Albert limped over to me, and Big Boy had run for his truck.

I looked up to see about travelers on the bridge, but there was no sign that any motorist had taken note.

Albert called 911 on his device and I patted Big Boy on the shoulder. I'd never seen a human sweat like he was sweating then, and I don't imagine I ever will again.

He held his little girl tight against him and hummed and did a little bobbing kind of dance with his knees, circling the pylon where the vandal had marked his bowel movement.

That little girl never did make a sound.

And all the while, the skinny boy moaned and wailed from inside the cab, like some drugged woman at a public funeral, stricken with a brand of grief and madness that can only come out by way of the windpipe.

It took me a while to make out what he was saying over and over. "She's my only niece," he said. "She's my only niece."

I looked at Albert and we nodded. We'd need to skedaddle before the authorities arrived, for there was no doubt the lingering smell of marijuana about us. I took the roach from my watch pocket and swallowed it.

I winked at the little curly-headed girl and patted Big Boy on his shoulder again. Then I squeezed it, hard, and I looked him in the eyes. "Remember," I told him, "a funeral procession is a solemn occasion, and if we don't yield right-of-way to its vehicles, we are worthless."

He nodded a little bit.

I thought momentarily of going on, of asking him to imagine how none of this washing machine foolishness would have ever transpired if he'd just stayed in line until the cortège had run its course. But he was doing that swallow again, the one that men do when they can't produce enough spittle to speak or make a move. I have always felt sorry for men with this condition.

"Let's get to gettin," Albert said.

He was already limping back to the car.

Vince Trimboli

SOLVO

The low sky, hung
low over the arboretum and

shattered with cries
of birds; say Loon

and let it sound
like someone lingering.

Say Sparrow—see
how it feels like sorrow's

letters in your mouth.
We rarely say the things we mean

or mean what we say,
see, Starling or Myna,

be un-fettered: Loon,
Starling, say Tern—

how the longest migration is
from there to here.

Jessie van Eerden

EDNA

It's not such a big world anymore, that's what they said, and I made fun, I said the globe does fit in your hands, but to me the world always felt large and I wanted all of it for myself. Elizabeth got the Internet on her computer; she read the news from fourteen different countries, could tell me the weather in London; the world's as small as this screen, she said. Esther could lie in the clover and swear she felt the pulse of children and mothers on the other side of the earth, straight through the middle, through all the lava and tar. How could the world be big when she could feel the heartbeat of anyone as if she held them in her arms? And Ron Malynn, my husband of fifty-six years, Ron said it was the transportation systems: the interstate highways that Eisenhower laid out, I-81 right over our town, Lace, Virginia, and anyone from California could zoom past overhead; then the flights, hop a plane for anywhere, like our son the newsman does, but Ron never flew anyplace, he never set foot out of Virginia.

They're all three dead, and only now am I the one saying it, that the world is not big, it is small. All places are one place, collapsed and brought into a circle. If I had to say what it looks like, I'd say it's a circle around a bullfight; all the world is that bull in the center of the ring and I am the bullfighter, maybe every person is, in their own vision of it. Of course, this is nonsense beyond an old woman's feeling, but I don't know how else to describe the way it feels to want the world—for my greed is still great—when that world will not be had.

My rest is fitful, I do not really sleep anymore, just catnap, so I am often in the bullfight, in that big circle that is, in truth, a small, small circle. I feel the hot breath of the bull on my face, and I smell the metal tang of the ring through its nose. The world that will not be had.

What I mean is, it is upon me, my lifetime, my fate, this world, and each time I'm in the center of the ring I think I'll win, it will all be mine, but I don't. I was a hungry young girl and I am a hungry old woman. The bull charges me, then escapes me, and in its eye, a gleam; maybe the world is so small it's the very eye of the bull. In its eye there is the soap, the turkeys, there is Jimmy Flax without a face.

It may be that what I want is someone to get me out of the ring—and maybe that means I want forgiveness, or death—but there is no one to do it. It's true I live here with my daughter, her husband, and my granddaughter; they are right in front of me in this big house, a nice house that Ron and I bought, the kitchen he repapered for me in a red apple and birdhouse design, the house in which I was twice unfaithful to him; there were infidelities for both of us. I live in this same house with them, but if there is an *other side of the world* they are on it; they know nothing of the eye of the bull. For me, here in my nightdress and old-woman blue skin like paper, fitful and hungry at night, in the center of the ring: all the world rushes at me. It is soap, it is turkeys, it is Jimmy Flax without a face.

I am not out of my head. I can explain such a world as this, even if I cannot claim it for my own and make its outcome something other. Do not think me demented, as Esther Nash was; a sweet demented girl from childhood, we knew it even then, in the forties. I can explain, and I can begin with Esther because it was she who brought me to meet Jimmy Flax at the county fair in Ridley.

We were fifteen. Esther had a hum and a giggle and a sigh, that was her way; she flopped at her pretty neck like a doll, and she had Jimmy and me meet under the bleachers where the marching band was playing. Elizabeth Maslow shunned boys but came with us to see the python snake in the Marvel Tent, and she got Esther to go with her. His thick hair went in black waves over his head, his face like a book I could read over and over, and strong arms, I could picture his arms and chest under his shirt the minute I saw him, and I could also tell he was penniless, the dusty smell of him, his thinness despite his muscle, a white shirt worn by many brothers before him, shoes too, for I had three brothers and that was also the way it was for us. We were poor, and the year I was fifteen, that was about the time I started to hate it. Jimmy didn't speak under the bleachers, nor did I. There was just brass and drums out on the field; we put our heads close together to look through the seats, through people's legs, at the blue band uniforms out there in rows. I was a well-shaped girl, and I could tell that, when he wasn't watching the blue band, Jimmy Flax could picture what was under my clothes too, the curves beneath my dress. Never in my life had I wanted to be touched by a boy's hands so badly, and his keeping-apart, his not touching me, was like warm water poured over me. We started to go together and we were steady for the summer.

That was also the summer I helped Janey Drummel make her soaps for a quarter a batch. Because this was around the time I began to understand that we, the Turners, were poor, I recognized that Janey Drummel was too and that she had no quarters to spare, but gave me work anyway, because the task was too detailed for her stiff hands and because she had sugar diabetes and her eyes were going weak. And because she was kind, and I did not like her kindness, for I knew I would not be so kind were I in her place. She gave me a quarter and, each time I entered her dismal kitchen, she gave me a kiss on my neck, below my earlobe; she was a small bowed-forward woman, stooped over. I could smell the cold beets she ate, and their bitter greens, and the pinch of Skoal pouched in her lower lip. I could smell the iron in the water heating in large pots on her stove, and I pressed my heel into the yellow linoleum that had a little give to it because of its black scarring from the coal and ash that coughed out each time a log was laid on the fire. And she was cold even in summer and I knew the bruises on her backside went wide and far, down onto her thighs, a dull violet, because she pressed so hard for warmth against the stove.

When I came on Wednesdays and Saturdays to work for her, the kiss she had for me, on my young-girl neck below my earlobe, it told me that we shared a secret and I did not want to know that secret, the secret of poor people.

Janey Drummel made soaps for rich women in Lace and Ridley. She bought cheap cakes of plain Ivory soap, and she collected Jackson & Perkins rose catalogs. My job was to cut out the pictures—yellow roses, peach, deep red, white—for she could no longer cut carefully around the small pictures. I filled her cigar box with cut-outs of roses, the real versions of which we could never order. They were blush tea roses and floribunda, with names like Champagne, Cornelia, Duchess, Scent from Above, Always and Forever. Janey Drummel took a pan that smelled of corn and burnt oil and she melted the paraffin till it gurgled on the stove. She squinted and took a wet rag and moistened the top of each Ivory soap bar and applied a catalog cut-out rose, then dipped the surface, barely, into the hot paraffin to make a soap picture, its rose bloom sealed in place, a pretty bar of soap to sit at the sinks of wealthier women.

One of those women was Lora Gibson whose husband had gotten rich drilling gas wells and they lived in the mansion once owned by the Laces, Loren and Harper Lace for whom our town was named. Along with cutting out roses from the catalog, I made Janey Drummel's deliveries for her. At summer's end—it was almost September and cold too early, for that time of year—I had to make a delivery to Lora Gibson, a basket of ten soaps for how many bathtubs, sinks, wash basins, lovely throughout that house? Janey Drummel gave me a kiss, gave me a quarter. Jimmy Flax said he'd walk me, and he held my hand, and I was feeling my youth, the way you do on such a cool day, but there was a gnawing hunger inside me, and I didn't confuse it with my body's burning for Jimmy Flax's hands touching me in the dark, no, it was something else, something he could not satisfy. It had to do with those soaps, my bouquet in the basket that smelled, not of roses, but of cheap Ivory and of flecks of snuff and of wax. We were fifteen and it was cold and the birds stirred; we saw a turkey hen in the woods, though it was too early in the year for turkeys to make themselves known. We were fifteen and Jimmy was talking of marrying me, how we'd build a lean-to off his parents' house at first but then get our own, and he would have a cordwood business, he thought that was the best idea, and maybe Janey Drummel would let me take over her soap picture business. The hunger in the pit of me turned sharp as a blade toward him, unkind. He said, The world is ours, Edna. That was the difference between Jimmy and me, he wanted for nothing, he thought he already had it all. I was greedy for everything and knew it would never yield itself to me, to my hands smelling of Ivory, paraffin, dull scissors, holding that basket.

I went alone inside the Gibsons' mansion with its pillars, its sure brick, its high ceilings. Lora Gibson came to the door in a silk robe, it was afternoon, she glinted for all the gold dangling from her ears, around her throat. Her daughter Bea, my age, sat there bored, her feet up on the table in perfect little slippers, and beside her sat some boy I did not recognize. He was older, his eyes metal-green, his hair thin and limp and gelled like older men did their hair and it made him look even older than he was. Miss Turner, said Lora Gibson, these are lovely, I love handmade things, come in, my daughter Beatrice you know from school, and this is my nephew Ron Malynn, he's come from Roanoke to work for Mr. Gibson in the office. Ron stood up and, like Jimmy, he looked at me as if my dress were not there, head to toe, and though he was not handsome, I was glad for the cold that had made my body, my breasts, so alert. Unlike Jimmy, this older boy had no simplicity in his face, no clearness that let you see deeply, read deeply; he had shoes shined black, uncracked, worn only by *his* feet, his gray trousers pressed so that, when he stood, they fell in a swoosh at the cuff, like Lora Gibson's silk. Watching me, he walked to the archway in the hall and stood, hand in his vest pocket, and I thought, Some stand in the archway and fill it up, and some stoop, bend their backs, cower and serve, and I would be the tall, vast, straight one, like this crisp unlikeable boy. We both knew what we wanted. I had found a greed that matched my own. I would not be Lora and Bea Gibson, I would be finer, Harper Lace herself, in the archway.

Mrs. Gibson gave me a whole dollar, and it shamed me.

Outside, I could not find Jimmy Flax. It was as if he'd read my thoughts, already saw me turning my back to him and his plans for us, so I started walking along the road alone, walking tall, then taking the path through the woods that we'd walked together earlier. I came to the rise that was hill enough to hide the woods floor ahead, and all at once there was a flock of turkeys filling the air, flying and squawking, maybe fifteen altogether, maybe more. They burst from among the trees, wild, a wide wingspan like that of a more majestic bird; they whipped fine young branches back so that the woods shivered, such a spectacle, feathers drifting down, birds above me, over me, over the rise into other trees, and here came Jimmy waving his arms and running behind them, scaring up this flock of turkeys for me. His face a beautiful book I could read cover to cover, beautiful pages, each one. The last turkey lighted in a tree and he laughed, Edna, how rich we are, he said. I wept, I put my Ivory hands to my face, my hunger so keen it cut, and I ran through the woods so fast that Jimmy couldn't catch me. I ran and ran and never gave Janey Drummel the dollar, I threw it in the weeds.

Ron didn't wait for me to graduate high school. We married when I turned eighteen in the October of my last year and I didn't finish, which enraged Elizabeth who would be valedictorian of our class, and which broke Esther's heart because she felt the breaking heart of Jimmy Flax. But I was intent, I married Ron Malynn and got a fine house and dresses and shoes and scarves and silk robes.

And Jimmy disappeared. It was Esther who told me, a year later, what happened to him, and because she was the way she was, crazy as a loon, I wrote to the newspaper office in Youngstown, Ohio, asking them to send me a newspaper, and I found out it was true: that Jimmy Flax had fallen in with thugs, he'd collected debts for them and had made good money, he was a high roller, then something went wrong and he was found in an alley in Youngstown beaten about the face, unrecognizable, his face, gone, his face.

That is the world as it rushes at me, that bull with barnacled horns, and such heat in its body, all of time and space a gleam in its black eye. No, do not think me demented, for that is the world that leaves me starved in my nightdress, in my restless rest, until one of these nights when its head will lower and it will charge and it will gore me, in the center of the ring, my blue old skin run through at last, and they will not throw down real roses, long-stemmed, from the bullfight stands, no, they will toss down the cut-outs from the Jackson & Perkins catalogs, they will shake them out from the over-turned cigar box, Champagne, Cornelia, Duchess, fluttering paper, light, too many to number.

Doug Van Gundy

COUNTRY MUSIC

———

It's a high trebly sound all piled up on the heart
until it's spilling out through the nose
of an AM radio, that sweet anguish
of knowing you're not crazy
for feeling so blue, that

while nothing is ever going to salve the wound
in your heart, at least there is someone
who has been down this way before
and had the wisdom & foresight
to bring along a guitar.

Late in the night, when the ache gets as bad as it gets,
and the moon is as pale & as gold as a draft beer,
the atmosphere takes on the hard
sheen of polished wood on a
VFW dance hall floor,

and the signal skips all the way across the sky from WSM, Nashville
to the blue hollows of the green Alleghenies, pushed hard by
fiddles and guitars and 50,000 crackling watts. Here,
brothers and fathers, sisters and mothers,
cousins and next-door neighbors

gather around the lighted dial of the vacuum tube oracle,
or sit alone on the bench seats of idling pickup trucks
to learn just how their cheatin' hearts
will tell on them, or be coaxed
into going honky-tonkin'

or simply lulled into sweet dreams by the whiskeyed honey
of voices that got just far enough away
from these mountains
to get flung back
home.

John Van Kirk

BEAR COUNTRY BLUES

———————

At first the bears were standoffish, not rude exactly, but distant, reserved, protective of their privacy. Ray had been warned about feeding them, but that was far from his mind anyway. In fact, he was largely unaware of the bears for the first couple of weeks, just trying to make a go of it, to get the cabin in shape, keep himself supplied with food and fuel. The nearest store was an hour away, half of that along a rutted jeep trail, passable only by the burliest vehicles with plenty of clearance. A heavy chain and padlock closed that trail off from the hard road. Ray didn't have a vehicle, anyway. He had taken a bus out from the city carrying his stuff, which he piled up on the front porch of the general store. It had taken three trips to get it downstairs from his apartment to the cab that took him to the bus station, and it took four trips to carry it all from the store to the cabin.

The bears, for their part, were aware of him as soon as he made that first trip up the path, carrying a large, odd-shaped case in one hand and awkwardly towing a suitcase on wheels, last year's leaves crunching under his feet. They knew something about the sort of people who came to the woods to live: survivalists, loners, refugees from the industrial world, often people who were broken in some way. Hunters they could recognize, too, but rarely did hunters actually move out into the woods; they just came for the day or, occasionally, a couple of days. And Ray, the bears could clearly see, wasn't a hunter or a survivalist—he didn't have the equipment and he didn't have the skills. The bears watched his lumbering treks up and down the trail with amusement and grudging compassion. They preferred that humans stay out of the woods, but it had long been clear to them that this was not a reasonable expectation, so they liked to know what sort of people had come to live near them. Ray seemed a good sort. That first night, after he'd finally carried everything inside, he'd simply disappeared. No lights shone from his windows; no smoke came from the chimney. But the next morning he'd opened up all the doors and windows of the cabin and spent most of the day sweeping, dusting, straightening the place out. He whistled as he unpacked the grocery bags of canned goods, and they liked that. They actually feared for him when they watched him chop wood, so careless and clumsy was he with the axe.

That second evening, after he'd eaten his supper of beans and rice cooked on a Coleman stove, Ray came out on the front porch with a cup of hot tea and his guitar. He took it out of its hard case, tuned it up, and began to play a song that he'd been working on ever since he'd watched his apartment building recede through the window of the bus:

> I could stay and wait for you, baby,
> But I know you ain't coming back.
> My days have all turned gray,
> And my nights are solid black.
> > So, I'm leaving, babe,
> > leaving the town where you left me
> > I know you won't come looking,
> > but if you do, you won't find me.

The nights were cold at first, but as the trees began to leaf out and the sunsets turned from gray to purple and red, the cabin seemed to hold the warmth of the afternoon sun well into the dark hours. The short gray evenings grew longer, and Ray would build his fire later and later. Before long, even if the fire had gone out by morning, which it nearly always did, he still woke comfortable in his bed, the dawn now a warm gold instead of the cold silver it had been when he'd first arrived. His ability to do his daily chores improved, and he gained fluidity and confidence, in only a few weeks time looking, if not like a seasoned veteran of rural life, at least not like a danger to himself. After eating his supper, he would sit out on the porch with his guitar, and the bears would listen from beyond the edge of the clearing, just out of sight, though sometimes he sensed that he wasn't alone.

He began to explore the surrounding woods, finding the scat of a large animal on his first hike, though he couldn't identify it. *I knew somebody was out there listening to me play*, he thought. It was some time, however, before he saw them. He'd dug out his harmonicas that evening, placed the rack around his neck, clamped one into it, and started to pick out his usual slow blues. No sooner had he begun to wail a little on the harmonica than he saw movement in the bushes. Then across an open space he saw what he thought was a huge dog, a Rottweiler, maybe, almost black with a brown muzzle. It scared him, the idea of a wild dog in his woods, and he instantly stopped playing. He stood up and walked to the railing, and he saw the animal again, this time moving more slowly, ambling off into the depth of the forest, and he realized it was no dog.

Ray's place was less than half an afternoon's walk from the bears' den, well within the territory they called their own. They'd spend their days foraging, feasting on willow catkins and new leaves until the catkins dried and the leaves turned bitter. By then they'd located the best rotting logs for grubs and ant larvae, and they watched for the first berries to appear. The woods were filling up with birdsong, and in the evenings with Ray's music. The bears adjusted their rounds to pass by the cabin at about the time he'd play, gradually becoming more casual about letting themselves be seen. The first time he caught a glimpse of the second, larger bear, he decided they were a pair and gave them names: Ursula and Bruno. He'd watch for them as he tuned up, peering into the bushes at the edge of the clearing around his cabin, and missing them on the occasional evenings when he didn't see at least some sign of their presence. And so the weeks went by, the days growing longer and the nights shorter, Ray adjusting to life in the woods, the bears adjusting to having him as their neighbor.

Ray was not a fisherman, but one of his friends had pressed a rod, reel, and a fancy box full of flies on him. "There's some little creeks back in there, and they're bound to have some brook trout in them," the friend had said. "I tied these flies special for these conditions." Now, in the green light of an early summer afternoon, Ray was trying to remember what his friend had shown him. Sneak up on the pool. Get the fly to float from the head of the pool to the tail. If nothing happens after a few tries, just move further upstream. It took a few tries before he got his fly into the water at all, but after losing several in the bushes, nearly falling into the first pool and thrashing the second with a hard slap of line, he watched the tiny tuft of feathers land softly on the surface of the water and float gently with the current. Splat. Something hit it, and he yanked back on the rod, snatching the fish—probably no more than six inches long—right out of the water and flinging it behind him into the woods. When he retrieved his line the fish was gone, and though he searched among the leaves, he never found it.

The bears had been watching from a discrete distance as he stumbled awkwardly over the slippery rocks, confirming their estimation of him as an outsider and pathetic woodsman. He sloshed right through the fishiest water, heading further up the narrow stream until he found one more pool. The smooth surface shone black under the canopy of leaves, and Ray took his time. He crouched down a little ways below the pool, moved his rod slowly through its arc in a test swing, and made a perfect cast. The fly touched down in the foam where a low waterfall poured into the pool from above. Then there was a splash, a flash of green tail, and the line went taut. Ray lifted the rod gently and felt the quiver of the living fish on the other end. Easy, he told himself, easy. The line moved about the pool, following the path of the fish, invisible below the surface, and it was like being connected to more than just a fish—it was like being hooked into the life force of the forest itself. He carefully worked the fish over to the bank and lifted it from the water. About nine inches long, its back was mazy with dark lines, its sides marked with lovely red and pale blue spots, and its dark fins were lined with white on their leading edges. He took it into his hand to get the hook out of its mouth, and it felt as smooth as satin. The hook was nowhere to be seen. He followed the line into the fish's mouth and, feeling uncomfortable, shoved his finger deep down its throat, trying to dislodge the hook, but to no avail. Impatient, he pulled on the line. The fish, which had been wriggling in his hand, shuddered and lay still. He felt something tear and then saw blood run from the gills. *You're supposed to cut the line when they swallow the hook*, he remembered, and fumbled for his pocket knife. When he put the fish back in the water, hoping against hope it would flick its tail and swim away, it turned belly up and floated downstream, a white dead thing.

Ray looked around and saw that the light was beginning to fail. He picked up the rod and headed back downstream, looking for familiar landmarks, wondering how far he had come in the course of the long afternoon, moving from pool to pool. He had killed two fish, both due to carelessness and inexperience. He stumbled into a hole, caught himself, then nearly fell the other way. The color had gone out of the woods; the gray of evening would soon melt into the black of night. He wasn't sure he'd make it back to the cabin before dark, but he had to be careful. He picked his way slowly along, staying to the creek, watching for the path that would take him back to his cabin, not sure he'd recognize it. The sky turned pink and gold, underlit by the sun that was already out of sight. As he looked up at the fish-scale pattern of clouds, his foot hit a slippery rock and shot out from under him. He flailed his arms, tried to catch himself, clawed at the air as he went down, landed briefly on his butt, slipped further and cracked his head... hard. He registered the impact, then all motion stopped and the last light seeped out of everything.

He came to with a terrible pain in the back of his head. It took him a moment to remember what had happened, figure out where he was. He had fallen in the creek bed, but as his eyes began to focus he saw that he wasn't there now. A broad expanse of starlit sky was visible above him. He lay flat on his back in the clearing in front of his cabin.

He crawled painfully up the steps and made his way into his bed without taking off his wet clothes. In the morning he found himself scuffed and bruised all over his body, his shirt nearly shredded at the shoulders and sleeves, but except for the serious lump on the back of his head, he had no other significant injuries.

That evening, having put the fishing gear away and promising himself he wouldn't try that again, Ray stood at the edge of his porch with his guitar in hand.

"I guess I've got to thank you," he said aloud, pitching his voice toward the opening in the bushes where he'd seen the bears. "So I've put you in my song." Then he sat down, with the guitar on his knee and sang the new verse he'd written that afternoon:

> Living with the bears, now baby,
> Up in the woods so far away,
> And you know I'm never lonely,
> No matter what those bears might say.
>> Yeah, I'm gone now, babe,
>> Left that town where you left me,
>> I know you won't come looking,
>> But if you do, you won't find me.

As the summer passed, the little glade in front of Ray's cabin was frequently visited by rabbits, who lazily chewed the tufts of wild grass. Raccoons got into his garbage one night, and after that he was careful to close the lid tightly and weight it with a heavy log. Ray would awaken in the morning to the chatter of chickadees and the singing of robins and cardinals; often at night he would hear the call and response of barred owls. And every evening he would sit out on the porch and play his guitar and harmonica, mixing old songs with new, ballads with folk songs, but always working his way back to the blues. One afternoon while walking in the woods he came upon a tiny glass bottle, like an old prescription bottle. It fit perfectly over his pinky. That night he tried it out as a slide, and at the new sound coming from his guitar, the bears once again let themselves be seen, Ursula, as before, less shy than Bruno, who never came fully out into the open. So the weeks went by, long dry days, warm evenings of fireflies, Ray's guitar and harmonica, and the accompaniment of the crickets and cicadas. Acorn season came, though it was not much of a crop, and the bears, foraging farther and wider as the woods dried up, still came to their spot just outside Ray's clearing nearly every evening, listened to him play, and waited for rain.

Early in the fall, Ray was walking a high steep trail where he could see the panorama of turning leaves, the forest from above a subtle palate of reds, yellows, oranges, and browns. He sat on a rocky overlook and unpacked his lunch of tuna fish and crackers. Below him the autumnal forest stretched out, and above pearly cloud formations roiled and swirled into constantly changing shapes, occasionally lit by pink and gold flashes of internal lightning. The rain first came in fat heavy drops, and Ray was soaked to the skin before he made it halfway back to his cabin. The trail turned muddy, and he slipped and fell several times before he finally scurried up the stairs onto his porch, chilled to the bone. He stripped down, built a fire, and crawled into bed, where he remained for the rest of the day.

The rain continued, heavy, soaking rain that filled the creeks and carved deep into their dry banks. Some of the oldest trees, their support carved out from under them, fell across the rushing brown water. Ray kept his fire going, waking up in the night to stoke it, until he ran out of dry wood. Then he nearly froze. He forced himself to go out into the rain and haul a stock of firewood up onto the porch, but it was soaked through and he couldn't get it to burn. Over the next few days, he opened the door from time to time to watch the rain fall and listen to the sound of the wind in the thrashing leaves. He tried to read, but often ended up falling asleep, curling up tight under all the blankets he had.

The bears lounged in their cave, looking out through the curtain of falling rain and thinking of juicy berries and fat hazelnuts and beginning to grow sleepy. It would be a hard winter, they knew, and the man in the cabin wouldn't make it without them to watch out for him. When the rains let up, they watched Ray's place closely, hopeful for signs that he would be heading back to the world of men soon, but they saw just the opposite. He was spending more and more of his day cutting wood, piling it up on the porch now, clearly stocking up for winter. He made an effort at chinking the cabin, and even climbed up on the roof to nail down a couple of loose shingles, very nearly falling off.

It was Ursula who made the first move. One night, after the light inside the cabin had gone out, she charged through Ray's clearing and took a swipe at the garbage can, flinging it up against the cabin with a noise that carried through the woods like an explosion.

The next day Ray cleaned up the mess, dug a deep hole, and buried the garbage. The can was bent almost in half, and bore the marks of Ursula's claws, two of which had actually torn through it. Ray banged it back into rough shape with a rock, scrubbed it out, and took it inside the cabin. But he showed no signs of leaving.

A week or so later, while Ray was out walking, the bears broke into the house, trashing the Coleman stove, shredding Ray's bags of rice and dried beans, punching holes in his can of cooking oil, breaking his lantern. The next day he headed down the path, the suitcase on wheels in tow. The bears were relieved until they saw him coming back a couple of hours later, the suitcase now overflowing with new supplies.

The first frost came, the days dawning with a sparkle of silver, the nights growing longer and colder. The bears felt the great sleep coming on. They gorged when they could on nuts and late crab apples. And they kept watching Ray. When he hadn't left by the first snowfall they knew something drastic had to be done.

Ray sat on the porch in the late morning sun, a cup of hot tea by his side. The night had been bitterly cold, and though he'd stoked the fire before he went to bed, he'd awakened shivering, curling up under the blankets and taking a long time to get out of bed. Now, though the sun shone brightly, the air burned his nostrils, cold as dry ice. About an inch of snow lay on the ground in front of the cabin. Tree branches were tufted with white. Only under the thick pines was the leafy forest floor visible. Ray was trying to make a song out of the beautiful scene when he heard a muffled shuffling in the woods. He immediately thought it was Ursula making her rounds, but she seemed not to be passing the cabin, but approaching, coming nearer and nearer. The dry branches of the once green bushes at the edge of the clearing parted, and there was Bruno, looking right at him. Ray had glimpsed Bruno before, noting that he was larger than Ursula; now he could see just how much larger. No one would ever mistake Bruno for a Rottweiler as he had Ursula when he first caught sight of her. Bruno was massive, his shoulders broad, his body deep as an oil barrel, and he was coming straight toward the cabin. Ray froze in his chair, having thought many times about what he would do if he ran into the bears in the woods, but totally unprepared to meet them on his front porch. Bruno reached the steps, and then stood up on his hind legs and bared his teeth in a snarl. He was huge, taller than Ray, and probably weighed at least three hundred and fifty pounds. Ray stood up, too. He was more confused than afraid, but he was still very afraid. "I thought you were my friend," he said, as if he expected the bear to respond.

Bruno looked at him. The man just wasn't going to leave. Bruno bounded up the steps and cuffed Ray on the shoulder, sending him flying across the porch and into a chair, which broke under him. Bruno, on all fours again, walked over to the chair and grabbed one of Ray's legs in his teeth. Ray felt the teeth tear through his boot and pierce his ankle. The bear dragged him down the stairs and into the clearing. Ray caught a movement out of the corner of his eye—it was Ursula coming toward him. Bruno had let go, and Ray rolled over and up onto his hands and knees, then wrapped his arms around his chest, tucked his head down as far as he could, and huddled in the fetal position, expecting now to be mauled by both bears. But what happened was not what he expected. Bruno cuffed him again, knocking him over, and each bear grabbed an ankle in its jaws and started dragging Ray toward the jeep trail. Ursula's bite was firm, but it didn't break through the leather uppers of his boot. Bruno's jaws held him harder, and he felt a tearing and agonizing crunch in his right ankle. Pain shot all the way up his leg, passed in a terrible wave through his loins. He shuddered and passed out. Over the next half hour or so, he drifted in and out of consciousness as he felt himself being dragged roughly down the path, until the bears left him at the padlocked chain a few feet from the paved county road, where, shivering and aching all over, he managed to signal a passing car before going into shock.

When the bears woke up, grumpy and sore, they immediately saw signs the winter had been rough; the woods were full of downed and shattered trees. Hard, brittle snow still lay beneath the pines. Ursula had given birth to a cub during the great sleep, and she had to look after it, so it was Bruno whose circuit of their territory first took him past Ray's place. A tree had fallen into the side of the cabin, breaking some windows, and the lock on the front door had been jimmied, the door left wide open. The place had been cleaned out, but there was no way of knowing whether Ray had come back to get his gear or someone else had taken it. There was no sign of Ray for many weeks, but then, as the days were growing longer, the dawns turning from silver to gold, the evenings from gray to purple and red, a truck came lurching up the old trail. A comfortable, woodsy-looking man had driven Ray and all his gear right to the door. The two men unloaded the truck, Ray looking even more awkward than he had the year before, when the bears had watched him drag his suitcase up the path. The two men studied the broken lockset and window and then got back into the truck. Later Bruno and Ursula and their little cub watched as Ray made his way up the path alone. If bears wept, Ursula would have wept to see him hobble up that long path with his cane. He spent most of the afternoon inside the cabin, and they could smell first the smoke of his fire, and later the aroma of his dinner. It was almost dark by the time he came out onto the porch with his cup of hot tea and his guitar. He took a long time settling his injured leg into a comfortable position, cradling the guitar now between his legs instead of just resting it on one. Then he tuned up and started to play a slow blues, and after working on the tune a bit, he began to sing:

> The city's fine for winter
> To stay home and keep warm,
> But when the winter's over
> I head out on my own.

Going to the country, babe,
Live free among the birds and bears.
I know you won't come looking,
But if you do, you'll find me there.

A round black furry animal about the size of a raccoon tumbled out from the bushes into the clearing. Then Ursula came out and picked it up by the scruff of its neck and carried it back into the cover of the brush. Bruno was there, too, Ray was sure, staying out of sight, but keeping his eye on Ursula and the cub. And keeping an eye on Ray.

Erin Veith

RELAPSE MEANS I FORGOT TO BE BETTER

———

My childhood is tied up
in a country-western song and my father's bullet,
same melancholy echo.

I'm wondering about
my bravery, if I was born with it. Aren't you beautiful?
my mother asked

the apple tree. After,
the woods I went into were not dark or dangerous;
the road was where all

our pets got run over.
When I say suicide, I wonder about your wondering.
I can't tell you

what she became.
She killed copperheads. She built a blue house. She
carried me back out.

Took me two decades
to discover my suffering was a choice. So no, honey,
I wasn't born brave.

Bravery is my heart,
a little barbed wire for show. Like everyone else,
I grew up in a

moment of after.
I was raised by a wolf and a saint. That's the danger
inside of me

I'm aware of.

Ryan Walsh

THE FIELD

———————

We're down 5–2 and I've been watching fog
creep into the outfield from behind me,
thinking about the way summer
has already made a ghost of itself.
And when the big guy with the neck tattoo,
who's already scorched a double down the third-base line,
nails another one toward me, I'm not ready.
There's no fence to keep the ball
from rolling into the deep and unmowed
corners of the park. So I follow it there

looking for the grass-stained Spalding my dad and I
threw back and forth and back until dusk,
so as to keep out of Papaw Carter's house
that smelled of death, which is to say it smelled
of urine and of raw chicken thawing on the kitchen
counter and the years of mineral oil worked into the dark
wood furniture of the living room.
One of Papaw's farm cats slinks by. Splash of blood
on its white face. And I am looking for the ball,
keeping my eyes away from the house and the man
in the house who shares my blood. Whose purpled toes
had to be cut off to save the left foot. Whose purblind
pony paced a circle in the bare grass. Whose papery
voice was kept thin under blankets in August.

When he dies, Mom says his heart will fly
home to Jesus. And I picture the bloody form
like the red bird the cat dragged into the dooryard
rising over the farm, over
the low grey skies of Pruntytown,
vanishing beyond the mountains.
Papaw died in a room with the TV on
mute. I can't recall what happened
to that swayback pony nor the ball,
nor even where to find the plot
of earth where he's buried.

Someone is crying *Home* as the big guy rounds
third. *Home!* I leg it out to the taller grasses
now damp with end-of-summer evening.
And there in the grass is the ball.
Home. It seems impossibly far.

Randi Ward

DADDY LONGLEGS

I'm tired
of asking
you where
the cattle
have gone—
stop pointing
at me.

GRANDMA

———————

What's left of her
paces
the sagging porch
wearing
one sock,
crying
for the dogs.

Meredith Sue Willis

THE ROY CRITCHFIELD SCANDALS

It was the summer of 2000, and the political season was heating up, especially in West Virginia, where we had a young woman running for governor. She wanted to stop mountaintop removal coal mining. This is a hard sell in West Virginia where the coal companies own mostly everything, including the politicians. We had seen the ugly pictures of what they do to the hills down in the southern part of the state, but where we live, in the northern part of the state, they've been strip mining for a hundred years, and maybe we just got used to it.

Besides, that summer, we had something much more immediate to think about.

My fifteen-year-older half-sister had a scandal to tell us about. Vashie had been my third grade teacher, which she counts as raising me, but I don't. She was a terrible teacher, indolent and whiney. I'm retired from teaching and a widow myself now, and I avoid Vashie. I talk to her, but I don't drive her to the doctor, and I don't pick up her groceries. Her daughter Ruth doesn't either, but Ruth is an agoraphobic.

Vashie was even worse as a mother than as a third grade teacher.

We're all widows now, Vashie, Ruth, me, and my friend Ursula Rose, who was having the tag sale in front of her late husband's mansion the day Vashie waded through the sale tables leaning on her walker, lurching dramatically from time to time and pausing to rest when she thought we were watching her.

"Well ye gods and little fishies," said Ursula, glancing up from the cash box. "Look who's coming. Do you see who's coming, Ann?"

"I see her," I said. "She's planning to stage a fall, and we'll have to call the ambulance."

"You're always so mean to her," said Ursula. "I can't give her my chair because I'm taking the money. You'll have to give her your chair."

Ursula is a full-time bridge and golf player, cocktail drinker, and shopper. She has gone to Pittsburgh to shop at Kaufmann's at least once a month since she married Mr. Rose, and after he died, she started having tag sales to get rid of her purchases. The Rose mansion is the biggest house in town, overlooking everything, the Masonic Lodge and County Courthouse, the high school and the old fair grounds. It's a wonderful view, and that day there was a fresh breeze.

As Vashie got closer, she called out in her tiniest voice, "I've been having palpitations. I know I look fine, but my heart has been doing somersaults all morning."

Ursula said, "Ann's going to give you her chair, Vashie. I have to sit here and take money."

I got up. I'd planned to give her my chair all along. I pulled over a five gallon Christmas popcorn can from the sale. I'm fifteen years younger than Vashie, but it's more than age: I walk and I garden. Vashie sits all day peering out her window. So I asked her how she got up the hill.

"Caliph Savage drove me."

"I thought you and Caliph weren't on speaking terms." Caliph owns a lot of property around town and has money in the mining supply company and a string of coal trucks. He's also chairman of the board of trustees of the First Baptist Church of Kingfield.

"I've been advising him on hiring the new minister, and of course he never listens to me, and he made sure I wasn't on the search committee. In fact," and here she leaned forward and cut her eyes right and left to indicate something important was coming, "in fact, he told me they've hired an interim pastor. And you will never believe who Caliph Savage picked. To be interim pastor of the First Baptist Church of Kingfield. It's a scandal."

"Somebody we know?" said Ursula.

I said, "How can Caliph hire a preacher by himself? What happened to the search committee?"

"It's an *interim*. Besides, the search committee does whatever Caliph says."

You need to know that the Baptist church doesn't provide leadership the way, say, the Catholics do, or even the Evangelical United Methodists. There is no Baptist Church hierarchy to send you a new minister. Baptists get their preachers by stealing them from other Baptists. Search committees go around listening to preaching, and then the church sends out a Call, and then the preacher prays to find out if he's supposed to accept.

Vashie waited for us to ask for the name, and when we didn't, said, "Frankly, I think Caliph is getting senile. He was so handsome and smart, too, when he was young, and he ended up a dry-as-dust old tightwad. I practically had to beg him to bring me up here today, and then he wouldn't wait for me, he just abandoned me to get back however I can."

I tried to catch Ursula's eye, but she was taking ten cents from a little girl for a princess mug.

Vashie paused until Ursula was finished with her commercial transaction. "Well, are you going to guess?"

I said, "Just tell us, Vashie."

"I'm not even sure this *interim* is an ordained minister. He's been doing something with juvenile delinquents and before that he was some kind of political radical which means a Communist if you ask me." She pressed her lips together one more time, looked at Ursula, then looked at me. Finally, she said, "He hired that hillbilly hippy Roy Critchfield. To be interim pastor at the First Baptist church!" Then she settled her chin back in her neck and narrowed her eyes to get our reaction.

Ursula said, "Who's Roy Critchfield?"

Vashie snorted. "Ann knows. She taught him."

"He was in the very first class I taught at the high school," I said. He had been big and gangly, all his height in his legs so that his knees and feet always seemed to be sticking out in the aisles. I remembered wide shoulders and a terrible haircut, and how he cringed when you called on him. "He was from up on Salt Lick Run. He went to some kind of church that didn't allow them to do perfectly innocent things like sing in the chorus."

Vashie gave me a tiny nod with her eyes glittering, the closest to praise that I ever get from her, when I verify something she says. "That was because of his father, Preston Critchfield. Preston died a couple of years back and left his little shack to the boy. It's right next to Caliph's back acres. I have to think Caliph has something in mind about the property, hiring the boy."

"Well," I said, "he's not much of a boy now is he? He must be forty-five if he's a day."

Vashie said, "Roy's mother ran off and left them, and oh it was the biggest thing that ever happened. Preston used to come into town and stand outside where she was staying and shout that she was going to hell. There was always some kind of trouble around the Critchfields."

"You sure do remember the good parts, Vashie," said Ursula.

I said, "I think Roy wasn't allowed to play baseball either. *That* was the scandal, forbidding that poor boy to do what the other kids did."

"And then," said Vashie, "Roy went off and became a Communist and a drug dealer and wore his hair down to his waist!"

I didn't remember any of that part. I had had a vague sense that things had happened to Roy, but I might have been confusing him with a different boy from Salt Lick, one who died in Vietnam. I said, "Vashie, are you saying Caliph hired a drug dealer for a preacher?"

Ursula said, "Caliph might if the drug dealer was cheap enough."

At this point a woman we didn't know came up to ask Ursula the price of a glass vase. The woman didn't sound like she was from here. We had already had two cars with Maryland plates and at least one from Pennsylvania. I don't know how people find out about Ursula's yard sales, but they come from all around.

"I don't know what to charge for it," said Ursula. "What do you think, Ann?"

"I don't know," I said. "Is it good glass?"

"Probably."

The stranger woman's eyes opened wide, which suggested to me that *she* knew something about glass even if we didn't. "I'd offer a dollar," she said.

Vashie was right on it. "A dollar? That thing's Waterford crystal! Don't sell it to her for a dollar! She's a dealer, I can tell. She's going to go off and get eighty or ninety dollars for it! I'll pay you two dollars myself for it!"

The stranger said, "I'd go five."

"Six!" cried Vashie.

"Five dollars will be fine," said Ursula.

Vashie brings out the worst even in kindly souls like Ursula. I think our last preacher left because he couldn't stand Vashie sitting behind her curtain watching his family come and go and calling him in the middle of the night because her heart was palpitating.

Vashie shook her head. "That woman was laughing up her sleeve at you, Ursula. Sometimes I don't think you have good sense."

"Oh," said Ursula, "I just sell stuff for fun. I don't need the money."

"I wish I didn't need the money," said Vashie. "I wish I was in a position to throw money away. Me with the roof falling in on that old house and half the window locks broken so any evil young man could come right in and do what they do to women."

Ursula took a deep drag on her cigarette. "You ought to get the windows fixed, Vashie."

I wish she'd stop smoking. She has that cough, and she's always getting bronchitis, plus there are the tiny burns in her expensive clothes. It's prematurely aged her skin, too. I don't want to think about her lungs.

I said to Vashie, "So did you see Roy Critchfield? He was such a skinny boy. Did he ever fill out?"

Vashie shrugged. Narrative, not description, is her strong suit. "His hair isn't long any more. But let me tell you Roy Critchfield was a rough customer for many years. He had a job with the juvenile delinquents, which is the blind leading the blind if you ask me. Caliph found him camping out in his Daddy's house on Salt Lick. No water, no electricity. Caliph thought it was a vagrant and went to chase him out. But they talked, and Caliph found out that Roy had gone to seminary for a while and become a youth pastor."

Ursula said, "That sounds sort of admirable to me."

"For the First Baptist Church of Kingfield? A youth worker? Maybe not even ordained? When my daddy was the chairman of the board of deacons at the First Baptist we would never of had anything like that."

I have to admit, she gets to me when she acts like Daddy was only her Daddy and not mine. So I said, "When *my* daddy was chairman of the Board we didn't have women deacons either. It wasn't so wonderful, Vashie. But what I want to know is, why would Roy Critchfield accept?"

"He probably lost his other job. I don't know. And he gets the parsonage—"

"With running water and electricity," said Ursula.

"—that beautiful yellow brick parsonage that has housed some of the finest Christian men who ever lived. And now this poor excuse is going to try to head up the First Baptist Church of Kingfield!"

"Vashie," I said, "aren't you and I related to the Critchfields?"

"You are. Not me. Through your mother. I think this *Reverend Critchfield*'s mother was a second cousin to your mother. We are certainly no relation on Daddy's side."

So the first scandal was Caliph hiring Roy Critchfield at all. The second scandal was how bad Roy's preaching was. We've been losing membership for years, especially to a couple of nondenominational churches out on Corbin Creek, but we had a nice turnout for Roy's first sermon. I always sit in the back, and Vashie does too, in her wheel chair on the opposite side from me. The big surprise was when my great-niece Becky walked in. She's Ruth's daughter, Vashie's granddaughter, a big girl who rarely speaks, almost as antisocial as Ruth is agoraphobic.

I waved to Becky to join me. "Did Ruth send you for a report?" I whispered.

Becky ducked her head and shrugged. She wears her hair short and doesn't make eye contact. There are those who used to think she was a lesbian, but whichever way she goes sexually, she was born with the worst case of morbid shyness I've ever seen. I had her in high school, and she sat in the back and never raised her hand for anything.

Caliph Savage in his shiny old blue suit introduced Roy, who was remarkably recognizable after all these years. Wide shoulders, long legs, short torso, a little less concave in the chest than when he was a teenager, but still thin. His hair was thinner, too, and his clothes were as all-wrong as they had ever been: a brown suit jacket short at the wrists and wrinkled khaki pants. When he began to talk, you couldn't hear a word he said. We take public speaking seriously in the mountains, and we expect volume. Roy mumbled, reading from sheets of notebook paper that he held in front of his face.

Vashie said out loud, the excellent acoustics carrying her voice to every corner, "What's he saying?" and then a little later, "I can't hear a thing!"

Finally, Caliph Savage walked across the platform in his deliberate grim-faced way and fiddled with the switch on the pulpit mic. There was a great rumble as of thunder, and suddenly we could hear Roy's mumbling, very loud. Not the words, but the rhythm of the mumble.

On the positive side, his first sermon was short.

We sang "Blest Be the Tie That Binds," and Roy gave an acceptably loud benediction, and marched up the aisle to stand at the door and shake hands. I half expected him to run out in humiliation, but, no, he seemed to be enjoying greeting people. In fact, the line moved slowly, as if people were having a chat with him. I would have asked Becky what she thought, but she did one of her disappearing dodges, which is remarkable for a woman as tall as she is.

It turned out that while Roy was a terrible public speaker, he was personable and pleasant and was trading jokes and greetings like the Chamber of

Commerce. He and the whole congregation seemed to be having a downright good time getting to know each other. Vashie jumped the line, or rather, rolled, right over people's toes. She stared up from the wheelchair at me accusingly, "That was Becky. What was Becky doing here? Why didn't she have the good grace to come and say hi to her grandmother?" But then it was Vashie's turn to speak to Roy, and she talked to him longest of all. "I couldn't hear a thing," she shouted up at him. "You have to enunciate more clearly, Reverend!"

Roy seemed to be sincerely sorry, "Several people told me that," he said.

"I'll help you," said Vashie. "I'm a professional teacher, you know. And when I was a girl we studied elocution, so I'll help you improve your public speaking skills."

Roy, poor lamb, seemed to think that was a good idea and thanked her in advance for any help she could give. Then he saw me and his face lit up. "Mrs. Harding, how great to see you!"

"Well, Roy, it's good to see you, too." I say that to all my former students and I almost always mean it. "You sound like you're surprised I'm still alive."

"Your mother used to come to church here," Vashie broke in. She had locked her wheels right beside Roy as if she were part of the reception line. "After she left your father."

The people behind me leaned forward expectantly to see Roy's reaction to that.

"That was a sad time for my family," he said.

"Well," I said, "It's good to see you grown up, Roy. You seem to have turned out very well."

He laughed and shook my hand again, and again I had that feeling of being genuinely liked, and I understood why the line had been so slow leaving church. "I do apologize about the sermon," he said. "I haven't had a lot of experience preaching."

"We'll take care of it," said Vashie. "I'll give you a little practice, milk and cookies, I always take care of the pastor. I live right across the street, you know. You can always call on me." I passed on by, and she was still talking. "I'll just wait here while you finish greeting everyone," she said, "and then I'll let you take me over to my house."

Ruth phoned later that afternoon. We speak on the phone almost every day. I ought to go see her, but it's painful to go in that cluttered house. She said,

"Well, I hear my mother already has the new preacher in her clutches." In spite of agoraphobia, Ruth always knows what's going on. "I'm going to make Becky come again next week to tell me if he does better." Ruth's other kids are out in the world as teachers and engineers, but Becky, who I sometimes think might be a touch autistic, rarely does anything more social than her job attending to the library stacks at the university.

The second week's sermon was a big improvement over the first. Roy was still reading, and I'm pretty sure it wasn't his own words, but you could hear him. Becky wore an aqua summer dress that showed off her shoulders. She left during the benediction again, and Vashie rolled over to me and said, "Becky was here again? And had a dress on? And what about her hair? Her hair is different. What did you think of the sermon? I worked on it with him. The parsonage has a whole library of sermons, so all he has to do is pick one out and practice."

A little later in the summer there was a scandal over the sermon that Roy wrote himself. Most people were pretty pleased with Roy's work, especially with the youth. He had them into the parsonage and organized some hikes and softball games. He had discussions connecting Jesus Christ to the environmental movement that not everyone approved of, and he let a couple of the boys play electric guitars during the service. That didn't go over too well with some of the older folks, but it didn't rise to the level of a scandal.

Roy even collected money and hired a bus for a weekend to take the youth downstate to help rebuild someone's house. The most unusual thing about this bus trip was that Becky went along as one of the chaperones. Ruth and I talked about it a long time, how Becky had gone out and bought an overnight bag and some new shorts and slacks.

The scandalous sermon was a week after the bus trip, and it was without a doubt the best one Roy preached all summer. It was about the possibility that Jesus experienced a loss of faith. I don't know how closely people were listening, but for those of us who did, it was an eye-opener. Who ever thought of things like that? And if they thought of it, who would ever say it?

"We all want to know that someone really understands us," said Roy. "We Christians are taught that Jesus is the only one who can do that, and we're taught that he can do it because he experienced what it is to be human. But if all Jesus experienced in the way of being human was physical suffering—well, what kind of suffering is that? The worst human suffering isn't about physical pain. Our bodies shut down when we hurt too much. We pass out. But our brains can suffer on without end. The worst kind of human suffering is to lose hope.

"So my question is, how could Jesus really understand us if he never experienced despair or at least had serious doubts about what he was doing up on that cross?" Roy waited a few seconds, and then said, "'My God, my God, why has Thou forsaken me?' Jesus said that on the cross, and I believe he really meant it. That he really knew what it meant to stop believing. Not just to have a test of physical endurance, but to lose hope of God. And if he didn't know what that feels like, well, he was never truly human."

It gave me a little shudder. I don't spend a lot of time thinking about these things, but I had wondered about that, about why Jesus getting crucified was supposed to be so much worse than someone else getting crucified or the torture you read about in the paper every day or for that matter the suffering people go through with cancer.

Vashie had cupped her hands over her ears, which didn't mean she was listening but that she wanted people to think she was. Caliph Savage had his eyes closed. I think most of them blocked it out, that someone paid by the First Baptist Church could be standing up there saying Jesus Christ doubted the existence of God.

The ending rambled a bit. Roy said that if there is a heaven (and I'm sure he used the word "if"), that Jesus will let us all in because he understands, that he'll forgive us our disbelief. So we should pay attention to one another and be kind and (I'm sure he said this) try to stop them from ruining the mountains because we're part of this world and we're all in this together. When it was over, I shook his hand and thanked him. Most of the rest of them seemed to ignore what he had said the way you ignore an old person passing gas in public.

The final scandals were about sex and politics. Vashie called me to complain that Roy hadn't come home the night before. I said he probably just came in really late, but she said, no, there hadn't been lights even at 3 a.m., and he didn't answer the phone either.

"Maybe he's staying out at Salt Lick."

"Something is going on," said Vashie. "Where is he? What if I have a heart attack? Who will I call? What if someone breaks into my house?"

I said, "How were you getting through the night before he came to the parsonage?"

"Not well," she said. "All I know is, I heard a noise last night and called, and he never answered. I could have been murdered in my bed." She paused, and I could hear her breathing. Then she said, "I'll tell you what *I* think. *I* think he was out tomcatting."

It took her a couple of days to figure it out. She called me again, and as soon as I answered the phone, she started shouting. "You and Ruth! The two of you! My own daughter and my sister I raised like a daughter! How could you treat me like this?"

I said "What are you talking about, Vashie?" Knowing exactly what she was talking about.

"You've known about it for weeks and kept it from me! Ruth doesn't have the sense she was born with. Letting that fat Becky do whatever she pleases—"

"Becky is thirty-five years old, and she isn't really fat anymore."

"I don't care! She's living in Ruth's house, and Ruth should keep a leash on her. To *have an illicit affair* with the temporary preacher! To have a preacher who is an adulterer!"

"I think fornicator is the word you want," I said. "I don't think either Roy or Becky is married."

"Sneaking around in the night! First Ruth told me Becky has a boyfriend, and then she says 'Becky is entertaining menfolk!' Like it was a joke! I said 'Ruth this can't be allowed!' And do you know what she said to me? She said Becky deserves some pleasure in this life!" She had to stop and pant for a while before going on. "And besides, he's a-way too old for her."

I bit my tongue so I wouldn't say, And you're too old for *him*, sister.

"And that's not all. He came over to my house today as big as life bringing me my groceries and offering to take me to the doctor!"

"And you told him you couldn't accept help from a fornicator?"

"I let him know how I felt. I didn't say it in so many words, but I hardly spoke to him the entire time I was in his car. He knew."

In spite of fornication, however, I don't think Caliph would have fired Roy until they had the next preacher lined up, if not for the Mountain Party people.

On Friday, I picked up the phone for Vashie's first call of the day. She hissed, "Becky is at the parsonage right now! In fact, there's a whole house full of people," she said. "People with banjos! They're sitting on the porch of our parsonage." She paused. "I think it's the Communists from the Mountaintop Removal Party."

Now I've mentioned that it was an extremely busy political year—this was the year West Virginia put George W. Bush over the top with our five electoral college votes at the same time we were electing the usual Coal Company Democrat for governor, but we also had that girl from down around Charleston running for governor on the Mountain Party ticket.

"Roy Critchfield is not only tomcatting at night," Vashie said with great satisfaction, "he's showing his true colors and turning the parsonage into a den for radicals!"

That week Roy turned the Sunday morning service over to these political people with anti-coal company ballads and a slide show of ugly pictures of mud and raw dirt where beautiful trees used to be. Everyone showed up: Becky looking like the cat that ate the canary, or maybe more to the point, like a woman who's been enjoying her body for the first time in her life. The teenagers were there, and people from the university, and there was even a reporter with a camera.

The Mountain Party people sat in the big carved chairs up on the platform with Roy, and they did everything except read the scripture. Roy did that, Psalm 46: *God is our refuge and strength. Therefore we will not fear, though the earth be moved, and though the mountains be toppled into the depths of the sea.*

They had a slide show and stories and songs about the awful things the coal companies had done to our state. Buffalo Creek where all those people drowned because of the faulty dam for waste water from the mines. But except for Psalm 46, there was no mention of God and no praying. The congregation ranged from bored to bemused to vaguely uncomfortable, except for Caliph Savage. He was outraged. Caliph has that part interest in the mining supply company, and I expect he would gladly sell the tops off all his mountains if anyone made him an offer.

By midweek, Roy was through as interim pastor. There was an emergency meeting of the entire church membership—deacons, trustees, and all the rest of us. One of our lawyer members, also a member of the Republican committee, said it was partisan politics and therefore endangering the church's tax status. Most of them just said it was not what they come to church for.

Vashie stood up in her walker and said she had supported Roy from the beginning and helped him in every way she could. As a Christian, she still had to love him, but he had gone too far letting in Communists. Roy sat through it all and nodded like he was in a counseling session, trying to understand their feelings. I voted to keep him on, but I wasn't all that sorry the way it turned out.

Before Thanksgiving, the First Baptist had hired itself a regular pastor with a wife and two kids. The wife, however, was a big disappointment to Vashie because she refused to let her husband run across the street every time Vashie's house creaked.

Roy stayed in town. He moved in with Becky and Ruth and spent a lot of time in the southern part of the state working with the Mountain Party. A few of us—Becky and me and Ursula because I told her to and Ruth by absentee ballot—voted for the Mountain Party. They never had a real chance, of course, and the regular Democrat won. He wasn't a bad governor, as West Virginia governors go, but he didn't run for a second term because he had an extramarital affair that came out in public.

After the campaign was over, Roy and Becky got married, which Vashie claimed was her doing. She said every time he took her to the doctor, she worked on him about the importance of holy matrimony. Roy planned to continue working against mountaintop removal, but when Becky got pregnant, he took a job at the grocery store and then applied for a teaching license. He teaches social studies at the new middle school now, and he does get in trouble from time to time when he has the kids do PowerPoint projects on mountaintop removal. He still works for the environmentalists, and he also runs errands for Vashie, who says she has forgiven him although she'll never forget.

I donate to whatever groups Roy says to, as I believe he's got righteous instincts. Roy and Becky have turned out be wonderful parents, better at babies in my opinion than at stopping mountaintop removal, but they don't give up, and I figure that as long as people like Roy and Becky don't give up, I'll at least keep donating.

William Woolfitt

ABSENTEE

———

I come from the careening wrong turn, Holy Rollers,
Queen Anne's lace, and fists;

siltstone and slate embossed with ferns; bituminous coal
that pocks our land with holes

and pits, makes an overseas company rich.
My trailer stands

at the end of a flood-prone road I never would have found.
Showers at night fill my gutters

with knuckles of hail, scattershot ice a bruising
reminder to me

that I am really in my body, and not in a dream,
when I go out to smell

the world set alive. Taking welts on my back,
I move past wood scraps

and junk cars to Buffalo Creek, where I fill my jug
with the true, the dark, the raw,

a speaking-forth of sulfur ooze.

TO TOIL NOT

———

Even on these nights of swelter,
when brine glazes our listless skins,
the gleaners pour out from the cool
recesses of Stillhouse Cave and comb the edge
habitats of karst country, where groundwater's

drippy metronome nibbles out maternity
caves and bachelor roosts. The bats must want,
as everyone does, to toil not, to open
their mouths in ardor, to shake off
liquid calcite, ceiling-spittle,

and fly like scarves of parchment
flung by some juggler's fraught hands,
and at the feeding grounds, to pack on fat
for the coming winter, tuck with gusto
into the hayfield's larder of moths.

CONTRIBUTORS

Winner of the Flannery O'Connor Award for Short Fiction for *The Purchase of Order*, **GAIL GALLOWAY ADAMS** is a professor emeritus of creative writing at West Virginia University, where she won several teaching awards, among them the CASE from the Carnegie Foundation for the Advancement of Teaching.

MAGGIE ANDERSON is the author of four books of poems including *Windfall: New and Selected Poems* and *A Space Filled with Moving*. Her new book of poems *Dear All* is forthcoming (Four Way Books). She has received two fellowships from the National Endowment for the Arts. Maggie Anderson lives in Asheville, North Carolina.

PINCKNEY BENEDICT grew up on his family's dairy farm in West Virginia. He has published four books of fiction. His work has been published in *Esquire*, the O. Henry Prize series, the Pushcart Prize series, the Best New Stories from the South series, and *The Oxford Book of the American Short Story*.

LAURA TREACY BENTLEY is the author of *The Silver Tattoo*—a psychological thriller with a magic-realist's edge set in mythical Ireland—and a short story prequel, *Night Terrors*. Her first poetry collection is *Lake Effect*. Laura's work has been widely published in the United States and Ireland.

MICHAEL BLUMENTHAL's most recent books are *"Because They Needed Me": Rita Miljo and the Orphaned Baboons of South Africa* and his first collection of short stories, *The Greatest Jewish-American Lover in Hungarian History*. His eighth book of poems is *Be Kind: Poems 2000–2012* (Etruscan Press).

ACE BOGGESS of Charleston, West Virginia, is author of two books of poetry: *The Prisoners* (Brick Road Poetry Press) and *The Beautiful Girl Whose*

Wish Was Not Fulfilled. He edited the anthology *Wild Sweet Notes II* (Publishers Place). His poems appear in *Harvard Review*, *Rattle*, and many other journals.

MARK BRAZAITIS is the author of seven books, including *The River of Lost Voices: Stories from Guatemala*, winner of the Iowa Short Fiction Award; *The Incurables: Stories*, winner of the Richard Sullivan Prize and the Devil's Kitchen Reading Award; and *Julia & Rodrigo*, winner of the Gival Press Novel Award.

Born in Miami, raised in England and West Virginia, and educated in Texas, **JOY CASTRO** is the award-winning author of two memoirs, two literary thrillers set in post-Katrina New Orleans, and a collection of short fiction. Editor of the anthology *Family Trouble*, she lives and works in Lincoln, Nebraska.

JONATHAN CORCORAN is the author of the story collection *The Rope Swing* (Vandalia/WVU Press). He received a BA in literary arts from Brown University and an MFA in fiction writing from Rutgers University-Newark. He was born and raised in a small town in West Virginia and currently resides in Brooklyn, New York.

West Virginia native **ED DAVIS** is the author of the novel *The Psalms of Israel Jones* (Vandalia/WVU Press) and the book of poetry *Time of the Light* (Main Street Rag Press). He lives with his wife in Yellow Springs, Ohio.

MARK DEFOE is professor emeritus at West Virginia Wesleyan College, where he teaches in the low-residency MFA Writing Program. DeFoe has won the *Chautauqua* literary journal's poetry competition and the Tennessee Chapbook Award. His tenth chapbook is *In the Tourist Cave* (Finishing Line Press).

CHERYL DENISE has two books of poetry, *What's in the Blood* and *I Saw God Dancing* (both with Cascadia Publishing). She has a spoken word poetry CD, *Leaving Eden*, available on cdbaby.com. She lives in the intentional community of Shepherds Field in West Virginia.

ANDREA FEKETE was born and raised in the southern coalfields of West Virginia, granddaughter to Mexican and Hungarian immigrants. Her novel

Waters Run Wild is historical fiction about the coal mine wars of West Virginia. In addition to a poetry chapbook, *I Held a Morning*, her work appears in many publications.

DENISE GIARDINA is the author of six novels, including *Storming Heaven*, *The Unquiet Earth*, *Fallam's Secret*, and *Emily's Ghost*. She has also written a play. Her articles appear in many news publications, including the *Nation* and the *New York Times*.

MAGGIE GLOVER is a graduate of West Virginia University. Her poetry appears in *Carrier Pigeon, jubilat, Ninth Letter,* and other journals. Her debut collection of poems is *How I Went Red* (Carnegie Mellon University Press).

CRYSTAL GOOD is an artist, advocate, and entrepreneur thriving in the heart of Appalachia. The inaugural Irene McKinney Memorial Scholar at West Virginia Wesleyan College, Crystal earned her MFA in poetry in 2016. She has presented her poems in readings and performance from DC to Dubai.

JAMES HARMS is the author of nine full-length collections of poetry, including *Rowing With Wings* (Carnegie Mellon University Press, 2017). He chairs the Department of English at West Virginia University, where he teaches in the MFA Program in Creative Writing.

MARC HARSHMAN's second collection of poetry is *Believe What You Can* (Vandalia/WVU Press). Marc is also an award-winning children's author; his most recent and thirteenth title is *One Big Family*. Marc hosts a monthly show for West Virginia Public Radio, *The Poetry Break*, and is the seventh Poet Laureate of West Virginia.

RAJIA HASSIB was born and raised in Egypt and moved to the United States when she was twenty-three. She holds an MA in creative writing from Marshall University and lives in Charleston, West Virginia. Her recent debut novel is *In the Language of Miracles* (Viking).

JOHN HOPPENTHALER's books of poetry are *Lives of Water, Anticipate the Coming Reservoir*, and *Domestic Garden* (all with Carnegie Mellon University Press). With Kazim Ali, he has co-edited *Jean Valentine: This-World Company*

(University of Michigan Press). For the cultural journal *Connotation Press*, he edits "A Poetry Congeries." He teaches at East Carolina University.

RON HOUCHIN was raised in Huntington, West Virginia, and lives in South Point, Ohio, just across the river. He says, "I sleep in Ohio and live in West Virginia." Houchin has published seven books of poetry. The most recent, *The Man Who Saws Us in Half* (Louisiana State University Press's Southern Messenger Poets Series), won the Weatherford Award for Poetry.

NORMAN JORDAN (1938–2015) was a poet and playwright born in Ansted, West Virginia, and associated with the Black Arts Movement of the 1960s and 1970s. The author of five books of poetry, he introduced a new form of poetry called "Stick Poetry" in *Sing Me Different*, his last publication.

LAURA LONG is the author of the novel *Out of Peel Tree* (Vandalia/WVU Press) and poetry collections *Imagine a Door* and *The Eye of Caroline Herschel*. She was born and raised in Upshur County, and her ancestors arrived in Randolph County, West Virginia, in the 1770s. She now lives at the foot of the Blue Ridge in Virginia.

MARIE MANILLA's books include the novel *The Patron Saint of Ugly* (Houghton Mifflin Harcourt), winner of the Weatherford Award; *Shrapnel* (River City Publishing), which received the Fred Bonnie Award for Best First Novel; and the story collection *Still Life with Plums* (Vandalia/WVU Press). Marie lives in Huntington, West Virginia, her hometown.

JEFF MANN has published three poetry chapbooks, five full-length books of poetry, two collections of personal essays, a volume of memoir and poetry, three novellas, five novels, and two collections of short fiction. The winner of two Lambda Literary Awards, he teaches creative writing at Virginia Tech.

MESHA MAREN is the author of the novel *Sugar Run* (Algonquin Books). Her work appears in *Tin House*, the *Oxford American*, and other literary journals, and she has received fellowships from the MacDowell Colony and the Ucross Foundation. "Chokedamp" was selected by Lee Smith as the winner of the Thomas Wolfe Fiction Prize.

LEE MAYNARD is the author of six books, including *Crum, Screaming with the Cannibals, The Scummers, Magnetic North,* and *Cinco Becknell,* all published by Vandalia/WVU Press. He has published and taught widely and is an avid outdoorsman and conservationist.

SCOTT McCLANAHAN wrote *Crapalachia* (Two Dollar Radio) and *Hill William* (Tyrant Books). His work has been featured in *Vice,* the *Oxford American,* and other publications. His most recent book is a graphic novel with artist Ricardo Cavolo, *The Incantations of Daniel Johnston* (Two Dollar Radio).

JOHN McKERNAN grew up in Omaha, Nebraska, and has lived in West Virginia for many years. He recently retired after teaching forty-two years at Marshall University. His poems have appeared in many periodicals from the *Atlantic Monthly* to *Zuzu's Petals.* His most recent book is *Resurrection of the Dust.*

LLEWELLYN McKERNAN is a poet and teacher who has lived and worked so long in West Virginia that she considers it home. Her publications include five poetry books for adults and four for children. Her poems have won eighty-five prizes, awards, and honors and appeared in thirty-seven anthologies.

IRENE McKINNEY (1939–2012) was Poet Laureate of West Virginia from 1994 till her death in 2012. Founding Director of the West Virginia Wesleyan College MFA Program, she was a gifted teacher and tireless advocate for poetry. Her many collections include *Unthinkable: Selected Poems 1976–2004, Vivid Companion,* and a posthumous book, *Have You Had Enough Darkness Yet?*

DEVON McNAMARA's poems, essays, interviews, and reviews have appeared in the *Christian Science Monitor,* the *Hiram Poetry Review,* and the *Laurel Review, I,* among others. She was the recipient of a Yaddo fellowship and is professor of English, Irish literature, and creative writing at West Virginia Wesleyan College. She is the author of *Driving.*

KELLY McQUAIN was raised on a dirt road in West Virginia that bears his family name. He has been a fellow at the Lambda Literary Retreat and a Tennessee Williams Scholar at the Sewanee Writers' Conference. His chapbook, *Velvet Rodeo*, won the Bloom poetry prize. His work appears in many magazines and anthologies.

RAHUL MEHTA is the author of the short story collection *Quarantine* (Harper Perennial), which won the Lambda Literary Award and the Asian American Literary Award for Fiction, and the novel *No Other World* (Harper). He lives in Philadelphia with his partner and teaches creative writing.

SHERYL MONKS is the author of *Monsters in Appalachia* (Vandalia/WVU Press), a collection of stories. She works for a peer-reviewed medical journal and edits the online literary magazine *Change Seven*.

Now retired from Marshall University, **MARY B. MOORE** is a native Californian who wrote herself into West Virginia. Her poems have appeared in *Abraxas, Birmingham Poetry Review, Poetry, FIELD*, and other journals. She is the author of the collection *The Book of Snow* (Cleveland University Press).

A dancer whose career was cut short by the onset of rheumatoid arthritis and author of *Roundabout Directions to Lincoln Center* (Urban Farmhouse Press), **RENÉE K. NICHOLSON** is assistant professor in the multidisciplinary studies program at West Virginia University and was the Emerging Writer-in-Residence at Penn State-Altoona.

VALERIE NIEMAN is the author of two collections of poetry, most recently *Hotel Worthy* (Press 53), and three novels. A graduate of West Virginia University and Queens University of Charlotte, Neiman is a professor of creative writing at North Carolina A&T State University and serves as poetry editor for *Prime Number Magazine*.

MATTHEW NEILL NULL is a native of West Virginia and a recipient of the O. Henry Prize, the Mary McCarthy Prize, and the Joseph Brodsky Rome Prize from the American Academy of Arts and Letters. He is the author of the novel *Honey from the Lion* (Lookout Books) and the story collection *Allegheny Front* (Sarabande).

ANN PANCAKE has published two short story collections, *Given Ground* and *Me and My Daddy Listen to Bob Marley*, and a novel, *Strange As This Weather*

Has Been. Awards include a Whiting Award, National Endowment for the Arts Fellowship, Pushcart Prize, the Bakeless Prize, and the Barry Lopez Visiting Writer in Ethics and Community Fellowship.

JAYNE ANNE PHILLIPS is the author of five novels, including *Quiet Dell*, *Lark and Termite*, and *Motherkind*, and two widely anthologized collections of stories, *Fast Lanes* and *Black Tickets*. A National Book Award and National Book Critics Circle Award finalist, she is the recipient of a Guggenheim Fellowship and numerous other awards.

SARA PRITCHARD is the author of the novel *Crackpots*, a *New York Times* Notable Book, and the story collections *Lately* and *Help Wanted: Female*. After living in Morgantown, West Virginia, for over thirty years, she now lives in Lewisburg, West Virginia, and teaches in the low-residency MFA program at Wilkes University.

MARY ANN SAMYN is the author of several collections of poetry, most recently *My Life in Heaven*, winner of the FIELD Prize (Oberlin College Press). She's professor of English at West Virginia University and, currently, Director of the MFA Program in Creative Writing.

ELIZABETH SAVAGE is author of two books of poetry, *Idylliad* and *Grammar*, as well as several chapbooks. She is the poetry editor for *Kestrel: A Journal of Literature & Art* and a professor of English at Fairmont State University.

STEVE SCAFIDI is the author of four books of poetry, most recently *The Cabinetmaker's Window* and *To the Bramble and the Briar*. He has won the Larry Levis Reading Prize, the James Boatwright Prize, and the Miller Williams Prize. He works as a cabinetmaker and lives with his family in Summit Point, West Virginia.

ANGELA SHAW was raised in Beverly, West Virginia. Her first book is *The Beginning of the Fields* (Tupelo Press). She lives in Swarthmore, Pennsylvania, with her husband and their two children.

KENT SHAW's book *Calenture* won the Tampa Review Prize. His poems appear in *Boston Review*, *Denver Quarterly*, the *Believer*, and other magazines.

He holds a PhD from the University of Houston. He currently teaches English literature and creative writing at West Virginia State University.

ANITA SKEEN grew up in Charleston, West Virginia, graduated from Concord College, and is currently the director of the Center for Poetry in the Residential College in the Arts and Humanities at Michigan State University. She is the author of five collections of poetry, most recently *The Unauthorized Audubon* with visual artist Laura B. DeLind.

AARON SMITH is the author of two books in the Pitt Poetry Series, *Appetite*, an NPR Best Book, and *Blue on Blue Ground*, winner of the Agnes Lynch Starrett Prize. His work appears in *Ploughshares*, *The Best American Poetry*, and many other publications. He is a core faculty member at Lesley University in Cambridge, Massachusetts.

IDA STEWART is the author of *Gloss* (Perugia Press). Her poems also appear in journals including *FIELD*, the *Journal*, the *Tusculum Review*, and *Connotation Press*. A native of Morgantown, West Virginia, she currently lives in Haverford, Pennsylvania, and teaches writing at the University of Delaware.

From Princeton, West Virginia, **KEVIN STEWART** teaches at Carroll College, Montana, and holds an MFA from the University of Arkansas. He is the author of *The Way Things Always Happen Here: Eight Stories and a Novella* and has published in *American Literary Review*, *Appalachian Heritage*, *Connecticut Review*, and *Shenandoah*, among others.

A. E. STRINGER is the author of three poetry collections, most recently, *Late Breaking*. He also edited and introduced a new edition of Louise McNeill's *Paradox Hill* from West Virginia University Press. His work has appeared in the *Nation*, the *Ohio Review*, and *Shenandoah*. For twenty-four years, he taught writing and literature at Marshall University.

NATALIE SYPOLT's fiction appears in *Appalachian Heritage*, the *Kenyon Review Online*, *r.kv.r.y*, and *Willow Springs Review*. She has won a Mid Atlantic Arts Foundations Fellowship, the *Glimmer Train* New Writers Contest, and the fiction contest for *Still: The Journal*. She teaches at Pierpont Community and Technical College in West Virginia.

GLENN TAYLOR is the author of the novels *A Hanging at Cinder Bottom*, *The Marrowbone Marble Company*, and *The Ballad of Trenchmouth Taggart*, a finalist for the National Book Critics Circle Award. Born and raised in Huntington, West Virginia, he now lives in Morgantown, where he teaches at WVU.

VINCE TRIMBOLI is a proud Appalachian native from Elkins, West Virginia. Trimboli holds an MFA in creative writing from West Virginia Wesleyan College and has published poetry in *Still: The Journal, Connotation Press*, and other venues. Vince Trimboli's first collection is *Condominium Morte* (Ghost City Press).

JESSIE VAN EERDEN is the author of two novels, *Glorybound* and *My Radio Radio*, and the essay collection *The Long Weeping*. Her work appears in *Best American Spiritual Writing,* the *Oxford American*, *River Teeth*, and many other places. Jessie directs the low-residency MFA program at West Virginia Wesleyan.

DOUG VAN GUNDY teaches in both the BA and MFA writing programs at West Virginia Wesleyan College. His poems, essays and reviews have appeared in the *Oxford American*, *Ecotone*, *Appalachian Heritage*, *Poetry Salzburg Review*, and elsewhere. He is the author of the collection *A Life Above Water* (Red Hen Press).

JOHN VAN KIRK is the author of the novel *Song for Chance*. His short stories and essays appear in the *Hudson Review*, the *Iowa Review*, *Kestrel*, the *New York Times Magazine,* and other publications.

Originally from Rock Cave, West Virginia, **ERIN VEITH** holds an MFA in poetry from West Virginia University. Her chapbook of her poems is entitled *I Closed My Eyes to Tell That Story* (Latham House Press). Currently, Erin works for the Statewide Adoption Network in Pennsylvania.

RYAN WALSH grew up in Elkins, West Virginia. He is author of the chapbooks *Reckoner* and *The Sinks* (winner of the Mississippi Valley Poetry Chapbook Contest). His poems have appeared in *Blackbird, Ecotone, FIELD,* and elsewhere. He is currently the Development & Writing Program Director at the Vermont Studio Center and lives in Burlington, Vermont.

RANDI WARD is a poet, translator, lyricist, and photographer from Belleville, West Virginia. She earned her MA in cultural studies from the University of the Faroe Islands and is a recipient of the American-Scandinavian Foundation's Nadia Christensen Prize. Her most recent collection is *Whipstitches* (MadHat Press).

MEREDITH SUE WILLIS, born and raised in Harrison County, West Virginia, teaches writing at New York University. Her books have been published by commercial, small, and university presses. The *New York Times Book Review* called her first short story collection "a[n] . . . important lesson on the nature and function of literature itself."

WILLIAM WOOLFITT is the author of the poetry collections *Beauty Strip* (Texas Review Press), *Charles of the Desert,* and *Spring Up Everlasting* (Paraclete Press). His fiction chapbook *The Boy with Fire in His Mouth* won the Epiphany Editions contest, and he won the Plattner Award for Fiction in *Appalachian Heritage.*

ACKNOWLEDGMENTS

Thanks to Marie Manilla, Ann Pancake, and Sara Pritchard for their early encouragement and insights about this project, and to Chip Hitchcock for decades-long talk about Appalachian literature. Thanks to Lynchburg College for its support, and to the English Department, Julie Williams, Sara Severens, Jasmine Smith, and my Fall 2015 Literature and Culture class. I am grateful to people and environments that nurture artistic communities, especially Jessie van Eerden and everyone at West Virginia Wesleyan's Low-Residency MFA Program, and the Virginia Center for Creative Arts. Mark Adams has helped throughout, and he's the bee's knees.

Most of all, thanks to Doug, my amazing co-editor.

—*Laura Long*

Thanks to West Virginia Wesleyan College for its support, and special thanks to my colleagues in the English Department and the students in my Appalachian Literature classes of 2015 and 2016. I echo Laura's gratitude to Jessie van Eerden and the faculty, guests, and students of the West Virginia Wesleyan Low-Residency MFA Program. I am also indebted to Marc Harshman and Maggie Anderson for their wisdom and counsel. Melissa Thomas-Van Gundy is in a class by herself, and I am grateful to her beyond words.

Finally, most special thanks to Laura Long, my co-editor and friend. Working with her was a joy, and I'd do it all over again.

—*Doug Van Gundy*

CREDITS

"Olives" by Gail Galloway Adams first appeared in the *Kenyon Review* XXVI, no. 3 (Summer 2004).

"And then I arrive at the powerful green hill" by Maggie Anderson first appeared in *The Autumn House Anthology of Contemporary American Poetry (2nd and 3rd editions)*, ed. Michael Simms, et al. (Autumn House Press, 2011, 2015) and the *Iron Mountain Review: Maggie Anderson Issue XXI* (Spring 2005). Both *"And then I arrive at the powerful green hill"* and "A Blessing" are included in *Dear All* by Maggie Anderson (Four Way Books, forthcoming).

"Mercy" by Pinckney Benedict first appeared in *Ontario Review* 65 (Fall/Winter 2006) and subsequently in *Pushcart Prize XXXII: Best of the Small Presses (2008)* and in *Miracle Boy and Other Stories* by Pinckney Benedict (Press 53, 2010).

"Vow of Silence" by Laura Bentley first appeared in *Grey Sparrow Journal* 15 (Winter 2013).

"Stone-Hearted" by Michael Blumenthal first appeared in *Poetry Porch* (2015).

"What If There Weren't Any Stars?" by Ace Boggess first appeared in the *Santa Fe Literary Review* (2015).

"The Rink Girl" by Mark Brazaitis first appeared in *Ploughshares* (Spring 2014).

"The Dream of the Father" by Joy Castro first appeared in *How Winter Began: Stories* (2015) by Joy Castro. Reprinted by permission of University of Nebraska Press.

"Through the Still Hours" by Jonathan Corcoran first appeared in *The Rope Swing: Stories* by Jonathan Corcoran (Vandalia/West Virginia University Press, 2015).

"The Boys of Bradleytown" by Ed Davis first appeared in *Ohio Writer* (2006) as the winner of the "Best of 2005."

"August, West Virginia" by Mark DeFoe first appeared in the *MacGuffin* 26, no. 2 (Winter 2010).

"Lettuce" by Natalie Sypolt first appeared in *Willow Springs Review* 67 (Spring 2011).

"Cortège" by Glenn Taylor first appeared in *Huizache* 5 (Fall 2015).

"Solvo" by Vince Trimboli first appeared in *Connotation Press* (2016) and subsequently in *Condo-minium Morte* by Vince Trimboli (Ghost City Press, 2016).

"Edna" by Jessie van Eerden first appeared in *Newfound* 2, no. 2 (July 2011).

"Country Music" by Doug Van Gundy first appeared in the *Oxford American* 67 (Winter 2009).

"Bear Country Blues" by John Van Kirk first appeared in *Best Short Stories from the* Saturday Evening Post *Great American Fiction Contest, 2015.*

"Relapse Means I Forgot to Be Better" by Erin Veith was published in *I Closed My Eyes to Tell That Story* by Erin Veith (Latham House Press, 2014).

"The Field" by Ryan Walsh originally appeared in the chapbook *The Sinks* (Midwest Writing Center Press, 2011).

"Daddy Longlegs" by Randi Ward first appeared in *Anthology of Appalachian Writers, Gretchen Moran Laskas Vol. V* (Shepherd University, 2013); "Grandma" first appeared in *Skidrow Penthouse* 16 (2014). Both were subsequently published in *Whipstitches* by Randi Ward (MadHat Press, 2016).

"The Roy Critchfield Scandals" by Meredith Sue Willis was published under slightly different titles and versions in *Out of the Mountains: Appalachian Short Stories* by Meredith Sue Willis (Ohio University Press, 2010) and in *We All Live Downstream: Writings About Mountaintop Removal* edited by Jason Howard (Louisville, KY: Motes Books, 2009).

"Absentee" by William Woolfitt appeared in *Talking Leaves* and *r.kv.r.y. quarterly* and subsequently in *Beauty Strip* by William Kelley Woolfitt (Texas Review Press, 2015). "To Toil Not" also appeared in *Beauty Strip.*

CPSIA information can be obtained
at www.ICGtesting.com
Printed in the USA
FSOW03n1405310117
30130FS